*You will
never forget.*

D1407443

"All right, Lance. Goodbye, love."

The phone call had taken a lot out of her. Too much, really. *It's been almost twenty-five years since I've heard that woman's name*, she thought. *It shouldn't bother me now.*

But it does. It does.

She sat on the edge of the bed and sighed loud and long as she smoothed the covers under her, remembering all that had happened in those early days. The running. The fear. All the name changes—so many times she'd lost count.

It had all been for nothing, really. She had only delayed the inevitable.

The evil *thing* had found her son.

the Supernatural

JOHN G. JONES

Tudor Publishing Company
New York and Los Angeles

Tudor Publishing Company

Copyright © 1988 by John G. Jones

This is a work of fiction. The characters, names, incidents, places and dialogue are products of the author's imagination, and are not to be construed as real.

All rights reserved. No part of this book may be reproduced or transmitted in any form or by any means, electronic or mechanical, including photocopying, recording, or by any information storage and retrieval system, without the written permission of the Publisher, except where permitted by law.

For information address Tudor Publishing Company, 255 E. 49th Street, Suite 25D, New York, New York, 10017.

ISBN: 0-944276-17-2

Printed in the United States of America

First Tudor printing-September 1988

Dedication

For my brother Glenn—we all miss you more than words can express.

As always, SPECIAL thanks to Brad Munsen.

To Kay.

To Carey.

To the kids: Ben, Kerren, Kellee, Nicole, Rod, Brad and Dean—your energy keeps the world eternally young.

And those who are still kids, if only at heart: Beryl, Anne, Tony and Bob . . . and, of course, Valerie, my ever-youthful Mum—thanks to her positive inspiration my life has always been, and still is, a non-stop journey through a gigantic funpark.

Prologue

It did not breathe. It did not move. It had no heart to beat or eyes to see. Yet it existed. In a way unique unto itself, it *lived*.

For eons it had drifted through the vast reaches of interstellar space . . . *seeking*. Always *seeking*.

Countless times it had touched down on some promising world only to be disappointed. Then it would be drifting through the void again.

Finally, countless centuries from its beginnings, it found what it had always sought. It touched down one final time and never rose again.

Now it lived a different life, as it had for numerous centuries, rooted deep in the Northumbrian earth of a small blue planet in a sparsely populated arm of the galaxy.

It had waited . . . *patiently*, its near-consciousness scouring the surface of its new world, searching for something more than a simple home.

And in the dim and distant past its vigil had been rewarded. It found signs: the first feeble and tentative sounds of life.

Life, it discovered, was an intoxicant—something to be nurtured and refined. Something to be *tailored*.

Certain traits were particularly fascinating—even pleasing to it. As time passed it manipulated these aspects, injecting an essence of itself into favorable strains, and closely monitoring the progress of these special projects, while all about it other experiments in evolution sang the chorus of creation.

It wondered at the unexpected advances and mourned the inevitable failures. And it waited. Always, it waited.

Then, in the recent past, major changes swirled about it with startling suddenness—a swelling advancement almost too swift for it to encompass: magic, machines, warfare . . . *life*. It struggled with new concepts, new conflicts, new surprises. It rejoiced. It raged. It mourned.

Yet through it all, that single line survived. The line carrying its precious essence continued without a break.

During its long habitation, it took on many forms: a massive horn of granite; a wicker hut twenty stories tall; an oak that could cover the sky itself. It had become the source of legends, and the key to dreams.

Its latest form was relatively innocuous, suited to the time. As always, it was two-sided, double-lobed, each of its halves identical to the other even in the smallest detail. And its ancient origins, its endless patience, its ageless, fundamentally changeless existence in this place gave it an aura that was preternaturally *native*—earthy, proper, *belonging*—despite the strange symbols that dotted its surface.

Its form was that of a beautiful, strangely designed house, with two vast and crenellated wings that were mirror images of each other.

And now, at long last, the wait was over. All the pieces were in place.

It was time for . . . *THE ONE*.

Chapter 1

Darkness kissed him. Darkness engorged him, embraced him, sucked at him like a hungry beast.

He strained to see: only darkness. Darkness.

Breath rattled in metered unison with his footfalls. Air murmured past him, cooling the sweat from his skin as he moved faster and faster.

Where am I? he wondered. He was running, but . . . to where? And why?

His heart writhed in his chest, fighting to pump blood through constricted arteries. It was cold, then hot, then cold again. He peered into the blackness, pupils straining to enlarge until his eyes stung and his head thundered.

Darkness. Only darkness, and a cold and bottomless sensation that swelled inside him.

He was . . . alone. Not "by himself" or "away for a while." But terrifyingly ALONE!

Faint light fluttered against him. Bloated irises rapidly contracted. A moment passed, and another. Slowly his surroundings solidified, colored a slate gray.

Images hovered in the dimness. Shadow-draped limbs, gnarled and twisted, reached out for him. He crouched and held up his hands to ward them off.

3

They were trees, yes . . . but not like any trees he'd ever seen. He touched one hesitantly, and it whispered rough and warm under his fingers.

It wasn't his imagination. He could feel them.

Suddenly, grotesquely, they moved again, knotting together over his head to form a canopy, a tunnel, a covered path.

An instant later, he felt something more—a thing setting sharp and solid against his spine. A thirsting, insatiable evil, poised, ready to slash deeply.

It was coming from the trees.

He pushed away from them and ran down the path. The air was thick and humid like syrup, but he kept moving, kept trying until the breath burned in his lungs.

He turned a tree-lined corner and chilling mist covered him, swooping in like an insubstantial wall, clinging hungrily as he ran.

A wailing moan—harpy cry, banshee wail—cut through the mist. It pushed and expanded in him like a living thing, crashing against the walls of his skull. And with the sound came a memory, a terrifying, painful memory.

He had done all this before. Had been here many, many times. And he knew what would happen next.

The roots at his feet stirred and separated, spreading like gray arthritic fingers. They were hiding something soft and supple. Warm tones glimmered against the shapeless ash.

It was the body of a woman. He didn't know her—they'd never met—but he loved her with a passion so intense it seared him. He longed to rush forward and take her in his arms. To hold her. To protect her. But he was helpless.

He watched in horror as the body turned, not of its own volition—it was limp and lifeless—but as if some invisible foot had hooked under the torso and turned it over for a better look.

The body of this woman twisted unnaturally. Her ankles, dark with blood, were pinned to the earth. Her gold hair swept across her breasts like a soft curtain. She was bleeding from a hundred tiny cuts that covered her from neck to knee like obscene tattoos.

Anger screamed in him, driving him to do something. But the sharp, awful thing was behind him again. It chuckled wickedly inside his head and surged past him, a reeking wind. The odor was thick as smoke, choking. Sweet and heavy, intense, it clutched at his throat like a fist.

The female corpse jerked and arched as the thing tore it free of the rootbed, then dangled it in front of him. It flexed and arched again. And again. Like a dancer, he thought. Or like a whore.

He strained to go to her but found himself turning, running from the body, from the smell, pushing forward through the heavy air as he searched for a light in the gray-green mist.

Tears streamed down his face. The pain in his chest pulsed and pulsed again.

A strange metallic ringing started somewhere in front of him. He turned aside, pushing through the woods in a different direction, afraid to investigate. Another crashing tone clattered to his left. And then to his right. The metallic intruder clanged into his consciousness, louder, more insistent. Then it was galloping at him, an invisible metal demon on an iron mount.

There was no place left to run. Nowhere to hide. It was coming for him, chasing him. He could feel its leaden weight above him, bearing down. He could sense it rather than see it: a hammer, a mace, a sharply honed ax. A weapon that could kill with a single blow.

"Let me die," he begged.

The weapon swooped down to split his skull.

Chapter 2

He broke from the dream with a brutal *snap*, sitting up against the sweat-soaked, overstarched sheets and biting back a scream.

I'm fine, he thought. *Fine. It's just a hotel room, like all the other hotel rooms. That's all. I'm fine.*

He lay back on the bed, his muscles rigid. Then he blinked and blinked again. Breath came in short, sharp jerks.

The dream hovered behind his eyes. For a timeless moment he refused to move, afraid it would reach out and scoop him up again. He knew he couldn't take that; not now.

Nothing happened.

He was awake.

Slowly, he relaxed. Air gushed from his aching lungs and he rolled onto his side, squinting blearily at the travel clock on the bedside table. Its bright red numbers winked at him, and he groaned at what he saw—it was 6:30 A.M.

I better get up, he told himself. *Up and at 'em.*

He eased himself to his feet and glared into the bureau mirror. His hair was mouse-brown. His eyes were the same colorless color. The skin under his eyes sagged unhappily, and his closely cropped beard did nothing to hide the beginning of a jowl that announced approaching middle age.

He scowled at the image, hating what he saw.

The hotel phone near his head buzzed again, and he dimly recognized the sound. He had heard it buried inside the dream. *That* was what had awakened him at the crucial moment. When the weapon came slashing down—

He shuddered. *Don't think about it*, he ordered. *Just . . . don't.*

He picked up the receiver on the next ring, thinking he should be grateful for it. Usually he hated phones, but not now—not today.

"Hello?" he said, stifling a yawn.

"Hello!"

He didn't recognize the voice. ". . . Yes?"

"Crossfire. Do you hear me? *Crossfire.*"

For an instant he sat frozen, the plastic receiver gripped tightly in his hand. Then he slammed down the phone and jumped to his feet.

Less than four minutes later he left the room for the last time. One hand held a large suitcase, the other a round leather traveling bag. He checked both ways in the hall, closed the door to room 526, left the key in the lock and hurried away.

He didn't even pause at the elevator doors. It took a moment to open the entrance to the stairs with both hands full, but he managed. He made sure the door was latched behind him before he quickly made his way downward.

When he reached the lobby level, he slipped behind the counter and moved swiftly down an austere hallway to the concrete stairs beside the loading dock. He was grateful for the half-light in the parking structure beneath the hotel. In seconds he had blended into the ghostly predawn shadows of Miami.

He had learned to be careful. It was all that had kept him alive.

Two days later, a small human-interest item appeared in the local paper. The man with the mouse-brown hair and heavy jowl never saw it, but it would have made him laugh if he had.

It told the strange story of Roger "Cappy" LaRouche, a janitor at the Miami International Airport, who was cleaning one of the stalls in the men's toilet when he found an unusual treasure: an unmarked, handmade Italian leather suitcase containing a brown wig, a pair of black shoes, a crumpled but expensive blue business suit, and a collection of brown hair that was later determined to be a recently detached beard.

Cappy LaRouche was trying to find the owner, hoping for a reward.

He never did.

Chapter 3

The automatic doors silently slipped open, and the deep-throated snarl of a heavily loaded truck echoed across the hotel foyer. Gears rasped, and the snarl rose to a whine. The door stayed open long enough to admit a contingent of Oriental tourists who gabbled among themselves.

The sudden blare of sound in the tasteful quiet of the hotel made heads turn. But the tall, gray-haired stranger standing at the reservations desk didn't move. He was concentrating on forging a signature.

The desk clerk barely checked the registration form when it was returned to him. "Will this be cash or charge, Mistah Avyaahn?" he said blandly, mangling the French name.

"Avignon," the man corrected. "Ah-veen-yon." He presented a credit card. "And it will be the ssscharge, Monsieur." His English was colored by a heavy accent.

The desk clerk smirked. "Of course."

A slight twitch tugged at the corner of Avignon's firm mouth. His lengthy, well-manicured fingers thrummed a soft, nervous beat on the side of his expensive Italian leather briefcase. He looked tired. Puffy rings shadowed the space under his heavily bloodshot, steel-gray eyes.

No one seemed to notice. He preferred it that way.

While the clerk validated the credit card blank with the practiced ease of the truly bored, Avignon's eyes drifted across the crowd in the foyer, constantly alert, constantly nervous.

There was a large, loud group in the patio restaurant, harassing the two mini-skirted waitresses who served them. A man in colorful, slightly ridiculous gypsy garb sliced among the tables, executing a passionately kitsch rendition of *O Sole Mio* on the violin.

Nothing out of the ordinary. And that was fine with Avignon.

He noticed a well-dressed woman with beautiful brown eyes sitting in the lobby. She returned his inquiring look and smiled warmly. *What is it you like?* Avignon thought. *The dashing gray hair? The world-weary look? Or perhaps the expensive tailoring?*

He slipped his attention by her without returning the smile. *There simply isn't time,* he thought. *More's the pity.*

The desk clerk cleared his throat for attention. "Would you sign here, sir?"

"Of course." As Jean Avignon reached for the forms, his nose wrinkled and twitched. A look of pure puzzlement passed across his face.

"Something wrong, sir?"

"Non . . ." He hesitated, then shrugged. "I thought I smelled some . . . sing. A very sweet smell."

The desk clerk gave him a strange look and shot a glance at a hovering bellboy that said, *We've got another kook on our hands.*

Avignon smiled and touched a long forefinger to his brow. "I have been perhaps traveling too much. How you call it . . . jet lack?"

The clerk smiled politely and nodded at the forms. This time Avignon signed.

As he straightened, a subtle movement halfway across

the lobby caught his eye. He looked to his left as he returned the signed forms to the desk clerk.

A thin, well-dressed man was lounging comfortably in an overstuffed chair, reading the *Wall Street Journal* and nursing a mint julep. His deep-blue eyes didn't move from the page when Jean Avignon glanced at him.

"You have Suite 2235, Mistah Av— sir." The desk clerk bit it off with a bitter smirk and handed the key to the bellboy. "Mark will see to your bags."

As they crossed the lobby to the elevators, Jean Avignon again shot a glance at the dapper man with the newspaper. This time the man looked up at him. No sign of recognition passed between them.

Well, well, Avignon thought. *Am I that good, or is he?*

He was locked in Suite 2235 taking out his eyes when the man with the *Wall Street Journal* came to call.

The contacts were always first. Lance had never quite adjusted to them, so they were last in and first out. He smiled at the bright blue that had hidden behind steely gray lenses and stepped back to examine his handiwork.

Not bad at all, he thought. He had put on ten pounds and twenty-five years, all in a public toilet.

With one swift motion he pulled off the gray wig and shook loose his own closely cropped blond curls. Then, very carefully, he tugged at the wrinkled area below his eyes. The edge of the plastic skin lifted up, and he peeled away the age lines from both cheeks.

There was a knock at the door.

He had the gun off the bureau and aimed at the door in less than a second. Slowly, bare feet scarcely brushing the carpet, he crept forward and took cover behind the couch.

"Oo eez eet?" he said in the overripe Avignon accent.

"It's Benny, Lance. *All clear!*"

Lance straightened and pocketed the gun. He shook noticeably. Pointing the weapon was one thing, but he had to admit—if only to himself—that he wasn't sure if he could actually *use* it.

Even as sure as he was, he left the chain lock on when he cracked open the door. Benny looked as dapper as ever in a brown wool sweater and coordinated chocolate slacks. He patted nervously at his graying hair and smiled through the crack in the door.

"I can't believe it," he said very softly. "I really can't believe it!"

Lance grinned and opened the door just wide enough for his old friend to slip inside.

"Kee-*rist*, Lance! I thought you were dead!" His accent was a strange mixture of tough Brooklynese and upper-class Manhattan that almost put the lie to his expensively tailored suit—almost, but not quite.

Before Lance could stop him, Benny threw his arms around the younger man in a viselike bear hug.

"Take it easy, Benny," Lance said, laughing. "You'll bust a rib."

Benny let up, still grinning.

"And why should I be dead? I mean, now anymore than last week or the weeks before that?"

Benny frowned. "You haven't seen the latest news?"

"No. I breezed through the paper looking for the horo-scope, but—"

Benny shook his head. "It wouldn't have made the papers yet, I guess."

Lance scowled and sighed. All traces of the dashing Frenchman had disappeared, accent included. Now he was a weary twenty-four-year-old with a flat Californian accent and a worried look. "You want a drink?"

"No, I *need* a drink!"

While Lance fixed a scotch for himself and another large julep for his friend, Benny described what had happened.

"A man was shot to death in the restaurant of the Fontainebleau Hotel in Miami this morning."

"The Fontainebleau?"

"Right. And the police initially identified him as Arnold Perpoint."

"What?!"

Benny took the drink off the small bar before Lance could hand it to him and flopped down into a nearby armchair. He was ashen with fatigue and relief. "I thought it was you for sure. I was *positive* it was you."

Lance moved to his side. "Are you okay?"

He nodded. *"Now,* I'm okay." He took a sip of the drink. "It's just that—"

Lance tried to put his friend at ease. "Three minutes after you called and gave me the high sign, I was up, packed and out of there."

Benny looked confused. "High sign?"

"Sure." Lance couldn't understand Benny's surprise. *"Crossfire.* The warning code we agreed on."

Benny very carefully placed his glass on the small table by the chair. "Lance," he said slowly, "I didn't call."

"Benny, you're not making any sense. Nobody else knew—"

"I didn't call, damn it!"

Lance held up his hands. "Okay, okay. But if you didn't, then who did?"

"I'm damned if I know."

They stared at each other for a long moment, then Lance sighed again. He seemed to be doing a lot of that lately. Sighing and running. Running and sighing. "Let that go for now. How did you find out about— Hell, who *was* it at the Fontainebleau?"

"The hotel desk clerk swears it was Arnold Perpoint. Says he saw him and a lady go into the restaurant, and a few minutes later told that to two gentlemen who asked for him. Seems this couple was having a quiet breakfast when two heavies walked up behind the guy as he was munching on his eggs Benedict and took his head off with one shot."

Benny gulped at his drink.

"The chick went looney-tunes—totally hysterical," Benny said. "A hotel doctor had to sedate her even before the cops got there. It so happens a buddy of mine on the Miami Force was one of the first to arrive. He owes me a favor or two, and I'd asked him to keep a watch out for the names you were carrying—just in case."

"I didn't know you did that sort of thing," Lance said, his brow furrowing.

"I usually don't. He's a special friend, and so are you." Benny swilled down the rest of his drink. "Anyway, the chick had no ID. But the guy was carrying some of the paper I made for you in the last batch—"

"*What!*"

"Name of Arnold Perpoint."

"But . . . that's impossible—" The words hung limply on the air.

Benny went on as if he hadn't heard. "Boris—the guy on the force—he gave me a call. Then I went a little looney-tunes myself. *Shit,* Lance, you scared me!"

Lance frowned even more heavily. "Benny, I wasn't with any woman. And I didn't have breakfast at the Fontainebleau. I *was* in Miami, sure, but I was asleep in my room when you—when someone called and warned me to get out. And I *got out!*"

"You weren't Arnold Perpoint?"

"Yes. I *was* Arnold Perpoint: a mousy little guy with a CPA firm in Detroit." Lance hunched his shoulders and twisted his facial features. Even without makeup, he suddenly looked like the pinched little man who had fled Miami after hearing the word *Crossfire*.

"God, you're getting good at that," Benny said admiringly. "I barely recognized you in the lobby just now, and I know what to look for."

"I didn't think you made me at first."

"It wasn't until you were getting into the elevator. Then something caught my attention."

Lance frowned and rubbed at his forehead. "Benny, I

destroyed the Arnold Perpoint ID, same as I always do, when I changed identities in the men's toilet at Miami International. I swear, I still had it. The cops *couldn't* have found it on this guy, whoever he was.''

Benny took another swallow of his drink, then pulled nervously at his chin. ''Yeah, well I couldn't quite believe you were dead. Didn't want to, is probably closer to the truth. Anyway, I asked Boris to send me a copy of the papers.'' Benny took another large swig before continuing. ''He called an hour ago. That's why I came here, just on the off chance. The papers . . . disappeared.''

''Disappeared?!''

''Yeah, it's crazy, huh?'' Benny rubbed at his chin again. ''Boris is adamant that he had them, and that they were in the name of Arnold Perpoint. But when he got back to the station and went to take them from the pouch, they were . . . *gone*.''

''I don't get it.''

''Me either, Lance. But it scares the *shit* out of me. Especially the part about the two heavies.''

There was an empty pause as they both stared at the wall, trying to absorb everything that had happened.

''Was it Raines?'' Lance asked as he started his second drink. There didn't seem to be anything he could say about the rest of it.

Benny nodded.

''What went wrong, Benny? The word on the grapevine was that Sammy was giving up on us—calling off the dogs.''

''We were faked out, Lance. Sammy didn't ease up, he doubled his effort. Stepped up the chase.''

''But we heard—''

''Exactly what he wanted us to hear,'' Benny finished. ''He probably figured that if we thought things were letting up, we'd get sloppy. Maybe even surface.''

''I wasn't sloppy, Benny. I didn't even slip out of character in bed.''

Benny stood up wearily and nodded. "I believe you, kid. And I don't see how anybody could have guessed it was you behind that fake skin you use." He walked to the bureau and fingered the scraps of latex and the hairpieces. "Incredible," he mumbled.

"So how did they fall to it?"

"I wish I knew."

"And who called me?"

"I wish I knew *that*, too."

Lance started to pace. It was a bad habit, he knew, but he always did it when things began to slip away from him. "Something is really wrong here," he said, low and tense. "None of this makes any sense. But we haven't got time to try and figure it out now. My cover's blown. Maybe yours is, too. They might know you're traveling with me—"

"Any suggestions?"

Lance stopped and looked at him, blank-faced. "No," he said shortly. "Not a one."

Benny smiled—a wry, twisted little grin. "Well, I been thinking of a certain reverse English on that scam we worked in Seattle a couple of years ago."

Lance remembered the game. European royalty bait and switch.

Benny kept grinning. "It would go smooth as shit through a snake over in Europe. Texas millionaire, looking for investors. Couple of phone lines to a boiler room in an empty office on the Champs-Elysées, and in a week or three—"

Anger suddenly flared in Lance. "Come *on*, Benny! Get serious!"

"I *am* serious!"

"I've never even been to Canada! How in the hell am I going to find my way around Europe?"

"What's to find your way around? Just move from jet set to jet set. Come on, kid, those mucky-mucks are always looking for an under-the-table score. We—"

"*We?*" Lance said luxuriously, drawing it out. "You're going with me?"

Benny jauntily tossed down the last of his drink. "What do you think, I'm going to let *you* have all the fun?"

Lance smiled weakly as he sat down and buried his face in his hands. *I'm so tired,* he thought. *So goddamn tired, it's hard to think straight.*

Benny put a comforting hand on his shoulder. "Don't worry about this, kid. We're gonna be fine. You'll see."

"I'm okay, Benny," he said, rubbing his face with one hand. "I just haven't been sleeping too well the last couple of nights, that's all. Probably just the change in time zones."

Benny squeezed his shoulder in agreement and fixed himself another julep. Lance was glad his old friend had accepted the story without question; it was one of his more threadbare lies.

It was the dream that was getting to him, and he knew it. Not Sammy Raines, not the endless travel, the *dream*.

It wasn't normal, having the same nightmare seven nights straight. And worse yet, he couldn't remember the details at all. Just that it was horrible. Horrible and violent. Every night it shot him out of sleep like a cannon, his guts twisted in a knot. And after he woke, he forced himself to stay up until the sun rose. He didn't want to risk it starting again; he wasn't sure he could take it twice in one night.

He wasn't sure he could take it once more *period*.

Benny was watching closely. "Lance," he said softly. "What is it?"

Lance tried to pull himself together. "Nothing. Really, Benny. I'm just tired." With an enormous effort, he pushed the echo of the dream away and forced a smile. Somehow it helped. He began to relax. "I'm going to take a shower, and then hopefully get some rest. There's nothing we can do right now—not until you rig up some paper that'll get us across the Atlantic."

"No problem there," Benny said, all business now. "I can have the layouts here by sunset."

Lance smiled in spite of himself. "You old buzzard," he said, admiring his partner-in-crime. "You've had this all planned, haven't you? The trip to Europe, the Texas millionaire scam?"

Benny shrugged, grinning again. "It's always been an escape clause. Just figured now might be a good time to use it."

Lance had to agree. Now *was* the time. And if anyone could get them out of the country in one piece, it was Benny. He was a veteran survivor, and the best damn counterfeiter on the North American continent.

Benny squeezed his arm and smiled. "Make sure you rest, kid. We have a long trip ahead of us, and we want you looking sharp for those ladies in Monte Carlo."

Lance smiled as Benny winked. Then he led the older man to the door and locked both locks behind him as he slipped out into the hall.

As soon as Benny was gone, the smile faded into a frown.

How could the dead guy have been carrying his ID? It hadn't been stolen, he was sure of it.

And who the *hell* had called and said *Crossfire?*

Chapter 4

Lance stared at his nude body in the full-length bathroom mirror and shook his head. It was a cool, objective assessment—an old habit, left over from years of college and semi-pro athletics.

The joys of jockhood, he thought. Even now, long after his last game, he still watched his diet, limited his intake of liquor, and kept up a rigorous daily exercise routine. *Have to keep moving.*

He had to laugh at that. *Sure. Keep moving. Or die at the hands of one of Sammy Raines's all-too-eager hired killers.*

And every day I change a little bit more. Every day less and less of the jock survives. There's more and more of the con man, the fast thinker, the fast talker. With every new identity, the past falls farther away.

He shrugged as he pushed the thoughts aside and opened the shower door, testing the water with his hand until it was just short of scalding. Then he stripped off the purple Yves St. Laurent robe and stepped gingerly into the bath, hissing at the water as it hit his bare skin.

God, that feels good, he thought as a stream of hot water like a pleasant shower of needles pummeled his broad, brown shoulders. It was a rhythmic tattoo that washed away tension.

Too damn much has happened. I'm starting to lose track . . . starting to lose control.

Steam billowed up in thick clouds, surrounding him on all sides and painting the translucent glass of the shower door with a silver coat of moisture. He was cut off now, pleasantly isolated from the unhappy world outside.

Always bothering me, he thought. *All the time. First this, then that. Back and forth. Up and down. Fortunes afloat on a murky sea.*

He sighed and closed his eyes, letting the warmth of the water against his back lull him into a state of sleepy nostalgia.

What would it be like—where would I be—if I'd never met Benny Haldane? Funny, Mom always wanted me to be an actor. Or a lawyer. Lance couldn't help laughing at that thought. He'd known a fair number of lawyers in the last couple of years, and even after all that had happened, all the scams he had pulled, he was still more honest than most of *them.* And acting? Maybe before, but not now. It could never give him quite the thrill he enjoyed in his chosen profession of basketball.

Mom was disappointed, he thought as he groped for the pink bar of hotel soap. *But at least she doesn't ask a lot of awkward questions. She just scolds me for not writing more often, and asks after Benny, and loves me in spite of it all.*

For a moment, he could almost see her tall, slim, tough good looks there in the mist: blazing blue eyes, just like his, and her shining brown hair pulled back from the cheekbones. A strong woman, and a staunchly proud one.

I'll call you soon, love, he promised silently. *As soon as this—*

Something touched his foot.

Lance jumped and looked down. *What the hell was that?* he thought. *It felt like something . . . alive.*

The steam obscured his vision. He couldn't see anything clearly—not even the rubber mat at the bottom of the tub. But it had been *real*—cold and slick, almost slimy. And it had disappeared as soon as it had touched him.

He wiped the water from his eyes and crouched down in the shower, squinting through the mist. *A piece of soap, maybe? No, it felt . . . pliable, somehow.*

There was nothing there.

He snorted to himself and straightened to his full height, leaning back into the spray and silently blessing the hotel for its apparently endless supply of hot water.

This is what I need, he thought. *This and a damn good sleep. I'm beginning to flip out—*

It touched him again. This time it wrapped around his ankle and *tugged* at him. It was impossible to disregard it.

Lance threw back his arms and fought to hold himself upright against the smooth tile wall.

"What the—"

For an instant the steam cleared and he saw it plainly. And as he shouted, he jerked his body away from what he saw.

But the pale blue tentacle with the white, sucking welts didn't let go.

He twisted to the side, half-panicked, and the steaming water hit him full in the face. Then he cursed and tried to reach the faucet, straining to keep his balance against the thing that pulled and pulled—

And another tentacle, as thick as his own muscled arm, appeared out of the shower door and snaked across his naked thigh, striving for purchase.

The tentacles were coming right out of the shower door itself, somehow surfacing from another world, through the misty glass door.

And they had him held tight now, were dragging him away. Dragging him *into* the glass.

The steam billowed up higher than ever, blinding him. His hands clutched at the smooth beige tiles, but there was nothing to grip. He turned, trying to see the things that were tearing at him, and thought he saw a third arm flailing about in the steam.

Then the vapor unexpectedly flew apart, as if shattered by a cold wind.

Lance froze at what he saw.

There was a *face*—an abhorrent, distorted, grinning face— rising out of the frosted glass of the shower door. It began as an abstract pattern, like rime on a winter window, and it expanded as he watched, swelling into three dimensions as the cold, fleshy arms tightened about him and pulled him down, forward, *into* the glass.

Lance screamed. He brushed his fists and hit the glass with both hands, right in the center of the obscene face, but it didn't shatter. It only shuddered like a sheet of steel, and the booming echo as it flexed sounded like inhuman laughter.

For a moment—only for an instant—the face lost its form, breaking into a scattered pattern of steam and light.

Lance seized this opportunity and made his move.

He gripped the shower door with both hands and *shoved*. The glass resisted, tried to trap him, but he shoved again with all the strength he could muster.

It flew open with a scream, and the tentacles squealed like tortured pigs. Something ripped and shuddered as the sliding door passed through the thing like a scythe through rotting wheat—and the clutching cold disappeared.

Lance didn't look for the face. He didn't look for anything. Instead, he ducked his head into his arms and hurled himself—shoulder first—through the open door and onto the bathroom floor beyond.

He hit the linoleum with a painful *thud* and rolled against the base of the sink. His head glazed the ceramic, and for a split second he saw speckles of light across his vision.

But a sudden rush of adrenalin urged him on, and he shook them away. Working on instinct alone, he struggled to his feet and backed out of the bathroom, dripping wet and naked, staring at the empty shower.

There was nothing there, of course. No tentacles. No face in the glass. Just scalding hot water roaring from the shower head and billowing steam that filled the room from the ceiling down.

That was ail.

Half an hour later he was still stark naked as he sat in the overstuffed chair in the living room, finished another drink, and tried hard to think about nothing at all.

It wasn't working.

It's the lack of sleep, he told himself. *The recurring nightmare. I've heard about it before. Not enough sleep, not enough REMs, and you have waking dreams. Hallucinations.*

That's what it was. I let my guard down for just a second and all the tensions, all the craziness since Raines started chasing me . . . it all came out.

It took on the shape of pale blue tentacles with livid white welts. It could just as easily have been pink elephants.

The metallic buzz of the doorbell made Lance jump like a frightened child. As the drink slipped into his naked lap he jumped up, cursing himself—under his breath—for being so clumsy.

He grabbed his robe from the back of the chair, wrapping it around his waist, then hurried to the door and peered through the peephole.

The gun was forgotten. The careful passwords were left behind. He was just too tired and shaken to remember.

The same bellman who had brought him to his room was standing in the corridor, looking very impatient.

"Who is it—" he stopped himself. *Damn it,* he thought. *I'm out of character.* One hand rubbed at his forehead as he fought to clear his thoughts. *Come on, come on. Don't blow it now.*

He cleared his throat and tried again. "Allo," he said, raising his tone a few notes. "Oo eez dere?"

"I have a package for you, sir," the bellman called from beyond the door.

Lance tried to sound befuddled. It wasn't hard. "Ah . . . well . . . I ham in the shower, *garçon*. Without the clothes." He cracked open the door a few inches—just wide enough to let the package in. "Could you please pass it to me, *s'il vous plaît?*"

The package appeared in the gap between the door and frame, and Lance snatched it, slamming the door as soon as it was inside.

"Sank you," he said pleasantly, his eye glued to the peephole.

The bellman waited for a moment, expecting a tip. When it wasn't forthcoming, he stomped away mumbling bitterly under his breath.

The parcel was wrapped in brown paper, the name and suite number written on it in clear blue numbers an inch high.

Good old Benny, he thought, grinning. *Best pen-and-ink man who ever lived. It's been, what—a couple of hours since he left and he already—*

DON'T OPEN IT!

Lance's head snapped up. *What the hell was that?* he thought. A soundless voice. A wordless command that seemed to come from outside and inside of himself at the same time.

He waited, frozen in place, listening so hard the sound of his own blood pounding in his ears was like continuous cannon blasts.

Minutes passed. Nothing happened.

Damn, he thought and sighed. *This lack of sleep is really getting to me.*

The seal on the package broke with a *snap,* and he fumbled with the wrapping paper, finally just tearing at it with both hands. It contained a large envelope—

DON'T OPEN IT! DANGER! He dropped the envelope and clutched at his head with both hands. *God, what was it?* Something was ordering him—trying to control him.

Fear gushed up inside Lance and crushed him like a vise. Then the smell was back: that cloying, syrupy-sweet smell from the dream. It clutched at his throat.

That proves it, he thought, watching his hands shake. *That proves it's a waking dream. I've got to get some sleep, that's all. I'm having the same damn nightmare, and it's not even waiting for me to sleep anymore. It's forcing itself into my waking thoughts.*

Slowly, he bent at the knee and gathered up the wrapping paper and the envelope. *I'll just take a quick look at Benny's layouts,* he told himself, *then stretch out for a couple of hours. That'll end all this craziness. These nightmares—*

His thoughts stopped short as he saw the front of the envelope for the first time.

Written there in large letters was the name: MR. LANCE SULLIVAN. Not Jean Avignon, the identity he had taken on the day before. Not Arnold Perpoint, either. And not Carson Benzer, or Stephen Ward, or Bernie Weinstein, or any of the other names he'd used in the last few months.

The envelope was addressed to his *real* name. And only Benny Haldane, in all of Dallas, knew it.

He wouldn't do that, Lance thought. He knew it as surely as he knew his own name. *Benny's a pro.*

DON'T OPEN IT! DROP THE LETTER! RUN! RUN!

Intense fear hit him like a sledgehammer. He nearly dropped the package all over again. Things shifted into slow motion as panic welled up inside him and his heart thumped like a dangerously overloaded machine.

I'm gettin' the hell out of here, he thought.

AWAY! GET AWAY!

The letter fluttered to the floor. He grabbed at a pair of

slacks hanging over a nearby chair, pulled on a shirt, and stumbled to the door, mumbling under his breath.

"Got to get away. Can't let it get me. Can't—"

THERE IS DANGER IN THE LETTER! RUN! IT'S YOUR ONLY—

"No!" he shouted into the air.

Touching the doorknob was like suddenly being connected to a live wire. It somehow sent a bolt of clarity raging through him, as sharp as an electrical charge. *What the hell am I doing?* he thought as the panic bubbled and churned inside him like a thunderhead. *What the hell is this? I'm running from a damned letter. Have I finally flipped—*

DON'T THINK! STOP FOR NOTHING! RUN! IT'S YOUR ONLY CHANCE!

The wordless compulsion was back, driving into his brain, forcing him to flee.

He hit the door with his fist as hard as he could. A knuckle popped under the force of the blow and the pain cleared his head for an instant.

Think, he ordered himself. *Consider your actions. Don't be driven by fear, particularly when you don't know where the hell it's coming from. Fight it, fight!*

In one convulsive movement, he turned back into the room, bent at the waist, seized the envelope, and ripped it open with a clumsy jerk.

The pressure cut off like a switch had been thrown. Lance swayed back under the sudden release, nearly losing his balance.

Insane, he thought, as he stumbled to the couch and sat down heavily. *I must be absolutely insane.* Sweat sprouted from his brow. *I feel like I've been beat up. Like I've lost a war inside my skull.*

He stared dumbly at the torn letter in his left hand. *Over this?* he wondered. *This? Okay, so it has my real name on it. That might mean that Sammy's found me—found us. But what else could it mean?*

Lance had had hunches before. They'd even saved his life. He remembered how a strange intuitive fear had compelled him to skip an airline flight from Boston to New York . . . and how the same plane had been high-jacked. And a second time, when he'd refused to board a plane to El Paso . . . and it had crashed into the Gulf of Mexico, killing everyone on board.

Benny had been mad as hell at missing that flight, until he'd heard about the seventy-three corpses they'd fished out of the sea. After that, he'd learned to trust Lance's hunches, just as Lance had learned to trust them himself.

And now that the madness had subsided—that chaotic, insistent pressure inside his head—he knew something important was hiding inside the envelope. He didn't care about *hows* and *whys*. He just *knew* it, with the same crystalline certainty that had saved his life at least twice before.

The paper crackled as he opened the letter. It was on the fancy legal stationery of a law firm in Sydney, Australia, named Wilcox, Cundy and Cook.

```
Lance Sullivan:
As executors of your great-grandmoth-
er's estate, we have the sad duty of
notifying you of her unfortunate and
untimely death. Be also notified that
you have been named a beneficiary in
her last will and testament.

Said estate is of considerable size,
and your participation in its full and
proper dispensation is essential.

Please contact Mr. Alex Ryder, our rep-
resentative in the United States. He
may be reached at his Beverly Hills of-
fices, telephone number (213) 555-0439.
```

It is essential you contact him as soon
as possible, so he may apprise you of
all the pertinent details.

Your prompt communication is impera-
tive. I eagerly await meeting you in
person in the very near future.

It was signed with a wide swirling signature: "Josh
Wilcox."

Lance stared at the paper until his eyes hurt—until he no
longer saw the letters at all, only a meaningless string of
dancing black specks.

It's a trap, he thought. *Some stupid trap set by Sammy
Raines. Does he think I'm dumb enough to jump at an old
con like this? 'You have inherited big bucks. Call me right
away and tell me where you are.' What kind of fool does
he think I am? I don't have any relatives other than my
mother, and she's safe and sound in Santa Barbara.*

Later, in a calmer moment, Lance would realize how
confused he really was. If the letter had found him, Sammy
Raines didn't *need* to draw him out into the open. He
knew exactly where he was, and he could come in any
time with guns blazing.

But staring at the letter, still feeling the shocks and
chills of that strange soundless voice, his thoughts were a
loud, tangled rush. *Nothing* made sense. Not the letter,
not the thing in the shower, not Sammy Raines's mad
vendetta—*nothing.*

A few minutes later, he called the lawyer in Beverly
Hills. He didn't really think about it; it just seemed the thing
to do.

The hotel operator came on the line. "Yes? May I help
you?"

"Oui. Zis iz Monsieur Avignon, Suite two-two-sree-
five. I would like to be placing a telephone call to Los
Angeles, *s'il vous plaît.*" His eyes were glazed and his

mind was in shock, but still Lance didn't fall out of character.

He gave her the number, and as the phone rasped and ticked in his ear, he held up his wrist and stared at the sweep second hand on his watch.

Three minutes, he decided. *From the moment they answer the phone, no more than three minutes. That way they can't trace me.* He still couldn't grasp the single impossibility that the letter represented: Somebody already knew where he was. They didn't need to trace any call.

The phone rang thousands of miles away. A pleasant middle-aged female voice answered, "Ryder, Fullhurst and Smith. Good afternoon."

"Could I speak to Mr. Ryder? This is Lance Sullivan." His eyes never left his watch as he fought to get control of his scrambled thoughts.

"One moment, please."

The line clicked.

"Mr. Sullivan?"

"Yes."

"Alex Ryder here." He had a deep, melodious voice that floated over awkward pauses with an oily ease.

The perfect lawyer's voice, Lance thought. *Maybe too perfect.*

"Mr. Sullivan, I must say I'm pleasantly surprised at your swift response. Good to see the information was correct."

"What information?"

Alex Ryder appeared not to have heard the question. "My orders are to tell you about the details surrounding the reading of your great-grandmother's last will and testament. I hope you will accept our condolences at her untimely—"

"I don't know what you're talking about," Lance said.

Once again, Ryder didn't seem to hear him. "Her instructions stipulate that the will must be opened and read in full on the 28th day of the August directly following her death. All the beneficiaries of her estate have been contacted—you're the last—and they must appear at the reading in the offices of Wilcox, Cundy and Cook on that day, or forfeit any and all benefits assigned thereby. Since that date is only two weeks away, I'm sure you realize how urgent it was that I speak with you."

"But I don't—"

Ryder kept on talking. "The estate is sizable—"

"I don't *have* any great-grandmother!" Lance shouted into the phone. "There must be some mistake."

Alex Ryder finally stopped talking. He paused. Then he said, "But the letter found you."

"I know that. But it doesn't change anything. You've got the wrong boy."

Lance started to hang up, then thought better of it. It was that hunch again—something telling him that there was more to this than a simple miscommunication. "Ah . . . Mr. Ryder. This probably sounds stupid, but can you tell me anything about this lady who's supposed to have been my great-grandmother."

"Well . . ." Ryder seemed confused, but tried to oblige. "Aah . . . I don't really know very much, except that her name was Elizabeth Beresford. I believe she was called 'Essie.' "

The receiver turned cold in Lance's hand.

For a long second he sat, staring blankly, no longer hearing Ryder's voice.

"Mr. Sullivan! Mr. Sullivan, are you—"

Lance hung up without a word. A memory, old and dim, was tugging at him.

Beresford. *Beresford.* He knew that name. Lance thought hard, and his forehead wrinkled into deep furrows as he searched his memory. *Why does that name sound so familiar?*

It came as if a dam had burst. Lance dropped heavily into the large chair, a look of astonishment filling his features.

*   *   *

Lance was only six when he found the secret paper. It was a rare rainy day in California, and he was bored and restless.

"You're spoiled," his mother scolded good-naturedly. "Too much sunshine, too much good weather. Why when I was a girl . . ."

She trailed off then. Lance wondered about that, as he would wonder many times throughout his life. Mum never talked about her past—her childhood. *Never*.

But this time, just to get him out of the way, she let him play in *her* room—that sweet-smelling, ruffled sanctum that belonged to Mum alone.

The bureau drawers—the ones he was told not to open— were full of clothing and a powdery, feminine, maternal smell. None of it interested Lance much . . . until he came to the bottom right-hand drawer.

It was a wonderland of forgotten bits and pieces: post-cards with fascinating, faded postage stamps. Costume jewelry she'd thrown in the drawer and forgotten. A torn snapshot of a man Lance didn't recognize. And lipsticks, compacts, pins, pens, berets, curlers, containers of eye-shadow and sticks of eyebrow pencil. There were earrings, broken bracelets, a watch with no hands . . .

And there, folded five ways and tucked into a corner of the drawer, he found a yellowed piece of paper. Just the sort of mysterious discovery to set a six-year-old's imagi-nation on fire. It could be a treasure map. Or the combina-tion to a chest of gold buried in the basement. Or any number of magical things.

He opened it carefully and read it a word at a time. Reading was still a slow process for him.

"CERTIFICATE OF MARRIAGE," it said at the top. And under that, names that meant very little to him.

It wasn't until much later that he realized the "James" it mentioned was his father . . . the father he'd never met. And he didn't know then that his mother Betty's name was short for Beatrice. Or that she had once had a different last name.

Why should it have mattered then? he thought as he stood in Suite 2235 of the Dallas Hotel and stared into space. Why should he have wondered at the yellowed legal document that bore the names of James and Beatrice *Beresford*.

Even my own memories are coming back to haunt me, he thought.

Chapter 5

As the sun set outside his hotel window, Lance Sullivan changed his face.

Blue eyes turned brown, flecked with gold. The tight blond curls were covered with a James Dean brush-back wig. Bits of thick aquatic tubing were inserted in each nostril, to widen and flatten his nose. A wisp of charcoal from the head of a burnt match gave him a five o'clock shadow in a shade wholly different than his real beard. Another thumb-streak under each cheekbone made him look gaunt and hungry.

Next he slipped on a sleeveless James Dean T-shirt, stove-piped Levis, and a pair of colored sneakers. His shoulders dropped, his thumbs hooked into the belt loops of his jeans, and he grinned at the stranger in the mirror.

Johnny Hancock gave him a crooked know-it-all grin right back.

The disguise had started during the scams, both to protect his identity and to throw the marks off balance.

Now he had to do it to stay alive.

It's almost a sin to enjoy this so much, he thought. *But I like it. And now it's not just the makeup and clothes and hair color that changes. I change inside, too. I'm not*

Lance Sullivan—not when I look like this. I'm Johnny Hancock, twenty-two-year-old chain-smoking high school dropout—unemployed, uninvolved, undesirable, and mad at the whole damn world.

He spun on his heels and slouched out of the room, hooking the door shut with his heel as he went.

Once he was out of the hotel, he worked his way toward a nearby drugstore and a pay phone. As he went, he took on a loping, slouching saunter, his head bobbing slowly as he surveyed the street.

"Should get me some gum," he said, running his tongue over his teeth. "Johnny Hancock would chew gum." He pulled a comb from his pants pocket and lightly adjusted his ducktail. "Yeah. Gum at the drugstore. Perfect."

The cashier looked him up and down when he leaned on the counter, slammed down three coins, and mumbled "Gum." She pushed the green-and-white package across the counter and scooped the money into her palm, and Lance couldn't help grinning when he saw her count the change very slowly.

But Johnny Hancock didn't think it was funny. John Hancock thought, *Shit. Like I would counterfeit a quarter and two nickels. Gimme a break.*

He kicked down a long linoleum aisle stacked high with shampoo, cough syrup, headache remedies, suntan oils and feminine hygiene sprays. *Looking for a phone*, he told himself as he moved, catching sight of the wide-eyed cashier in the shoplifting mirror over his head.

He flipped her the bird and she looked away quickly. *Damn straight*, he thought, enjoying the game. *Damn fuckin' straight*.

Johnny Hancock was a lot of fun, Lance decided. A little out of control maybe, but a lot of fun.

The phone was an old-fashioned black monster mounted on the back wall. It looked as if it had been there for years, untouched during the bright plastic-and-chrome renovation that had transformed the rest of the store in the recent past.

Lance dug into his tight jeans, plunked a handful of coins on the top of the metal box, and pushed a quarter into the coin slot.

He wasn't about to call from his hotel room. He'd worked too hard keeping his mother's whereabouts from Sammy Raines and his boys, and he wasn't going to risk leaving a record of her number in some hotel computer. Not now.

The phone beeped four times and the operator's nasal voice—accentuated even more by the phone line—chirped in his ear.

"Please deposit four dollars and fifty cents for the first three minutes."

He fed the phone quarters until it beeped again.

"Thank you. You have credit for three minutes," the operator chirped again.

"Thank you *so* much," Johnny mumbled. *Like she was doing me a fuckin' favor or something.*

Lance was a little surprised at his own hostility. But he put it behind him when the phone at the far end of his connection began to ring.

All right, Johnny thought. *Good deal.*

"Hello?"

The coin dropped into some secret place inside the pay phone with a loud clang.

"Mum? This is Lance."

"*Lance!*" Betty Sullivan cried. "How are you, love?" She sounded delighted to hear from her son.

"I'm okay, Mum," he mumbled as he patted his DA.

"It seems like months since I've heard from you," his mother said. Then she laughed. "It's not, of course. It's been, what, five days, but—"

"Ah, look, I gotta ask you," Johnny Hancock butted in, "who is Essie Beresford?"

There was a long pause. Lance tried hard to listen to the

silence, to gauge what was going on in her mind . . . but the other part of him, the Johnny Hancock part, wasn't really interested. He barely knew the broad at the other end of the phone. He wanted to get moving. And as he waited, his fingers idly traced the old graffiti and phone numbers scratched into the wall next to the phone.

KATHY BLUMFORD SUCKS!

SURF NAZIS FOREVER!

JAMES DEAN WILL NEVER DIE!

LULU WILL DO IT WITH ANYONE
FOR A BUCK: 555-9928

Well all right, Lulu! Johnny Hancock thought, grinning.

Lance shook his head and bent into the phone. "Mum—"

"W . . . what do you mean, Lance?"

He sighed, exasperated. "Don't do that, Mum. Come on. Who is Essie Beresford?"

Johnny Hancock jiggled the quarters in the fist of his right hand. *Come on, lady. Come on. Gotta go, gotta move.*

"W . . . where did you hear that name, son?"

"You know her, don't you?"

"I—"

"She was my great-grandmother, wasn't she?"

"Lance—"

"Wasn't she?" Lance said.

God damn it, Johnny thought. *Never get nothin' straight. Never get nothin' the way you want it with damn parents and damn teachers and damn everybody trying to keep you—*

Lance passed a hand over his face. *What the hell's happening to me?* he thought. *I can't let the characters get away from me like that. It's only a pose, it's only—*

"Yes," his mother said, very softly. "Yes, she was your great-grandmother."

God . . . damn . . . it. Now Johnny was really upset. "All those years," he said into the phone. "All those years I thought we were alone. You *said* we were. And you were *lying* to me, you were just *lying!*"

"I had a good reason, love. You've got to—"

"You know what I been through?" Johnny shifted from one foot to the other, scowling as his eyes scanned the store. "You know what it's like, having no relatives, no family? Kids make fun 'a ya. They treat you like *shit*, Ma."

"Love, I—"

"And all the time, I had a *grandmother!* All the time! And now she's *dead,* before I ever knew her. She's goddamn dead! How the hell could you do that to me?" Johnny whined. *How could she cheat me, lie to me, God damn it—*

God damn it!

Lance stopped himself—he stopped Johnny. He gripped the handset of the phone until his knuckles turned white. *What's the matter with me? I didn't mean to say any of that—*

"Are there any others?" Johnny said, his voice still hard and mean.

"Lance," his mother said carefully. "How did you find out about Essie?"

"A lawyer called me. Said I was in her will." But he didn't want to talk about that. He wanted to talk about how the bitch had lied to him, how *everybody* lied to Johnny Hancock. "How many others?" he demanded. "How many?"

"How did they find you, Lance? How could they possibly know who you were? Or *where* you were? *I* didn't even know that."

For a moment—only a moment—cold reason cleared Lance's mind. Johnny Hancock's bubbling resentment faded, and he stuttered into the phone. "I . . . I don't know, Mum. I guess . . . No, I don't know."

"I do, Lance. Oh, my God, I'm sorry, but I *do* know."

She sounded terrified. "Mum? What's the matter? Look, it's only a letter. A phone call. I—"

"I'm scared, Lance. I'm really scared."

For an instant, Johnny's anger tried to boil up, but Lance stopped it fast. "Okay, Mum. Okay, it's a mystery. But I'm sure there's some logical explanation." The lie felt sour on his tongue. The truth was, he didn't know what was happening. Ever since those dreams had started, it had been one thing after another, and another—

"What did they say?" his mother asked.

"What did who say?"

"The lawyers. The ones who found you?"

"She *died,* that's what they *said.*" *Shit,* Johnny Hancock thought, *what was this, the third fuckin' degree?* He was mad now, really mad that she kept asking all these goddamn questions. He was the one with questions; *he* was the one who wanted to know what was going on. "She left a big estate, and I'm in the will, okay? You want a cut or something? You want a piece of that, too?"

"Lance, is something—"

"They want me in Australia, okay? Satisfied?" Johnny was shouting into the phone now. The cashier at the front was staring at him through the mirror, but he didn't give a rat's ass. "I gotta go to Australia, or I'll lose—"

"Nooooo!"

Lance stopped short. He had never heard his mother scream like that before—never heard her sound really frightened before. The shock of it snapped him out of his strange dual role, and for an instant he was terrified. *Something's wrong with her,* he thought, chilled to the bone. *Something's wrong . . . with me.*

"What is it, Mum?" he said suddenly. "What's the matter?"

There was another long pause. Lance tried to hang on,

he tried to concentrate on staying himself. *Say something,* he thought desperately. *Don't leave me here alone, or—*

Johnny rushed back to fill the silence—and Lance's mind.

"What is it, goddamn it? What, what, *what?*" He hated the old bitch, hated it when she did this to him!

"There's no way you can understand," Betty Sullivan said. Her voice was cool and controlled—far more distant than the miles that separated them. "You weren't even born when it happened. Lance, there are good reasons—important reasons—why I left Australia, and why I never told you. And please, listen to me: *you can't go back there.* Not now. Not *ever.*"

Johnny shifted the phone to his other ear. He leaned on his other leg and sneered. "You don't tell me what I can do anymore, Ma. Remember? I'm *out* now. I'm *free.*"

"Lance, why are you saying things like that? What is it? Are you all right?"

For a moment, Johnny faltered. There was too much gentleness, too much love in her voice. He couldn't—he couldn't—

"It's okay, Mum," Lance said and rubbed at his face with his free hand. "I'm just . . . I'm not sleeping very well, that's all. Look, if you don't want me to go to Australia, I won't go."

She sighed with relief. "Thank you, love. But we have to talk about all this. We *have* to. I want to try and explain, but not on the phone. Not this way." She hesitated a moment. "Can you come home, love?"

Lance didn't answer for a long time. There was a battle going on inside him.

Seething anger from Johnny Hancock was filling every corner of his being, and he couldn't control it. He couldn't even think straight with the hatred and heat from the juvenile delinquent—who was somehow a part of Lance himself—roaring through him. Still, he didn't give in—not right away. He held on a moment longer through sheer will.

"Yes, I can come home, Mum. But it'll take me a few hours to straighten things out here and get away. I'll call and let you know what flight I'll be on, as soon as I know."

"Thank God, Lance. Thank God." She sounded impossibly relieved. "I just wish you were coming home for a happier reason."

Sure you do, Johnny thought. *You always want me home where you can get at me, pick at me, make me do whatever you want—*

STOP IT! Lance shoved the wild thoughts away for one last moment. "I love you, Mum," he said hurriedly, before Johnny could come back and twist it. "I'll see you real soon."

"All right, Lance. Goodbye, love."

Johnny slammed down the phone so hard it almost snapped off in his hand. *Damn it,* that old bitch made him mad! And damn it if he was gonna shag his tail out to California just 'cause she was feeling lonely again. No way. No chance.

Lance was being swamped by the Johnny Hancock persona. He found to his horror that he couldn't control his own body, as one thumb rubbed at the phone numbers etched into the wall and Johnny grinned at a sudden thought, locked somewhere between *East of Eden* and his own childhood fears and dreams.

Always felt like a geek when I was a kid, he thought. *Everybody always askin' questions like 'Where's your pa?' 'Where's your grandpa?' 'How come no relatives, huh?' Huh?*

All those forms they made you fill out. All that crap about next of kin. Well, I ain't got no goddamn next of kin, okay? At least not until today. And I don't know whether to be happy or not. I don't know anythin', don't know nothin' and never did. Never—

I have to call Benny. Lance struggled frantically to regain control. He turned toward the phone and put a hand on the receiver. *I have to call Benny and tell him what's happening. Ask him to come and get me—*

The moment he touched the phone Johnny came back.

"Gotta get me some more gum, man. This shit's all chewed out." Some small memory tapped at him—something about calling somebody . . . or something.

Johnny shrugged it away. "Hey, it can wait. Gonna get me some beer. Gonna cruise a little, see if I can find some action. Maybe call ol' Lulu. Yeah, call little Lulu."

He sauntered through the drugstore and slapped down the coins for some more gum. Then he slouched into the street. So cool. So *cool*.

Betty Sullivan was completely forgotten. He wouldn't have recognized Benny's name if he'd heard it. And Lance was just some kid he used to know. A real loser.

But Johnny Hancock was on the move. Johnny Hancock was goin'. And meanwhile, the street was alive; the street was happening. He could see that everything he needed was just straight on down the road.

If he had looked up, he would have seen a phosphorescent cloud, visible only to him, drifting directly over his head. But he didn't look up. He didn't want to look up. He only wanted to cruise. And when something did seem odd to him, when he did sniff at the sickly sweet smell that surrounded him, he figured it must be the exhaust from a Harley-Davidson passing by.

Nothing to worry about. Nothing for Johnny Hancock to do but cruise.

Chapter 6

"All right, Lance. Goodbye, love."

Betty Sullivan stood in the bedroom of her Santa Barbara bungalow and listened to the long-distance line disconnect. Her thoughts were a million miles away; she forgot the phone was still at her ear until the harsh burr of the dial tone pulled her concentration back to the room.

She hung up very slowly and frowned to herself. "Who am I kidding?" she said aloud. Her voice sounded odd in the empty room. "He'll never believe me. I'm not sure I believe it myself anymore."

She suddenly felt very old and very tired. The heavy flowered drapes hanging in the furnished room seem to swallow up her words like a hungry sponge. The air felt almost too thick to breath.

She caught a glimpse of her reflection in the full-length mirror mounted on the far wall, and leaned forward, scrutinizing all five-feet-six-inches of her slim, wiry frame.

"Not a bad-looking old girl," she said aloud, trying to recapture some spark of her normal ènergy. "You can still make it on your own, can't you? And he will believe you. He has to. It's the only lie you ever told him."

The phone call had taken a lot out of her. Too much,

really. *It's been almost twenty-five years since I've heard that woman's name,* she thought. *It shouldn't bother me now.*

But it does. It does.

She sat on the edge of the bed and sighed loud and long as she smoothed the covers under her, remembering all that had happened in those early days. The running. The fear. All the name changes—so many times she'd lost count.

It had all been for nothing, really. She had only delayed the inevitable.

The evil *thing* had found her son.

Lance had said that Essie Beresford was dead now, but Betty didn't believe that. The old witch would never die. Maybe she *couldn't.* But how did she find them? *How?*

Betty's shoulders slumped in defeat as she looked away from the mirror. How didn't really matter. What was done was done. What mattered was that now, after a quarter of a century, she would have to tell Lance the truth about his father—and his father's death. And she would have to tell him about the crazy, evil woman she feared more than anyone else on the face of the earth.

Betty wandered aimlessly around the room, fussing at her graying hair as her thoughts drifted back to the long ago. Back to 1957, when her skin was still smooth and pretty. When Australia was her home. When Jim Beresford was alive and by her side.

What a handsome man he was! Trim, golden blond hair like his boy's would one day be. And though he wasn't truly tall—just a hair over five-foot-ten—there was something about the way he held himself, about the sparkle in his bright blue eyes, that made him seem much taller.

They lived in a small rented house in Newtown, a suburb of Sydney. One day, only a few months after they were married, Jim got a call from Grandmother Essie. She wanted him to visit her at Beresford Hall, her huge estate at Parramatta.

Jim didn't even think of refusing. A request from Essie Beresford was akin to a royal decree.

Still, Beatrice didn't like the old lady. She never had. There was something . . . well, strange about her. And she was sure the old matriarch was highly offended at their insistence on making a life for themselves away from the rest of the Beresford clan. After all, every other member of the family seemed quite content to leech off Essie's fortune; why should Jim and his young bride be any different?

Yet they were different. They wanted to be. But Essie had summoned Jim to Beresford Hall, probably to try once again to convince him to accept her "generous help," whether they wanted it or not.

The invitation came in a long, grim telephone call between Jim and the old woman. After it was over, he hung up the phone heavily and turned to his wife. "Beat," he said. (He always called her that, though no one else dared.) "Beat, you're not going to believe this."

He gave her the details of the Beresfords' strange legacy, just as Essie had described it to him.

She must have been afraid he wouldn't come, Beatrice thought, *to tell him so much over the phone.*

Jim was right: Beatrice didn't believe him, not a word. Not then, anyway.

"It sounds like a cheap Edgar Allen Poe novel," she said. *Or the ravings of a sick and desperate old woman,* she added to herself.

Jim grinned. What a lovely smile. "You're right. It does. But Essie didn't sound like she was joking. She says she wants me to spend the next few days with her at Beresford Hall, so she can explain it more fully."

His eyes were flashing with a fire that Beatrice had come to love. It was like the light in a small child's eyes when driven to discovery, or in the eyes of a wise man who has seen more than he can hold. And there was something more there: a bottomless energy. A *power*. It sounded melodramatic, she knew, but it wasn't. It was exactly the right word to explain Jim: *power*.

"Essie says we're in danger, Beat."

"Who is 'we'? You and me?"

He nodded. "And all the family, I think. But right now she says she's most afraid for me."

"I don't understand."

"I don't either." His eyes were blazing. "But I believe her."

Beatrice quirked her mouth and made a small sound of derision. "Your intuition again?"

He grinned, half-embarrassed. "I know, I know. My hunches seem crazy at times—"

"Yes, they do. But they also have a habit of being right." Beatrice reached out for him. She couldn't keep her dark frown hidden. "Jim, I'm afraid."

He held her close and whispered to her. "I am too, Beat."

He had never talked down to her, never tried to pretend things weren't serious when they really were. "There's something . . . I don't know, *eerie*, I guess, about old Essie this time."

Beatrice pulled away an inch and tried to laugh. She made it to a half-smile. "Oh, really?" she said wryly, loving him so much it tore at her.

He smiled now. "More than usual, I mean." The frown returned. "I've never known her to be so grim. So worried. She says we're in real danger, but that she'll show me how to protect us from . . . whatever it is she's afraid of."

He stopped and took Beatrice's face in his hands. Warmth flooded over her, and she trembled under his touch.

"If you don't want me to go," he said, "I won't."

"I love you, Jim." Beatrice held him tightly.

"I love you, too, Beat."

She gripped him, refusing to let him go for the longest moment. "You don't think this is just the ravings of a senile old lady, do you?"

"No, I don't."

She nodded and sighed. "When will you go?"

The decision was made.

"She said I should come right away."

"I'll pack you a bag," she said, taking his hand and leading him toward the bedroom.

An hour later she waved good-bye to her husband as he drove off in their 1956 Holden sedan.

She went back into the house after the car had disappeared, and the silence and loneliness in every room pressed in like darkness. She wanted to relax, to sit and not think at all. "A bath," she said to herself. It had always been one of her favorite pastimes, and today she had the tub filled and the soap bubbles white and frothy in record time.

It was glorious. She stayed in far longer than she had intended. But after the better part of an hour, she sighed, climbed out of the bath, wrapped herself in a huge orange towel and padded down the long hallway to their bedroom.

The sun had set while she had dawdled in the tub. Now the room was black and warm before her, and she had to fumble about just inside the doorway to find the light switch.

She couldn't find it. She eased her hand over the wall again and again, groping . . . and it just wasn't there.

The skin on the back of Beatrice's neck suddenly prickled. An icy tension trickled down her spine.

The darkness never bothers me, she thought. *Why—*

"Beatrice."

She spun and faced the darkness, terrified by the voice.

Someone was in the bedroom, calling to her. She backed away, almost into the hall, and peered into the room.

It was a woman. She could tell that from the voice. But it was dark in there. Completely dark.

This time she found the light switch on the first try. She snapped it on and stepped forward, ready to face whoever waited for her—

But nothing happened. No light blazed; no filament popped. Nothing.

"I have to talk to you, Beatrice."

The voice still waited in the darkness.

There's a flower pot in the hall, she thought. *Only three or four feet away. If I can reach it, I might be able to hit—*

"Beatrice—"

A sudden realization swept over her with physical force. *That voice!* she thought. *I know that voice!*

It was Essie. Stronger, somehow younger than she remembered . . . but it *was* Essie.

That was impossible, she knew. Essie was miles away, in Parramatta. She—

"It *is* me, Beatrice. It *is* Essie."

She searched the blackness, trying to locate the source of the voice. But it seemed to hang in midair.

"I'm sorry to have frightened you, but I had no choice. I had to warn you quickly." There was something soothing in the old woman's tone. Beatrice found herself slowly walking forward.

Then, in the heart of the darkness, Essie appeared.

Beatrice stopped, frozen in horror. No. It wasn't Essie at all. The figure before her was years younger than the hateful old woman in Parramatta. And she could actually see through the apparition, as if it were a reflection in an invisible mirror. The figure stood five feet before her, feet not touching the floor, glowing soft and full.

It should have terrified her. But Beatrice's hands were steady, and her heart beat calm and steady in her breast. *Why am I so peaceful?* she wondered. *Why aren't I running out of the house screaming like a madwoman?*

"Because you have nothing to fear from me," the apparition explained. "You know that instinctively."

The thing's lips didn't move. She heard the voice only in her mind.

"M . . . maybe so," Beatrice answered, her voice shaking. "But give me half a chance, and I'll run like hell."

The apparition smiled weakly, pulsing in the darkness.

"Am I dreaming? Did I fall asleep in the tub?"

"No."

"But Jim said he was meeting you at Parramatta—" Sudden fear flooded through her. "Where *is* Jim? Is something—"

The apparition didn't move, or speak.

Beatrice slowly started to move away. "I'll call him there. I'll call Parramatta, and he'll—"

Light enveloped her and she froze again. She looked down in horror as her feet lifted from the floor and she spun slowly in the air to face the Essie-thing again.

"I *am* asleep," she said carefully. "I'm asleep in the bathtub, and this is a dream. Any second now, Jim will call and I'll wake up and—"

"Jim won't call, Beatrice."

"Where is he?" she cried. "Please tell—"

"He's dead, Beatrice. He died a few minutes ago in his car."

Beatrice stared at the apparition. Anger and fear and hate welled up in her. "No! No, don't say—"

"It was quick. He didn't suffer."

"*Nooooo!*" She screamed it, trying to drive the voice out of her mind. It couldn't be true, it *couldn't*. She was just *dreaming* all this! "You're lying! You're just saying it to hurt me!"

The glowing thing wouldn't let her go. "He won't be coming home," it said. "And you are in danger as well. You have to leave here, Beatrice. Now, while you still can. Jim's death was no accident; he was sacrificed. And *you* will be sacrificed as well, unless—"

"What are you talking about?" Beatrice didn't want to listen to any more of this. It was mad, completely mad.

"He was a threat to . . . to that . . . *sick* and *evil* part of me," Essie said, struggling with the words. "You are a threat as well, because of the baby you carry."

"Baby? *Baby?*" Beatrice clutched at her stomach. "I don't—"

"You're pregnant, Beatrice. And the child you are carrying is a threat to—"

A cold rage filled Beatrice. "You couldn't know that. There's no way you could know that. The tests won't be complete until—"

The apparition gestured at her, and the words died in her throat. She suddenly *knew* that Essie was right. There was something growing inside her. Something very precious.

In the midst of the fear and confusion, she smiled. *Jim will be so happy,* she thought. *We both want it so much.* She could see his smile when he heard; she could feel his arms around her, and see the two of them making love with a passion born of this new togetherness.

"Jim . . ."

Energy crackled around the ghostly apparition, and Beatrice felt a cold bolt of fear run through her all over again. This *thing* said Jim was dead. "An evil part of herself," she said—

"No." Beatrice shook her head. "You want to split us up; you always have. You're just trying to frighten me, and I won't be frightened. Not by you or anyone." She tried to take a step back, forgetting the bonds of purple light. "You're a frustrated old woman who's used to getting her own way, but you won't get it! Not this time! Go away! Go back t—"

A lightless, soundless explosion rocked the room, and Beatrice screamed.

Essie was gone, blotted out . . . and a twisted, malevolent face was taking form in the center of the blackness. It reflected every sick and frightened thought she had ever had. It was pain and disease and hatred, crushed into a single set of features.

She watched it grow and groan and open its mouth to swallow her. Blood and saliva dripped from its fangs.

The light that had held her was gone. She screamed her throat raw and ran from the room, the towel dropping to the floor as she fled. There was a housecoat by the front door. She clutched at it as she ran out of the house, then threw it on as she stumbled down the porch and across the yard, screaming and screaming.

As she went, Essie's words echoed in her mind. "Jim is dead, Beatrice."

Beatrice was crying his name. She couldn't stop running, couldn't stop weeping.

"I know you can't understand any of this, but run. *Run*, Beatrice," the voice told her. "I'll keep it from you as long as I can. I'll give you time to hide. Take your baby to safety."

Beatrice tripped and nearly fell. She pushed at the sidewalk with one hand and scrambled up again, running and running. The tears stung her cheeks.

Much later, Beatrice would wonder what Essie had meant by "keep it away." After all, she had said it was a part of her. But that was later. As she ran, it was all she could do to keep her mind blank. She just had to *run*, that was all. Run and run and run . . .

"I'll keep track of you." Essie's voice was back. "I'll always know where you are. And when the time is right—"

"*NOW! The time is now!*"

It was a different voice—deep and distorted, thick with evil. "*Don't run, little one,*" the new voice said, and it terrified Beatrice more than anything that had come before. "*Running won't help.*" It oozed into her as she ran, and for a moment her steps faltered. "*You have to die, don't you see that?*"

"No . . ."

"*Yes!*" the new voice hissed. "*But I will make it a joy, little one. A pleasure to make all other pleasures you've known pale in comparison.*"

"NO!"

She could feel its presence like slavering jaws only inches away. Its hot breath burned her. But she turned and ran toward the light, toward the church at the end of the block.

When she crashed through the door, the priest kneeling at the altar turned in surprise. His face betrayed shock at her appearance: her hair was matted into knots; her feet were cut and streaked with filth; her naked body was clearly visible under her flimsy housecoat.

Beatrice didn't care. Only inches inside the door, the pursuing presence seemed to disappear. She felt safe here, somehow, at least for the moment.

The priest came forward and put his arm on her shoulder. It was strong and cool and dry. Calm coursed through her when he helped her to her feet. "Come along," he said. "Let me help you."

Later that night she learned it was true. Jim was dead. It was a simple car accident, the police said, and they could not be bothered with an investigation. "No foul play," they had told her. "No foul play."

The next day she buried him in an unmarked grave, and after the funeral she withdrew what little money they had and left Australia forever on the first available flight, a flight to Hawaii.

The insurance money helped. While she was waiting for it, she took a temporary job in a hotel in Waikiki, but the moment the check from Australia cleared, she was on a flight to the American mainland without so much as a "good-bye."

She was still haunted by memories of Essie.

"An evil part of herself," she had said. "There's no way you can understand," she had said. But Beatrice understood well enough. *Essie* had killed Jim. Not a truck, *Essie*.

Lance was born eight months later, in a small town in Wisconsin that Beatrice could barely remember. As soon as he was old enough to travel, she'd begun moving again. She never stayed in one place long enough to put down any kind of roots. She changed her name with every move. And even when Lance got older and needed schooling, she kept moving. They never stayed more than a year in one location. She never stopped looking over her shoulder. And for years, she was terrified of the dark.

When Lance was thirteen, Beatrice, now Betty Sullivan, had come to rest in the small, affluent Southern California community of Santa Barbara. For twelve years she had hidden there. Sometime during those almost twenty-five years of hiding the terror had faded. It almost seemed like a vague nightmare now. At least it had until Lance called about . . . that woman.

Essie Beresford. The old woman haunted them still . . . even after death.

"Of course he won't believe me," Betty Sullivan said to the dusty sunlight streaming into her bedroom in Santa Barbara. "Truth to tell, I'll be lucky if he doesn't try to have me committed." She buried her head in her hands. "Oh, Lord, what—"

The fine hairs on the nape of her neck stood up. A trickle of ice-cold fear moved down her spine, and she straightened very slowly.

She had felt that sensation before. A long time ago. In their cozy little house in Sydney, Australia.

It can't be, she thought, holding tightly to her sanity. *Essie's dead.*

But the tickling fear grew. The muscles in her back and thighs began to twitch, and sweat filled the hollows of her face.

No, she told herself. *No, no, no, no . . .*

Her mind was still screaming when she turned and stood face to face with—

Essie Beresford.

The apparition was coruscant with energy, bright with

evil light that sparked from its eyes and its hair and even the tips of its fingers.

"I thought you were dead," Betty said. "I prayed we were rid of you."

Essie Beresford smiled.

"What do you want from me? From *us?*" But Betty already knew the answer. Essie had told her, twenty-five years ago. And nothing she said now could change that.

Essie stared at her. Her eyes twinkled merrily. And she began to laugh.

Bile rose in Betty's throat. She pushed herself to her feet and vaulted for the door. *It worked before,* she thought. *Maybe—*

A malignant purple beam of light snaked out in tendrils and tripped her as she reached the door. She sprawled on her knees and the heels of her hands, skidding on the polished hardwood floor.

"Damn you!" Betty Sullivan cursed the evil thing that hovered in the center of the room. "*Damn* you!"

She started to rise, and an invisible pressure held her down. She straightened against it, tried to force herself to her knees, but it pushed harder. And harder. And *harder*.

Her arms and legs gave out, and Betty hit the hardwood floor with an agonizing thump. The air gushed out of her. Pain tore at her chest. Then the pressure increased again, until her cheek crunched against the floor.

She looked up, her eyes pleading for mercy. Her mouth worked, but the pressure was too great for her to be able to speak.

The apparition's eyes were bottomless pits. She was staring into two endless doorways to hell. The only movement behind Essie Beresford's eyes was the flickering of hungry, unearthly flames.

I'm dying, Betty thought. *Dear God, I'm dying at the whim of this disgusting thing.*

Betty looked again at her executioner, and the image

wavered. For a moment, it wasn't Essie at all. It was . . .
a beast? A man? An almost handsome man. A—

No. It was Essie. Essie with her hands stretched out and
her palms down. Essie who slowly, slowly lowered her
palms and pressed.

An hour later, she was still alive. She writhed on the
floor of the bedroom, agonizing convulsions pounding at
her over and over. Her eyes bulged from their sockets.
Blood oozed from the self-inflicted wounds in her hands,
where fingernails had dug deep into soft flesh.

But the invisible force from the glowing figure would
not let her die.

At each involuntary moan, the fragmented parts that had
been Betty Sullivan coalesced again . . . only to break
apart once more from the pressure, the pain. The beast that
was Essie savored every moment. With each groan, the
luminosity surrounding the apparition expanded with an
explosion of color.

It was *enjoying* it, Betty realized. Enjoying her pain,
feeding on it like a pig at a trough.

Betty thought again of Lance, as she had so many times
during the endless hour. He was so much like his father,
she thought dimly. There was so much warmth there, and
understanding. And yes, *power*.

She smiled through the convulsive twitch of her muscles. *It had been worth it. You hear that, old hag?* she
thought. *It was worth it. All the worry and the pain. All
the days I was sure I couldn't go on. The work, the
friendship, the love, it was worth it. Worth it.*

The glowing thing reared up angrily. The defiance in
Betty Sullivan infuriated it.

I love him, you witch-thing. Love him. She threw her
thoughts at the beastly hag, filled with rage and defiance . . .

Betty suddenly smelled something in the room. Something that opened the door to a pleasant memory.

Betty Sullivan smiled.

The evil apparition bellowed and swooped down toward her, trying to bring back the fear . . . the terror . . . the feelings it had kept her alive to savor. But it was too late. The woman had found something special in her memories, some new strength. The apparition *hated* it. It struck out in anger and crashed the full weight of its power at the hapless form of Betty Sullivan.

Betty never heard the raging bellow; she never saw the arrival of her death. Instead she saw her mother huddling with her at the warm stove hearth in their home. And her father, who reminded her so much of Jim, wise, calm and strong, had his arms around his daughter, while his eyes looked deeply into the endless dance of the flames before him. He was smoking a pipe with the tobacco she remembered the best.

The smell, she thought. *That sweet, sweet smell.*

A single joyful tear trickled down Beatrice Beresford's face, and she smiled as she died.

Chapter 7

The twin-engine Hadley Page Jetstream rumbled around him, lulling Lance Sullivan into a half-dream.

Below him, a dotted line of headlights snaked along Highway 101, only inches from the Pacific Ocean. Out in the channel the oil platforms winked on and off in starry constellations of colored lights, like thousands of miniature Christmas trees.

He lay back in his seat and tried to untangle his jumbled thoughts.

He had left Dallas eight hours and two people ago. The first disguise—Eric Nordstrom, a strapping Norwegian exchange student—had gotten him to Los Angeles without incident. For a while, he had considered using Johnny Hancock again, but there was something . . . *wrong* with that disguise. Something very strange.

Hancock had somehow taken him over for a day and a night. When Lance tried to mentally reconstruct everything that had happened, he found a perplexing blank in his understanding of the events.

He remembered getting the letter from Alex Ryder and making the ensuing phone call. He remembered putting on Johnny Hancock and going to the drugstore to call his mother. The call itself was strangely hazy—disjointed and hostile, though he couldn't say why—and the last thing he remembered was the decision to call Benny and let him know that he had to leave for California immediately.

The next thing he knew it was morning and he was waking up in his bed in Suite 2235.

And a full day had passed.

Even now, the thought of it sent a chill through him. As soon as he realized what had happened, he called Benny and tried to sort it out. His old friend had been even nearer to panic than he had been when Lance first arrived. He had nearly wept with relief when he heard Lance's voice. But when Benny asked what had happened, where Lance had been for almost twenty-four hours, Lance simply couldn't remember.

He thought about it until his head raged with pain. But there was only a brief, twisted recollection of a disco, a fragment of a song from a new wave group, a girl with dark eyes and a wide painted mouth . . . and nothing else. Nothing.

So Johnny Hancock was retired. Permanently.

At the Los Angeles International Airport, he took advantage of the stopover to visit the men's room and shed his skin. When he emerged he was Leo DePizzo, an attractive and overly tan high school principal. He mingled with the airport crowds, wandered past different gates, and slowly circled all three major terminal sections. After visiting a dozen different coffee shops, he had a meal in the restaurant atop the futuristic, arched centerpoint of the airport. Then, finally sure he wasn't being followed, he bought a ticket on a commuter flight to Santa Barbara and went to the nearest men's room.

Seconds before they closed the door to the Jetstream, he arrived as himself—Lance Sullivan. It was the first time he'd been out in public without makeup in over a year.

For the first few minutes, he felt oddly naked. It was unnerving to be unprotected after so long. But there were only nine other people on the flight to Santa Barbara, including the pilot and copilot, and none of them paid him any notice at all.

Suddenly the plane lurched under them as it hit an air pocket, and an elderly man near the cockpit gripped the arms of his seat until his knuckles almost glowed.

Lance could sympathize with him. He had never had much trouble with flying, but he often wondered about aerodynamics. Who didn't? Of *course* it could all be explained perfectly, but the truth was that it *had* to be magic. Huge chunks of metal and paint couldn't fly through the sky like birds—not without some kind of enchantment.

He looked out to his right as the lights at the tip of Summerland's stubby peninsula passed beneath him. To the right was Montecito, and beyond that, to the north, Santa Barbara.

Home.

Mum would be waiting at the airport, he knew. Good old Mom, with the lively eyes and the nut-brown skin. He frowned momentarily, remembering how he hadn't been able to contact her when he called from Dallas, or again from Los Angeles. But the neighbors, the Hawks, had an answering service. At least she would know when he was arriving.

She would be standing there, smiling. The tears would flow, however reluctantly—she was a tough old bird—and the first embrace would say everything that their words couldn't manage.

She knows I love her, he thought. *It's strange that it took me so long to realize how much.*

"Ladies and gentlemen. We will be landing at Santa Barbara Airport in a few minutes. Please fasten your seat belts and extinguish all smoking materials. Thank you."

The twin engines changed pitch and the plane banked to the right as it began its descent.

"Lance, I've got bad news."

Bill Meador met Lance in front of the small Spanish-styled air terminal. The minute Lance saw him he knew something was wrong. Bill was his mother's finest friend, one of Lance's oldest father figures, and the family doctor. But even standing in silhouette, backlit by the orange glow from a nearby lamppost, it was obvious he was deeply troubled.

Lance glanced around, taking in the flower beds and the milling passengers waiting for luggage. He didn't see any sign of his mother. His intuition was screaming at him, but he was afraid to ask the question he knew was waiting.

"It's Mum, isn't it?"

"Yes."

He hated that tone of voice. It immediately told him how serious it was.

"What happened? I talked to her yesterday. I mean . . . a few days ago." It was yesterday for Lance, but Johnny Hancock had stolen precious hours from him.

"She—" Bill stumbled on the words. "She's dead, Lance."

Lance's mind slipped out of gear. He was almost ready—*almost*—to hear that she was sick, or that she'd been hurt in an accident. But . . . dead?

"I . . . don't . . . how? *How?*"

"A heart attack," Bill lied. "Sometime last night. Meg Hawk found her this morning."

Tears filled Lance's eyes.

"I'm sorry, Lance. I didn't know where to find you." Bill was fighting tears of his own. He'd been a close friend of the family since they'd arrived in Santa Barbara, and he'd loved Betty Sullivan in his own way for most of that time.

The two men stood staring at each other for a long moment. Then they reached out and hugged, crying unashamedly.

Finally Bill broke away. He sniffed lightly, but he didn't wipe away the tears as he picked up Lance's bags.

"Come on," he said. "I'll take you home."

Streaks of light from the dying afternoon sun streamed through the louvered blinds in Betty Sullivan's bedroom. Lance stared out the window at the long shadows staining the street.

He was dressed in a black suit and tie. His mother's body was already buried. *At rest forever,* he thought.

With a deep sigh, he turned to look at the quiet room behind him. It looked as it had always looked, but it wasn't the same. That special something—the essence that was uniquely his mother—was gone now.

He didn't fight the tears when they came again. They whispered down his cheeks in slow rivulets.

"*Mum!*" The pain he had kept locked inside during the funeral broke free, and he let himself cry long and hard, without control. And behind the grief and hurt, the anger and loss, he found an unexpected joy. Joy at having known her, at having been a part of her.

A tide of relief and gratefulness swept over him, making him cry new tears . . . better tears.

After a while, he lay back on the bed and let the memories flow through him for a long time. Crying, then laughing, then crying again, he relived many of the good times and the bad times they'd shared.

When the last wave of remembrance was spent—when he could stand again, breathe again, *see* again—he found that he had burned away the grief. It would come again, he knew—when he saw a special color, or heard a particular laugh. But for now, and forever after, there would be love and fond memories in place of the pity and emptiness, and that was far better. It was what Betty would have expected of him.

The room was rapidly darkening as evening approached, and as he switched on the lights in the room his eyes fell on the dressing table near the bed.

Without really thinking, he knelt in front of it and

opened the bottom right-hand drawer. His fingers remembered better than his brain, and they instantly went to the proper corner and found the folded piece of paper.

As he opened the certificate, he thought about his last conversation with his mother. She had been frightened—really frightened at the mere mention of Essie Beresford's name. But they had shared the same surname, a long time ago. Why should her dead husband's grandmother, forgotten for so long, terrify her like that?

Betty had always told him that his father had been an American, that he had died in the Army just a few months before Lance was born. But the piece of paper he was holding said different. According to the certificate, Jim Beresford was an Australian. He had never set foot in the United States.

His mother had lied to him, and he didn't know why.

All right, he decided. *Maybe it wasn't the truth. But if she lied, there must have been a damn good reason.*

He tapped the paper against the edge of the drawer and said it aloud: "If only I knew what the reason was, it might make things easier to understand." He shook his head as he heard his words echo slightly in the room.

It's no use, he thought wearily as he crouched down and returned the marriage certificate to its drawer.

Suddenly, soundlessly, an eerie purple light glowed at his back, outlining his shadow on the bureau.

Lance jumped to his feet and turned, shocked, involuntarily sucking in a huge gasp of air.

Betty Sullivan was hovering in the center of the room, glowing with a strange purple luminescence. Lance could see the half-obscured lines of the window beyond her—*through* her.

"You must not go to Australia," she said. He heard the words ring in his head, though the apparition's lips didn't move.

"M . . . Mum." Lance moved forward to embrace his mother.

"You must not go—"

As he reached out to touch the image of his mother, it disappeared. Its words cut off in mid-sentence.

Lance stared at the empty air for a long time. Then, still stunned, he sat heavily on the edge of the bed. Only then did he notice the thick, sickly sweet smell—almost familiar, somehow—that lingered after the apparition had faded. It must have arrived when the . . . whatever-the-hell-it-was did.

His thoughts raced. The metronomic ticking of his mother's old clock was all he could hear, and he let its rhythmic beat fill his thoughts. This time there was no need to search for an answer. It came of its own volition—a crystalline, rock-solid burst of intuition that left no room for doubt of any kind.

The—ghost? The luminous specter had looked like his mother. It had moved like her, sounded like her. It had even repeated the warning about staying away from Australia.

But an essential part of the feeling and warmth he knew and loved had been missing. It had *not* been his mother. The floating thing had not been Betty Sullivan or Beatrice Beresford. He was certain of it.

It had been . . . *something else*.

Bill Meador looked tired. He tried to put on his best face for Lance—Lance could tell—but the grief and weariness in his eyes was all too obvious.

They sat opposite each other in Petrini's, a small Italian restaurant near the house Lance had once called home. It was a friendly, nostalgic place for both of them. Lance remembered coming here after basketball practice at the University.

The wine-red booths hadn't changed at all. Neither had the enlarged black-and-white photographs of Italian scenes and cities that hung on the walls. He felt oddly comfortably inside Petrini's.

"Bill, I need to talk."

Bill smiled. "Well, we've always been good at that."

Most of Bill's soft brown hair had disappeared in the last few years, and his body had lost some of its athletic firmness. But he had taken on a distinguished bearing that Lance didn't remember from before.

Lance smiled and toyed with the ice in his water glass as he remembered the endless conversations they'd had over the years—many of them right here. Bill was the one he always came to with his *man* questions. And then there was politics, and sports—lots of sports raps.

"Lance, what is it?" Bill was frowning at him.

Lance hesitated as the waitress brought them both a beer and they ordered a medium pizza. As she left the table, Lance started to talk.

"Bill, a lot of . . . strange things have happened to me since the operation on my knee."

The doctor looked down and played with a button on his silk shirt. He, better than anyone, knew the details of the operation that had ended Lance's basketball career almost before it had begun. The memory of it apparently still made him nervous. He fussed with the paper placemat featuring the caricatured portraits of the Petrini Brothers before he spoke again. "Your mother never really said what you were up to, but she did tell me that she was . . . concerned."

He looked up quickly, locking eyes with Lance. "Are you in trouble?"

Now it was Lance's turn to look embarrassed. "I have been for almost two years," he said. "But lately it's taken a weird twist. I'm not sure . . ." His words trailed off.

Bill smiled grimly. "Look, Lance. We've known each other for a long time. I don't know what you've gotten yourself into, but it doesn't really matter. I'm here. I'll help if I can."

Lance nodded. He knew from long experience that Bill

meant what he said. It was just hard to know where to begin.

"Do you remember Benny Haldane?"

"Benny . . . Haldane." Bill frowned as he tried to place the name. "Wasn't he that artist friend of yours—the one you brought home some time back? Watercolors, as I recall."

Lance grinned in spite of himself. "Memory's still as sharp as ever," he said. "But *artiste* would be more accurate. The watercolors were a cover. Benny's actually one of the best counterfeiters in the world."

"You're into counterfeiting?" Bill made it a hoarse whisper.

"No, Bill, it's not that exciting."

Bill laughed, more from relief than anything else. "Well, I'll be damned!"

"I know it's kind of unusual, but . . . Benny saved my butt before you even met him. And he's helped me out of a hundred bad situations since then. Dishonest, honest—I don't know what those words mean anymore. But he's a good man and a good friend." He glanced at the doctor, measuring him up. "In fact, in a lot of ways, he reminds me of you."

Meador ignored the compliment. "Saved you from what, exactly?"

"After I got tired of the 'poor little me' bit—you know, having to give up the idea of being the world's next basketball superstar—I . . . well, I went a little crazy, I guess." Lance sighed heavily.

Bill frowned, saying nothing.

"I found myself in Fairfax, not far from San Francisco. I was broke and pissed off at the world. Got drunk a lot. Did plenty of drugs. Nothing really heavy, Bill, just enough to keep reality away from the door."

Bill nodded without looking at him.

"I was staying at a guy's place, guy by the name of Ray Stiller. He was into a lot of shady things, and he knew I was getting low on funds. One day he asked me if I wanted to make some easy money." Lance sipped at his beer and grimaced. "I said yes without even caring what it was."

"Jesus, Lance," Bill sighed. It wasn't a condemnation. He was just surprised.

"I know. It was dumb. But you had to be there." It was a small attempt at a joke, but it failed, miserably. Lance shrugged. "Anyway, before I knew it, I was up to my ears in the trade."

"Trade?"

"Con games, Bill. Running all sorts of scams to swindle people out of money. Some of the first ones— Well, I'm not too proud of those today. Roofing deals, scams on lost dogs and found relatives. Some mail-order fraud, too. It was bad news. It hurt innocent people."

"Lance, I don't know if I should be—"

Lance waved him off. He wanted to tell it all now. "But then I started to get good at it—particularly at some of the slicker stuff. Real estate scams on people who were trying to keep their money from the government, or their wives, or their companies. Look, I wasn't Robin Hood, but— damn it, Bill, I had fun. And except for those first few months with Ray, I wasn't hurting anyone. At least not anyone who didn't deserve it."

"You're a pretty amazing character then, my friend. To be smart enough to know who deserves what." Bill looked mad. "We regular mortals, we need courts of law to decide that sort of thing."

They were getting off the subject. "Look, I don't want to debate morality with you, Bill; not right now. I was just saying that— well, it's what I did. For a long time. And then about a year ago, it all fell apart."

He looked hurriedly around Petrini's, to see if anyone was listening. No one seemed to be. "Ray was getting more and more hungry," he said. "One day, he set up a big scam that I wasn't in on—something he knew I would never have agreed to. The next thing I knew I was knee-deep in a major-league drug deal.''

Bill was trying to take it well. ''How major is major?'' he asked, doing his best to sound calm and disinterested.

''Three million dollars.''

''Jesus!'' His exclamation didn't sound too objective.

''Yeah, mind-boggling, ain't it?'' His try at a smile was weak at best. ''But that's not the worst of it. Right in the middle of the drop, three total strangers, armed to the gills, suddenly broke in and *whoosh*. No drugs. No money. And one very angry criminal-type, bent on killing the creeps he *thinks* set him up. And guess who this criminal-type thinks is the Head Creep?''

''You?''

''Right the first time.''

''But how?''

''My old buddy, Ray Stiller. The son of a bitch set up the whole scam in my name—even *posed* as me, the bastard—and an hour after the hijacking, he left for the sunshine south of the border. But he did pause just long enough to finger me as the mastermind.''

Lance smiled in spite of himself. ''It must have been a beautiful performance, beginning to end. Because Sammy Raines believed it hook, line and sinker.''

''Who's Sammy Raines?''

''The angry criminal-type with blood in his eyes. The one who was out three million bucks.''

''Oh!''

'' 'Oh,' is right.'' Lance looked incensed as he swigged down the last of his beer. ''Damn, Bill. I was the perfect patsy.''

''Didn't you try to explain?''

''Sure. But Ray had done a *great* job. Sammy hadn't only lost three million big ones, he'd lost face, too. And he figured the best way to regain both was to make an example of me to my accomplices, who would then promptly return the money.''

Bill Meador didn't say anything for a long time. He just drank his beer and scratched at his chin—an old habit Lance had seen a hundred times before.

"So how did you resolve it?" he finally asked.

"It isn't resolved. I was in the process of going like a lamb to the slaughter—naive little me, I actually thought I could explain and Sammy would understand—when Benny popped up for the first time . . ."

"I was wondering when he would show up."

"He'd heard about the whole screwup—don't ask me how—and since we'd worked together on some games earlier on, he'd decided to try and help. Beside, Sammy Raines had killed two old friends of his before; I think he had his own ax to grind. Anyway, he talked to Sammy, tried to explain, but Sammy didn't want to know. All he wanted was his money back and a body. *My* body. Benny suggested that disappearing might be infinitely more pleasant than dying." Lance smiled wanly. "He didn't get much argument from me."

"Disappearing?"

"Yeah. He had this sweet scam all worked out. I would change my appearance, using wigs, clothes and makeup. Then we would travel around the country, living on credit cards and IDs he would fake up. Benny would fence the goods and we'd split the profits."

"Out of the frying pan into another fire," Bill said sourly.

"I guess so," Lance shrugged. "But at the time it seemed like my only chance. Sammy wasn't joking when he put out the contract on me. And he's still not joking." He licked his lips nervously. "Two days ago in Miami, his heavies blew a man's head off because they thought he was me."

"*What!*" Bill turned pale, and Lance wondered if he'd believed any of it until that moment. "Lance, you've got to go to the police."

"What was that you just said about 'out of the frying

pan'?'' Lance looked away, only half-seeing the old wine casks and plastic grapes that lined the restaurant's walls. "No. Even the cops couldn't stop him. Turning myself in would only tell Raines where I was."

Neither of them spoke for a while. Finally Lance sighed and ordered another couple of beers.

"And on top of everything else, a lot of *weird* things have started happening."

"It isn't weird enough already?" Bill said.

"It's gotten a lot weirder," he said. Lance started with the nightmares—what little he could remember of them. Then he talked about the strange telephone call in Miami, and wondered aloud how Raines had found him in spite of his disguise. He told Bill about the hallucination in the shower, the voices in his head, the sudden appearance of a long-lost relative with a wealthy estate. He described the strange "possession" by one of his own characters, and the blackout it created.

". . . and then there's Mum's death."

Bill Meador froze with a drink halfway to his lips. "What about it?" he asked quietly.

"It's too coincidental, Bill. Just too damn *pat*."

"I don't know what you mean."

"At first I thought Sammy had found her. Hell, I was already figuring out how to get to him and kill him for it . . . until last night."

"Last night?"

He told Bill about the apparition in Betty Sullivan's room and how sure he was that what he'd seen had *not* been his mother at all.

Bill just stared at his beer. Lance couldn't tell what he was thinking about all this.

"Did you ever hear my mother mention the name 'Beresford'?" he asked.

Bill looked confused. "No, I don't think so. Why?"

"That was her real name. My father's name."

"Are you sure?" The doctor was astonished.

"Yes," he nodded. "And it might have something to do with why she wouldn't marry you, no matter how often you asked."

Bill blushed to the roots. "You . . . know about that?"

"Sure. And I think she cared about you as much as you did about her, but there was something holding her back. Something to do with Australia, I think. To do with the Beresfords. It kept her from ever relaxing, from ever letting go."

Bill nodded solemnly.

"Bill, do you believe *any* of this?"

The response was quiet, very measured. "Yes, I do."

"How much?"

Bill looked him square in the face. "I don't know, really. I just don't know." He shrugged, then added, "Lance, you and I have always leveled with each other, so I'm going to level with you now. But I want your promise you won't push me for specific details."

Lance nodded.

"I've always believed there are things in this world we don't—*can't*—understand. And I admit, normally, I'd think you were off the rails after what you've just told me. Counterfeiters. Drug smugglers. Master criminals out to kill you. Not to mention the long-lost relatives and the visits from beyond the grave." He snorted and took another drink. "I don't know. Nothing about this whole—*affair*, if you can call it that—has been normal. Betty's death wasn't normal."

Lance sat in stunned silence.

"She didn't have any reason to die, Lance. Her blood tested normal. Her heart was in good shape. The autopsy on her brain and vital organs showed up negative, negative, negative. *She should be alive.* But . . . but—"

Bill Meador wiped the tears out of his eyes with the back of one hand. When he spoke again, his voice was hoarse. "Well, your story explains one thing, anyway. Or at least verifies something."

"What?"

"The smell you mention. You caught a whiff of it in your dreams, and in one of the hotels. Well, when I first visited her room, when I— when I first saw her— there was a strange odor I couldn't place. It was gone in a few seconds, but . . ." he trailed off.

"Damn," Lance said softly. "*Damn!*"

Bill finished his beer and swallowed hard. "So what are you going to do, Lance? What's next?"

Lance sighed heavily as he pulled his wallet from his inside coat pocket. "I'm damned if I know, Bill. But I think I'm going to have to seriously consider a trip to Australia. To see if I can find any answers there."

Bill Meador nodded. "You'll be careful, of course."

"Of course."

The old doctor looked straight into the eyes of his dead lover's son. "If I can help in any way—"

His words hung in the air as Lance just nodded. There didn't seem to be anything left to say.

Chapter 8

Alex Ryder swung his legs from the driver's seat of the metallic gray Mercedes 450SL sedan and firmly planted both feet on the concrete surface of the underground parking complex. Then, with a grunt and a loud wheezing breath, he heaved his bulbous frame from his German status symbol.

It took him an extra moment to find his balance—*damn dizzy spells!*—but after a deep breath he reached through the open door and scooped up his handmade Italian leather briefcase. It took a few more seconds to carefully close and lock the car, then he was huffing and puffing his way past row after row of decadently expensive sedans and sports GTs, working his way to the elevator bank at the center of the structure.

He buzzed for the elevator and pulled a white silk handkerchief from the pocket of his dark-blue suit, dabbing at the sweat beading his forehead. As he waited for the elevator to make its way down from the twenty-three-story tower directly above his head, he studied his reflection in the full-length mirror by the elevator doors.

God, what have I let myself become? I'm five-seven. I'm forty-seven. I have a great practice, a good marriage, wonderful friends . . . and I look like a bloody clown. He fastidiously straightened the edge of the lapel of his immaculate six-hundred-dollar suit. *Even Mario's expert tailoring can't hide it anymore. How in hell did it happen? How did I let it happen?*

Three hundred pounds. He'd finally hit the big Three-Oh-Oh.

Almost against his will, he let his mind wander back to his breakfast conversation with Annie, just this morning.

"I don't know how you can stand looking at such a blimp," he had said.

"I love you, silly," Anne had answered without hesitation. "I wouldn't care if you were five hundred pounds."

"But shit, Anne, I'm not old! It hasn't been that many years since I was on the damn track team at USC. And I played tennis and racquetball damn near every day. What is it . . . fifteen, twenty years?"

"More like thirty. But it doesn't *matter,* honey."

"Remember when we first met?" He smiled at the memory, and so did she. Anne was the only woman he'd ever really cared about in his life, and with her as a stabilizing force for his boundless energy, everything seemed easy.

"At a track meet," Anne had said, her eyes growing soft as she let her mind wander back. "You were so dashing—"

"And *thin,*" Alex said, frowning.

The edge in his voice brought her back with a snap. "Don't do this to yourself, Alex. You've done so much since then. Your incredible grades and passing scores on the bar exam. Only four years until your junior partnership in Aldous, Stannard and Stannard. Then going out on your own. That was a huge gamble."

"And look at me now. I'm making out wills for the rich and famous, and occasionally rescuing one of their snot-nosed kids from a drug bust. Can you believe I actually thought this was exciting when I first started? 'A breath of fresh air to my staid profession.' Shit, most of them are like spoiled, petulant kids themselves—kids who don't have a clue to what life's about, with so much money they can get away with damn near anything they want. Face it, Annie, I'm a glorified diaper service."

"You're a respected member of your profession, who owns one of the most prestigious law firms in Beverly Hills," Anne had insisted. "And I'm proud of what you've done." When he had tried to turn away from it, she had walked over and grabbed him in a bear hug. "I love you just the way you are, Alex."

"I couldn't have done any of it without you," he had told her—and he'd meant it. "Marrying you was the most sensible thing I ever did."

The loud hissing of the elevator doors sliding open broke into Alex's reverie. He stepped into the car and pressed the button for the penthouse offices of Ryder, Fullhurst and Smith. *Success*, he decided. *Success was my downfall.* The thought flashed into his brain as the elevator doors opened to show the plush waiting room of his law firm. *That, and a deep and abiding love of pasta.*

"Good morning, Mr. Ryder," the receptionist chirped happily as he made his way through the solid oak doors that led to the main suites.

"Morning," Alex called back, trying not to notice the distinguished and expensively dressed gentleman seated in the waiting room.

No doubt waiting to have his last will and testament written or amended. God, I hate to think how many wills I've written, or witnessed, or been executor for.

At first, it *had* been exciting. But now, like so many things in life, it had dulled with repetition. His job had become a plush-lined prison. The names were different, the terms of the estates changed slightly each time, but it was all the same—all the bloody, boring same.

He nodded mechanically to the secretaries of his numerous associates as he made his way down the hall toward the master suite. Their "Good morning's" hardly reached him.

When he was almost to his office door, Merle Long broke him from his doldrums.

"There's a Mr. Lance Sullivan on the phone for you, Mr. Ryder."

Ah! He quickened his step as he thought about this Australian case. Now that had actually brought a breath of fresh air into his work.

When the first long-distance call had come, he had never heard of Wilcox, Cundy, and Cook of Sydney, Australia. But they'd obviously heard of him and would not be turned from their intent to have him handle this case for them.

After hearing the details, Alex had thought they were more in need of the services of a good private investigator than those of a lawyer, and he'd told them so. His words had had no effect. He even quoted an absurdly high fee, in hopes of discouraging them—but Josh Wilcox insisted Alex was "the only one for the case."

"Money is no object," Wilcox had bluntly stated. "We have been told to have you handle the job, so that's how it has to be."

Alex was never really sure who had told Josh anything, including his name, but he finally acquiesced—with the understanding that his fee would be paid regardless of results. He would try to do as asked, he told them, but he made no guarantees.

Twelve hours later, a heavily wrapped and sealed parcel sat on Alex Ryder's desk. Inside the parcel was yet another equally heavily wrapped and sealed package—already addressed—and a set of detailed instructions for its delivery. It was not the first—and would definitely not be the last—time Alex Ryder was confused by this case.

The package was not addressed to Lance Sullivan, the man Alex had been asked to find. The address read:

Monsieur Jean Avignon
Suite 2235
The Hotel Dallas
Peachtree Center
Dallas, TX

A second set of instructions dictated exactly what Alex was to say to Mr. Lance Sullivan when he called. They also contained a sharply worded admonition—unnecessarily sharp, to Alex's mind—not to deviate from the instructions, "in any way, shape or form."

He didn't consider his call to the hotel in Dallas a deviation. And more important, it had been unsuccessful. The hotel reservations desk assured him there was no Mr. Lance Sullivan, or Monsieur Jean Avignon, currently staying at the hotel. What's more, they had no advance reservation in either name.

So, he thought at the time, *I'm sending a sealed package to the wrong person in the wrong place.* But he did as he was told—the money was worth it. He had Merle Long send off the package by special messenger and forgot all about it in a sudden flurry of requests for his services as executor that kept him busy for the following two days.

One phone call quickly changed that.

In all his years as an attorney, Alex Ryder couldn't remember a phone call quite like it. The person identifying himself as Lance Sullivan sounded almost . . . skittish—like a horse that was ready to bolt at any second. His voice had quivered and he appeared not to grasp much of what was happening. And he had flatly stated that he didn't even have a great-grandmother. As soon as Alex had started to explain about the trip to Australia, the man had hung up. Just like that.

That was when the dizzy spells had started, Alex realized now. The first wave of nausea had washed over him as soon as he'd lost touch with this Lance character. He had placed a call to Josh Wilcox and asked for further instructions. "We'll just have to wait and see if he calls back," the Australian lawyer had said. He hadn't seemed concerned—at least not at first.

That had been five days ago, and there had been nothing since. Nothing except for two calls a day—morning and night—from the Australian attorney. Wilcox seemed less placid with each communication. In the previous afternoon's call, he had insisted on sending new instructions by Courier Air-Express.

But now, finally, Lance Sullivan had called back. Alex eased his bulky frame behind his huge desk and massaged his right arm as he picked up the phone. He was unaware of the gesture—and barely aware of the pain.

As he went to answer the call, Merle Long hurried in with a package, placed it on the desk in front of him, and left.

Alex quickly punched the red HOLD button. "Mr. Sullivan?" he said as he opened the package and looked down at the new instructions from Wilcox, Cundy, and Cook. They had arrived even faster than either party had expected, Alex thought as he spoke again into the phone. "Mr. Sullivan, are you there?"

In the fraction of an instant before Lance Sullivan answered, Alex Ryder saw the note accompanying the new instructions. It wasn't addressed to him at all. It was addressed to his senior associate, Leon Fullhurst.

Then he saw the P.S. at the bottom of the letter.

At first it didn't make any sense—it had to be some kind of error. Then the pain in his arm cut through him, and a vise closed on his lungs, and Alex Ryder, all three hundred pounds of him, knew that the postscript wasn't a mistake.

It was a prediction.

Oh, God, he thought.

Lance Sullivan was talking on the other end of the line, but Alex couldn't understand him. The pain was too much to bear. The pain in his chest . . .

"Mr. Sullivan," he choked out, and bile rose in his throat. "I'm . . . I seem to be . . . having a heart attack."

He passed out at his desk before he could buzz for Merle. No one was aware of what had happened until Lance Sullivan called in on another line and told them to check Mr. Ryder's office.

They found him slumped over the package of instructions from the Australian attorneys. One hand clutched the note, just below the postscript.

The notation was only two lines long. It read, "P.S. Our hearts go out to you at this sad time. Please extend our condolences to Mrs. Ryder and all of Alex's family."

Chapter 9

Lance Sullivan put down the phone very slowly, though he never consciously remembered doing it.

I just heard a man die, he thought.

He couldn't be sure of that—not yet, at any rate. Lots of people survived heart attacks these days. And Mr. Fullhurst, the other attorney, had sounded very confident, very controlled.

But . . . no. He had listened to that man's voice, and he *knew*.

He had listened to a man die.

It suddenly seemed as if the walls of his mother's California bungalow were coming closer—like the house was trying to swallow him whole. He didn't want to be there anymore. He wanted *out*. Without another thought, he grabbed his jacket and lurched down the porch. Moments later, he had climbed into the family jeep and gunned it down the driveway, out into the street, and away from the house.

A little over twenty minutes later he was nearing the top of San Marcos Pass. At Camino Cielo he eased the jeep off the main road and quickly negotiated the first of hundreds of winding curves that made up a magnificent drive along the top of the range separating Santa Barbara from Santa Ynez Valley.

About eight miles past the Painted Cave area, famous for the drawings by ancient Chumash Indians, he spied the small dirt trail he used as a landmark, and he pulled the jeep to the side and parked it by a clump of brush.

It only took a few seconds to disconnect the rotor button from the motor and throw it into his pack—a simple but effective way to discourage anyone from "borrowing" the jeep while he was gone. Soon he was climbing the front of a nearby ridge, and moments later he was out of sight of the road.

As a boy, Lance had often felt the need to be alone. But he and his mother had moved so regularly that he rarely got the chance to find a personal retreat—a special place all his own . . .

Until they had arrived in Santa Barbara and finally settled down. There, only a few weeks after their arrival, he was introduced to the Los Padres National Forest on a school outing, and he had found his spot.

Even in adulthood, it remained a mystery to him. Why should a single space in hundreds of thousands of acres of forest, lakes and holiday campsites mean so much to him? Why did he still dream about it, years after his last visit? *No answers,* he thought. *Only questions.* But from the first time he had seen it, he had somehow felt at home.

Lance dropped the pack beneath *his* tree and flopped down next to it. Then he let his eyes range out over the unbelievably beautiful vista in front of him.

Across the valley floor the trees were sparse, and fields of hay and wheat covered vast sections. The deep olives and warm browns added to the blue of Gibraltar Dam and Lake Cachuma, and a thin black ribbon of road snaked down from the pass, which looked deep and severe. Lance watched a stream of cars racing off toward Santa Ynez and Solvang, and let his breath out in long, deep sighs.

Even up here, he knew civilization wasn't far away. A

few feet behind where he sat, he could top the ridge and look out over Santa Barbara and Goleta and see the University of California, Santa Barbara, perched on the point at Isle Vista. Even his special place wasn't as isolated as it had been. Many people—maybe too many—called Santa Barbara home these days. The president of the United States lived only a few miles off to his left.

Still, he thought, *life never seems to change very much around here. And that's all my life has ever been, change and change.* He watched two large hawks soaring on the wind currents just a few feet from the edge of the ridge. It was somehow comforting to know that they had been riding the updrafts since long before men of any color had made their homes in this area.

And, as he always did when he was here, Lance marveled at how peaceful he felt just watching the birds glide and dip, rise and soar, fall and rise again. He let his mind drift, trying to forget, and let the soft breeze heal the pain he still held locked inside.

Crossfire, he thought. That was the moment when the nightmares that had been troubling him for months suddenly broke into the waking world. When that voice—not Benny's, not anyone's he knew—whispered his secret code word into the phone: *Crossfire.*

His thoughts were spinning. Everything that had happened in the last six days tore at him. The news about missing relatives, his possession by one of his own characters, his mother's death, his accidents and dreams . . . and now a lawyer in Beverly Hills, a man he had never even met, dying as he spoke Lance's name.

He eased his body back against the tree trunk behind him and looked deep into the bright morning sunlight, willing the tension from taut muscles, relaxing the worry lines that furrowed his strong forehead. His breathing eased to a faint whisper. The blood coursing through his veins slowed its headlong rush and became a gentle rhythmic throb.

Lance's body had always been in his command. That was what had made him a good athlete, and a natural actor. Since his earliest days, he had been able to control his body through a strictly personal form of meditation, a half-dream state that cleansed him and opened him simultaneously.

It was a unique form of alpha-state induction—that, at least, was what the psychology professors in college had called it. All he knew was that it clarified his thoughts and reordered his life . . . and that he needed the strength and serenity of it now more than ever.

Without thinking how, he closed his eyes and let his mind swim free in the darkness—the soft, warm darkness.

His consciousness surged forward into the void, hunting the illusive tendril of a thought that waited only a hair's breadth out of reach. There *was* some sort of answer to this—some connecting theme that could force all the death and delusion into a recognizable pattern. He only had to find it. He only . . .

There was a shape in the internal darkness. It was huge, double-lobed and imposing. He saw it crouching on a hillock, surrounded by brush and clouds. He saw . . .

A house!

He floated toward it like a spirit. The mansion opened before him, and a figure stood there to greet him.

The figure was not as clear as the house itself. The coruscation of power around it, the brilliant shards of light and energy that glittered at its edges, made it difficult to see clearly.

Was it a man? A woman? Was it even *human?* He only knew that it directed vast power . . . and at the moment, its attention was riveted on Lance.

Its hand reached up. It pointed. It spoke—

And the image swirled away, ripped from him, receding . . .

Retreating, Lance thought. *As if I came too close.*

He stood up, and stretched mightily. There was a new strength in him, a sudden certainty. There was a decision to be made, and now, quite suddenly, he knew what it was.

He knew what he had to do.

"Okay," he said into the air over the ridge. "I'll go to Australia for the reading of the will . . . and to try and find some answers."

A smile returned to his face as he took one last look at the view stretched out in front of him. *Who knows,* he thought, *maybe Great-grandmother Essie actually remembered the American relatives in the will. Maybe I'm a rich man, and I don't even know it.*

"Not much chance of that, eh?" he called playfully to the hawks still soaring nearby.

It was a shame they hadn't kept in touch, he thought wistfully. A hell of a shame. It would have helped to have had relatives, even distant ones, during all those years. And now . . .

"*Three hundred and fifty million dollars!*" That's what the attorney, Mr. Fullhurst, had said the estate was worth. He said it aloud one more time: "*Three hundred and fifty million dollars!*"

As his words echoed across the ridge and he bent and swung his pack up onto his shoulder, he tried to comprehend just how much money that really was. He couldn't. It was just too much.

Finally, shaking his head, he let the thought go and called out again to the hawks as they swept away on a thermal updraft.

"That's a hell of a lot of tacos, amigos!"

Then he turned and headed back toward the jeep.

Chapter 10

Torrika slowly lifted her head and let her eyes take in the scene that stretched out before her.

The crystal blue Pacific waters washed gently at the white sandy beach. The sun had just reached its zenith and she had to shade her eyes against the intense, glittering reflections that played across both water and sand. Above her head the trade winds ruffled the fronds of tall coconut palm trees.

These were familiar sights to her; she had lived with this beauty since the day she was born. But now she had to fight to keep it all in view.

The vision was strong today.

It came on her suddenly, like a hurricane wind, like a tsunami. One moment there were the distant sounds of the booming surf crashing against the reefs, the whickering of the wind, and the lazy buzz of insects.

Then all she could hear was the sound of a car, its engine screaming.

The sea, sand, and grass hut here on the beach were gone for her. Though her body still sat, cross-legged, on the southwestern shore of Nacula, an island in the Fijian Chain, her mind was picturing the paved street of a distance city in a future time, in a land far to the southwest.

The warmth of the early-morning sun was replaced by the light chill of early evening.

The bright sunlight faded to eerie blue-black shadows, lit by a moon fast approaching its fullest face.

She could see the ghostly glowing images in a spot halfway between the shade of her hut, where she sat without speaking, and the waters of the Pacific. It should have been a patch of clear, virginal sand covering the circumference of the island. Instead it was a scene more real than her home.

There was a woman with hair the color of sunlight. She stood with him—the *light carrier*.

He was the one the ancients had spoken of since Ulu, the great bird of time, had first flown from the high heavens to grace the human world. And he had come as she had always prayed—while she was still alive, while she could still help him.

It mattered very little to Torrika that her most important task, the one she had been born to carry out, would occur when this vision of future things finally came to pass, in a world she no longer inhabited. That was unimportant. Only *his* survival mattered.

It did not occur to Torrika to wonder how she knew this—how she knew this strange-looking man could be the *light carrier*. The knowledge was simply a part of her, just as the visions that came upon her were.

It was a simple, powerful thing: she was the last of The Chosen, a direct descendant of the God Kings. *Lutunasobasoba* and *Degeis*, who rode the giant war canoe *Kaunitoni* from the lap of Heaven to the top of the sacred mountain, *Nakauvadra*, were blood of her blood.

The *people*, the Fijians of today, spoke of the past with whispered awe—if they spoke of it at all. Most worked in the tourist business at one of the many hotels. Torrika had seen them there. She remembered how some buildings were luxurious, how many others were less exotic—and how they all boasted of steadily increasing business. She

had seen other Fijians at the airport, working for the
airlines or car rental businesses or any one of hundreds of
other tourist industries. It made her very sad. Few remembered more than a smattering of their heritage, and what
broken pieces of the past still remained had been molded
into showpieces for the tourists.

Even her father gave lectures on the lawn in front of the
Hyatt Regency Hotel. Standing there with a cane pointer,
he recited small sections of the history of Fiji—twice
daily—to visitors from the far corners of the world. During
his stories, most of the tourists oohed and aahed in all the
right places; then they hurried off to the nearest air-
conditioned bar for a cold drink, no wiser or happier from
what they had heard.

Torrika would have none of it. She had kept the old
memories pure in her heart. She believed with every fraction of her spirit that the way of the People was the True
Way.

Now she was vindicated. The vision had shown her *The
One*.

In the vision, he was crossing a street. His concentration
was split, she sensed. His energy was undirected. Part of
his soul was enveloped in fear—fear of something Torrika
could not begin to understand. Part of his energy was
diverted to speaking—pointless speaking, meaningless
words. And part of his power was subsumed in the puis-
sant aura of Golden-Hair. He was in danger. Torrika could
see that, *sense* that: *he was in danger.*

He did not see the vehicle racing toward him at high
speed through the darkness. He kept walking, head down.
The vehicle came closer, roaring like a living thing. In an
instant, it would strike him and drive the life away, back
into the Void, perhaps forever.

She could not let it happen. She *would* not let it happen!

Torrika opened her mouth to cry out, and she heard
it—heard the vision: "*Light Carrier, beware!*"

He turned. In an instant that hung, suspended, for all eternity, he simply *stood*, balanced.

Then he called on the power.

A beam of light so intense that it overshadowed even the light of Father Sun leapt from him. It struck a mortal blow at the approaching vehicle, and the metal creature flew away, brushed aside like a straw in a hurricane.

Torrika recognized the scene now. She had seen parts of it before—this and many other scenes, time and again over the last ten years. A prickling sensation came over her. In an intuitive flash, filled with anticipation and fear, she realized the final Truth.

It was time. The days of waiting were over. Her small part in the great destiny of the *light carrier* and his Golden-Hair was about to unfold.

It was not new to her. She had watched it happen in the visions from the time she was a little girl. She had laughed and cried over it, had felt every nuance of pain, fear and joy. And she had welcomed it, even knowing the final outcome.

So, she stood in the shadows of her family's hut and smiled at the sea, then nodded, just once, and turned toward the rutted road that led to the lagoon where her father's boat was waiting.

It was time for Torrika to leave Nacula for the last time.

"*Australia?*" Benny Haldane sounded distant and tinny—and mad as hell—at the far end of the pay phone line. "Christ, kid, what the hell's in Australia?"

"I'm not sure," Lance told him, glancing nervously over his shoulder, "but I have to check something out."

He was standing at one of the pay phones in the Bradley International Terminal at Los Angeles Airport, talking to Benny Haldane in Chicago, and was hating every moment of it.

No disguise. No concealment. No *nothing*. It was one thing to kick around the deserted hills of his hometown without protection . . . but *here?* LAX during peak flying hours? And now Benny was giving him trouble about the trip, too.

"I don't buy it," Benny said stubbornly. "Something's goin' on here. Who is this again?"

Lance sighed. Not that old password–no password crap. He knew Benny was concerned. He appreciated it. But not now. Not when he was trying to keep both eyes peeled for *real* trouble.

"It's Lance Sullivan," he said wearily. It was the only time he would use his real name—the only phrase that would prove to Benny that everything was all right. If he'd said it any other way or used any variation on the name, his old friend and partner would be alerted. "You remember him," he added. "Tall kid, good-looking, but not very bright."

It wasn't a very good joke. Benny didn't laugh. It just made the pause before Benny spoke again seem longer than ever. "This must be *real* important, kid," the older man said. He sounded angry about the breach of security. "You know you're takin' a hell of a risk."

Lance nodded and scanned the terminal for the hundredth time. "I know, Benny," he said softly. "And it *is* important. You'll have to trust me, it *is*."

It must have been something in the way he spoke—or maybe Benny was actually starting to listen to him. But when his partner spoke again, it was different: calmer somehow. Concerned, but not angry anymore.

"Okay, kid," he said through the long-distance hiss. "Is there anything I can do?"

"You can not worry," Lance said, trying to make it sound light and easy. It didn't work. "I've only been in the terminal two minutes, and the check-in and seat assignment was all taken care of before I even got here. There are advantages to going first class, you know?"

"Sure, kid." He still sounded sour.

"Benny, really, don't sweat it. I'll be on the plane in another two minutes."

"Australia, Lance?"

"Yes. I've found out I've got relatives there. On—on my mother's side." Mentioning his mother sent a wave of sorrow over him. He knew it was going to take a long time for that wound to heal.

Benny sensed it. He always sensed that kind of change in Lance. "Are you okay?" he asked.

"I'm fine." Lance quickly glanced around again. The currents of travelers, visitors, parents and children continued to flow like water. No one seemed to be paying the slightest attention to him. Still . . . "Look, Benny. I better go."

There was another long pause. When Benny spoke again he sounded gruff, his voice harsh with unspoken concern. "Yeah, do that. But keep me posted, right?"

"I will Benny. Bye."

"Lance—"

Lance hung up quickly, before either of them could say anything more. Then he turned and headed for the security check-in at the far side of the terminal.

As he went he scanned the area, searching for the slightest hint of an observer. Nothing appeared to be out of the ordinary . . . but he knew that airports were filled with idlers waiting for departures, or waiting for arrivals, or just killing time in a relatively clean, relatively warm place. It was the worst possible location for security. Lance was painfully aware of that every time he tried to penetrate the crowd around him.

He reached the wooden arch of the metal detector, ominously positioned between the terminal and the departure lounges, and quickly stepped through. No bells, no whistles—not that there should have been—but he couldn't afford to be stopped and searched, not even for an over-sized set of keys.

Without losing stride, he grabbed his shoulder bag from the moving belt and hurried through a set of huge glass doors, moving quickly down the hall that led to the plane that would take him to Australia.

Only when the hallway grew narrow and comfortably deserted, when the crowded terminal was out of sight, did

Lance finally slow down. And even then, he waited until he was safely standing in front of Gate 16 before he let loose a huge pent-up sigh of relief.

Vincent Fender was a weasel . . . and he *liked* it that way.

He was about as skinny as a human being could possibly be, with a pair of squinty, dark eyes, set too close together, and bushy eyebrows perched below a beetle brow. His nose was too long; his nostrils were too narrow. He really *did* look like a comic-book version of a humanoid rat, right down to the cheap, shiny black suits he affected.

And it was true: Vincent Fender *liked* the image. He'd started with what God, "the bastard," had given him, and he'd made the most of it. Now, after years of working at it, his look fit what he did for a living, and that was part of the plan, too. Vincent Fender was a stoolie, an errand boy, a gunsel, and a general low-life runabout for Sammy Raines. He was The Weasel, and he took a perverse pleasure in the nickname.

One thing he *didn't* like, though, was airports. Too many people, too much noise. Trying to keep a line on a mark in a crowd like this and not get spotted at it—hell, it was barely worth the effort. But here he was, and so far luck had been with him. Lance Sullivan had been looking over his shoulder all morning, like he was waiting for the boogeyman to jump out, but he still hadn't spotted Vincent once. Hell, during that long talk on the phone, The Weasel had been only a few feet away, watching him and sipping a beer. But the kid still hadn't made him, hadn't thought to look up to the restaurant and bar perched above his head.

He stayed at the bar as Lance made his way to the departure terminal. It was getting to be just about that time, Vincent thought, grinning. The kid would get out of the crowd, down to the gate, and he'd think he was safe. But The Weasel had a ticket, too—an all-purpose counterfeit tab that would get him just about anyplace in the airport. And he could look as much like an innocent passenger as the next guy—for a few seconds, anyway. Long enough.

Down at the gate. Where the people thinned out, and everybody was half asleep with boredom anyway. That's where he'd do it.

He sighed happily and looked around the new terminal. *Classy,* he thought. *Real classy. Maybe I don't hate airports so much after all.*

He hurried to the nearest phone—the same one Lance had used—and punched out Sammy Raines's private number in New York City. While he waited, he counted up the different ways he could do Lance Sullivan.

It could be quick and quiet. That was one of his specialties. But Sammy had made it clear that this one was to be made an example of. Maybe he *should* break tradition and go big on this one. Real messy. Headline stuff.

Either way, he was equipped. He patted his breast pocket and felt the familiar, comforting shape nestled under his lapel . . . and he smiled.

"Please dial your telephone calling card number, or slide your credit card through the marked slot, or dial 'O' for an operator."

As the metallic, synthesized voice of the automated operator droned in his ear, Vincent slid his credit card through the slot marked by the phone company and waited, balanced on the balls of his feet. The burr of the dial tone changed to the series of clicks and beeps that signified the card being accepted and the call being placed.

He touched his breast pocket again and felt Little Amy. He had named her after the first girl he'd ever done, back when he was sixteen and a half. He never liked the Spic name everybody used: "sty-let-to." Sounded like some Eye-Talian food or something like that. No, Little Amy was something better than that.

He had made her himself, and he was proud of that. Fashioned from superhard plastic, she would pass through any metal detector without a peep, but she was every bit as deadly as her metal counterparts. Hell, she was *better*. If things got tough, if he had to ditch her, a few seconds of heat from a fire or even boiling water would melt her down, twist her into an unrecognizable lump.

The perfect weapon, he thought. *My Little Amy*.

As he heard the purr of the first ring, he had the strangest feeling. A ripple flowed over him like a cool breeze, but he was inside an air terminal. There were no breezes here.

There it was again. The phone had only started its second ring, but the feeling was back and this time, as it washed over him, he found it hard to breathe. He tried to inhale, but it was as if he was suddenly standing in a vacuum. Then a weird smell assaulted his nostrils. Whew! It smelled like something had died nearby! He looked around, half-expecting to see some overdressed woman wearing way too much perfume. But it was worse than that. Nastier, somehow.

Besides, there was no one near him. He had used the last phone in a group of four, and there weren't many people traveling tonight. He was alone.

Just me and my stench, he thought, grimly amused.

Then Sammy Raines answered the phone.

"Hello."

The Weasel opened his mouth to speak. He formed the words in his mind and set his tongue in motion. *Hi, Sammy,* he was going to say. *I got him for you. No problem*.

But something was wrong. The words caught in his throat, as if he was trying to bring up something hard and hot out of his stomach, something he couldn't get past his constricted throat.

He couldn't talk.

Shit— shit, he couldn't breathe at all.

His head was down all the time—looking at the phone, looking at his shoes, trying to appear harmless and small. So he hadn't seen the sparkling gold mist swoop in around him. It came with the choking. It came as the smell got so bad he couldn't think straight.

"Hello?" Sammy Raines said. "There somebody there? *H'lo?*"

He started to gasp. He could feel himself turning blue.

The glistening golden vapor started to swirl, agitated and shimmering. It expanded and convulsed like the lungs of a dying asthmatic.

Like Vincent Fender's lungs.

"Hello?" Sammy sounded pissed off. "Goddamn it, if there's anybody there, you better *talk* to me!"

The receiver dropped from The Weasel's hand and dangled, swinging slowly back and forth at the end of its metal-covered cord. He tried to speak one last time. He clawed at his collar, he worked his jaw like a hooked fish, but nothing came in, and nothing went out. Not a breath.

Vincent Fender died.

He didn't feel his body expand like an inflatable doll. He didn't feel it lift from the ground and hover momentarily, then plop to the floor like an empty, lifeless sack. He was past that already. He was past everything.

The instant his heart stopped beating, the golden mist evaporated. A businessman trying to call his family on Long Island found the body a few minutes later.

It looked like a heart attack, or a stroke. Nothing new. Nothing unusual, really. The coroner's office barely bothered with the autopsy.

"Mr. Sullivan! *Mr. Sullivan?*"

Lance came to consciousness, locked in the grip of a crushing fear. As he blinked, trying to see, the voice spoke again. "Are you all right?"

Finally Lance's eyes focused enough for him to make out the dark-haired air hostess. She was standing over him in the dimmed light of the first-class cabin, a look of genuine concern filling her features.

He wasn't in the forest. There wasn't any girl. He was on a 747, bound for Australia. Everything was all right.

"I'm . . . aah . . . fine," he mumbled. The memory of the dream slipped away, and part of him was grateful for its loss. He rubbed his eyes and tried to straighten up in the huge airline seat.

"I'm sorry to wake you, but you were beginning to shout," the hostess said. "I thought you might prefer to be awake."

Lance managed a smile. "You're right. That was some nightmare. Thanks."

He tried to straighten himself in the seat, again, but couldn't seem to manage it. The hostess leaned down and pulled on a lever near the floor; the seat hissed lightly and swung into an upright position. "When I saw you'd drifted off, I tilted back the 'sleeper' to make you more comfortable," she explained. "Is that better?"

She smiled, showing a beautiful set of white teeth, and Lance smiled back. *Now that was nice,* he thought. There were definite advantages to flying first-class. He saw others, too, now that the nightmare was passing: three other hostesses to assist only ten passengers, including Lance.

He stretched his long legs out, and they didn't even touch the seat in front of him. Then he smiled as he thought of how cramped it must be in the rear of the plane—in the economy section.

"I appreciate it," Lance said. He realized he meant the space, and the flight, and being awake—and being alive. He appreciated it all.

The hostess smiled again. "Can I get you anything?"

"A large cup of strong black coffee would be nice. I don't want to sleep again right now."

That much is true anyway, he told himself. *I definitely don't want to sleep again.* The pretty, dark-haired hostess went off to get his drink, and he rubbed his eyes again, looking for the first time at the shadowy forms of the other first-class travelers. All of them appeared to be sleeping soundly.

He found he was jealous of their ability to pass the flight

so peacefully. He was even jealous of the fact that they could sleep at all, without finding death and fear in their dreams. That's all sleep held for him anymore. He had learned to hate it.

"There you are," the hostess said as she returned. She placed a tray with a small pot of coffee, a jug of cream and a bowl of sugar on the wide space next to his right elbow. "Is there anything else I can get you?"

"No, that's fine, thanks. How long before we reach Fiji?"

The dark-haired girl checked her wristwatch. "We should touch down in Nadi in a little over two hours."

"Thanks," Lance said, groaning inwardly at the thought of fighting off sleep for two more hours. The combination of the darkened cabin and the constant hum of the engines made it hard to stay awake.

"Just buzz if you need a refill . . . or anything else," the hostess said, and went off to join her three friends, who sat idly in a group of vacant seats at the rear of the section, chattering happily to each other.

Lance squeezed his eyes tightly closed, then stretched them open to their limit. He shook his head and sighed heavily. Then he lifted the cup to his lips and took a long swallow of the black liquid, hardly noticing the burning heat in his mouth and throat.

Torrika waved good-bye to the man and woman from Paris as their rental car slowly eased off the grassy area in front of the Hyatt Regency's driveway and sped away from Kora Levu, toward Nadi.

She had been traveling for two days, island-hopping with friends as far as Suva, and had made the final leg from Suva to Nadi in the same way many island people traveled—by hitchhiking.

A short walk down the asphalt road by the tennis courts soon brought her to the large lanai entranceway to the main hotel.

Torrika wanted to see her father—she *needed* to see him. She had missed him at home—one of her rides had taken longer to get than she'd planned—and she knew he would be here.

After climbing the steps, she hurried past the rental car desk, and skirted by the large stairwell. A quick look over the balcony facing the beach revealed her gray-haired father on the grass under the large palm trees, giving the tourists an easy-to-swallow version of Fiji culture.

Some of it didn't make much sense to the visitors, she knew. Some of it, Torrika had to admit, didn't make much sense to her. Many of the legends had been damaged beyond comprehension by time and by missionaries who tried to make the "heathens" into God-fearing Christians.

Torrika went back into the main foyer, moving swiftly past the gift shops, half-running down the long ramp to the beach, the pool and the pool-bar.

She stopped by the edge of the downstairs lunch area and listened to her father. He had been taught by her grandfather, as she had been. But in him, the light seemed weak and changeable. He spoke endlessly of The Old Ones, but he understood so little.

She loved him very much . . . but how was that possible? How could he see so poorly?

She sighed heavily, realizing it was the *lali* of the gods and not her place to try to understand. She loved him very much, that was all that mattered.

He saw her standing, half in shadow, and he nodded lightly. The hint of a smile flickered across his face as he swept into the last part of his lecture.

"Fiji has many modern heroes, also," he said in his deep, soothing voice. "In World War II, Corporal Sefanaia Sukanaivalu was awarded the Victoria Cross for bravery . . ."

She had heard it often. Now the words flowed over her like water—soothing, cool water to protect her from the coming heat. He hoped they had enjoyed his little talk. He hoped they would enjoy Fiji. He hoped they would come back and visit again soon.

She hardly noticed the twenty-odd people who sat listening to him. She was looking at him . . . only at him.

Perhaps he never had understood, but he had taught her so much over the years. He had seen her special talent early on, had taught her what little he knew, and then had made sure she found the teacher she needed. Soon after, the visions had started and no further teaching was necessary. But he was always there whenever she needed to talk. He was always there, ready with comfort and love.

He shook the hands of the visitors who offered—some even gave him some bills as tips—and as the last of them drifted away, he hurried over to her side.

Torrika's eyes filled with tears.

"Bula, Torrika," he said warmly. He looked concerned, but he did not ask why she wept. He had learned not to question his daughter's strange and powerful gifts. He only accepted . . . and loved.

She threw her arms around him and hugged him close, her tears flowing freely now. "Bula, Daddy. I love you," she sobbed.

He wrapped his huge brown arms around her and held her tight. She told him nothing—there was little she *could* have told him that he would have understood. But he knew she was going away. And he was sure she would not be back.

They stood there together until the shadows grew long and dark around them. Torrika could not let him go. She drew strength from him, and warmth.

It would all be all right. She would do what she was destined to do, and the world—*her* world, *everyone's* world—would be better for it.

Nadi Airport was calling. The *light carrier* was drawing near. But for now, for this moment, there was only Torrika and her father.

She already missed him.

Chapter 11

The long, dark hallways of the ancient manse echoed with the piercing, inhuman cry. It bounced from marble statues that were ancient when Richard the Lion-Hearted led his doomed crusades to the lands of the Saracens and rebounded from stone floors worn down by the tread of countless thousands of feet.

Tapestries woven with gold and silver absorbed some of the sound. One twisted hanging depicted hooded revelers cavorting about a huge fire and feasting on the remains of an unlucky comrade. Others showed different but equally debauched, demonic motifs.

The scream continued, passing through the heavy material, through the cold stone walls themselves. It spread throughout the massive structure.

But no one heard it.

The entire estate was deserted except for the thing that raged down its long ornate hallways, that rushed through the glittering ballroom, that crashed in and out of room after amazing room, wailing its contempt for all living creatures . . . and one being in particular.

The creature despised the left hand of its right hand, the negative to its positive. It hated the *bitch* who sprang from its own bosom and tore away the power, ripped it asunder, leaving only the hint of what might have been.

It hated the other side of itself, the part that had robbed it of the ability to easily quench its . . . *unusual* desires—its need for life-force.

But soon the chance would come to rectify the situation. Then the creature's cursed sibling would feel the wrath of a hatred unknown to mortals, a loathing that had festered for almost six hundred years in the twisted mind of this beast that was once a man.

All that time, it had searched for the answers, painstakingly sifting and resifting, pondering even the slightest inflection of words once spoken by a learned uncle, dead now almost six hundred years. It had recited, over and over, the words locked deep in its memory, taken from written pages that had long ago faded and crumbled to dust. It fought to understand and control the bizarre symbols that were a key to the power.

Then, quite suddenly, it understood. A final piece fell into place. A certain set of phrases, a single syllable spoken at precisely the correct instant—and it *knew*.

Now everything was different. Now it was *free*. It loosed another shrieking wail—a blend of frustration, hatred and fulfillment—that echoed throughout the house that was not a house.

At last! At last it understood at least enough to strike back.

Now we will see how well you can stand the torture, the thing thought. For an instant its ancient and long-abandoned human form reasserted itself, and with that momentary reemergence came human memories: plots hatched through the centuries, schemes joyously and carefully orchestrated over hundreds of years. It howled at the thought of the depredation it would loose against its hated enemy. The joy it felt was nearly orgasmic.

Though not really understanding the whys and wherefores, it stretched out and mentally touched one of the glowing strands of the energy-field web that was the real essence of the mansion.

The body of the beast-human shimmered for a long second, coruscating with intense flashes of color. Then, suddenly, it was gone.

The ancient manse breathed an immense sigh of relief.

Brenda Kaye was in her late sixties, gray-haired, wrinkled, stoop-shouldered, "one of the Geritol set," as she often put it. Still, she thought as clearly as she ever had, which was damn clear. And she saw with a sharpness that would astound most thirty-year-olds. It certainly astounded her doctor, who swore up and down that it was impossible.

It wasn't. It was just Brenda at sixty-eight.

Brenda lived in a tiny one-bedroom Housing Commission house in the Sydney suburb of Winston Hills. She often sat out in front of her tiny unit, in a deck chair fitted with a large sun-umbrella, reading.

That was where she was, as usual, when the odd thing happened.

It was a sweltering, humid summer day—a day that reminded her of her childhood, for reasons she couldn't quite pinpoint. Something about holidays, and freshly squeezed juice, and her loving and stern old mother.

She closed her book for a moment to remember, then looked at the lurid cover in her hand and smiled. "Old Mum, God rest her soul, would turn in her grave if she saw what I read these days," Brenda said aloud to herself. Then she turned the page of the torrid romance, eager to find out if the heroine had given in to the amorous advances of her handsome suitor.

She'd worked hard all her life, and now, in her second year of retirement, she was enjoying the strangest things. Like these novels that would have been banned when she was a girl. And the soaps, both in the daytime and at night. "Days of Our Lives," and "Dallas," and "Falcon Crest," and "Dynasty" and "A Country Practice." She loved them all and remembered every detail of each of the plots.

Even her biweekly trips to nearby Parramatta to pick up her pension check were planned so she wouldn't miss a single episode unless it was absolutely unavoidable.

Brenda turned the page and to her delight found that the heroine had indeed given herself totally to the handsome suitor. She hated herself for hanging on every passionate, lustful word of the encounter. *I know better than this,* she tried to tell herself. *I'm a bright—*

Something moved at the edge of her vision, but she ignored it.

". . . the handsome dark-eyed captain lifted her to feelings she had never known, in a climactic experience that defied description."

Something moved again. Brenda sighed in exasperation and finally looked up.

Her mouth dropped open in disbelief.

Across the street, hanging in the air a good two feet above the far footpath, was a ball of colored light. It seemed to be expanding and shrinking with a pulsing beat as the colors whirled furiously, becoming more and more agitated. Brenda thought it looked for all the world like a special effect from one of those movies by Spielberg.

Before she could decide what to do, the ball silently exploded into a huge puff of smoke. And as the smoke cleared, the old lady's shock grew even more.

Standing on the pavement, large as life, was a man. He was dressed in a dapper tweed suit, cut in a safari style, wearing a soft felt hat and smoking a briar.

For a moment, he seemed somewhat confused, almost as if he didn't know where he was or how he'd gotten there. But his confusion quickly passed and in his face came something that would send chills down Brenda's spine every time she ever thought of it.

It sounded melodramatic, even to her, but Brenda couldn't shake one thought. This man was *evil*. And even from this far away, his just standing there made her stomach knot in fear.

The strange old gentleman finally looked about and his eyes met Brenda's. With a flourish, he tipped his hat to her, then turned and hurried off around the corner and out of sight.

For the longest time Brenda stared at the empty corner, not quite believing what had happened.

A part of her wondered if she shouldn't call the police, or someone, and tell them what had happened. After very little consideration she realized that would not be a good move.

She was in her sixties, comfortable, and except for the degrading experience of having to beg for her pension, despite having worked hard for forty years and paid in much more than she could possibly spend before she died, she was content. With her little house, her television shows and her friends, she had a good life here. She wasn't about to risk all that. She didn't fancy being committed to an asylum somewhere, because she told stories about suddenly appearing balls of light and evil, disappearing elderly men.

No, it would be her secret, she thought as she looked back to her novel.

For a moment she thought she would never pick up the thread of it. All she could think about was that beautiful, terrifying globe of light . . . and the evil look in that gentleman's eye. That intensely evil look . . .

Then a word in the novel caught her eye—a word that Brenda Kaye would never even *think* of saying out loud.

"Oh, my goodness," she said, chuckling to herself.

She looked up quickly, as if she half-expected the gentleman to be eavesdropping. But there was no one there.

There was only Brenda at sixty-eight, in the midst of her torrid lovemaking with the dark-eyed sea captain.

Chapter 12

Lance Sullivan made his way along the exit ramp of the jumbo jet and out into the Fijian night air, recoiling at the stifling humidity.

"Good God, Harold," a heavyset woman a few steps ahead of him whined to her trembling husband. "It's two-thirty in the goddamned morning. What must it be like here in the *day*?"

What indeed, Lance thought to himself as large beads of sweat formed all over his body.

The entire group from the plane quickly made their way along the open ramp toward the terminal, and Lance took a deep breath of the earthy, moist air. It reminded him somewhat of Bimini, in the Bahamas.

He passed under the WELCOME TO NADI sign that stretched over the entrance to the immigration desk and tried to put some distance between himself and the noisy woman, but her voice still reached him a second before he entered the air-conditioned transit lounge.

"It's a good thing I didn't let you talk us into staying here—"

The automatic glass doors hissed shut, cutting off the nasal voice. Lance sighed gratefully and made his way to the far end of the top level of the huge waiting area.

The cool, dehumidified air chilled the perspiration that rose from his skin. Lance stood for a short second to enjoy this wondrous alternative to the oppressively normal humidity of the Fiji Islands.

Finally, he sat at a small table in an alcove formed by the hall to an unused set of glass doors and looked about the lounge. It was designed solely for tourists. This section only opened when the overseas planes touched down to refuel and load and unload passengers, and it stayed open just long enough to accommodate eager duty free shoppers.

Except for a tiny bar that also served sandwiches, the duty free shops took up most of both levels of the transit area. Since ongoing travelers were not allowed to leave here until the plane was ready for takeoff, they were effectively trapped and bored and usually found themselves wandering through the stores even if they hadn't planned to.

Lance noted these things from his somewhat secluded spot in the far corner. He was so deep in thought he didn't notice the tap on the glass of the door behind him.

The second knock caught his attention. He turned and saw a Fijian woman standing outside, motioning to him.

She was an intense chocolate brown, tall, with a strong face and jaw and a thick, sculptured nose. The sulu wrapped tightly around her body was a furious, precisely patterned combination of earth-browns, white and black. A red flower adorned her dark, Brillo-Pad hair.

She saw that she had caught his eye and looked nervously about, then motioned to him again, even more insistently this time.

Without really thinking, Lance turned and looked behind him, sure she couldn't mean him. But there was no one else nearby, so he turned back to face her.

Saying good-bye to her father wasn't easy for Torrika. Though she couldn't really tell him anything, even his limited ability with the *power* was enough for him to know something was going on.

At first he had tried to learn what it was. But then somehow he sensed that questions would only waste the precious time they had left, so he dropped his interrogation and made their short visit together a happy one.

When she finally stood to leave, he took her in his arms and hugged her close for a very long time. Then, without speaking, they walked together down the hotel driveway toward the main road.

Torrika was relieved when one of the guests stopped to give her a ride to the airport even before they reached the blacktop. Saying good-bye was always hard for her.

As she looked back at her father through the rear window of the rental car, she saw him standing beneath the hotel sign, waving and smiling. She whispered a soft prayer to the *Old Ones* to give him peace in the last years of his life.

Once at the airport, she made her way down the long hallway leading to the customs office, waving to a friend in the currency exchange of the Fiji Bank as she went. She went over her plan again.

They rarely had anyone watching the customs desk. She would slip past it, out through the deserted baggage claim section—before it hummed to life—and up the wide staircase leading to the transit lounge. It was the only way for her to get into the departure area without causing a commotion.

Her plan began to go wrong, however, when she found the door to customs unexpectedly closed and locked. She was forced to slip out onto the tarmac and shinny up the metal ironwork of the multileveled walkways leading to and from the departure gates.

She was both surprised and awed as she approached the sealed glass doors of the second level. There, through the shimmering glaze of the sheet glass, she for the first time saw the centerpiece of her visions sitting just a few feet away. She expected the sight, of course, but it was one thing to have visions of the *seeing* and totally another to actually be standing looking at *The One* in real life.

One look was all she needed to confirm what she had always surmised when trapped in her visions. The glow of the *power* was still faint in him. He was still not aware of what he was to become.

She hesitated an instant, thinking about the final outcome of this meeting. The hot tropical breeze tickled the uncovered skin on her body and sent an inexplicable chill through her, but she pushed her fears aside. This was her destiny, she knew. Her part in a sequence of wondrous events, now, at last, set into motion.

She tapped at the glass.

At first, Lance Sullivan couldn't figure out what this Fijian woman wanted, but her continued motioning finally got the message across. She wanted him to open the doors.

He knew the idea was preposterous. She could be any sort of crazy person, or thief, or beggar. Yet he found himself looking closely at the solid steel, manually activated release bars firmly secured across the entire width of the exit doors.

He shrugged at her, motioning that he was sorry, while she persisted in her wild gyrations.

"I'm sorry," Lance whispered, mouthing the words to her. "I can't do it."

There was no way he could make her understand the warning printed in large red letters on his side of the door:

**Emergency Exit
Alarm Door. Must Not Be Opened
by Any but Authorized Personnel
Except in Case of Extreme Emergency. Infringement of This Order Is a Punishable Offense.**

The Fijian government obviously isn't overjoyed by the idea of people arriving or leaving without official sanction,

Lance thought. And the last thing he needed was trouble with the officials of a country he was visiting for little more than an hour.

But the Fijian woman wouldn't go away. She locked her startling blue eyes on his and stood staring intently at him.

Lance found himself moving forward.

Thinking back on it later, he would wonder again and again, what had prompted him to do it? But at this moment he never gave it a thought. He simply moved forward and put his hand on the cool, heavy metal.

One solid push on the bar released the emergency door. Instantly—true to the printed warning—an incredibly loud clanging filled the area, hammering at his eardrums.

Lance was shocked from his near dream state, but Torrika didn't hesitate for an instant. As soon as the doors were released she pushed them open, slipped inside the transit lounge, and began speaking to him in rapid, staccato bursts.

"I have co . . . as instru . . . by . . . visi—"

Lance could see her mouth shaping words, but the loud ringing of the alarm made them unintelligible.

It took a moment for Torrika to realize what was happening. When the reason for her master's puzzled look finally dawned on her, she aimed a vicious curse at the alarm, leaned in close, lips almost touching his ear, and tried again.

Lance wanted to run, to be anywhere but here. He could see two customs officers rushing toward them at full sprint, and he *knew* this could only be trouble—exactly the kind he didn't need. But something made him stay. And the same something prompted him to listen closely to what this woman was trying to tell him—whatever it was she thought was important enough to risk a brush with the law.

"Scion!" she was saying. "I am here as the visions instructed!" Torrika shouted just inches from his left ear. "You must know of your heritage before you—"

One of the two customs men, a burly Fijian, grabbed

Torrika and pulled her roughly away from Lance. She was still shouting to him, but he couldn't hear her at all now over the blaring noise of the alarm. And even if he could, he thought to himself, he probably wouldn't be able to make any more sense of it than he had made of what she'd just said.

When the second customs official, a painfully thin Indian man with a waxed black moustache, placed his hand on Lance's chest, motioning to him to stay where he was, he did exactly that.

Meanwhile, yet another member of airport security began waving interested gawkers away, and the burly Fijian bodily dragged the strange, blue-eyed woman down the stairs leading to the baggage claim area. Lance shook his head as she fought the man tooth and nail, kicking and scratching, all the while shouting back at Lance.

Suddenly Lance knew—as so often he just *knew* things— that it was important for him to hear her words.

The Fijian was too much for Torrika, even driven as she was. He lifted her into the air and carried her down the last few steps.

The frail Indian smiled tightly at his colleague's brutish solution to the incident. Then he stepped to the glass doors, slammed them shut, and reset the alarm.

Lance started to make a break for it. He didn't think of the consequences. He didn't even know why it was so vital that he get away. Still, his body tensed as he prepared to sprint down the stairs after the strange woman. To hell with the consequences.

The sudden cessation of the mind-scrambling bell made him balk. In the next instant the Indian man was back, standing between him and the stairs.

The Fijian carrying Torrika was only a few feet from the entranceway to the baggage area when she screamed to Lance.

"Lance Sullivan! Lance *Beresford!* Listen to me!"

She couldn't have gotten his attention any better if she had thrown a brick at his head.

"Be of strong resolve, Lance Beresford! Death is waiting in the illusion of kinship! But you are *The One!* The guardian of the white-light sword! It may—"

"Passengers for Flight 663 to Sydney, Australia, are requested to make their way to Boarding Gate Three on the top level of the transit lounge."

The amplified PA announcement drowned out the Fijian woman's last words.

Before it ended, she was whisked out of sight by the burly customs agent.

Lance began to go after her, but the Indian got in the way again. He pushed the palm of his hand against Lance's chest, and for the briefest instant, Lance actually contemplated hurling the little man aside and going after the woman. She somehow knew *both* of his names. How the hell could she know them? He had to find out, he had to—

Good sense raced to his rescue. It was a tremendous effort, but he contained himself.

"You will come this way," the Indian said curtly, pointing a bony finger at an office on the far side of the waiting area.

"I have a plane to catch," Lance said.

"Yes, yes. We will see about that," the Indian chirped, nodding his head and sounding for all the world like a Peter Sellers impersonator.

Lance took one last look down the stairs, then sighed heavily. This wasn't the time to make waves, he realized. He headed off across the top level of the transit lounge with the two customs officers tightly flanking him as passengers from his flight began milling around Gate Three.

"Welcome back, Mr. Sullivan," the dark-haired hostess said when Lance stepped aboard the plane to Sydney. Her name was Nancy, he knew. He had read it off the name tag she had pinned onto her uniform as they were approaching the Fijian island chain. He was the last one aboard. The main door swung shut with a loud thunk and was firmly secured by a male supervisor before he had even reached his seat.

Nancy helped him get settled quickly. His briefcase—filled with little of importance—went under the seat. His suit bag, crammed with make-up and false hairpieces, hung in the closet at the front of the cabin.

"Thanks!" he said to her as he slipped into his seat, genuinely grateful. "For a while there I wasn't sure I'd make it."

"So I heard," she smiled. "You'd best fasten your seat belt. We were delayed waiting for you. The captain will want to get into the air as soon as possible."

"That's fine with me," he said. Then, as she hurried off to check on her other passengers, he shook his head and mumbled to himself, "Damndest thing, that woman going to all that trouble to babble a lot of gibberish at me!"

Less than five minutes later, the huge plane was lifting into the air and racing away from the islands of Fiji.

Jesus, that was close, Lance thought, easing back into the comfortable, cushioned chair. *It's a damn good thing I was traveling first class and as an American citizen, or it might have gotten hairy back there.*

The sudden release of tension, the purring of the jet engines, and simple exhaustion from twenty-two hours without sleep finally became too much for him. Lance closed his eyes. Seconds later, he fell into a deep sleep.

Torrika stood in the doorway of the customs office for a long minute, even though she was free to go. She breathed in the warm, muggy air . . . and it felt good.

She watched for a moment as the soft, heated breeze playfully set the edge of her sulu dancing to and fro. She let her eyes drink in the activity and bright lights of the bustling airport, then she gazed longingly at the distant hills that were part of her Fiji.

There were no more visions of the *seeing*. No more

magical looks at people she had never known, and places she would never visit. There was only the sure and certain unfolding of her destiny as she had seen it so many times during her short life.

The two customs officials had detained her for almost three hours, repeating the same questions over and over: "What were you trying to do? Why did you try to accost the American?"

She'd told them the truth with the same tenacious rapidity they used to ask the questions, not wavering or changing her story once during the entire interrogation.

The man of Indian descent had scoffed at her words, though she'd noticed the big Fijian said very little. Finally, it was he who had convinced his partner she was harmless enough. "It comes from all those old fools spouting Island legends," he had said, his words carrying no conviction. "Makes the gullible ones a little crazy."

When the Indian had agreed to let her go, the Fijian officer had walked her to the door and shown her the respect usually given only to elder relatives.

Torrika noted the faint strains of deep blue seeping into the blackness of night and felt the ever-so-slight changes that heralded the approaching dawn. She knew Lance Sullivan was only hours from the beginning of his awakening to the truth. Just as she knew she was even closer to hers.

Finally, she sighed heavily and made her way along the brightly lit airport concourse, out into the last hour of darkness. She knew what waited there for her . . . and she was ready to face it.

Chapter 13

Darkness kissed him. Darkness engorged him, embraced him, sucked at him like a hungry beast.

He strained to see: only darkness. Darkness.

Breath rattled in metered unison with his footfalls. Air murmured past him, cooling the sweat from his skin as he moved faster and faster.

Where am I? he wondered. He was running, but . . . to where? And why?

His heart writhed in his chest, fighting to pump blood through constricted arteries. It was cold, then hot, then cold again. He peered into the blackness, pupils straining to enlarge until his eyes stung and his head thundered.

Darkness. Only darkness, and a cold and bottomless sensation that swelled inside him.

He was . . . alone. Not "by himself" or "away for a while." But terrifyingly ALONE.

Faint light fluttered against him. Bloated irises rapidly contracted. A moment passed, and another. Slowly the surroundings solidified, colored a slate gray.

Images hovered in the dimness. Shadow-draped limbs, gnarled and twisted, reached out for him. He crouched and held up his hands to ward them off.

They were trees, yes . . . but not like any trees he'd ever seen. He touched one hesitantly, and it whispered rough and warm under his fingers.

It wasn't his imagination. He could feel them.

Suddenly, grotesquely, they moved again, knotting together over his head to form a canopy, a tunnel, a covered path.

An instant later, he could feel something more—a thing setting sharp and solid against his spine. A thirsting, insatiable evil, poised, ready to slash deeply.

It was coming from the trees.

He pushed away from them and ran down the path. The air was thick and humid like syrup, but he kept moving, kept trying until the breath burned in his lungs.

He turned a tree-lined corner and chilling mist covered him, swooping in like an insubstantial wall, clinging hungrily as he ran.

A wailing moan—harpy cry, banshee wail—cut through the mist. It pushed and expanded in him like a living thing, crashing against the walls of his skull. With the sounds came a memory—a terrifying, painful memory.

He had done all this before. Had been here many, many times. And he knew what would happen next.

The roots at his feet stirred and separated, spreading like gray arthritic fingers. They were hiding something soft and supple. Warm tones glimmered against the shapeless ash.

It was the body of a woman. He didn't know her—they'd never met—but he loved her with a passion so intense it seared him. He longed to rush forward and take her in his arms. To hold her. To protect her. But he was helpless.

He watched in horror as the body turned, not of its own volition—it was limp and lifeless—but as if some invisible foot had hooked under the torso and turned it over for a better look.

The body of this woman twisted unnaturally. Her ankles, dark with blood, were pinned to the earth. Her gold hair swept across her breasts like a soft curtain. She was bleeding from a hundred tiny cuts that covered her from neck to knee like obscene tattoos.

Anger screamed in him, driving him to do something. But the sharp, awful thing was behind him again. It chuckled wickedly insiae his head and surged past him, a reeking wind. The odor was thick as smoke, choking. Sweet and heavy, intense, it clutched at his throat like a fist.

The female corpse jerked and arched as the thing tore it free of the rootbed, then dangled it in front of him. It flexed and arched again. And again. Like a dancer, he thought. Or like a whore.

He strained to go to her but found himself turning, running from the body, from the smell, pushing forward through the heavy air as he searched for a light in the gray-green mist.

Tears streamed down his face. The pain in his chest pulsed and pulsed again.

Gravel suddenly crunched under his feet. He was running down a wide driveway toward . . . something. For an instant it began to take shape, but then it disappeared back into the gray fog. No matter how hard he tried, how fast he ran, the shape was always just beyond the next billow of grayness.

Then a plaintive, echoing voice called through the dank air.

"Lance Sullivan!" it called. "Lance Sullivan!" it wailed. "LANCE SULLIVAN!" it screamed.

He stopped, confused. As he shuffled his weight from one foot to the other, the sound of the gravel under his feet momentarily caught his attention.

But then the voice was back—louder, more insistent. It surged at him, the words lapping over each other, crashing down on him, dragging at him, tearing him in all directions.

His being stretched to its breaking point, unable to fight back—helpless even to understand. Still the words attacked, slamming at his consciousness.

"Sullivan! Beresford! Sullivan! Beresford! Sullivan! Beresford! SULLIVAN!"

The words turned into a solid, slamming mass, pounding incessantly at his innermost self.

"Beresford! SULLIVAN! . . ."

"Let me die," he begged.

"SULLIVAN! . . . SULLIVAN! . . . MR. SULLIVAN? MR. SULLIVAN!"

"Let me die!"

"Mr. Sullivan! Wake up—"

Lance thrashed out, trying to drive away the pain, and connected with something.

In that instant, a gentle purring filled his ears. His eyes snapped open and he saw Nancy standing in front of him. A look of shock filled her features. She was holding her mouth with her left hand, and a trickle of blood seeped between her fingers.

Lance was suddenly awake. He instantly realized what he had done. "Oh my God! I'm really sorry," he said. "Are you all right?"

He released his seat belt and went to get up, but Nancy backed away slightly. "I'm fine," she said quickly. "You were having another nightmare." Her voice quavered as she used a handkerchief to wipe the blood from her split lip. "You were breathing funny, and I was worried about you. I guess I shouldn't have stood so close, but I couldn't seem to wake you."

"I *really* am sorry, Nancy," Lance said, frowning. "I don't know why I keep having these nightmares—"

"It's all right." She smiled now, and the tension between them began to ease. "But if you start dreaming again, I think I'll get someone else to wake you."

Torrika's sandals flipped, flopped and slapped on the soft red earth of Viti Levu, the largest of the Fijian islands.

She hardly noticed them. She no longer thought of the trees, or the flowers, or the birds, or her Fiji. She was preparing herself, steeling her emotions, so that she would not disgrace herself in her most important moment.

When the eerie purple glow began to shimmer in the air a few feet in front of her, she was not startled.

As it began to ooze and pulse, then grow in size, she didn't run like a frightened native.

She had seen it all in the visions.

She played her part exactly as she had to: the seed was now planted and would flower at the crucial moment. Her life was of little further importance; there was just one small thing left to do.

The sickly purple oozed a disgusting stench that wrinkled her nose, though she tried not to let it affect her. As the smell became more and more putrid, she found herself unconsciously backing away a few steps. But when the swirling ball of color finally took shape, she planted her feet firmly in the red earth and stood her ground.

Still, the sight of the grotesque beast that now appeared sent an involuntary ripple of fear coursing through her. She sucked in a frightened gasp.

It might have been human once, but the strange pustules lumped all over its gnarled and twisted form made it hard to be sure. A disgusting yellow fluid bubbled from the sores. There was no doubt where the smell that sent wave after wave of nausea washing over her came from.

Knowing what was to come, and being prepared for it, was not enough to stop the fear. It rose in Torrika unbidden as a deformed, taloned hand reached out for her.

The vicious claws ripped her, tearing deeply into her soft flesh. She began to scream. But the searing pain that assaulted her every molecule was like a cold splash of water on her face. She caught the scream in the back of her throat and refused to let it surge into the moist air. She was defiant. She would not let this *thing* have the pleasure of seeing her break.

Even as the beast crushed the life from her frail form, she kept her lips tightly clenched and performed the last of her duties.

With every ounce of her will, she concentrated on one intense, living thought. When it had reached a fever pitch, she mentally hurled it forth into the ether, a beam of consciousness, spiraling through the vortex of time and space, racing toward a preordained moment in the future.

It is done! she thought. Then, smiling through the pain, she embraced the end of this existence, basking in a wondrous glow as the melodious voices of the *Old Ones* sang her a welcoming chorus.

It is done, she thought again . . . and she smiled as she died.

Chapter 14

A whimper of frustrated rage broke from her ghostly lips and echoed around the empty old room.

"How could I have done it?" she said for the thousandth time. "How could I have made such a fundamental error?" Again, the only response was her own words, bouncing back at her from the ancient furnishings.

She flickered from one side of the room to the other in the ethereal equivalent of pacing. "I must be getting senile, *really* I must," she told herself. Then she snorted, half-amused. "Still, after six hundred and fifty years I suppose that's to be expected."

The early-morning sun sprayed through the weather-beaten slats of the room's only window and formed crazy-quilt patterns on the bookcase that stretched the entire length of one wall. A bright shaft hit the gold-leaf binding of a huge book sitting alone on the second shelf, sending honey-colored geometric shapes across much of the far wall. She winced as she looked at the title: *A History of the Family Beresford.*

"Why *now*?" she said, suddenly angry. "He's arriving today, *this minute,* and I can't even let him know the danger he's in!'' She lashed out in frustration, her clenched fist sweeping at the bookcase.

The hand went right through it.

For a long moment she stood there, buried to the wrist in the ancient oak, struggling to control her rage. Finally, after too long a time, she shrugged her shoulders and sighed bitterly. ''Lance . . .'' she whispered, and pulled her hand from within the wooden bookcase. She spread her fingers and peered through the ghostly outline of her palm. The rest of the room was clearly visible through it. ''When you most need me, I'm helpless. Totally, wretchedly, *stupidly* helpless.

''Lance,'' she said again. ''I'm so sorry.''

Chapter 15

Lance Sullivan looked down from the window of the Boeing 747 at the city of Sydney sprawled out below. Until now he hadn't really thought much about how it might look. There were too many other things occupying his mind.

It was 7:45 on a clear morning, and myriad tiny reflections from the summer sun danced wildly on the waters of the huge natural harbor that stretched off in all directions. A massive, single-span bridge joined the central area of the city to the northern section, its huge legs set into four solid-rock pylons, each over fifteen stories high. Nearby, the sail-like wings of the world-famous Opera House swooped into the sky, making it the most recognizable landmark in the city. Off to its right was a crystalline blue inlet, where a mad variety of boats visited and departed from a long row of jetties. Above the quay hung a suspended railway, and beyond it the metropolitan skyline was a linear chaos of every conceivable skyscraper design. Deep-green parks were scattered over the landscape, from directly below him to the golden horizon. Some were barely larger than vacant lots, others covered many blocks—and all were filled with flowers, glittering with open water.

It was one of the most beautiful cities he had ever seen.

The plane banked and began its descent to the runway stretched along the edge of a large blue-water bay off in the distance. Lance found himself wishing that they had to circle the city once more before landing. It would be worth the spectacular view.

The cabin speaker came to life as they passed over the Sydney Harbor Bridge. "Ladies and gentlemen, we are beginning our final approach to Mascot Kingsford-Smith Airport. At this time, please extinguish all cigarettes, bring your seat backs and tray tables to their upright positions, and make sure your seat belt is securely fastened."

Lance involuntarily clenched his teeth as he heard the high-pitched whir, then the loud clang, of the giant plane's wheels dropping down from the undercarriage and locking firmly in place. As the pitch of the engines changed, he stretched the muscles of his face and drew in a deep gulp of air, struggling to rise above the blunted feeling that suddenly dragged at him.

Hell! I'm about to start out fresh, he thought as the engines of the 747 began to roar. *I'll get to be myself, for the first time in ages, in a place where no one knows me. Where no one's hunting me. I should be happy, not exhausted.*

The attempt to lift his spirits was only partially successful. As the wheels touched down on the runway and let out a staccato squeak, he felt the apprehension rise all over again. It built as the engines were thrown into reverse, and the airplane roared and shuddered around him.

This is the worst part, he told himself. A few moments later, the plane slowed, the roaring stopped, and the expectant hush of the crowd was broken by relieved chattering and bustling. Lance sighed tiredly.

"Welcome to Sydney, Australia. Captain Waters and all of us in the crew would like to thank you for flying with us. We hope it has been an enjoyable experience, and that when considering your next flight, you will give us the opportunity to once again be of service.''

The cabin attendant's chirping voice only made Lance feel more exhausted. She went on to tell them Australia had strict quarantine regulations and that government agriculture agents would soon be coming aboard to spray the cabin.

Lance was only half-listening. Fifteen hours on a plane, the strange experience in Fiji—hell, the strange experiences *everywhere*—were finally taking their toll. He had to blink his burning eyes over and over just to keep himself from nodding off.

He sagged heavily in his seat as the airliner finally reached the end of the runway and rumbled into a wallowing turn. His pain-filled eyes stared blankly out the window, disappointed that his excitement at seeing the vista of Sydney stretched out below him had disappeared so quickly. Now there was only a dull ache in its place, and the lead-weight heaviness of exhaustion that made it hard for him to hold on to much of anything.

Without thinking, without speaking, he sat during the long taxi up the concrete apron to the airport terminal and just stared vacantly out the tiny, double-paned window.

He heard the booted feet of the men from the agricultural department thumping heavily down the aisles. He heard the hiss of the aerosol cans loosing their contents into the air. He even smelled the sharp chemical odor rising from the cloud of fungicidal spray. But none of it really seemed to reach him. He never consciously gave it a thought.

Instead, his glazed stare took in the groups of happy people packed onto the terminal's outdoor viewing platforms. They waved frantically in his direction—though it was impossible for them to know where the objects of their attention might be seated, or if they were even actually on the plane. Lance was too tired to care if somewhere in the crowd might be someone sent to meet him. He simply

hung in a weary, fuzzy limbo—unthinking, uncaring, un-
concerned about anyone or anything.

The group on the platform was quite a collection: old
women holding tight to grandchildren and windmilling
their arms. Men in sharp, well-tailored suits, jumping up
and down and waggling their hands like children. A huge,
fat woman with her massive bulk pressed hard against the
railing, so tightly it looked as if it would cut her in half.
Two—

It rushed at him like a dream, or a scene shot with a
powerful zoom lens: A man in his fifties, wearing a tweed
suit and a stylish English country hat, stood off to one side
of the group, puffing at a large pipe that jutted from the
corner of his mouth. Lance gaped as the man bit down on
the pipe and broke into a wicked grin.

The other people were still there, still milling about,
waving, shouting silently. But none of them were like this
man. The others seemed to be hidden in a fog, covered by
gauze. *This* man was crystal-clear—*unnaturally* clear. And
without knowing exactly why, Lance felt a sudden, fundamental premonition of evil.

The man removed the pipe from his mouth. His lips
moved, silently forming words, and Lance heard them
echo in his mind.

"Leave here, Lance Sullivan!"

He didn't believe it. He *couldn't* believe it. It was the
weariness, the jet lag, the fear—

*"Do not enter the city. Do not even leave the terminal.
Simply take the next plane back to where you came from,
or you will DIE! There will be no further warning . . .*

"LEAVE! . . . NOW!"

Lance opened his mouth to speak, or shout— or scream—

The scene jerked and shifted. He felt a jolt of something
sweet and electric pass through him.

And the unnatural clarity passed. He was looking at
a crowded observation platform, still filled with people,
but . . .

The stranger was gone.

The passengers from the 747 hurried down the long hallway that led from the arrival area to customs and immigration. Lance was swept along with the group, like a twig on a swollen river, as exhaustion sapped the last remaining energy from him.

He was in a thick, aching daze. Even thinking seemed to be too much trouble as he plodded blindly past a series of huge advertisements extolling the wonders of particular states or areas on the Australian continent. He was only minimally aware of them, or of the huge WELCOME TO SYDNEY, AUSTRALIA sign that stretched across the arch leading to the line of immigration desks.

Without really thinking about it, Lance handed his traveling pouch to the man at the nearest desk. It contained both his passport and letters from Wilcox, Cundy and Cook that explained his presence in Australia.

The redheaded immigration agent wore a look of perpetual disbelief. He grunted a few times as he sorted through the documents, and with a final look of disgruntlement, he stamped the American passport and handed the pouch back to Lance.

Lance's movements were completely automatic. As he slipped the pouch into his bag, then slung it over his shoulder and turned, he bumped into an overweight man in a white seersucker jacket who said something to him. He didn't respond. It didn't seem to matter, really.

He retrieved his two patent-leather suitcases from the huge metal baggage carousel, in the area just beyond the immigration desk. He would have stumbled toward the taxis then, if it were possible. But there was only one exit from the baggage claim area, and to get to it, he had to go first through customs.

Later, Lance would have no recollection of the curt questions asked by the customs inspector, and even less idea what his replies were. Whatever he said must have satisfied the man; he made only a perfunctory search of Lance's shoulder bag, then waved him through without even attempting to open the pair of larger suitcases.

So Lance Sullivan officially entered Australia by the simple act of walking through a sliding door and into the passenger arrival section of Kingsford-Smith Airport.

It was like entering a madhouse.

A sudden babble of noise rushed at him in a solid wave of sound. Lance *felt* it more than *heard* it. He was in a dream now, a wild and uncontrollable dream that was becoming a nightmare.

A sea of strange faces glared and shouted, motioning at him from behind a metal barricade. The crashing sound of their voices hammered at his ears, and he lunged forward, pushing his luggage trolley before him, desperate to escape.

The jeering countenances swam at him, then swooped away, then raced back. His head spun. Sweat broke out all over his body, beading heavily on his face. He turned, fighting to keep a hold on sanity. But it seemed to hang just out of reach.

The brightly painted, incredibly wrinkled face of an old woman filled his vision. Her gold-capped teeth glinted as she leered at him and shouted words he didn't understand.

Lance couldn't take it any longer. He felt the top of his head lift away, felt his arms and legs go cold as unconsciousness called to him. He knew he was going to faint, but he didn't fight it. He almost welcomed it, some—

In that instant, as his body began to crumple to the floor, a sharp force slammed into his back. He straightened, suddenly and inexplicably wide awake, as something both powerful and insubstantial came over him.

In that same instant, he saw the bizarre faces and raucous noise for what they really were: hundreds of excited people waiting for friends and loved ones to clear immigration and customs.

He stood there for a long time, shuddering and catching his breath. He was *better* now. Not quite right, not really, but at least sane again. And strong enough to slowly turn and scan the crowd, searching for the source of the almost living energy that had just touched him. For a brief instant—before it was lost in the crowd—he caught sight of a face he knew frighteningly well.

It can't be! he thought. *The golden blonde hair looked the same. The shape of her face was—*

No! He cut off his own thought. *It couldn't be her. But . . .*

He found himself searching through the swirling crowd of tourists and reunited families, refusing to believe what he had seen, but refusing to stop his search. He almost crept down the alley made by the barricade, hoping beyond hope that his mind had not been playing tricks on him.

He found nothing.

After a few minutes, the weariness started to return. He sighed heavily and eased the trolley toward the exit near a row of taxis that waited at the curb.

He felt the soft touch of a hand on his right arm.

"Lance Sullivan?"

The voice was female, but deep and rich—almost sultry. He turned to face the woman who had spoken, and his mouth dropped open in a gaping stare.

She was about two inches shorter than his six feet, with long, burnished golden hair that matched the suntanned brown of her soft skin. Her flashing green eyes seemed to dance as she said, "I'm Angelique Beresford. I believe we're distant cousins."

Her incredible beauty would have stunned Lance even under normal circumstances. But these were *not* normal circumstances—not by any stretch of the imagination.

Angelique Beresford was the girl from the dream.

There was absolutely no doubt of it. Lance had seen those incredible eyes pleading at him; he had watched that flowing golden blonde hair swirl about her soft pink shoulders; he had seen every inch of her perfectly proportioned, naked body as it gyrated in the air like some sick marionette.

And now he truly realized for the first time that in those nightmares that had turned his sleep into endless hours of terror, he had fallen hopelessly in love with the golden-haired woman.

And suddenly she was a reality.

He couldn't find any words to say. He simply stared at her, mouth open, until she stepped closer and offered her hand.

"Welcome to Australia," she said, and her beaming smile turned her already lovely face into a thing of rare beauty.

"Th . . . thanks." Lance couldn't seem to drag his eyes away from her. His tongue flopped like a lead weight in his mouth.

"You must be bushed," she said quickly. Her words were tinged with the unusual twist that made the Australian language different from its ancestral British, but her accent lacked the heavy cockney ring of the customs inspector and the immigration agent.

"Why don't I take you to your hotel, so you can freshen up." She didn't appear to notice his speechlessness. She simply went on as if everything were perfectly normal, lifting the heaviest of his bags with leonine ease and pointing towards the parking lot. "The car's over this way."

He finally found his voice as her stylish, vaguely American-looking auto rumbled out of the parking lot. "W-what kind of car is this?" he asked, knowing how stupid he sounded.

"It's a Holden sedan," Angelique Beresford said. "They're made and built here in Australia."

Lance had been fighting to get out one entire sentence without sounding like some stuttering moron ever since they'd met in the airport arrival area. He hadn't trusted himself as they made their way to the car, and even now he felt like a fool for asking such a mundane question. *At least I'm talking,* he thought slowly, as he felt himself nod and heard himself say, "Looks real sharp."

He sounded like an idiot, and he knew it. There were so many things he wanted to ask, so many other things he wanted to say to her.

But how? he thought. *How the hell can I expect her to understand?*

He stared at Angelique's profile as she turned the car onto the four-lane highway and urged it out into the flow of speeding traffic.

She's the most beautiful creature I've ever seen, and I'm madly in love with her, he thought. *And until five minutes ago she was a figment of my imagination.* He knew there was no way he could tell her how he felt. It would seem schoolboy-stupid to anyone but himself.

Then he looked up. Suddenly all thought of Angelique was brushed aside, and he was instantly gripped by fear.

The freeway traffic lane merged into normal two-way traffic, but there was something wrong here, something horribly *wrong.* Everything was twisted around. The cars seemed to be coming straight toward him. And even as he gasped and jerked in his seat, he knew what it was: they were driving on the *left*-hand side of the road instead of on the right. He was seated on the *left*-hand side of the car. The traffic was careening at them from the *left.*

The overall effect was more than disorienting—it was downright terrifying. He had to bite his lip not to cry out as Angelique swung the car into a turn and accelerated out into the traffic . . . on the wrong side of the road.

At least . . . *his* wrong side. She didn't seem to be bothered by it at all.

The hotel suite was enormous. As Lance walked from the bathroom into the living room—his hair wet, a towel wrapped around him—even his tired mind couldn't help but be amazed.

He had been given the penthouse suite on the thirty-fourth floor. It was the biggest and most elegant suite he had ever seen, beginning with this huge living room that sported a bar covering one entire wall. Behind him were two separate bedrooms, and off them were two massive bathrooms—one fitted with a sunken tub that could easily accommodate four people.

Lance stood in front of the huge windows—they filled two entire walls of the living room—and looked out over the bridge, the aerial railway and freeway, and the wharf Angelique had called Circular Quay. As he watched the ferries arriving and leaving, he finally began to realize, at least a little, the kind of immense wealth the Beresford family had.

He had stayed in some chic hotels himself as he had fled across America. Counterfeit plastic and a snotty attitude could buy a lot in the land of plenty. But that was just to slip into the background, to withstand casual examination as yet another well-off, bored-to-distraction traveler.

This was different. This kind of wealth defied anonymity. The Beresfords didn't *care* if anybody noticed how rich they were. They were even too rich to care if *other* rich people noticed them.

This is the elite of the elite, he thought as he picked up a jade figurine from the table by the couch and examined its subtle beauty. *It really is a shame we didn't keep in closer touch.*

He had followed Angelique's advice and hadn't gone to sleep at such an early hour. Instead, he had opted for a long, hot shower, to be followed by a personal tour of Sydney. "That way you'll be able to adjust to our time a lot better," she had said.

Lance had accepted this without even thinking. He was still boiling with questions—about the Beresfords, about Angelique, about the horrible recurring dreams. He didn't know how many she could answer—or *would* answer—but somehow it didn't really matter. He knew that he would take advantage of any chance to spend time with this vision from his dreams. Part of him knew he *had* to, regardless of the outcome.

Who knows, he thought, as he headed back to the bedroom to get dressed. *Maybe I'll get some kind of clue as to what the hell is going on here.*

Chapter 16

It took only a few hours with Angelique for Lance to become reasonably accustomed to the strangeness of Australian driving habits, though he still found himself flinching involuntarily from time to time. He found, too, that his fatigue had unaccountably lifted. He didn't feel nearly as tired as he had at the airport, though six hours had passed and he still hadn't slept a wink.

Angelique was concentrating on her driving, deftly maneuvering the large sedan through busy traffic, as he smiled at her across the wide, plush front seat of the car. And suddenly he knew why he wasn't so weary. It was Angelique herself. There was an infectiousness about her, an *up* feeling, a positive energy that seemed to wash from her over him, brushing away all negativeness.

She caught his stare out of the corner of her eye and gave him *that* smile. Lance felt his heart melt for what must have been the thousandth time.

She had picked him up at the hotel almost four hours ago and had been playing tour guide ever since. The first stop had been the revolving restaurant atop the Centerpoint Tower, a needlelike structure that towered over the city skyline. The buffet lunch had been light, fresh and delicious—much like Angelique herself.

As he'd eaten the crab-and-prawn salad entree, Lance had stared out the restaurant's floor-to-ceiling glass windows at Sydney's natural beauty, stunned by its power a second time. Angelique had seemed delighted by his reaction. She'd spent the meal pointing out local landmarks.

"This Centerpoint Tower complex sits near the middle of the city proper," she'd said. "Over the Harbor Bridge is North Sydney and the northern suburbs. That's where I live."

She'd turned and pointed to the east, and the sun had glittered in her loose, full hair. He had been having a hard time with her, he'd realized. A hard time not staring at her. An even harder time not touching her, holding her . . .

Stop it, he'd ordered himself.

"Those tall buildings on the hill are in King's Cross, and over the other side of it are a running series of bays. Beyond that are the eastern suburbs and a string of eastern-area beaches."

Lance had torn his eyes away from her and cleared his throat. "Which way is the Beresford estate that Mr. Fullhurst mentioned?" he'd asked.

Angelique had frozen for a moment—an unnatural, telling pause. Then she had wheeled about a complete 180 degrees and pointed off over buildings and houses that seemed to stretch on forever. "*Beresford Hall* is near Parramatta, over that way a good twenty miles." There'd been a nasty, bitter edge to her voice for the first time—as unnatural in her as the sudden sharp move and the angry grimace. Lance had started to say something about it, to apologize—though he couldn't guess for what—but she'd cut him off. "Oh, don't worry," she'd said shortly, as the frown grew deeper. "You'll see it soon enough!"

He'd started to speak again, and she'd stood up at the table. "I'm off for dessert," she'd said quickly, and even Lance had been able to tell it was a lie. "Be right back." She'd stalked away before he could say a word.

All right, he'd thought, well aware of what had caused the sudden change in her. *No more questions about the Beresford family.*

Angelique continued to drive him around Sydney, showing him an amazing array of sights: Hyde Park, with its numerous, intricately decorated fountains and its long tree-lined paths; Wynyard Square, with its statues, fountains and underground shopping complexes; Circular Quay, where "Sydneysiders" and tourists alike hurried aboard ferries that would take them to destinations on every part of the harbor; Sydney Opera House, more spectacular up close than from the air; the Botanical Gardens, a huge flower-like park overlooking the harbor; King's Cross, with its back-alley "businesses" and its combination of glitz, glamour and porn—the Greenwich Village and Times Square of Sydney all wrapped into one; and Double Bay, a fashionable suburb made up of little streets filled with fancy clothing stores and restaurants—a little like Rodeo Drive in Beverly Hills. They ended the tour by exploring a series of large and small eastern-area suburbs, all dotted with fresh fruit stands and other equally quaint-looking stores of every shape and size.

Lance kept his promise for three hours, but that was all he could stand. *I've come a long way for some answers,* he told himself as they took a circuitous, leisurely drive toward a place called Watsons Bay. *Damned if I'm going to be put off any longer.*

Since leaving Bondi Junction, they'd been driving on a road that passed quaint brick houses and occasional apartment buildings. The wide street seemed to wind along one edge of the harbor, and more and more often Lance caught breathtaking glimpses of the city of Sydney over his left shoulder.

He was staring back at this view of city and harbor when Angelique pulled the car to the curb and opened the door. "Come on," she said, her eyes sparkling. In the next instant, she was out of the car and gone.

By the time Lance had eased out of the vehicle, she had crossed the street and was standing at a small fence in front of a stark white lighthouse that perched on the edge of a large, grassy cliff.

"This is Macquarie Lighthouse, the oldest lighthouse in Australia. It's been operating since 1818," Angelique said as he reached her side.

"It's very nice," Lance said. He stood beside her for a long moment without speaking, enjoying the cool, slightly salty sea breeze that rippled over his face and bare arms.

Finally, he took a deep breath, and without turning toward Angelique, he said, "Tell me about Essie Beresford."

Angelique continued to stare at the lighthouse. It was a full minute before she spoke, and when she did her voice was tight with the same icy bitterness he had heard before. "What do you want to know?" she said shortly.

"Anything . . . everything."

"You know about the money. What more do you really need? That's all that really *matters*, isn't it, the damn *money?*"

"Hey!" Lance turned toward her, smiling. He raised both hands in surrender, palms up. "I'm not the enemy, you know."

Angelique wouldn't look at him. She just kept glaring at the distant water without speaking, and finally Lance spoke again. "Look," he said, "I'd be a liar if I said I hadn't wondered what it might be like to have all that money. Or even *some* of it." He shrugged and smiled again. "But there's no chance of that. I don't think she even knew we—my mother and I—existed. Hell, I never knew about *her* until two weeks ago."

Angelique wheeled to face him, her surprise obvious. "*What?*"

"It's true. My mother never told me about any of you guys until after I received a letter telling me Essie was dead."

"But— but *why?*" Angelique couldn't hide the fact she hadn't known this before. "Why didn't somebody tell you? Your father—"

"Died before I was born," he said shortly.

"Then your mother? Why hadn't she told you before?"

"I don't— I never found out. She . . ." Tears misted his eyes. He turned away abruptly and headed back toward the car. "She died before she could tell me."

Angelique followed him across the street. Neither of them spoke as they slid into the large front seat of the Holden sedan.

As she eased the car out into the flow of traffic, Angelique said softly, "I'm sorry, Lance. I didn't know."

They drove in silence for the next few minutes. Finally Angelique pulled the car over and eased it to a stop at the curb.

Lance was deep in thought, remembering. His mother . . . the father he had never known . . . the feeling of grief and relief he had experienced in the mountains near Santa Barbara.

"Lance . . . ?" Angelique said hesitantly. He looked up, aware of his surroundings for the first time. He hadn't even noticed that they had stopped.

The car was parked on a steep incline in front of a row of houses, but he only noticed that later. At first all he saw was the breathtaking vista: 270 degrees, showing Sydney Harbor to the left, and, to the right, the blindingly beautiful Pacific, vast, smooth and hard as beaten metal, beginning less than forty feet beneath their feet and rolling endlessly to the horizon.

The entrance to the harbor was directly in front of them—a natural opening less than a half mile wide. Across this stretch of water was another monolithic headland, as huge and imposing as the one on which they stood, its sheer face dropping straight down to the water hundreds of feet below.

"The Sydney Heads," Angelique said as they climbed

from the car. She put her arm through his and they walked across the street to a wooden fence that ran along the top of the cliff. "Any ship, any size in the world, can sail through here. And even in the heaviest storm, they can be in the smooth protected waters of the harbor in minutes."

She'd proud of the city, Lance thought. *This is her home, and she loves it, and from what I've seen, she has damn good reason.* He peered at the distant horizon, and a wave of melancholy swept over him. *I wonder if I'll ever have a place like this myself,* he thought. *A home . . .*

The two distant cousins stood in silence, drinking in the scene as a large sailing yacht skipped across the waves in the blue waters of the Heads. Its huge orange spinnaker billowed in front of it as it silently turned into the harbor and headed toward Sydney.

"She was an amazing lady," Angelique said very quietly. Lance nodded, but he didn't speak. "I guess she seemed like a tyrannical matriarch to most of the *others* . . ."

There it is again, Lance thought. *That bitterness in her voice that just doesn't seem to fit.*

"A bunch of *leeches,* anyway!" she mumbled, and looked at her feet, frowning.

He could hear tears in her voice—angry tears, harshly suppressed.

"They hovered around like a pack of dingoes, Lance," she said. "Pretending to care about her, pretending to *love* her. But they were only waiting for her to die so they could get their grubby little hands on her money. That's all it was. *Money.*" Angelique looked at Lance, hatred and rage in her clear blue eyes. "That must be it," she said harshly. "That's probably why your mother didn't tell you about us. By and large, mate, we're a rotten bunch of relatives to be stuck with. Sounds like the lady had good sense."

"Come on," Lance said, smiling, trying to lighten the mood. "You're exaggerating."

She smiled back, but she shook her head. " 'Fraid not,

mate,'' she said, breaking into a heavy Australian accent.
''You've got a right lot a' bludgers in your family tree.
An' they ain't gonna be too happy ta find out there's
another sheep in the mob. One more ta split the swag with,
eh?''

Lance couldn't help grinning. Now *that* was a new
sound out of her.

''Did you understand that at all?'' she asked, grinning
back.

Lance laughed. ''Pretty much. But it can't be that bad,
can it?''

Her expression grew serious all over again. ''Worse,
I'm afraid.''

''Oh.''

They stared out at the water a moment longer, then she
seemed to shake off her gloomy mood. ''Still,'' she said,
shrugging and sighing, ''I could be prejudiced. Lord knows
I have reason to be. You really should decide for yourself.''

He nodded. ''Okay. When will I meet them?''

''They'll all be there for the reading of the will. The
whole sorry lot.'' Angelique ran her hands through her
hair, and in a few seconds the smile was back. ''Anyway,
that'll come soon enough. Let's enjoy ourselves while we
can.''

''Great,'' Lance said. ''But maybe you could tell me a
little more about the history of the Beresfords? I've got a
lot of catching up to do.''

''I could do that,'' Angelique said, and took his hand in
hers as they walked slowly along the cliff top.

An hour later they were sitting on a small wooden bench
overlooking the Pacific and slurping on huge ice creams
that were rapidly melting in the warm sun. ''A lot of our
history's been lost to time,'' Angelique mumbled, her
mouth half full, ''but it's certain the original Beresfords
came from England. It's said we were among the first
noble-blooded settlers, but I wonder how much of that
might be wishful thinking.''

Lance watched an enormous tanker make its way out to the open sea and tried to balance the cone so that the sticky chocolate cream didn't drip onto his clothes. It was hard to juggle and listen at the same time.

They had walked along the cliff and looked out over "The Gap," a place where people who couldn't stand the thought of living had often thrown themselves to their death on the rocks below. Then they had sat on this bench and just gazed out at the edge of the earth's largest body of water. For almost three-quarters of an hour, they hadn't spoken a word.

It didn't seem necessary, somehow, Lance thought. Then he felt the weirdness again.

Three times, while they had sat quietly, he'd felt a strange tingling sensation in his head—something like prickly heat, only on the inside. Now, as Angelique finally began to speak about the Beresfords, here it was again. He shook his head, feeling silly. But it was taking a conscious effort to concentrate on Angelique's words.

"Anyway, there aren't any records of the beginnings, but someone back there must have either been rich or made a lot of money in the early colony days." Angelique took another long slurp of her strawberry ripple, then suddenly looked over at Lance. He was swaying slightly, his eyes half-closed. "Are you okay?" she asked.

He straightened up, blinking. "Yeah," he grunted. "Why?"

"Oh, nothing. I just thought you looked a little—"

"I'm fine. Keep going."

Angelique stared at him for another few seconds, then brushed her concern aside. "Robert is convinced there's a book chronicling the complete history that Essie was keeping from him."

"Robert?"

She laughed shortly. "Sorry. I forgot you don't know about your illustrious relatives."

"Just Essie," he said, passing a hand over his forehead. "And now you."

"Well, why don't I run down the list and tell you a little about each?"

"That would really be helpful."

"You hungry?" she asked.

He nodded. "Yes. The ice cream's great, but it isn't exactly a wholesome meal."

"Good! There's a nice fish restaurant down the hill. Let's have dinner. Besides, I'm not sure I could stand talking about the family on an empty stomach."

She laughed, only half kidding. Then she stood up and started for the car.

Lance sat there staring at her for a moment, the world swimming around him.

There's something in my head, he thought numbly. *There's something . . . telling me . . . making me . . .*

She stopped and turned to face him. The sun was golden and brilliant behind her. Her lithe figure glimmered with light. "Lance?" she said. It came out low and sultry, deep with meaning. "Are you coming with me?"

He nodded very slowly. "Yes," he said, and stood up, still swaying slightly. "Yes, I am."

He followed her back to the car, and they left without another word.

Chapter 17

Lance Sullivan walked from the dark hallway into a wood-paneled conference room fitted out with an oversized desk and surrounded by deep cushioned leather chairs.

Angelique—he had begun calling her "Angie" at her request—was a short step in front of him.

They had just left the warmth and freshness of yet another gorgeous Sydney day, and the shadows and mustiness in the offices of Wilcox, Cundy and Cook, Attorneys at Law, were an unpleasant contrast to what lay just outside the antique walnut doors. Though he fought against it, Lance couldn't help feeling depressed by that fact. *Still, what the hell*, he told himself. *This reading of Great-grandmother Essie's will should be over in an hour, at most. Then Angie and I can get back out into the warm sunlight.*

For the last two days, he had been happier than he could ever remember being. Angie was like a fresh breeze that had blown into his life and changed everything. Her smile, her laugh—her simple presence—pushed all the sordid details of his past into some tidewater section of his memory, to be duly forgotten.

She was all he had been able to think of for the last four

days, ever since his arrival. Perhaps the fact that he had barely been able to doze, let alone sleep, during that time had something to do with it. But Lance was sure it was more than exhaustion-induced euphoria. He enjoyed her, enjoyed being with her.

They had been together most of every day. She had shown him Sydney; she had tried to explain some of the customs of Australia; she'd even tried to prepare him for this meeting with the rest of the Clan Beresford. Somehow, Lance didn't care about any of it. Nothing really mattered except being with her—not the sightseeing, not the details, not even the family.

"They're a rum lot, I can tell you," she had said more than once. Each time she had smiled broadly, realizing he couldn't help but laugh at the overly exaggerated Australian accent she used.

And as she had spoken, with every smile, he had fallen more and more in love.

He perched his hand at her waist as they entered the large conference room and silently observed her smile at his touch. *I love the way she smiles*, he thought as he surveyed the stolid faces of the four people seated at the large table in front of them.

His mind raced on. *It's more than just her smile. I'm in love with Angie*.

He was astonished at how easily he accepted this realization. It seemed a perfectly normal statement, with none of the terror a thought like that might have held for him just a few weeks before.

He glanced at her, and she turned to him, as if sensing his thoughts. Then she smiled—a special, secret smile.

I'll be damned, he thought. *I think she's in love with me, too*. This thought almost took his breath away.

As he watched Angie seat herself in one of the high-backed chairs, then motion him to the seat next to her, he felt . . . content, somehow. There was a special something in her . . . something more than simply beauty and intelligence . . . a *power* that struck a chord in him. It was something much more than lustful attraction—though there was plenty of that, too. It was . . . no, he couldn't define it. Not yet.

He sat at the long conference table, pulling the chair in under him, and tried to focus his attention on the proceedings. It didn't matter too much; he knew his being here was just a rather boring formality. But even the heaviness in the room couldn't dull the warmth he felt when he looked at Angie sitting beside him. *Formality or not,* he thought, *I'm glad to be here. Otherwise I might never have met her.*

He pushed his awareness of her into a warm, distant corner of his mind and concentrated on Josh Wilcox, the solicitor, as he entered the room and seated himself at the head of the long table.

"You all know why we are here," the portly, bald-headed Wilcox said brusquely. He patted the top of his hairless head and adjusted the vest of his dark blue suit. Then he lifted the top page of a thick bunch of legal-sized papers and held it up as if he were showing off Exhibit A. "I would like to welcome Mr. Lance Sullivan," he said with great ceremony, scanning the other members of the family, "and thereby introduce him to those of you who might not know him." His chilly blue eyes held Lance's for a brief moment. "I realize it was a long trip for you, sir, with seemingly little apparent reason. And that this trip may well have been somewhat of an inconvenience, since you had to travel so far. If such is the case, please forgive us. We—that is, our firm—were only following the stipulations laid down by your great-grandmother."

"He's no *Ber*esford!" a nasal, rather tinny voice snapped. "And I, for one, think he should leave."

Lance turned to face a stocky, dark-haired man with bushy eyebrows that barely thinned above his nose. The man scowled at Lance as he spoke again.

"How do we even know he's who he says he is?" the man said to no one in particular.

"Mr. Beresford!" Josh Wilcox said, a trifle exasperated. "We've already been through this. As I told you, our firm followed Essie Beresford's wishes, *to the letter*. We—and you, for that matter—are subject to those wishes."

The man across the table huffed loudly.

"And, if there are no other . . . *objections*," Josh Wilcox said firmly, "I would like to begin."

The man across the table from Lance huffed again, even more loudly, but said nothing further.

Wilcox gave a tiny, bitter smile. "I am instructed by orders *clearly* spelled out in the will . . ." He looked up and frowned, then quickly went on, "to read one of two different sets of instructions, depending on who is present here today. Toward that end, I shall start the formalities with a roll call." The attorney glared down the table, as if expecting further complaints. When none came, he began reading from the paper in his hand, looking briefly at each attendee as he spoke his or her name.

"Angelique Beresford," he said. "Jessica Beresford. Monica Sheerlow. Douglas Beresford. Robert Beresford. And Lancelot Sullivan-Beresford."

As the solicitor spoke, Lance tried to remember what Angie had told him about each member of the family. But her words about one relation in particular seemed to wash all memory of the others aside.

Robert Beresford.

It was Robert, the imposing man with the thick, brushed-back hair seated across the table from him, who had opposed his being there. According to Angie, Robert was a fervent practitioner of the black arts—a self-proclaimed warlock—who was incidentally convinced that the entire Beresford fortune should be his. "The only one with enough character to deserve it," he was in the habit of declaring, to anyone who would listen. "His exact words," Angie had said.

Josh Wilcox's voice pulled his attention back to the head of the table.

"I shall now, as duly authorized executor of the estate of Essie Thelma Beresford, read her last will and testament." Wilcox picked up one of two sealed manila envelopes from the desk in front of him and broke the seal. Then he pulled out a small batch of papers and a smaller sealed envelope.

"My first instruction . . ." he said, reading as he spoke, "is to hand this letter to you, Mr. Sullivan." Josh Wilcox looked at Lance and held out the small envelope. "You are requested not to open it until after the reading of the will. And then, to please do so in total privacy."

The attorney reached forward to pass the letter to Lance, but Robert Beresford suddenly reached out and grabbed it from him.

"Let me see that!"

"*Mister Beresford!*" Josh Wilcox snapped. "You are going *too* far!"

As he spoke, Robert placed the envelope between his open palms and caressed it, sliding his hands back and forth over its entire length.

"You appear bent on totally disrupting these proceedings," Wilcox said, his wattles turning a dangerous scarlet. "And I, for one, am offended by your rudeness. This letter is *not for you.*" Josh Wilcox leaned over and snatched the envelope from Robert's hands. "If you intend to continue like this, then I will have to ask you—"

"I was just checking to see that the seal hadn't been broken," Robert said gruffly.

Bullshit, Lance thought. He found himself more bothered by the hint of a smile that flicked across Robert's face than by his rudeness. There was something . . . *evil* about it. And as his distant cousin eased back in the chair, and the smile spread across all his features, Lance felt even less comfortable. *Like the cat who ate the canary,* he thought, not quite knowing why.

Josh Wilcox handed Lance the envelope. Lance looked at it briefly, then slipped it into the inside pocket of his green sports jacket.

The attorney stared at Robert Beresford for a long moment, then opened the pages of the will itself and began to read.

Later, Lance would not remember much of what followed. He kept finding his attention drawn to Robert.

Then, as the attorney droned on through the formal jargon that surrounds most wills, he began to nod off. It didn't involve him, he knew. He barely paid any notice. In the warm, stuffy room, with Wilcox going on and on without a pause, he found himself drifting in a halfsleep. Someplace far away, he knew, someone was talking about the "faithful servants . . . loving grand-niece . . . cousin . . ."

"*Lance Sullivan-Beresford . . .*"

Lance snapped from his reverie at the mention of his name.

"—have always been sorry that one of my favorite relatives, Beatrice, found it necessary to take her infant son, Lancelot, and leave us so soon after the untimely death of her husband, James," Wilcox said, reading from the will. "Since James was my favorite, I have decided to leave the bulk of my estate to his son and heir, Lancelot."

Josh Wilcox looked up from the will and caught the look of total, complete astonishment on the face of the young man from America. He allowed himself the tiniest of smiles before he continued.

"But for the small amounts mentioned earlier in this will, set aside for faithful retainers and my direct heirs, and excluding the sum left Angelique—who will always be a part of me—all my assets, holdings, and possessions are to go to Lancelot Sullivan-Beresford on the day of his twenty-fifth birthday . . . if, and only if, he takes possession and full title to Beresford Hall *on that day*."

Robert was on his feet and shouting. One of the women

let out a deep moan. Angelique simply sat and stared at Lance.

Josh Wilcox raised his voice. He had to shout to finish the last sentence of the will. "Should Lancelot fail to take possession of Beresford Hall on the day of his twenty-fifth birthday, for *any* reason, the inheritance, in its entirety, will revert to Angelique Beresford."

"*This can't be true!*" Robert screamed. "*It's some kind of sick joke.*"

"It is no joke, Mr. Beresford," Josh Wilcox said, and Lance thought he could see just a hint of smug satisfaction in the solicitor's expression. "This is Essie Beresford's last will and testament, duly witnessed, signed, and recorded, as she dictated it to me just a week before her death."

"*I'll contest it!*" Robert shouted.

"That is your prerogative. But I can tell you, as the family attorney, I don't believe there to be sufficient grounds for a successful action."

Now the attorney made no attempt at all to hide his smile of satisfaction.

"I believe your twenty-fifth birthday is in five days, is it not?" Josh Wilcox asked Lance.

Lance swallowed. Hard. "Yes," he answered, dimly aware that the attorney was only doing this to upset Robert all the more.

Robert leapt to his feet and hurled the heavy chair backward. It slammed into the wall behind him.

"*Bastard!*" he screamed at Lance. "*Cretin!* Do you really think I will allow my heritage to be stolen?" His bushy eyebrows rose, and the skin beneath them grew beet red. For an instant, Lance was sure that Robert was going to throw himself forward, go for the throat . . .

Then, just as suddenly, the stocky man became calm. He leaned forward very slowly, his hands tightly clenched. Lance felt Robert's eyes bore into him like a dull auger.

"Go back to America," Robert whispered deep in his

throat. "If you want to live through the next five days, *go back to where you came from.*"

Before Lance could do anything but be astounded by his outburst, Robert Beresford turned and stormed out of the conference room.

There was a moment of complete, uncomfortable silence. Then the tall, good-looking man that Wilcox had called Douglas cleared his throat and leaned forward. "I . . . apologize for Robert's outrageous behavior, Lance," he said, running a hand through his mousy brown hair. Then he reached across the table, his palm outstretched. "I'm Doug. It's good to meet you."

"Same here," Lance said, and shook his hand. There was a soft warmth in this man's eyes, and Lance believed that Douglas was actually sincere in wishing him the best.

"Don't judge us all by Robert. He's a little crazy. It comes from thinking he's entitled."

There was nothing for Lance to say, so he said nothing.

Douglas glanced at the others, then back at Lance, and said, "I hope the inheritance brings you joy and peace." Again Lance was sure that he meant what he said.

"Thanks."

Doug quickly stood up. "I'm sure I'll see you again, soon." Then he turned and strode from the room with barely a glance at the remaining members of the family.

Josh Wilcox rose as well and took center stage with an easy, practiced grace. He swept around the table and pointed a palm at the two women still seated at the far end of the room. "Lance," he said, "I don't believe you've met your cousin Jessica Beresford, or her companion, Monica Sheerlow." Monica was the first to speak—or even move. She appeared to be in her late forties, her graying, black hair pulled severely back and tied in a bun. Lance thought her hairstyle and her choice of clothes made her seem old-fashioned. She had the look of a spinster aunt, old before her time.

"Monica," Wilcox continued, "Lance is Jessica's distant cousin."

"There seems to be no end of cousins in this family," Monica snapped. Without acknowledging the introduction, she turned and took the arm of the beautiful young woman with the empty eyes who was still sitting at the table, staring blankly into space. The younger woman's expression had not changed once since Lance and Angelique entered the room.

"Your cousin Jessica," Josh Wilcox said to Lance. Then he turned to the young girl, his tone soft, as if talking to a very young child. "Jessica, this is your cousin, Lance. He's just come from America to visit."

Jessica continued to stare into space, not even acknowledging Monica's tug on her elbow.

So, this is Jessica, Lance thought, remembering Angie's description. *It's hard to believe someone who looks so normal can be an idiot savant.*

In fact, Jessica was more than just normal. She was quite beautiful—as beautiful as Angelique herself, though more mature, despite being mentally little more than a dull four-year-old. And yet, as with others of her rare breed, she had some amazing abilities.

"Idiot savants have the ability to focus almost superhuman concentration on random, inexplicable things," Angie had told Lance at dinner the night before. "In Jessica's case, she can barely speak a full sentence, but she can make mathematical computations at near computer speed. And when she sits at the old Beresford piano that Grandmother Essie gave her, she can play anything." There had been a tear in her eye as she had continued. "Except for her . . . *problem,* she could be a concert pianist. Maybe one of the best."

At the time, Lance hadn't said what he was thinking: *if she weren't an idiot savant, Jessica might not be able to play at all.* But now, seeing her, he realized it didn't matter. She was a beautiful woman, and her life might have been wonderful.

"Hello, Jessica," Lance said gently, and for just an instant he thought he saw a flicker of response in her large, brown eyes.

"She won't understand you," Monica said flatly. Then she again tugged gently at Jessica's arm. "Come on, Jessica."

As his mentally retarded cousin slowly climbed to her feet, Lance couldn't help but notice the change in Monica. She spoke gruffly to everyone else in the room, but when she turned to Jessica, there was an unexpected gentleness in her—an almost maternal smile.

As the two woman left the room, Josh Wilcox put that thought into words. "Don't let Monica's bark offend you. She cares for Jessica like her own daughter, and this was their only chance to live in Beresford Hall. Monica believes she's related to the family, but the connection has been so obscured by time that she can't prove it. I think she hoped Essie would leave it all to Jessica, and then they would both get what she feels is due them." He offered Lance a wry smile. "Like everyone, she can't believe Essie would leave everything to a member of the family they never even knew existed."

Lance grinned back. "I'm more shocked than she is," he said. "Than *anybody* is. Frankly, Mr. Wilcox—I don't understand any of this."

Josh patted him on the shoulder. "Maybe the letter will explain. Your great-grandmother was a very precise woman; I'm sure she had her reasons."

Lance shook his head, still unable to believe what had happened. "So," he said, trying to clear his thoughts. "What's next?"

"There are some formalities, naturally, but they won't take long. Then you can move into Beresford Hall and take over the running of *your* estate."

Lance stared at the attorney and scratched at his ear. Then he shook his head in disbelief one more time.

He turned to Angie. "Can you believe this?"

"Why not?"

"I don't know. I just never expected . . ." Lance stuttered. "Oh, maybe a couple of thousand dollars, just to be nice. But this . . ." Then he touched his coat pocket and felt the envelope nestled in there. "I think this letter will make *fascinating* reading."

Lance slit the envelope open. Then he turned it upside down to allow the letter to fall out.

A thin trickle of black ash poured from the white envelope, making a small pile on the hardwood table.

He and Angelique stared at it for a long time. "What do you make of that?" he finally asked her.

They were sitting on an ornate lounge in the hotel suite living room. They had hurried straight back to his hotel after leaving the offices of Wilcox, Cundy and Cook just to open the letter . . .

And now . . .

"It looks like . . . ash," Angelique said.

"It is."

"Is there anything else in there?"

Lance tipped the envelope, but nothing else came out. Then he held it up to his right eye and peered inside. Finally, he tore the envelope open, to make doubly sure.

"That's all there is."

"But that doesn't make any sense," Angelique said. "Why would Essie leave you a pile of ash?"

"Beats me."

Lance dropped the useless envelope onto the table next to the mound of dark residue and sat staring off into space.

"So, what will you do next?" Angelique asked.

He shrugged. "I haven't really thought about it. It's all happening so fast. I'm still trying to adjust to the whole idea." He rubbed at his eyes with his right hand, then looked up at her. "I guess the first move is to go take a look at Beresford Hall, since it's going to be my new home."

"Lance, I . . ." Angelique's words faded off.

"What is it?"

"I . . . I just wish you didn't have to go to Beresford Hall."

"*What?*" Lance stared at her, astonished. "But you heard the will. If I don't take possession of Beresford Hall, I'll lose everything."

"I know. But . . ." Again her words trailed off into silence.

"What is it?"

"I don't know. There's just . . . something about that place, since Grandmother Essie died, that frightens me."

Without really thinking about what he was doing, Lance pulled her to him and held her close. "Come on now," he purred into her soft blonde hair. "Nothing can go wrong from now on. We're on a roll. You'll see."

Angelique wrapped her arms around him, and as he held her shapely body even closer, Lance could feel her shivering. *How could a house make an intelligent woman like Angie so afraid?* he thought. But then the nearness of her, her warmth, helped him push the chilling thought aside.

What more could I want? he thought. *A huge estate, 350 million dollars, and Angie in my arms. Hell, everything's bloody perfect, mate.*

Chapter 18

"I swear, Benny, it's the truth," Lance said into the white and gold telephone receiver. It was 3:00 A.M. and he was sitting up in the bed in his suite at the Australiana Hotel in Sydney. Benny Haldane was in the United States.

"A 350 *mill*, Lance?" Benny's disbelief was clearly audible above the hiss of the overseas line. "Are you sure you haven't been drinking too much of that strong Australian beer I keep hearing about?"

"It's the truth, I tell you." As he spoke, Lance could almost picture the look of astonishment on Benny's face. "And to prove it's on the up-and-up, I'm sending you a first-class plane ticket and enough money to pay all your expenses."

"For what?"

"I want you to come out here and help me celebrate."

There was a long silence on the phone. For an instant Lance thought the connection between Sydney and New York had been broken.

"Benny?"

"I'm here, Lance." This time Benny was silent for even longer, but finally he spoke again. "This isn't a joke, Lance?"

"No, old buddy," Lance said, sighing heavily. "It's true. Hard to believe, I know, but true."

"Well I'll be damned," Benny said, his voice full of laughter. "*God damn!*"

Lance started to laugh along with his friend, but he had to quickly pull the phone from his ear.

"Yeeeeeehuuuuuh!" Benny's shout hollered from the phone.

"Will you come?" Lance laughed, his ears still ringing from the yell.

"Are you kidding? Do you think I'd trust *you* to look after that kind of money?"

"I'll call you tomorrow and tell you where to pick up the tickets and the cash."

"I'll be waiting," Benny said. "Oh, and Lance?"

"Yes!"

"Congratulations."

As he hung up the phone, Lance was smiling. Then he thought of how quiet Angie had been before she left. He'd asked her to go with him to Beresford Hall, and for a minute he'd thought she was going to say no. She didn't, but the "yes" had been sullen and sad.

Strange that she should be so afraid of a house, he thought, as he switched off the lights and eased himself down in the huge hotel bed. *Really strange.*

The drive was uneventful, and very quiet.

Subdued would be an understatement, Lance thought as he looked at Angie across the front seat of the car. Oh, she'd been polite. And she'd arrived at the hotel at exactly 10:00 A.M., just as she'd promised. But she wasn't the joyous, exuberant Angie he'd come to love in just a few days.

"How much farther?" he asked, as Angie piloted the car onto the freeway onramp near Parramatta and headed north.

"About ten minutes," she said shortly.

They had driven out of Sydney on the Parramatta road, a street Lance thought was only wide enough for two cars that had been made into a dual-direction four-lane highway. The rushing vehicles seemed only inches away from each other on one side and even closer to the curb and telephone poles and buildings on the other. Sometimes they seemed to be *on* the road, not beside it. The overall effect was terrifying.

He knew he was being foolish. And he would have liked to have joked about it, if only to ease his apprehension. But somehow it didn't seem appropriate this morning.

When they reached a place called Homebush, they were suddenly on a wide, spacious freeway. Lance relaxed—but the wide road lasted less than four miles, and then they were back on the crazed streets again.

Lance realized the Australian freeway system was still young, and still something of a dangerous patchwork, but he found himself praying this new section went all the way to Beresford Hall.

They didn't speak another word until they had turned off the road, crunched up the long gravel driveway, and come to a halt in front of one of the largest houses Lance had ever seen.

"Welcome to Beresford Hall," Angie said without smiling.

"Jesus!" Lance would have said more, but he was stunned.

It was huge, and unlike anything he could have possibly imagined. And yet there was something almost . . . *familiar* about it.

Bizarre was the only word to describe the architecture. It was a mad mixture of brick, mortar, and wood, with gargoyle statuettes incorporated into the design in the most unusual ways. Strange symbols and writing were etched into the walls themselves, and even splashes of bright paint couldn't dispel the ominous feeling one got just by looking at the structure.

The huge windows, placed as they were, seemed like eyes—eyes that stared intently at anyone who approached the hall on the winding gravel driveway.

No wonder the entire place is surrounded by high hedges and tall trees, Lance thought. *It looks like something Bela Lugosi might call home.*

"What do you think?" Angie asked.

"It's a bit much, isn't it?" was all Lance said. But he was thinking much more.

There was a . . . a *cold* numbness emanating from Beresford Hall. A kind of spiritual draining. It reminded him of only one thing—the terror he felt when he was trapped inside those nightmares, the ones that kept coming back to plague him.

He wanted to scream a warning at Angie—get her to turn the car around, get them out of there as fast as she could. But the words caught in his throat. He wasn't able to speak them.

Instead, he heard himself say, "I guess we better go in."

Something has taken over my body.

Lance fought to break free from it. He strained until sweat broke across his brow, but he couldn't speak as he chose, he couldn't *move* on his own.

Get me out of here, Angie, his mind screamed. *Help me!*

Angie turned and stared intently at him. "Are you all right?" she asked.

No! Help me, his mind screamed.

"I'm fine," he heard himself saying. "Why?"

"I don't know." A puzzled frown pulled at Angie's brow. "I . . . had a . . . funny feeling just then. Sort of like a . . . voice in my head."

Listen to the voice, Lance screamed with his mind, while his mouth said, "It's probably this place. It's enough to give anyone the creeps."

"You must think I'm a real idiot," Angie laughed nervously, as they both got out of the car and headed for the huge metal and wood door at the front of Beresford Hall.

"I'm sure we'll both feel better once we're inside," Lance heard himself say, as his arm reached out and rang the ancient doorbell.

Lance wondered if maybe he was dreaming—if this was the dream he had never been able to remember. Whatever it was, he was trapped. There was no point in screaming at himself. He would have to go along, whether he liked it or not.

The front door seemed to glide open with remarkable ease, Lance noted from inside the prison of his skull. *It must be fitted with some special pulley system,* he thought.

A heavily wrinkled man with iron-colored hair stood just inside the house. "Good morning, Mr. Beresford," he said. "I've been expecting you. I'm Wilmont, the butler." Then he turned to Angelique. "Good morning, Miss Beresford, I trust you are well."

"I'm fine, Wilmont, thank you."

"Please come in," the butler said and stepped aside.

For an instant Lance felt an intense resistance rise in him. He fought with all his being to turn his body and run—run and not stop until he was miles from this place.

But the pull from the house was too great. He found himself moving forward, stepping over the threshold.

And suddenly, he was himself again. The urge to run away was not only gone, but he felt an incredible warmth rush over him: a feeling of belonging as he had never belonged to anything before. The interior of Beresford Hall seemed to whisper a silent welcome to him. The light from the small chandelier hanging in the entranceway danced and sparkled like fire.

Lance felt as if he had . . . *come home.*

"Lance, what is it?"

"Uhh!"

"Is something wrong?" Angie persisted.

"Uuuumm, no. No, I'm fine."

"Would you perhaps like a cup of tea, Mr. Beresford?" Wilmont asked.

"Yes, that would be nice, Wilmont."

"Very good, sir. If you would both come this way to the small lounge room, I'll have Mrs. Sallinger prepare tea and scones."

As Lance followed Wilmont to the second floor, the feeling of *déjà vu* became almost overpowering. It was as if he had always known this house, as if he had always been a part of it.

After Wilmont had served the tea and scones—on bone china that looked to Lance as if it were worth a small fortune—he took them on a tour of the house. First he showed them through the kitchens, then the dining hall, then the den and the endless supply of lounges. And that was just the first floor.

With each new revelation, Lance's feeling of being a part of it all grew stronger, more compelling.

"The bedrooms are each decorated in much the same way," Wilmont said, as he opened the door to the first room on the second floor. "The Madam believed it was more important for them to be serviceable and comfortable than distinctive."

Lance could see what the butler meant. The bed was large and open, with a full eiderdown cover. Two large chairs sat facing the hearth. A table, with a bowl and pitcher, stood beside the bed, and full-length curtains hung from the windows. It was far from ornate or overdone, but there was a warmth about it that couldn't be ignored.

Wilmont closed the door as Lance rejoined Angie in the hall.

"Which room was my great-grandmother's?"

"The Madam's rooms are entered from the last door on

the left,'' the butler said. Lance could hear a hint of sadness, well-disguised, in the servant's careful diction.

As Lance briskly walked down the long hallway, he felt incredibly alive. Even the light chill that seemed to permeate every inch of Beresford Hall—that prickled at the soft skin on his face even now—could not dampen his enthusiasm.

He reached the door of the last room on the left and tried the doorknob.

It was locked.

"Do you have the key?'' Lance asked as the butler and Angelique caught up to him at the door.

"Yes, sir. But I'm afraid I can't open it for you."

"Why not?"

"It was the Madam's expressed wish. No one may enter until the new owner takes possession." Wilmont coughed lightly. "That would be you, I suppose, sir."

Lance frowned, an unaccountable annoyance taking hold. He shrugged it off with some effort. "I guess I can wait a few days," he said. Angie slipped her arm through his, and he made himself smile easily.

"Can we go now?" she asked.

Lance noticed the look on her face for the first time and realized she was still disturbed by this place. He had been neglecting her, ignoring her uneasiness since they had arrived. "Sure," he said, and squeezed her arm. "I've seen enough."

They turned to leave—

And a powerful surge of energy slammed into Lance. He staggered back, air rushing from his lungs, and nearly fell against the wall.

"What is it?" Angie asked.

He gulped in new breath and straightened very slowly. "I . . . don't know," he said, and shook his head, trying to clear away the confusion that clouded his thinking.

"Can I be of help, sir?" Wilmont asked.

"No, Wilmont. I'm fine, thank—" Lance stopped short

and stared in disbelief at the door to Essie Beresford's rooms.

A strikingly beautiful woman walked *through* the closed door, straight through the wood itself. She stood directly in front of him, facing him.

She smiled.

Lance opened his mouth to speak, but nothing came out. He watched wordlessly as the ghostly woman gestured toward the sealed rooms. Her lips moved soundlessly.

"Lance?" Angie called to him, but he didn't hear her. He was trying to understand what this beautiful, transparent vision was trying to tell him.

"*Lance!*"

He ignored her. He simply watched as the ghostly young figure gestured again, tried to speak again, then finally reached out to touch him.

Her hand passed through him as if she were fashioned from a cloud.

"What is it? What do you want?" Lance said.

"I just want to know what's the matter," Angie said, misunderstanding.

The phantom woman gave up. An expression of deep, almost painful melancholy showed on her transparent face. She slowly turned away and drifted back through the door.

"What is it, Lance?"

He pointed at the closed door. "Didn't you see her?" he said. "Angie, didn't you *see* her?"

"See who?"

"That woman! The one who just—" Lance stopped, realizing how silly his words would sound.

"What woman?"

"You . . . didn't . . ."

"I don't know what you're talking about," Angie said.

"Wilmont, did you see a young woman just now?"

"I saw Miss Angelique, and you, sir. You appeared to be bothered by something," the butler said.

"And nothing else?"

"Nothing else, sir."

"Open this door, Wilmont," Lance snapped. "I have to go inside."

"I'm sorry, sir. As I explained, I can't do that. My orders were very specific."

"But this is different. I just—"

"I have my orders," Wilmont said firmly, holding his ground. "I cannot defy them, for any reason."

Lance looked at them both as if for the first time. He saw Angie's concern—and fear, as well. He saw Wilmont's unswerving resolve.

He couldn't explain it. He wasn't going to try. He simply sighed heavily and gave up.

"I guess it can wait a few days," he said to the butler. Then he took Angie's arm in his. "Let's get out of here."

"I am *so* glad to hear you say that," his distant cousin said.

They hurried off down the hall toward the front door.

"I told you you'd like it," Angie said to Lance.

"It's really amazing."

They were standing on the viewing platform at a place called Katoomba, looking out over a breathtaking scene. Less than ten feet from the steel and wire mesh fence where they stood, the sheer edge of the mountain suddenly dropped off to the valley floor, one thousand feet below. The tree-covered valley stretched out from the base of the precipice, farther than the eye could see—broken only by three huge stone monoliths, known locally as "The Three Sisters."

"Makes you feel a little insignificant, doesn't it?" Angie said.

"I was just thinking exactly that," Lance answered.

Angie had returned to her old self the moment they'd left Beresford Hall. She had even suggested this drive up into the Blue Mountains, to Katoomba.

Lance was happy about that . . . but he was less than happy about everything else.

He couldn't shake the memory of his uneasiness—his *fear*—when they had first approached the place. It hadn't seemed so important when they were inside the house, but *now* . . .

He had somehow been trapped in his own body and had been forced to enter the hall against his will.

It had been different inside—different, but not necessarily any better. He had been filled with only one emotion—that overwhelming sense of *belonging,* so strong that it had crowded out every other emotion and thought.

What the hell went on there? he thought. *What have I fallen into?*

"Would you like to go back to my place for tea?" Angie asked as they dragged themselves away from the mesmerizing view and headed back to the parking area.

"I think I've had enough tea for one day."

"Noooo," Angie laughed. "A lot of Australians still call the three meals of the day, breakfast, dinner and tea."

"Huh?"

"Never mind," she laughed again. "Why don't we go to my place and I'll fix us dinner."

"Now *that* I understand," Lance said, as they climbed into the car and headed toward the road that led out of the mountains. "And it sounds like a great idea."

The view from the full-length windows of Angie's Kirribilli apartment was magic. When he switched off the lights and looked out across the waters of the harbor, Lance felt like he was in Disneyland. The entire city, including the Harbor Bridge, Circular Quay, and the Opera House, was a spectacle of twinkling, multicolored lights.

When Angie had pointed over in this direction from the restaurant in the Centerpoint Tower—one of the most brilliantly lit of all the city's buildings—Lance hadn't realized she'd meant she lived on the edge of the harbor itself. *And on the nineteenth floor, no less,* he thought.

Dinner had been incredible. By the time they had gotten back to Sydney from the Blue Mountains, Lance had been ravenous, and he'd wolfed the meal down. Now a warm glow permeated his entire body, courtesy of three glasses of fine Australian-made Barossa Valley wine, sipped slowly while the food settled.

Angie came back into the room and stood next to him. "It's beautiful, isn't it?" she said.

Without thinking, Lance turned and took her in his arms.

The first kiss was powerful and frantic. The second was no less urgent, the passion growing in them both.

As they broke from a very long kiss, Lance leaned forward and lifted Angie into his arms.

"Angie—"

"Not a word," she said, her voice a deep husky growl. "The bedroom is the door on the left."

He didn't have any trouble finding it.

Chapter 19

Darkness kissed him. Darkness engorged him, embraced him, sucked at him like a hungry beast.

He strained to see: only darkness. Darkness.

Breath rattled in metered unison with his footfalls. Air murmured past him, cooling the sweat from his skin as he moved faster and faster.

Where am I? he wondered. He was running, but . . . to where? And why?

His heart writhed in his chest, fighting to pump blood through constricted arteries. It was cold, then hot, then cold again. He peered into the blackness, pupils straining to enlarge until his eyes stung and his head thundered.

Darkness. Only darkness, and a cold and bottomless sensation that swelled inside him.

He was . . . alone. Not "by himself" or "away for a while." But terrifyingly ALONE.

Faint light fluttered against him, and he flinched away from it in surprise and pain. A moment passed, and another. Slowly his surroundings solidified.

Images hovered in the dimness, colored a slate gray. It took him a moment to realize what he was looking at.

They were trees . . . but not like any trees he'd ever

seen. He touched one hesitantly, and it whispered rough and warm under his fingers. They weren't imaginary, he realized. Not some figment of his imagination. He could feel them. The limbs were draped in shadows, gnarled and twisted . . .

And they were reaching out for him. He crouched and held up his hands to ward them off.

Suddenly, grotesquely, they moved again, knotting together over his head to form a canopy, a tunnel, a covered path.

An instant later, he could feel something more—a thing setting sharp and solid against his spine. It was more than a simple sensation, more than a vague premonition. It was a thirsting, insatiable evil, poised at his back and ready to slash deeply.

It was coming from the trees.

He pushed away from them and ran down the path. The air was thick and humid, but he kept moving, even though he felt as if he were wading through syrup, even though his breath burned in his lungs.

He turned a corner and chilling mist covered him, swooping in like an insubstantial wall. It clung hungrily as he ran.

A wailing moan—harpy cry, banshee wail—cut through the mist. He lurched to a stop as the screaming expanded inside him like a living thing, crashing against the walls of his skull. With the sound came a memory—a terrifying, painful memory.

He had done all this before. Had been here many, many times. And he knew what would happen next.

He looked down in horror as the roots at his feet stirred and separated, spreading like gray arthritic fingers. They were hiding something soft and supple. Warm tones glimmered against the shapeless ash.

It was the body of a woman . . . a woman he . . . he knew.

It was . . . ANGIE.

He longed to rush to her and take her in his arms—to hold her, protect her. But he was helpless.

He could only stand in mute horror and watch her lifeless body turn, as if some invisible foot had hooked under her torso and turned her over for a better look.

Her ankles, dark with blood, were still pinned to the earth. Her golden hair still swept across her breasts like a soft curtain. She was still bleeding from a hundred tiny cuts that covered her from neck to knee with glittering, obscene tattoos.

Anger roared inside him, urging him to do something, do anything . . .

But the sharp, evil thing that had been pursuing him was suddenly at his back again.

It chuckled wickedly inside his head. As it attacked, a reeking wind, a putrid odor as thick as smoke, snatched the air from his lungs. The stench was sweet and heavy, foul and intense. It closed his throat like a clutching fist.

The body at his feet disappeared in a sheet of pain. He stumbled aimlessly forward, fighting for every breath.

Tears streamed down his face. The pain in his chest pulsed.

Suddenly gravel crunched under his feet, and once again he remembered it from before: He had been running through a gray fog, down a wide, gravel driveway, toward . . . toward . . . he couldn't remember what. But he knew there had been something waiting for him before—a hundred times before. And even Satan himself was preferable to this endless emptiness. He would only go a little farther, a few more steps before the last of his energy and hope drained away.

A plaintive, echoing voice called through the dank air.

"Lance!"

It was Angie. He knew that, he could tell, somehow. He stopped in confusion.

The sharp, evil thing struck out at him.

Pain drilled through his skull, an evil laughing force as

rigid as stressed steel. Intense heat roared through his body and seared his mind, tearing him in all directions at once. But he lived. God help him, he lived.

Then the voice came back to him, louder and more insistent. It surged at him, the words lapping over each other in a desperate tide.

"Lance! Open your eyes!"

His consciousness pulled apart like stone stressed beyond its breaking point. He was unable to fight back, even to understand. The pain kept slamming into him in monstrous, echoing waves.

"Lance, please! For God's sake, open your eyes!"

The words became solid things for him—a counterforce pounding against the incessant, evil rhythm. He could feel them pulling him away, trying to drag him from the pain.

"Let me die," he begged.

"LANCE! OPEN YOUR EYES!"

He tried to help. He thrashed out blindly, trying to drive away the pain . . .

And he connected with something.

His eyes snapped open to see Angie, her naked body glistening in an eerie green light. She was standing in the doorway of a strangely familiar house, her hands stretched out to him.

"Take my hand, Lance," she said. "Let me help you."

He started to move forward . . . and a darkness more intense than night gushed forward, blotting her from view. He was trapped inside the cloud, so blind his outstretched hands were invisible only inches away. He heard the evil thing at his back laugh. The pain swept through him again.

Without thinking, he thrust his hand forward, fingers groping in the blackness . . . and he felt a soft warmth wrap itself tightly about his palm and wrist. It was a fresh, pure sensation, doubly eerie in this evil place. It spread through him like a breath of spring air.

The endless pain within him began to fade. Slowly, very slowly, it disappeared altogether.

"Wake up, Lance," a sweet voice murmured. He recognized it now. He loved it. *"Leave the nightmare behind. Come back to me. Please, please come back to me!"*

He was suddenly awake, sitting up in the bed where he and Angie had made wild, wonderful love just a short time ago. At least he *thought* it was a short time ago. It could have been hours. Days.

Angie sat facing him, her eyes tightly shut. She was holding his hands firmly in her own, whispering one phrase over and over again with a hoarse, rasping intensity.

"Come back to me. Please, come back to me!" she whispered.

"Angie . . ." he said. His throat was dry and brittle, and the sound was more a croak than a human voice. He swallowed hard and tried again. "It's all right. I'm back."

Angie's eyes flew open. It took a long moment for her to focus, for her to *believe* that he was awake and sitting before her. Then it fell into place—Lance could *feel* it as she suddenly understood. In the next instant she was in his arms, weeping with relief.

"Thank God," she said. "Thank God."

For a long while they held each other tightly, not saying anything.

Finally, Lance cleared his throat. "Are you okay?" he said.

"I'm fine," she said quickly, her voice quavering. "It's just—you, you were having a nightmare. You were screaming, and breathing funny— God, I thought you were going to *die,* Lance! I was so worried." She slowly released her hold on him and eased back on her haunches. Tears welled up in her eyes. "I couldn't wake you. I just *couldn't.*"

"But . . . you did," Lance said, frowning as he tried to remember. "I don't understand it myself, but I— I heard you calling. Then I felt your hands holding mine." He looked down at their fingers, still twined tightly together.

Then he looked up, deep into her eyes. "How did you do that?"

She shook her head and took in a long, shuddering breath. "I don't know, love," she whispered. "I really don't know." But a single tear, a tear of relief, trickled down her soft, suntanned cheeks.

Then, with painful suddenness, the memory rushed to Lance. He sat bolt upright. His hand flew free and clutched at his temples.

"God!" he said, "God . . . I— *I remember the dream!*"

Angie stared at him, and her eyes narrowed. "Lance . . ."

He barely heard her; he was frantically searching his memory for every scrap of recollection. This had never happened before. It had always faded too quickly to hold, no matter how horrible it had been. But now . . . part of it, at any rate, was still with him.

He remembered the fog, and the bizarre, living trees. Then, in a tortuous flash, the fear came back to him. The fear—and the pain.

His hands tightened on his skull. He felt the breath lock, hot and acidy, in his throat. "No," he said. "God, *no . . .*"

He collapsed on the bed, huddled in a knot of pain. Angie gasped and reached out to him, pulling this trembling man she loved to her and cradling him like a child.

He couldn't feel her at first. There was only the pain, and the fear, and nothing more.

"It's all right," she said, rocking slowly back and forth on the bed. "It's all right, now. You're safe, here, with me."

He didn't answer—he *couldn't*. She clutched him more tightly than ever, as if the simple, human contact could hold him together.

"It hurts," he rasped. "God, Angie, it *hurts*."

"It's over," she whispered, stroking his hair. She tried to pull him even closer. "Just let it go, love. It was only a nightmare, and it's over now, it's gone. I'm here with you. You're awake. Let it go.''

Even as she spoke the words, Angie knew they weren't true. This was no ordinary bad dream. There was something more to it—something to do with Essie's death, and the house, and . . . all of it.

Somehow, by some terrible and frightening mechanism she simply couldn't comprehend, she had joined him in his nightmare. She had actually entered his dream . . .

And she had saved him. This time, she had somehow saved him.

But what about next time? she thought. *What about next time?*

Chapter 20

Angie tilted the tall Old Country Roses Royal Bone China coffee pot and topped up Lance's cup, her hand carefully holding the fragile lid. "I'm sure it's got something to do with Robert," she said.

Lance slurped gratefully at his second cup. "What makes you think that?"

They were sitting at the table in the cozy dining area of her apartment. The early-morning sun glittered on the blue-green water of the harbor and sparkled off the burnished cutlery Angie had scattered across her sky-blue tablecloth.

It was all very lovely, Lance thought. Perfect.

Too damn perfect by half, he decided. Two hours ago he had been battling for his life in some nightmarish landscape that had been more real than Australia itself. Now he was politely sipping café au lait with his pinkie pointing up, and none of it, *none* of it, made one damn bit of sense.

"He threatened you, remember. And he's into that Black Magic mumbo jumbo."

" 'Black Magic'?" Lance echoed. "Isn't that a little farfetched?"

"What else would you call what happened last night?"

"I don't know," Lance said, shaking his head. "Mass hypnotism? The power of suggestion? Something like that. But whatever you call it, I was having those same dreams *weeks* ago. Robert didn't even know I existed then."

He and Angie had tried to get back to sleep after the nightmare, but there had been no point to it. They'd ended the night sitting up in bed, holding each other and watching the sun rise over the city of Sydney, trying not to talk about what was happening to them.

This first coffee of the day, poured and consumed just before six A.M., brightened things considerably. Now, in the clear light of this brightly polished morning, they could turn and look, however briefly, at what had happened there in the darkness.

"Well, I can't explain it," Angie insisted quietly. "But I'm sure Robert's involved."

"Female intuition?" Lance smiled lightly.

She gave him a killing look. "Call it what you like," she said. "I just *know*."

He couldn't help but laugh at her intensity. "I do believe you do," he said.

She took a sip of her coffee and smiled in spite of herself.

The sharp chirp of the telephone interrupted them. Angie reached over, grabbed the receiver from its white plastic wall mount, and held it to her ear. "Hello?"

Lance stared out the window, marveling at the thousands of tiny points of light that flashed at him from across the harbor. Just a few seconds earlier they had been normal office-building windows. Now they were magic.

He was too enthralled with the view to see the look of deep concern that crossed Angie's face when she recognized the voice on the other end of the line.

After a few long seconds, she covered the mouthpiece with her hand and spoke to Lance. "Guess who?"

He turned from the window and raised his eyebrows, still distracted by the panorama.

"It's Robert," she said curtly. Lance frowned, and she smirked at him. "Still think he had nothing to do with last night?"

"Don't be a smart ass."

"Don't be so naive."

They both laughed, and he sat down next to her. "What's he want?"

"He's inviting you and me to his house tonight for drinks. What should I tell him?"

"Tell him I—" Lance stopped in mid-sentence. "I think *I* should go. Maybe I can find out what the hell's going on. But it might be safer if I go alone, in case you're right about him."

"Oh, right, mate. The big strong man who can't even wake up by himself is going to keep *me* out of trouble."

"Look, Angie, I just—"

"I'm coming along. Just try and stop me."

Before he could say another word she spoke into the uncovered mouthpiece, "Robert, we'd love to come." She listened, then added, "Eight o'clock? Fine, we'll see you then."

She hung up and turned to glare at her lover.

"Do I hear any argument?"

Lance grinned. "Not from me," he said . . . but he couldn't keep himself from worrying. Part of him wanted her along—*needed* her by his side—while part of him couldn't stand the thought of anything happening to her.

And there was no doubt in his mind that this little "tea" with Robert was going to be anything but safe and sound.

"Another cup?" Robert Beresford lifted the sterling silver tea pot from the ornate oak table and looked his guest squarely in the eye.

"No, thanks." Lance looked over at Angie, then brushed absentmindedly at a crumb that lay on the delicately patterned crochet tablecloth. "I'm still not used to tea, I'm afraid."

"I'm sorry I don't have any coffee to offer you," Robert said, not looking the least bit sorry. "I don't have many *Yank* visitors."

Lance didn't like the way Robert said "Yank." In fact, he didn't like Robert at all. *Our first meeting got us off to a rotten start,* he thought. *And the more I get to know him, the more I dislike the guy.*

The three of them were seated at the table in the breakfast room of Robert's impressive house. From the outside it looked for all the world like a castle—an authentic, Old English *castle*—that had somehow magically zapped itself from the past to the present, making the trip unscathed. It looked as if the builders had completed construction only days before.

"Quite right," Robert had said dryly when they'd first arrived and were staring up at the vast, stone facade. He was obviously pleased at their bewilderment. "Actually, it's only just been finished by my own little regiment of workers. Had it built precisely to my own specifications, you know. Broke champagne over the bow, as it were, barely a fortnight ago."

Lance tried not to look impressed. He didn't want to give Robert the satisfaction.

The interior was every bit as impressive as the exterior. Twenty-five-foot-high, solid oak beam ceilings hovered over every room on the lower floor. Huge tapestries, reminiscent of those that had adorned the castles of the feudal lords of Europe, hung in the dining room, the living room—even the den. Matching leather chairs and couches were everywhere, apparently all from the same craftsman's hand. The ornamentation was primarily silver and gold—*real* silver and gold, Lance had no doubt—and there was plenty of it in every room.

"Does it meet with your approval?" Robert had asked as the tour of the mansion's bottom floor was completed.

"It'll do," Lance replied, trying his best to sound nonchalant. "In a pinch."

"Ah," Robert said, sniffing. "That renowned Yank wit."

Yeah, Lance thought, *and screw you, too*.

He was growing tired of the oh-so-dry repartee. It was verbal fencing, he realized—two tomcats circling around, each getting the measure of the other before the battle began.

It would help, Lance realized, if he could know *why* a battle was necessary, and how it would be fought. But whatever the reasons, and whatever the weapons, he knew it was coming. He could smell the tension in the air, like a storm brewing on the horizon.

"No coffee in the house *at all*, Uncle Robert?" Angie said, prodding him purely for spite. "I thought coffee was pretty much an Australian drink these days." She didn't even try to hide her distaste for Robert and his poor manners.

"Perhaps in *some* circles," Robert said, allowing a trace of impatience to show through the arrogance. "But here in the Manor, we hold with the old ways."

The Manor? Lance thought. *The "old ways"? Isn't that stretching it just a wee bit, Robert old chap?*

Lance could see Angie girding for battle and decided to intervene before it got messy. He started to rise, clearing his throat nervously . . .

He needn't have bothered. Robert seemed to have tired of the badinage as well. He was already on his feet, pushing back his chair from the table and saying, "Why don't we adjourn to the den for something a little more substantial?"

The three of them made their way through the archway into the den.

Robert was doing his best to ignore Angie entirely and was succeeding rather well. "Do you drink port, Lance?" he said, pointedly excluding Angie from the conversation.

"Once in a while," Lance said casually. *Once, to be*

exact, he said to himself. *And I hated it. But I'm not leaving you any openings, you puffed-up bore.*

"Oh!" Robert seemed genuinely surprised. "You didn't strike me as a 'port' sort of chap."

That's one for me, then, Lance thought.

Their host walked across the room to where a cut-glass decanter and six glasses sat on an ornate silver tray. Lance took the opportunity to look around the den.

Robert's preoccupation with his role as "Laird of the Manor" was particularly obvious here. There was a stag's head brooding on one wall, a thick brocade carpet sporting an intricate coat of arms beneath their feet, and a line of gold and silver chalices mounted on the hardwood hearth above the huge rock fireplace at the far side of the room. *I must remember to ask Angie where he gets his money,* Lance reminded himself.

Robert turned back to them holding a glass of port in each hand. There was a strange, hard look in his eye, as if he was thinking about something particularly pleasing—or particularly cruel. "So," he said, "how are you at games?"

Lance sipped at the port and forced himself not to make a face. "Nice," he said briefly, hating it. "What kind of games do you mean?" *As if we weren't playing one right now,* he added to himself.

"It's more like a parlor trick, really." Robert sipped at his port and a smirk twisted his top lip. "Something I devised myself. I call it 'The Mind Game.' "

Lance wondered if Robert was aware of what the same term meant in American slang—how it implied cruelty, manipulation, arrogance. He decided that even if Robert *weren't* aware of it, the associations would please him.

Robert simply stroked the side of his fine cut crystal and described his little recreation. "Most people have too much trouble freeing themselves from their inhibitions," he said. "But one must, really, to play my little game." He looked at Lance again, with the same hard, almost birdlike glittering in his eye. "Now *you*, Lance, I think you might be very capable."

A sudden, cold certainty overtook Lance. *This is what he wanted us here for,* he thought.

He knew without a doubt that he should take Angie by the arm and walk her out of there without a backward glance. But he couldn't bring himself to do it—not yet. *If I do that, I'll never find out what's going on—and I have to; it's too dangerous to stay ignorant. At least this way I'll be ready.*

Robert was waiting for him, still stroking the side of his goblet and smiling. *Again like the cat who ate the canary,* Lance thought. He forced himself to smile back, feeling anything but brave, and said, "Sounds like it might be fun."

"Oh," Robert told him, "it might be a great deal more than *that.*" He could barely suppress a sneer as he sauntered over to a nearby desk and took a pack of oversized cards from the top drawer.

In the moment his back was turned, Angie put her long-fingered hand on Lance's sleeve and flashed him a meaningful glance. It didn't take vast mental powers to see she was trying to warn him about Robert. *Another premonition?* Lance wondered.

It's all right, he thought grimly, and let his own hand gently squeeze her tightening fingers. *We'll get through it.*

She removed her hand quickly before Robert could see, but there was a greater sense of calm from her now—as if the simple touch had strengthened them both.

Robert seated himself at the large card table and pointed to the chair across from him. "You take the chair opposite me," he said. Then he motioned negligently to one of the side chairs. "Angelique? There." It was almost as if he couldn't be bothered with her presence.

The pattern on the top card caught Lance's eye. The design was ancient, intricate . . . fascinating. He reached out to spread the cards for a better look, but before his fingers could touch them, Robert swept the deck away, lifting it from the table and almost clutching it to his chest.

"No!" he said, with ill-concealed panic. Then he visibly calmed himself. "N—no. You mustn't touch the cards until the game begins. It would spoil things."

What "things"? Lance wondered. He had an uneasy feeling in his stomach that he would find out all too soon.

Five minutes later, Lance sat relaxed in his overstuffed leather chair, one finger tracing a small, intricate pattern on his right temple. He wasn't even aware he was doing it, and if he had noticed it at all, he probably wouldn't have acknowledged that the pattern his finger was tracing was identical to the design on the back of Robert's playing cards. In any event, it was beyond him. He was concentrating on a scene that was unfolding behind his eyelids.

"Your basic fairy-tale real estate," he said, frowning slightly. "Green fields with a tall castle in the distance and a mounted knight approaching it. The knight has a . . . red? . . . plume on his helmet. His horse is black."

He opened his eyes and looked expectantly toward Angie at the far side of the table.

She dropped the card she was holding onto the soft velvet surface, a quizzical expression on her face.

The landscape that Lance had just described was illustrated there in perfect detail: castle, field, knight, and horse. Even the red plume sprouting from the knight's helmet.

"That's the fifth time in a row," Angie said, dumbfounded. "Five out of five." Angie appeared to be trying to understand what her own words meant. "That's . . . amazing."

Robert looked anything but pleased. "Yes, quite." He pulled the cards back quickly and shuffled them with a vicious snap. "Well, enough between *you* two," he said. He glanced sharply at Lance. "Now it's *our* turn."

Lance reached out to take the cards himself, but Robert

snatched them back. He half turned away as he shuffled again and again, frowning furiously.

As he shuffled the cards, Angie said, "Is that a normal score, Robert?"

At first he didn't seem to hear her.

"*Robert,*" she said, louder and more insistently than before. "Is that a *normal* score we got on your little 'game'?"

He humphed and mumbled, "It's higher than most, actually."

"How much higher?" Lance asked. Now he was curious himself.

"Oh . . . I don't know," Robert snapped. "What does it matter?" With a fierce abruptness he lifted a card and looked at it. "Now, which card am I holding?"

Lance wouldn't be put off. "What *is* the average?"

Robert sighed heavily. "Really," he said. "If you *must* know, three positive guesses out of five, in a repeated series, is considered unusual. You and Angelique did . . . very well."

"Very well" is a gross understatement, Lance thought. He glanced in puzzlement at his friend and lover. *It's the damndest thing. First I dream about her before I even know she exists, and now this.*

Angie smiled back at him. *It's almost as if she can tell what I'm thinking,* he thought. *And if it's true, she'd be blushing right now . . .*

His mind was still caught up in the thought when Robert spoke. The man's words seemed a thousand miles away.

"What card am I holding?"

Only half thinking, Lance turned his attention back to the game. His wariness was all but forgotten in his preoccupation with the woman he loved, and when he reached out with his mind as he had before, with Angie, he did so almost automatically. "I sense— "

Pain sliced through his head like a hot knife.

Automatic responses saved his life. Mental defenses he

wasn't even aware he had slammed down impenetrable walls and blocked the pain out.

For an instant Lance felt relieved. Whatever it was, he had managed to ward it off; now he could—

The pain smashed into his thoughts a second time, even more intensely than before.

Lance gripped his head with both hands and fell back in the chair as if he had been physically struck.

Angie jumped from her chair in shock. "Lance . . . ?"

A horrible, bubbling scream leapt from his constricted throat; flashes of pure, agonizing light crashed behind his eyes. Conscious thought was a distant thing. If he was aware of anything within the agony it was . . . color. He seemed to be drowning in a sea of it, choking on it.

Somehow, impossibly, the pain was wrapped in a cloak of *purple*.

He couldn't keep his fingers from digging into his skull, as if they were trying to pull the pain away, to order his thoughts with a brutal directness. But nothing helped. Nothing.

"*Lance!*"

Scorching heat pierced his temples. His brain was melting from a nonstop series of explosions that blossomed inside his skull in a purple cloud.

I . . . I . . . have . . . to . . . stop . . . it! I . . . have . . . to . . . do . . . SOMETHING!

He seized on a tiny fragment of consciousness. He tried to build a full thought, one tiny oasis of sanity inside the pain. And then he saw it.

A bolt of purple energy was streaking toward him.

He opened his eyes and saw a dim, ghostly vision of the room around him. He understood it now: the pain was an *external* thing, a power coming from outside him. If he could look at his surroundings, look at them in some special way, he could locate the source. He could—

The pain redoubled. He screamed again, and his eyes squeezed shut against the agony.

No, he thought. *No, I have to do this . . .*

He forced his eyelids open a fraction of an inch. They felt like burnt parchment, and waves of needle-sharp pain grated against the whites of his eyes, but he refused to give in to it.

He could see again, however dimly.

Angie was kneeling at his side, her eyes filled with fear and confusion.

Sorry, Angie. Can't . . . talk . . . yet . . .

The table before him was alive with waves of purple energy, a sea of beautiful, horrible power. And beyond the rippling cloth, at the far side of the table, Robert sat straight-backed in his chair. His eyes were closed. His mouth was forming a series of silent syllables.

He was glowing with a roiling purple energy, so bright that Lance had to close his eyes against it.

The searing purple light swelled and tried to engulf Lance again, but he was ready for it this time. He used the defenses that had saved him before. He built on them, reinforced them, pushed back at the force with all his will.

He suddenly understood what was happening—a strange, crystal-clear realization. The pain was real—not an illusion, not a dream. It was *real* . . . but only a secondary product of the real process.

The central battle was taking place on some purely mental plane. And it was a struggle to dominate Lance Sullivan.

It was a battle for his soul . . . and at the moment, Lance was losing.

Knowing that somehow made it easier to fight. With new determination, Lance reached his own awareness out, searching for Robert's.

The purple mist cleared, showing a strange, unearthly scene. A vast plain of dust, illuminated by a purple sun, stretched off in all directions. The emptiness and "aloneness" Lance had felt in the nightmares gripped him again.

This was the same place, he knew. A different region—a different "landscape," perhaps—but the same place.

Then he saw Robert, standing in the near distance.

A thin glowing ray of intense purple light beamed down from the sun and illuminated Robert's body. It seemed to fill him with power. He *glowed* with purple energy.

He turned to face Lance directly. He seemed to focus on him with a terrifying acuity, as if his entire consciousness was drawn to a single, white-hot point.

A bolt of energy leapt from Robert's forehead, near the center of his thick eyebrows. It streaked a jagged path straight toward Lance.

Lance warded off the blow again—but this time the defense was a conscious thing, *directed*. He felt himself raise a mental hand. He saw it in his mind.

The purple bolt hit the imaginary hand and bounced away without damage, a harmless beam of light. Lance felt a tiny charge of energy, a minor electric shock. Then his thoughts cleared and in a flash he saw Robert straighten, surprised at the sudden defense.

Robert took one step back, as if staggered. For a moment the beam of light from the purple sun seemed to falter, then it grew stronger than ever—a conduit of power, a lifeline of energy. Robert laughed, loud and hard, and . without warning, without preface . . . he disappeared.

The crushing mental pressure vanished with him, so suddenly it made Lance dizzy with shock.

He staggered and gulped in air. *Maybe it's over*, he thought. *Maybe if I can find my way back to the real world now, I'll have passed his little test, won this impossible war—*

The air directly in front of him, tinted purple from the dusty plain, began to roil and twist like a cloud of steam. And as suddenly as Robert had disappeared, a new creature took his place—only this time, directly in front of Lance, only a scant few feet away.

It was a giant leopard, its eyes glowing purple.

Before Lance could move, it leapt at him, jaws wide, fangs dripping. Lance threw up his arms in a purely physical defense and managed to turn the maw aside even as the animal hit him with all its weight.

He struck the flat purple sand with tremendous force, but he kept fighting. His hands shot up and clamped around the beast's neck, holding it back, but its slavering jaws were only inches from his face. He held its neck tightly, their power perfectly balanced. He could feel the immense muscles of the beast over him, straining to kill, coiled to strike. He held tightly . . . but knew he couldn't do it forever. Only seconds into the fight, he felt his arms already beginning to weaken.

The leopard roared at him—a deep, rough, choking sound as it forced its head forward, intent on tearing its victim to shreds. Lance found himself looking directly into the beast's glowing eyes, staring deep into the glittering purple and black . . .

Robert.

They were *Robert's* eyes.

Lance was as sure as he had ever been about anything in his life. Behind the deep, blazing purple eyes of this wild beast was the mind of Robert Beresford . . .

And *something else.*

In the instant he made contact—in a moment so brief he wasn't even sure it actually happened—Lance thought he felt another presence. Something more than the boundless ambition and cruelty of Robert Beresford. Something worse—something far older and more powerful. Something dark . . . and evil.

An instant later the contact was broken, the thought crushed. The big cat roared and lunged forward, its jaws snapping shut an inch from Lance's face. And though he strained every muscle, the best Lance could do was to hold the crazed beast where it was. Its hot, foul breath gushed over him. Saliva began dripping into his eyes. He couldn't hold it for long. In a moment his arms would give out, and the beast would take him, *kill* him . . .

"Angie!" he shouted—a tiny sound, lost in the foul wind of the dusty plain, weak against the bellowing of the beast. "Angie . . ."

Angie was frantic. She shouted at Lance for the tenth time, and she shook him as hard as she could.

Nothing. He was slumped back in the chair, in some kind of trance. The only sign of life was the horribly mobile expression of fear that twisted at his features.

Robert sat across the table, also slumped in his high-backed chair. But there was no fear on his face—only a light, almost merry smile, as if the world in which *he* was lost was infinitely more pleasing than Lance's.

It had all gone wrong. From the moment she had touched those bloody playing cards, it had gone *wrong.* But it had been so amazing to her. Each time Lance had looked at the card in his hand, it was as if she heard his voice—Lance's actual *voice*—describing what he saw . . . and then *she* saw it, too. Each time she had simply repeated what she "heard" in her mind, without stopping to think. And each time it had been right. When they had changed about, the process had seemed even easier, though surely it couldn't have been. Angie didn't know much about ESP—it had never interested her, really—but she knew enough to know that this was unusual . . . *impossible.*

Then Robert had intervened, and in an instant everything had crumbled.

One moment, Lance had been smiling at her. The next his face had suddenly twisted into a grimace, his hands had shot to his temples, he'd screamed and collapsed.

She clutched her lover's hand and wept. "What am I going to do? Oh, God, *God,* what . . ."

Stop it, she told herself. She forced herself to sit back, to breathe deeply. *Get a hold of yourself, girl. Being hysterical won't help anything.*

"Angie . . ."

She straightened up in surprise. *What was that?* she thought. *Someone called my name?*

She looked down at Lance, but nothing had changed. He still slept fitfully, trapped in a dream.

But I did hear him call. And it sounded like he was in agony.

Angie grabbed Lance's arm as tightly as she could. The night before, when he was terrified and in pain, she had been able to help. She didn't really know how she had done it, how it had *happened* . . . but maybe, somehow, she could do it again.

"Lance," Angie said, her mouth close to his ear. "I'm here. I'm here. I'm holding you."

Everything went *purple*. Pain tore at her. Huge slobbering fangs formed in her mind's eye, hissing at her, filling her with fear. With terrifying suddenness, she was fighting for her life, and she didn't know why . . . or how . . . or even *where*.

But Lance was there. Lance was . . . was . . . *her*. She was . . . *Lance*. They were somehow *one*.

There was no time to think about how it was happening. She could feel Lance's fear. She knew he was only seconds from collapsing under the beast's attack.

And if he faltered, they would *both* die.

A surge of energy rushed through him.

Lance jolted under the impact. The influx of power was so sudden, so shocking, he almost lost his hold on the leopard.

But now he was suddenly *renewed*.

For an instant he was too confused to respond. What was happening? How had he—

Lance . . .

Ah.

He felt her now. He *felt* Angie with him, *inside* him,

and he understood. She had come to help him again. She had given him new strength.

And he used it.

With relative ease, he inched the leopard back from his face. For an instant he thought about tossing it away, fifty feet down the dusty plain . . .

But no. Robert would only change his form again, turn into something larger and more powerful—into something Lance couldn't handle even with Angie's help.

So, instead, he gathered his strength and held the beast tight. Now he was finally able to take a good look at the leopard, clamping it between his hands.

It was obviously Robert. His essence permeated the beast. But again, there was that . . . *something else*.

It seemed to be an external presence—a surreal, almost nonhuman kind of power that somehow fed Robert, like the beam of light from the purple sun still connected to the creature, feeding it energy.

Robert has no power at all, Lance suddenly realized. *It's all coming from this . . . thing . . . whatever it is.*

Lance reached out and tried to touch it with his mind.

Darkness kissed him. Darkness engorged him, embraced him, sucked at him like a hungry beast. He strained to see: only darkness. Darkness.

Lance reeled back. *God!* he thought. *God, it's the nightmare! It's the thing from the nightmare!*

No! No, he realized. This thing was the *source* of the nightmares. The power that had been pursuing him for weeks, infecting him like some horrible disease . . .

And he knew how strong it was. He knew that he couldn't confront it—not yet, not now. The leopard that was Robert still hung only inches from his face. *That* was his first priority.

I have to cut Robert off from the thing. It's my—our— only chance. He would have to build a singular defense, a protection that couldn't be breached.

A wall, he told himself. He pictured it: *An impenetrable wall. A wall that blocks out everything. A wall so strong that nothing can get through. No light. No sound. Not even thoughts. A wall. An impenetrable wall.*

Over and over, like a mantra, Lance repeated the words in his mind. With each repetition, he concentrated more and more on the combined power of his mind and Angie's.

After a moment, he opened his eyes. There, hanging in the air above the purple plain, directly behind the beast, a wall was slowly forming.

It was the blackest of black—a barrier unlike any other. The purple illumination of the plain could not weaken the apparition. Light was swallowed by its chitinous surface.

Lance wasn't sure exactly how they had brought this thing into being, but it didn't matter. He concentrated on the task at hand.

He moved the wall. Without sound or warning, he made it drift quickly forward, hover over the place where Robert and Lance were still frozen in battle.

He made the wall move between Robert and the steady beam of purple light that shot from the sun . . .

And in that instant of separation, Lance gathered all the strength that remained in his double-mind and hurled it at Robert.

Everything happened at once.

The leopard flashed out of existence as Robert suddenly changed back to his human form. He pulled away from Lance's grip, cursing and howling more like a beast than a man, and lurched to his feet. He stared about in disbelief, suddenly afraid.

A blinding flash leapt from Lance's forehead, scorching the air as it struck Robert full in the chest.

The self-proclaimed warlock opened his mouth to shriek in agony as he was bathed in the full force of the flash, but the scream was abruptly cut off.

In a single heartbeat, Robert was vaporized. One moment he was there, shrieking at the purple sun that had fed him. In the next, there was nothing to show he had ever been there.

A wailing moan—harpy cry, banshee wail—carried across the purple sky. It reminded Lance of the nightmare, but he didn't want to think about that now. He only wanted to get out of the evil place. He only wanted to wake up . . .

Lance opened his eyes. Pain thundered through him. His vision swam and tilted. He got a brief, blurred look at the room, but couldn't really make out anything except a golden splash of Angie's hair against his cheek as she lay collapsed against him.

Then, mercifully, he sank into blackness.

Chapter 21

The doctor looked grim and very tired. "I'm sorry," he said. "There was nothing we could do."

Lance felt the pressure of Angie's fingers on his arm. He nodded and let his gaze wander around the hospital waiting room, not wanting to look the doctor squarely in the eyes. "It's all right, Doctor," he said. "We understand." What he wanted to say was, *"He was a filthy son of a bitch who tried to kill me, and he deserved what he got,"* but it wasn't in him. Anyway, he wasn't sure *how* he felt.

All he knew for certain was that Robert Beresford was dead.

"Look," the Australian doctor said, moving them away from the noise and tension of the emergency room. "There's nothing more you can do here. Why don't you go home?"

"We'll do that," Lance said, still not looking directly at the medical man. He took Angie's arm and started for the door, and the doctor called after them.

"I'm sorry!" he said. "It happens this way sometimes. So quickly we can't even tell what—"

Lance turned back and finally looked at him, and there was something in his look, in his eyes, that made the doctor stop, mid-sentence.

"We understand, Doctor," he said softly. "Really. It's all right."

The doctor said nothing, but continued to stare at him, as Lance turned away and left the hospital with Angie.

At first, Lance had thought Robert was sleeping. He had looked so relaxed in that chair, so content. But he hadn't responded when Lance had tried to wake him. And when Angie felt strong enough, she had tried to wake him, too. There had still been no response.

They had tried to find a pulse, but there was none to be found. Then came the ambulance, and the hospital, and that poor doctor who felt so sorry about the middle-aged man with the cerebral hemorrhage who shouldn't have died so young.

But Lance remembered. He remembered the purple plain, the leopard, the vision from his nightmare. He remembered how Angie had somehow merged her mind with his to allow him to defeat Robert. And he remembered the strange presence that had been feeding Robert with power. He remembered it all.

Angie didn't. She couldn't remember anything after their guessing game with the cards—or if she did, she wasn't telling.

When Lance had first awakened, he had found her collapsed on top of him, where she must have fallen when her mind merged with his. She was breathing normally—he would have noticed anything else immediately—but it still took almost half an hour to draw her from her coma. Lance himself hadn't felt much better. For hours later his head continued to pound, his body ached from top to toe, and he felt as if he had been in a war.

Now, the next morning, they were on their way back to Robert's house. They didn't say more than a few words as they drove, but Lance knew it was all right.

There are a lot of things I know about Angie without having to speak, he thought. *How does that happen? Why does that happen?*

The house seemed filled with an almost solid tranquility—as if silence itself was a sound, and that sound penetrated every corner of the structure.

Without a word, Lance and Angie began to search. They started in the front hallway of the "castle" and worked their way back through room after room, looking for something—*anything*—that might explain what Robert had become, and why he had tried to kill them.

It took them four hours to reach the study. There they found Robert's ancient rolltop desk, crammed with papers and notes. At first, Lance thought they had finally stumbled onto something . . . but all the documents were purely legal or financial: work agreements for the castle, canceled checks, business letters. All the paraphernalia of a wealthy man with diversified holdings, and not a scrap of anything that was out of the ordinary.

They finally gave up on the study and went back into the room Robert had taken them to for drinks the night before.

"This is hopeless," Angie said, flopping down in a chair across the room from the one where Robert had died only a little over twelve hours before. "He had to have *some*thing. He had to— Hullo."

She straightened up, and Lance turned to her. "What?"

"Look there."

There was a crack in the corner of the room, where two walls met at right angles. But it wasn't a *normal* crack—not the jagged separation of plaster, or a product of stress as the house settled. No, this was a tidy, straight, *machined* separation. As if the wall had been cracked on purpose.

Angie moved a floor lamp to get closer to the gap. She put her eye against it and squinted. "Can't see a thing," she said. "But . . ."

She put her fingernails into the tiny space and pulled, then jumped back with a shout.

Lance was at her side in an instant. "What is it?"

"Damn it!" she said. "I broke a nail!"

Lance laughed from relief. "God," he said, "I thought the Creature from the Black Lagoon had come to get you."

"Well, this is just as bad," she said, sucking at her index finger.

"Let me try." He stepped forward, thrust his fingers into the half-inch gap, set his feet, and gave a hard, fast jerk.

The wall moved. The entire wall, pictures and all, slipped out and away to reveal a five-by-ten-foot alcove hidden behind it.

As the wall moved, a light in the alcove went on automatically. After a long moment, Lance and Angie stepped inside.

Three walls were filled with books—expensive, leather-bound volumes that looked ancient and smelled even older. An ornate cedarwood cabinet was off to one side, crammed with bits and pieces of bone, china, paper, ivory—objects Lance had never seen before, and whose function he could only imagine. A wooden three-drawer filing cabinet sat next to it; one half-open drawer had misfiled documents spilling onto the floor.

A surprisingly simple, almost rough-hewn pentagonal table sat in the exact center of the room. Notes and hand-written letters were scattered across it. A fifty-year-old fountain pen and a blotter sat too close to the edge, where Robert had undoubtedly left them when he closed the room and prepared to greet his guests.

If there were ghosts at all, Robert's would be in this place, Lance thought. His essence still permeated every inch of the room. This was *his* place, *his* territory. It made Lance's skin crawl just to be there.

But they stayed and searched. If there were any answers to be found, he knew, they would be found *here*.

Looking through this room, however, wasn't quite as simple as looking through the others. There was a vast amount of material—books upon books, notes upon notes.

They had spent only a few minutes in the room before it became obvious that a lifetime wouldn't be long enough to read everything.

"Stick to the more recent stuff," Lance decided. "What's on the table, I guess, and the first layer of papers in the cabinet."

They were fifteen minutes into it when Lance came across the loose-leaf notebook labeled *history*. He browsed through it slowly and found that it was a series of documents specifically about Beresford Hall, the house Essie Beresford had owned—that *he* owned, now.

The book began with Robert's own notes—speculations on when Beresford Hall might have been built and on who the architect might have been. There was a copy of the original registration paper from the previous century, but the document didn't indicate how old the house had been when bureaucracy finally caught up with it. Certainly, it was complete at the time of its registration—it said that much.

"Just how old *is* that place?" Lance asked.

Angie was as enthralled as he was. "I think that's what Robert was trying to find out."

They found copies of historical reports about the land itself dating back to the first British settlers. They found letters from Robert sent to every conceivable government body, and polite, unedifying responses from the same, but none of it amounted to much. Robert apparently hadn't been able to find any reference to the actual construction of the house. Even the architectural drawings submitted when the house was officially registered in 1816 were not the originals.

"Weird," Lance said, as Angie drifted off to sort through another pile of papers. "If you believe this, you'll believe the house was here when the English *got* here. Like it predated them. That's crazy."

"Everything about this is crazy," Angie muttered.

Lance turned another page and found a series of handwritten parchment pages, carefully mounted and preserved. The first page, done in the flourishes of the seventeenth century, announced that this was the "Log & Personal Journalle of Alexander Tefton of His Majesty's Royal Expeditionary Forces, in the Year of the Our Lord 1788."

"That's not 'Tefton', you dope," Angie said when he read it aloud. "That's '*Sef*ton.' Tees were esses back then, remember?"

Lance simply nodded, already absorbed in the narrative— or what he could make out of it. Apparently Sefton had been a member of an expedition that had scouted the Rose Hill area shortly after the British settlement was established in Sydney Cove in 1788. He had even been something of a teacher, working with the local aboriginals, trying to explain English life and the English language to them.

" 'It waf—' excuse me, *was*, '—with great surprise that I observed the savages' reaction to my many pictographs,' he says here." Lance had to read slowly; the handwriting was crabbed to begin with and badly faded after almost two hundred years. " 'Upon observing my etching of a simple English country home, D'Nai, my best pupil, grew sorely agitated and commenced to babble in his simple tongue, pointing first to my drawing, and then to the hills to the south-southwest. Query upon query could not enlighten me as to the poor child's infirmity . . .' Hmm . . . more and more . . . here, Robert's taken some of the natives' words that Sefton wrote down and had them translated. 'M'c'—no, 'Dor'—Hell, I can't read it. But look, Robert's note says that, loosely translated, it means 'The Goddess' or 'She who always was.' "

Angie sighed as she went through yet another stack of papers. "Does that make any sense to you?"

"Not even a bit."

"Me neither, mate."

He continued to read the journal, frowning over the handwriting and ancient diction. Ten minutes later, Angie found a pencil sketch at the bottom of a pile of notes.

"That's strange," she said, holding it up and looking at it from different angles.

Lance was still concentrating on the adventures of Alexander Sefton. He only partly heard her words. "What's that?"

"It looks as though Robert has drawn two Beresford Halls, one joined to the other." She frowned and turned the drawing again, trying to make sense of it. "Why would he bother doing that? It looks like a . . . sad face." She noticed a set of scribbled lines on the lower right. "And look at this— Hoo, what handwriting! It appears he believed Beresford Hall had some kind of— what, 'inherent energy,' whatever that means. I guess that's why he drew these two houses. Twice as many houses, twice as much power." She laughed lightly and passed the picture to Lance. "I warned you he was a little off the track."

Lance glanced at the sketch . . .

And everything else froze. All he could do was stare at the crude illustration, numb with shock.

It's the house from my nightmare, he thought. *The one that's been chasing me for so long. The dream that the Presence infected me with. Damn, the house must be a part of it!*

He dropped the picture and backed away. Angie looked up, puzzled at his reaction.

Darkness was threatening to engulf him. *No wonder Beresford Hall seemed familiar*, he thought frantically. *What the hell is this? What have I gotten myself into?*

"Lance? What's the matter? *Lance?*"

Angie's words seemed to float somewhere in the distance. Lance couldn't hold on to them; he couldn't hold on to anything. He was trapped. He knew that now. Hunted.

I have to get out . . .

Without thinking he turned and hurried for the door.

"Lance! Where are you going?"

He didn't answer. He could only get out—*now*.

"*Lance!*"

He was running by the time he reached the huge front doors of Robert Beresford's "castle."

It was hours before he stopped.

Benny Haldane made his way across the O'Hare Airport terminal, heading for Air New Zealand Flight 200. He walked with a light, almost jaunty step, but his eyes scoured every inch of the airport as he moved.

He was going through the same ritual he had taught Lance years before. "Stop every once and a while," he'd said, "just for normal things. You know, tie your shoe, get a drink of water, check out a pretty lady. But use it to look behind you, look around you. *Always* keep looking, Lance."

It was a foolproof method for inducing paranoia, too— Benny knew that. Before long, *everybody* started to look suspicious. That fat woman with the three tiny children and a cartload of baggage. The tall dude in the Stetson and the lavender boots. Even the Catholic priest a few feet to his right. But what else could he do? He had to get out of the country clean—one hundred percent *clean*.

He finally headed for the security gate that would lead him to Flight 200. In a crowded airport, Benny knew he could miss someone tailing him. But if they followed him through security, they would become a lot more obvious.

No one seemed to pay him any mind as he passed through security and made his way down the long bare hall. *Another ten minutes*, he thought, *and I just might start to think about feeling relieved*.

In the boarding area he sat as far from the entrance ramp as possible, watching latecomers. He waited through the first call, and the second, and the third, ignoring the pointed looks from the flight attendants.

Finally, after the last call, Benny boarded the plane, convinced he'd done as much as humanly possible to cover himself.

A pretty young airline hostess, smiling in spite of his tardiness, directed him to his seat in the first-class section and asked that he fasten his seat belt. He cinched it tight, feeling reasonably secure.

There was no reason for the counterfeiter to look at the nondescript man in the three-piece business suit seated three rows in front of him. After all, he had boarded Flight 200 even before Benny had reached the departure gate. Besides, the man was the epitome of the traveling corporate executive—very proper, very bored. He hadn't even looked at Benny when he'd boarded the plane late, or given him a glance since.

But Joel Thanner knew Benny was there. And he was sure Benny would lead him to Lance Sullivan.

Lance Sullivan wandered aimlessly. It had been a long time since he'd bothered about where he was. He didn't care. He had needed to run, to burn off the terror that had suddenly closed around him when he saw the pencil sketch. So he had run. And when he had tired, as he eventually did, he walked.

It's amazing, he thought as he made his way across a major intersection and along the pavement that led under a railway bridge. *Just amazing*. Above him a double-decked commuter-train sped by. Normally, that would have been quite a sight—there was nothing remotely like it in the States. But Lance wasn't feeling normal at the moment. He watched the dull-brown train, followed by a shiny silver one, rattle into the nearby station without really taking it in at all.

I never would have put my finger on what was so familiar about Beresford Hall, he thought. *Not by itself*.

But Robert's drawing had changed that. Now there was no doubt. Lance couldn't pretend any longer. This wasn't some set of weird coincidences, or shared hallucinations. This wasn't some simple "mass hypnotism" scam. There were too many coincidences, too many hallucinations! Too damn much *power!*

No, he thought. *I'm caught in the middle of something I don't understand . . . and it could kill me. It could really kill me*.

Still . . . knowing that made it easier, somehow. At least he had accepted the reality of it. At least he could *fight* it now.

He looked across the road at an old Australian pub, The Star Hotel. There was a sign hanging on a concrete telegraph pole nearby. It had a colored painting of an aboriginal standing in the water next to a canoe and beneath it the words. PARRAMATTA—FOUNDED IN 1788.

So, he was in Parramatta.

I must be ten miles or more from Robert's place, he realized. He had run and walked and wandered quite a distance . . . and right into the center of his dream. Why had he walked to Parramatta? Why not Sydney, or the open countryside? What had *drawn* him here, nearer to that house?

Lance stopped walking and concentrated, trying to shake loose the fog that clouded his thinking.

Listen to yourself, Lance Sullivan. You're turning into a classic paranoid. If you don't stop it soon they'll be putting you in a padded cell. He took a long, deep breath and slowly exhaled. *I was freaked out. That's all. I wasn't watching where I was going and I ended up in Parramatta. No big deal*.

The thought seemed hollow, even to him. But he knew that he needed to rest, if only to slow his thoughts. He just needed to sit for a while.

He scanned the area. To the left of the Star Hotel was the town hall, a picturesque old white and brown turn-of-the-century building. A fancy brick memorial with a clock embedded in it perched in the center of the street a few yards away. There were flower beds everywhere, and there, at the end of the block, was a wooden seat. A place to rest.

Then Lance noticed the old church, directly to his left. Suddenly, without thinking, he turned and walked to it instead.

The plaque on the front said that Saint John's Anglican

Church had been built in 1802. There was something comforting about its solid brick structure, something heavy and simple and *solid*, somehow. It drew Lance to it. He crossed the lawn and sat on one of the old benches under its tall spire and listened as the bells played a hymn he couldn't remember the name of, but had heard many times before.

He might have stayed there a few minutes or a few hours—he was never really sure. He just sat and listened to the bells and drifted. People hurried by him on the street a few yards away. Some even tarried in the churchyard. To Lance, it was all one huge, comfortable blur. The warm sun made him drowsy. He even dozed off a time or two.

"Hello, Lance."

The voice came from next to him on the bench. He was actually too drowsy to think much about it at first. He just shifted slightly and said, "H'lo . . ."

"How are you?"

It slowly dawned on him how odd it was. Someone knowing his name. Someone passing the time with him, when he hadn't even noticed them sit down.

Lance turned to see who it was . . .

That was the end of his short, relaxing break from reality.

Now he knew that his theory about being drawn to Parramatta wasn't just paranoia. It was true. All true.

Because there was a man sitting next to him. A man in his fifties, wearing a tweed suit and a stylish English country gentleman's hat, puffing at a large pipe that jutted from the corner of his mouth.

Angelique Beresford sat in her apartment and stared at the living room wall. She was thinking about "The Connection."

That's what she'd come to call it in her own mind—using a capital T and a capital C. The Connection between her own thoughts and Lance Sullivan's.

It was impossible—unreal. But at the same time, it seemed so natural she hadn't even questioned it when it was happening. Now she wondered at the ease with which they joined minds.

There was a large blank in her memory. She remembered reaching out to him, *linking* with him . . . but that was all. Oh, Lance had told her everything—as much as he could put into words. But she couldn't remember. And for some unexplained reason, she felt as though . . . as though she had been *violated*.

And she hadn't told Lance quite everything.

How could I explain a bloody feeling, Angie thought to herself. *Especially this feeling. I don't even understand it myself. But I feel like we're a part of each other now. And I'm damned if I even know what I mean by that.*

She had hurried back here to Kirribilli after an hour-long search of the streets around Robert's house had turned up no sign of Lance. And now she waited, and worried. There had been a crazed look in Lance's eyes when he'd rushed from Robert's office. The memory of that look— the pain and confusion there—made her stomach tie itself in knots each time she thought of it.

She lifted the pencil sketch from the table at her side and stared at it for the hundredth time.

How could a dumb drawing like this have terrified him? Angie realized it must have something to do with Beresford Hall. But *what?*

A thought rushed into her mind. She had no idea how or why it came, but she knew, with certainty, that it was fact.

The dreams. It's somehow connected to the dreams.

The thought didn't make Angie feel any better about Lance's absence. She got to her feet and began to pace worriedly back and forth.

Come home, she thought. *Come home.*

"Warwick Beresford is the name," the tidy little man said pleasantly. "We've not met, but I'm a rather . . . *distant* relative."

Lance identified the accent immediately. He'd faked it himself often enough. "I have family in England, too?" he asked, not able to hide his surprise.

"Only me, I'm afraid," the man in the tweed suit answered.

Lance stared long and hard at the old man sitting next to him on the bench. There was no doubt that it was the same man he'd seen before under very strange circumstances.

"You were at the airport. You tried to frighten me off. What the hell did you mean? And how did you speak into my mind like that?"

Warwick waved it away and shrugged. "Oh, a parlor trick, really. Something I learned many years ago," he said.

That's what Robert had called his "Mind Game," Lance thought. *A parlor trick.*

Warwick's smile was warm and friendly. "So," he said, leaning forward conspiratorially. "How are you liking your visit to Australia?"

Lance was in no mood for pleasantries. "What the hell do you want from me?"

Warwick looked mildly surprised. "Well. Down to business, then." He frowned slightly and said it straight out: "I'd like to buy Beresford Hall."

"What?" Lance couldn't hide his astonishment.

"I live in the original Beresford Manse," Warwick Beresford explained, "in Northumberland, England. It is remarkably similar to the house you're about to inherit. So similar, in fact, that I would like to purchase it. I made this offer to Essie Beresford, your great-grandmother, but unfortunately she died before we could . . . consummate the arrangement, as it were."

"She agreed to sell?"

There was a tiny crack in the friendly facade. "You doubt me?" he said. "Of *course* she agreed. Otherwise, I—" Warwick stopped himself. He paused. Then the smile switched back on again. "And now, before you even sign the ownership papers, I am quite ready to make you the same extremely generous offer.''

The old British gentleman lit up his pipe and stared expectantly at Lance. ''So, what do you say?''

Lance sat and stared at Warwick, unable to give any serious thought to his request. With all the other things cluttering his mind, there was no room for something like this. Not now. *A real estate deal?*

It was as if Warwick had read his thoughts. ''I can see you have far too much on your mind at the moment to be bothered by such trivialities,'' he said, and got to his feet. ''No matter. I'll have my solicitor contact you. Good day, Lance. It was good running into you like this.''

Before Lance realized what was happening, Warwick had wheeled about and was striding off toward the corner of the church.

Lance sat for a long moment, not thinking much about anything. Then the absurdity and importance of the meeting that had just taken place crashed down on him. He had questions—*thousands* of questions—and the priggish old man from Great Britain just might have the answers to all of them.

He leapt to his feet and ran for the corner where Warwick had just disappeared. ''Warwick!'' he called. ''Warwick, wait—''

When he reached the flower beds nestled at the cornerstone of the church, there was no sign of the Englishman.

He had vanished.

The parking lot stretched off for a good hundred yards, but Warwick was nowhere to be seen.

''What the—'' Lance spoke to no one in particular. ''Where the hell did he *go?*''

After a long moment, he turned and sprinted back to the front of the church.

The old man wasn't there either.

He hurried to the edge of the pavement. A large truck trundled by, closely followed by a steady stream of cars.

Numerous people hurried along the footpath. But there was no sign at all of the man who had called himself Warwick Beresford.

"*Damn* it," he said, only to himself. "What now?"

"I've never heard of any Warwick Beresford," Angie said. "And I thought I knew *all* our illustrious relatives by now."

"Well, *he* knew *me*," Lance said. Then he sighed and eased back into the soft cushions of Angie's living room couch. "And about my inheritance."

After the episode at the church, Lance had taken a cab from Parramatta to Angie's place. It had been a long, weird day, and seeing her soft smiling face waiting at the apartment door had helped to erase some of the frustration and the confusion that were tearing at him.

She didn't care where he had been, or what had happened, as long as he was with her, and safe. Still, this story about the mysterious old Englishman who claimed to be a relation . . .

"How could he know about the will?" she said, her nose wrinkling as she frowned. "It just doesn't make sense. And you say you've seen him before?"

Lance shrugged and looked uncomfortable. "Sort of. He—or something *like* him—was at the airport the day I arrived from the States."

He went on to tell her about his first encounter with Warwick. When he finished she said nothing. There was nothing she could say.

They were sitting, holding each other, when the doorbell chimed. Angie went to answer it, and returned with a letter addressed to Lance.

He really didn't care who it was from. He was too weary from everything that had happened, too filled with emotions and confusion to take on anything new. But he tore it open anyway and found a short typewritten letter on legal stationery attached to an even shorter handwritten note.

After quickly scanning both letters, Lance read the hand-written one aloud.

" 'My dear boy,' " he read, " 'I am aware of the pain and danger you have suffered since your arrival in this country. Believe me when I say that Essie Beresford herself is the cause, in ways I hesitate to explain. You are in great danger, as is your cousin Angelique. If you wish to save yourselves, you must *both* leave Australia immediately. I hope for your sake you do just that, and that before you leave you see fit to sell Beresford Hall to me. Yours very sincerely, Warwick Beresford.' "

Lance looked at the other letter. "This one is a formal offer to buy Beresford Hall."

He dropped both letters into his lap and looked over at Angie. "What do you make of it?"

Angie slowly shook her head and climbed to her feet. "I don't know, Lance. I'm just too tired. Do we have to make anything out of it tonight? Can't it wait until tomorrow?"

Lance smiled and stood up. Then he reached over, put his arms around Angie, and pulled her gently to him. "You're right," he said. "There's only so much a person can take in any given day." Then he kissed her.

She smiled as they finished the kiss, staying very close to him. "Now *that* I can take," she whispered. Then she took Lance's hand, switched off the living room light, and led him down the hall to her bedroom.

Chapter 22

Joel Thanner hurried through the solid-steel sliding doors leading from the customs hall. His medium-sized suitcase sideswiped a tall Australian who was intent on getting to a large, boisterous group hollering, "Welcome home!" Then it bounced off the restraining rail near the automatic doors and nearly jerked his arm off.

Joel barely noticed. His cobalt-blue eyes were scanning the arrival area, looking for Benny Haldane.

He peered at the long line of windows on the far wall. The currency exchange was a likely possibility; so were the car rental companies.

But Benny Haldane was nowhere to be seen.

Be cool, he told himself. He gently but firmly forced his way past the tall Australian, trying not to look too frantic about it, and hurried to the wide glass exit doors.

An instant before leaving the terminal his eyes flashed to the flower stall and the souvenir stand. Still no Benny. Then, without breaking stride, he left the Kingsford-Smith Airport and hurried out into an already hot and sunny Sydney morning.

The terminal's huge open-air parking lot sat on the other side of the wide perimeter road and stretched off in all directions. He strained to pick out the faces of departing visitors, but there were too many and they were too far away. A line of trees cut off part of the view as well. No help there.

Joel Thanner stood at the curbside and cursed the Australian customs service for at least the tenth time. This was all *their* fault.

The plane ride had been uneventful. Haldane had barely stirred from his comfy first-class seat. But he had been almost the first off the plane and by the time Thanner had caught up to him, he was already at the head of the line in customs.

Joel had tried to follow, but a burly customs agent had directed him into the longest possible line. He had tried to argue, but the agent would have none of it. He had almost pushed Joel into line behind a long-haired, bushy-bearded man just returning from Nepal.

The woman agent checking bags had taken one look at the long hair and backpack and had proceeded to go through every single item in the bearded man's baggage. She had asked questions about everything she hadn'. recognized—and she hadn't seemed to recognize much.

Joel had tried to change lines, but the burly agent at the back had called out, "Hey! No changing lines, cobber."

Joel had no idea what a "cobber" was, but the intent had been plain, and the burly agent had checked regularly to see if Joel was still in his assigned place.

He had been forced to watch helplessly as Benny Haldane breezed through customs and sauntered out the sliding doors. It had been enough to make Joel contemplate breaking all the rules and blowing away the customs agent, just for the pure satisfaction of it. But no. Not then. He had waited patiently in line, and answered all the questions very politely, and remembered that his gun was disassembled and concealed in various parts of his luggage. He definitely had *not* wanted to draw undue attention to himself.

It had taken an eternity—but he finally cleared customs. Now, standing at the side of the curb with no Benny Haldane in sight, he knew it hadn't been fast enough. Not nearly.

It's been a good ten minutes, he thought as his eyes restlessly swept over hundreds of cars, all with names he'd never heard of and styles he had never seen before. *Damn it! He could be almost anywhere!* Now he had to count on blind luck: that Haldane would check into a hotel in downtown Sydney, where he could be easily located. Otherwise, tracking him could be an impossible job, and Sammy wouldn't like that. Above all, it was important to keep Sammy happy. Very, *very* important, if one wanted to stay alive and healthy.

The tall Australian and his large group bustled by Thanner, an older woman still crying tears of joy. "It's so good to have you home, love," she said and dabbed at her eyes with a floral handkerchief. The kids in the group were all talking at once, jabbering happily as the family made its way across the road and into the parking lot.

Joel Thanner hated them. But he swallowed the anger as he always did, and hid it behind his cool executive facade. Then he hailed one of the nearby cabs and started planning his next assignment: finding Benny Haldane.

"This is a joke, right?"' Benny said, grinning. "Some kinda Australian thing, sorta like an initiation. Am I right?"

Lance looked over at Angie and shrugged. "I told you it would be hard," he said, smiling sadly.

They had met Benny at the airport and taken him straight to the hotel to check him in. Then they'd left him to relax for the afternoon. Now the three of them were having dinner in the restaurant of the Australiana Hotel, where they had already eaten their way through soup and lobster tails while they told Benny everything—*everything*—about Lance's adventures since leaving the States.

It was no use. Benny was convinced of only one thing:

that the entire story was concocted for his benefit, as some sort of game to entertain the newcomer.

"It's not a story, Benny. I wish to hell it were, I really do." Lance placed his wine glass on the white tablecloth and nervously ran his finger around its rim. "But it's the truth, buddy. And believe me, if I'd known what was going on I would never have sent for you."

"Oh, come on, Lance," Benny said. He still wasn't buying any of it. "You don't really expect me to buy any of this occult crap, do you?"

Lance was right about Benny, Angie thought as the waiter approached their table with dessert. He seemed to be a talented artist, but he was basically a simple man, with a simple view of the world. All this talk of other planes and dark forces was obviously more than he could handle.

Aloud, she said, "Ah, the crêpes suzette has arrived. Wait until you taste this, Benny. Lance and I had it here the other night. It's one of the best in town."

During dessert, Benny tried to poke holes in their story. He tried to get Angie to contradict Lance; he tried to get Lance to change his story, or at least break into guilty laughter. It didn't work. *None* of it worked. By the time they were sipping their after-dinner drinks, he was actually beginning to think that they weren't playing some game— that they actually *believed* their own incredible story.

But even as they got their coats and headed for the door of the restaurant, Benny wasn't buying it. "There has to be some *logical* explanation," he mumbled to himself, shaking his head. "There *has* to be . . ."

Benny, Lance and Angie made their way under the covered entranceway in front of the Australiana Hotel and out onto the lower end of George Street.

It was well after midnight and the street was deserted except for Angie's car, parked at the opposite curb, and a large garbage truck nearby.

The sanitation men working on the truck were emptying

large containers into the rear hopper, where the machine hissed loudly, crushed the refuse, and then scooped it into its gaping maw. The sound seemed very loud on the quiet city street.

It was obvious to Lance and Angie that Benny simply couldn't come to grips with what he'd been told—at least not yet. They had agreed on the way out to let it drop for the moment.

Benny seemed relieved by the change in scenery. "You sure can't beat the weather here, Lance," he said as they made their way across the street to Angie's car. "This late at night and it's still warm."

He had insisted on walking them to the car. Then he planned to take an evening constitutional, since he'd been assured it was a safe thing to do in Sydney. "Not like the good ol' U. S. of A. *that* way, thank God," he'd said.

Lance had smiled at his friend. "That's not the only thing you'll like around—"

He never got the rest out.

A face suddenly appeared in his mind. It was disembodied and ghostly and seemed to be coming to him from somewhere far, far away. "*Lance Beresford! Light Carrier! Beware! You are in grave danger!*"

Lance instantly remembered the face. It was the girl in the airport. The one who had tried so desperately to warn him of impending danger when his plane had landed in Fiji.

This time Lance never waited to ask questions. It was obvious, in retrospect, that this woman had been right the first time. It was obvious to Lance that she had gone to great trouble to reach him with this message of warning. He wheeled about and moved into action.

The roar of a car engine broke into the rhythmic grind of the garbage truck.

Angie and Benny looked up to see a huge Holden sedan racing from the darkness, its headlights out.

But Lance had already dived to the side and shoved Angie as hard as he could.

"What are you doing?" she cried out as she stumbled toward the curb.

Lance ignored her. Still working on automatic, he spun back and rammed into Benny Haldane. The little man fell back, sprawling onto the far sidewalk directly in front of the hotel.

The car didn't veer from its original course. It was still racing straight for Lance. But if it hadn't been for Torrika's warning, the car would almost certainly have hit all three of them. It was likely, since they were deep in conversation, that they might not have heard the approaching vehicle until it was too late.

Until that moment, everything had seemed to reel out in slow motion for Lance. He had heard the warning, and heeding it somehow he had moved into instantaneous action.

But now, with his two companions safely out of the way, he found himself standing in the center of the road as the car hurtled toward him.

And he couldn't move.

He tried desperately to run—even to jump to the side. But his legs were like lead. They just wouldn't do what he told them.

I'm not in control. Something's holding me. He knew with a terrifying certainty that some outside force had taken over his body. There was no point in fighting it; he was caught like a fly in a web.

And the sedan was still coming straight for him.

"Lance. *Look out!*" Angie shouted from the curb.

Benny struggled to sit up, shaking his head in surprise.

Lance screamed deep in his mind. He strained every muscle and fought to move, but he couldn't even blink an eye.

The sedan was barely fifteen feet away and was gaining speed.

He saw his own death in his mind's eye, as clearly and

painfully as if it had already happened. The car would hit
him dead-on. He would vault twenty or thirty feet into the
air and land squarely on the pavement half a block away.
The blood would burst from his body like air from a
broken balloon. Everywhere, blood *everywhere*—

"*Your mind, Great One,*" Torrika said, speaking into
his mind one last time. "*Direct the power of your mind.
Use it, now!*"

Something happened that made no sense at all. It would
make no more sense days later when he tried to remember
it, to explain it. Maybe it was the vision of death that
triggered it; maybe it was simple fear and desperation. Or
maybe, more likely, it was Torrika's inducement to use his
mind.

Whatever the reason, Lance found that one moment he
was trying to get his legs to move, and the next he had
shifted his attention. Suddenly he was focused on trying to
make the car *go away*.

He felt the power rise up inside him. He felt it burning
in his lungs, convulsing his throat. He took in a huge
breath, clenched his teeth, and bellowed the most extraordinary scream of his life.

"*Noooooooo!*"

And with the release of the scream, Lance released the
full force of his terror directly at the car. He actually *felt* a
bolt of mental force leap from him and slam into the
vehicle.

It lifted off the ground. It moved sideways—exactly
sideways—without the slightest turn of the wheel, as if
some huge invisible hand had reached out and slapped it
aside.

The sedan was completely airborne for a full five seconds. Then it slammed into the side of the garbage truck at
high speed, bounced even higher into the air, flipped over
as it flew and crashed down on the concrete, roof first,
with the sound of a thousand metal drums exploding.

Sparks sprayed from the collapsed steel as it scraped

along the tarmac for more than a hundred feet. Finally, agonizingly, it came to rest against the edge of a temporary wooden walkway farther up the street.

Lance was still standing in the middle of the street, frozen by astonishment now rather than some hidden external force.

Torrika's face appeared in his mind one last time. Without saying a word, she smiled, then her image slowly faded and was gone. It was probably just part of the entire crazy episode, but for an instant Lance thought he heard a choir of deep voices rejoicing in the arrival of one of their own.

Angie rushed to his side and threw her arms around him. "Lance! My God, I thought you would be killed!" She buried her head in his chest, weeping with joy and relief.

Lance swallowed hard. "So . . . so did I," he said. He let his head bow for an instant, weighed down by the realization of what had happened, what he had *done*. Then he looked over Angie's soft hair to the car smoldering in the street.

Two of the sanitation men had reached it now, and a third was looking for a telephone to call an ambulance.

Lance hugged Angie to him. He felt drained, emptied, as if most of his energy had left with the scream. Part of him wanted to leave—now, immediately, before the police arrived with their questions and reports.

But he couldn't go. Not yet. Something told him to keep looking at the sedan. Something . . .

Without knowing why, he eased Angie aside and stumbled over to the wreck.

The two men from the garbage truck had ripped open the door on the driver's side, but the driver was pinned beneath the steering wheel of the upturned vehicle, his chest crushed to half its normal thickness. Both men cursed to themselves, then ran back to their truck to find tools that would help them free the injured man.

Lance found himself alone, kneeling over the battered, blood-soaked body and staring into the face of the man who had tried to kill him.

My God, he thought. *It's Douglas. Douglas Beresford.*

His distant cousin slowly opened his eyes and saw Lance. He coughed twice, and blood seeped from between his clenched teeth. Then he drew in a deep wheezing breath and fought to speak.

The best he could do was a whispering rattle. Lance knelt close to him, straining to hear what he had to say.

"Dreams," he said. "I . . . I sent the . . . dreams." More blood seeped from his punctured lungs. He reached out with his free hand and clawed at Lance. "But not . . . enough. Wouldn't let me stop there . . . Not . . . my . . . doing."

Douglas dragged another wheezing breath into his dying lungs and fought to speak. "Something . . . took me over. Didn't want to . . . hurt you, Lance, but . . . couldn't help it. Couldn't care less . . . about . . . money . . . from . . . estate . . . myself—"

His last words were an agony for him, but he forced them out. He tried to say more—to apologize, perhaps, to ask forgiveness—but a series of coughs wracked his body. He could speak no longer.

He coughed one last time. Then a gurgling rattle came from between his lips . . . and he died.

Lance leaned over the car for a long moment, barely breathing himself. Then he heard the workmen approaching again, shouting instructions to each other. He straightened and stood looking down at Douglas. Tears burned his cheeks.

He had never had a chance to know his cousin. For years he hadn't even known he'd *had* one, but he liked the man. In the short time he'd known him, he'd *liked* Douglas.

And he believed he was telling the truth. He *hadn't* wanted this to happen—not to any of them. Someone—*something*—else had forced him to do it.

And now it was too late to change that. Too late for everyone.

Lance knew, with a inner certainty, that it had also cost Torrika her life to warn him. To save *his* life. Why she had thought it important enough to make such a sacrifice was beyond him. She had called him "Great One." Maybe she'd mixed him up with someone else. Whatever the truth, he felt he owed her a debt he could never repay.

Angie and Benny reached the car and stood beside Lance, looking down at the dead driver.

Angie recognized him and gasped. "Why, Lance?" she said, her voice trembling. "Why would Douglas try to kill you?"

Lance turned away from the car. He couldn't stand to look at the body of his dead cousin. Without thinking about what he was saying, he spoke the truth: "He didn't want to kill me," he said. "He just didn't have a choice."

Benny looked at them both, his eyes wide and white. "Come on," Lance said, his voice weary and full of resignation. "I need a drink."

Benny Haldane sat on the bed in his hotel suite and tried not to worry.

It wasn't easy. Lance had assured him the hit-and-run thing had had nothing to do with Sammy Raines, but somehow that hadn't been very reassuring.

If not Sammy, he thought, *then who?* Benny wondered about that as he loosened his shoelaces and pulled off his soft leather shoes.

He was just beginning to realize how much Lance had changed. He actually *believed* all that occult bullshit. All that black magic.

"Shit," Benny said to the empty room. He pulled off his socks and got to his feet. "I need another scotch."

A sudden, subdued sound made him stop short. He pricked his ears and listened. There it was again. A deep, humming sound. It seemed to be coming from the other room.

He walked into the lounge area of the suite . . . and found a pulsing light hanging in the air over the couch.

"What the hell . . .?" Benny said aloud.

The hum was coming from the light. And it was growing louder as the light began to expand and change shape . . .

In the blink of an eye, the light had solidified. It wasn't a light at all now. It was an old, gray-haired woman hovering in the middle of the room, looking down at Benny.

It wasn't really there at all, he knew. Hell, he could see the far wall right through it.

He tried to get his thoughts together, but fear held him tightly in its grip. He would have shouted for help, but he couldn't find his voice. All he could do was stand there and think, *It's a ghost. An honest-to-God ghost.*

The luminous apparition hung in the air, its form shifting and waving like leaves in a light summer breeze.

"*BENNY HALDANE. THIS WILL BE YOUR ONLY WARNING.*"

The lips of the specter never moved. Benny heard the words in his mind.

Then the damned thing lifted its arm and pointed at him . . . and Benny *flew*.

One second he was standing in the center of the room looking in awe at the ghost. The next second he was flying through the air. Some unseen force lifted him and hurled him back through the open bedroom door.

He crashed against the wall and slid down to the floor, his bones ringing.

When he looked up, the specter was floating in the doorway.

This can't be happening, Benny told himself. *I must have fallen asleep. I must be dreaming.*

A lamp levitated from its spot on the bedside table and hung for a second in the air. Then it shot forward, and

Benny ducked as it slammed past him, narrowly missing his forehead.

"Son of a bitch," he said stupidly, straightening up and shaking his head. A guy could get *killed* here . . .

He heard the bedclothes rustling behind him. Then he turned and stared at the bed in disbelief.

The spread was moving about under its own steam. He started to move toward it, to keep it from flinching like a living thing, and the fabric lifted from the bed and snaked out through the air. It flapped like a pair of bodiless wings, flying towards him, and suddenly it wrapped itself around Benny's neck.

"Get . . . *off!*" he mumbled, tearing at the cloth.

It was too late. It was beginning to tighten.

Benny tore at it with both hands. This was no dream, he knew. Dreams didn't hurt like this. He was fighting for his life—fighting with a goddamn *bedsheet* for his life.

He squirmed and struggled and pounded at the fabric, but he couldn't get it away from his windpipe.

His air was slowly cut off. His head began to spin.

What a way to go, Benny thought as he started to black out.

Then, just as suddenly as it had started, the pressure disappeared. The bedspread went limp in his hands, fresh air gushed into his lungs, and he dragged the whispering noose away from his throat.

He lay on the ground for a long time—eyes closed, chest heaving—simply gasping for breath.

For a long moment he was afraid to look up—afraid that the ghostly figure might still be there. Finally curiosity got the better of him.

He rolled over and looked toward the door.

And the insubstantial gray-haired woman was still there.

Benny's breath caught in his throat. Damn it all, it wasn't over. She was going to try to kill him again.

She pointed one long gray finger at a spot directly between his eyes. "*BENNY HALDANE*," she intoned.

"THIS WILL BE YOUR ONLY WARNING. TAKE YOUR TWO FRIENDS AND LEAVE AUSTRALIA . . . OR YOU WILL ALL DIE."

Again the lips didn't move. Benny heard the words inside his head.

"Who are you?" he rasped. "Why are you—?"

Benny's words echoed across the empty room. The apparition had vanished between one syllable and the next.

Benny slowly got to his feet and went to the door. There was no sign of the ghost. It was gone.

He weaved noticeably as he crossed the room to the wet bar. His hands shook as he poured himself a stiff scotch.

After two more drinks he finally went back into the bedroom. He even went so far as to change into his pajamas and climb into bed.

But he didn't sleep a wink. Not the entire night.

"What the hell's going on, Lance?" Benny sputtered. "I thought you two were flipping out with all the stuff about the occult, but now . . ."

His words trailed off as he glared first at Lance, then at Angie.

He looked terrible. His eyes were heavily bloodshot, and there were deep rings under them. His gray-green pallor made his skin look like old parchment.

The three friends were seated at the table in Angie's apartment. Benny had arrived over an hour ago, and Lance and Angie had spent the whole time trying to calm him down.

"Have another cup of coffee, Benny," Angie said gently. "You look like you need it."

"What I need is an explanation. First you two tell me some wild story about hocus-pocus. Then a car driven by one of your relatives tries to run us down. And the next thing I know I'm being attacked by a lamp and a bedspread in my hotel room. Lance, come on. *Please.* What in God's name is all this about?"

"I wish I could tell you, Benny." Lance lifted his cup

of coffee to his lips and sipped lightly at it. "But I'm damned if I know. We told you everything in the restaurant last night. It's all been happening so fast, Angie and I are just as much in the dark as you."

Benny sighed heavily and sat staring at his old partner. Then he slowly got to his feet. "I need to use the head," he told them, his voice heavy with fatigue. "Where is it?"

Lance pointed to the hall. "First door on the left."

When Benny had left, Lance sighed himself. "He looks terrible," he said to Angie. "Between jet lag and no sleep, he's out on his feet."

But when Benny's voice hollered from the hallway it sounded wide awake.

"*Lance*. Come here . . . *quick!*"

Angie and Lance were on their feet and into the hall before the echo of Benny's cry had finished ringing through the apartment.

Benny was standing, staring at a framed picture that hung on the wall in the hallway. His mouth was open wide; one shaking finger was pointed at the image in front of him.

"Who the hell is *that?*"

"That was my grandmother, Essie Beresford," Angie said, puzzled by his consternation. "Why?"

"Your— your grandma? Really?" the counterfeiter stuttered, still pointing at the photograph of the elderly gray-haired woman. "Well, that's the old broad who visited me last night."

"Are you sure, Benny?" Lance quickly said.

"Are you *kidding?*" Benny snapped. "I'm telling y' Lance, the last time I saw that puss, it was floating in my bedroom . . . and I could see right *through* it."

Chapter 23

Angie and Lance sat across the table from each other, both quietly sipping their morning coffee. This was usually a time for conversation, but this morning neither of them felt much like talking.

Angie was feeling particularly uncertain on this bright, clear Sydney morning. She was wondering, against her will, exactly where she and Lance stood.

Too many bizarre things had happened over the last few days—the last few *hours*. She hadn't been able to tell friend from foe, truth from lies, fantasy from reality. But one thing hadn't changed. One central fact had served as an anchor for her in all the madness. She had been sure, absolutely *sure*, that Essie Beresford was a good woman. And now, if Benny Haldane's story was true, even *that* was called into question. Angie didn't know if she could take that particular truth. She was afraid it might be the final straw—the one fact that could break her open completely.

Angie had always been Essie's favorite. But even taking that into consideration, Grandmother Essie had been something more. She was a woman who felt . . . *right*. Her smiles were genuine. Her touch was warm and reassuring. Her words always held truth.

Damn it, it was simple. Angie *believed* in Essie Beresford. But now . . .

They had finally quieted Benny down enough to get some sleep, but he had refused to go back to the hotel. That had been fine with them; Angie had just made up the bed in the spare room.

Benny had stretched out on the mattress in there, just to please them. ''I can't sleep, though,'' he had stated firmly. ''Not after all that's happened.''

In ten minutes he had been sleeping like a babe.

That had been almost twenty-four hours ago, and except for a few short trips to the bathroom, he had been asleep ever since.

''Lance,'' Angie said. Her voice was thick with weariness and confusion. ''What do we do now?''

''I don't know,'' he answered, sighing. Then he took another sip of coffee.

That's not exactly true, he thought even as he was still saying the words. *I know one thing. I don't want that damned house. In fact, I don't want anything to do with any of this bullshit.*

He looked over at Angie and knew that even *that* wasn't exactly true. Not anymore. He was confused, he knew, but he couldn't push away what he felt for this woman. He understood the risk; he knew she might be an integral part of the evil things that were happening around them—and he knew that refusing the house might mean losing her. After all, if he passed up the inheritance, it would all go to her. She was next in line. Maybe that was all she wanted.

Lance shook that thought from his head. He couldn't believe it. He *wouldn't* believe it. *No*, he thought. *I love her. And she loves me. That's the only sane thing in this whole mess.*

He reached over and put his hand on hers, and Angie smiled for the first time that morning.

Lance was thinking how much better he suddenly felt just because of that smile when the phone rang and Angie hurried to answer it before it woke Benny.

It was Monica Sheerlow.

Angie listened silently for a few minutes. Then she mumbled into the receiver, "I'll call you back in a few minutes, Monica," and hung up.

"What is it?" Lance said. He couldn't help noticing the concern on Angie's face.

"It's Jessica." Angie walked over and sat opposite Lance again. "Monica says she's been having more seizures."

"I'm sorry to hear that," Lance said. Then he thought about it for a second and frowned. "How come she called you?"

"She was actually looking for you. It appears Jessica had a bad seizure two nights ago. *Very late.*" She gave him a significant look. "In the middle of the fit, she screamed out your name. Monica said it was as if she were trying to warn you that you were in danger."

"Two nights ago, about the time we were leaving the Australiana Hotel?"

Angie nodded her head. "Right. And it appears this wasn't the first time Jessica has shouted your name. She's been doing it a lot since you got to Australia."

"You're joking." Lance didn't want to believe any of this. He didn't want to get any further involved. No more mystery, he pleaded. Answers instead. Please, God, put an end to it all.

"Afraid not." Angie sadly shook her head.

So, it isn't over yet, Lance thought. *Even if I want to forget the inheritance and get the hell out of here, I'm still going to have to go see Jessica. After all, she's an innocent bystander, and somehow I've dragged her into this thing, too. I'm damned if I know what I can do, but I have to try to help.*

"Damn it," he said, trying to rub the sleep from his eyes and failing. "I guess you better call Monica back, and tell her I'm on my way."

"Would you like me to come with you?"

He smiled and squeezed her hand. "I know you're tired, my love," he said. "Just as tired as I am. But I'd really appreciate it if you would."

He got to his feet and walked around the table. She pushed back her chair and stood. As if acting on an unheard signal, they reached out and held each other close.

Angie's car made its way down the wide northern expressway leading to the Sydney Harbor Bridge.

From this spot on the expressway the view of Sydney, across the harbor, was extraordinary. But Lance wasn't in the mood for sightseeing. His eyes turned left, to sweep the harbor front along the northern shore. There was a zoo tucked away in the tree-covered area just over the farthest hill he could see. Taronga Park, Angie had called it.

They had laughed about the name, and she had promised to spend the day there very soon. But that had been before both their worlds had been thrown into turmoil.

Could it really have been only a week or two ago? Lance thought as his eyes vacantly scanned the beauty, barely seeing it. *God, it feels like years.*

"A penny for your thoughts," Angie said, flashing a brief smile at him.

Lance went to tell her what he was thinking about, but he stopped himself. It was too beautiful a day, and there had been too much serious business already. He felt like being stupid, being *normal*, if only for a few seconds.

"What the hell good's a penny, these days?" he said and laughed.

"When I was a little girl we still used pennies," Angie said, smiling with the memory. "Brenda Philips and Nancy Medhurst and I used to go to the Tuck Shop with a few coppers and buy all sorts of lollies."

Angie's eyes lit up as she reminisced, and Lance felt a warmth begin to flow over him as the car crossed the bridge and made its way around onto the overhead Cahill Expressway. The view of Circular Quay and the city of

Sydney was breathtaking, but Lance barely noticed it. He was too busy looking at Angie.

"Sometimes we could even afford to buy a Hoadley's Crumble Bar, or a Polly Waffle. We'd eat a few of the lollies and save the rest. Then, after school, we would buy sixpence worth of chips wrapped in newspaper and a half a loaf of Promax and go down to Duck Creek. We'd pull the center out of the bread and fill it with hot chips, then we'd tear it into three pieces and all sit and eat it and watch the dumb boys in the creek lifting old cans from the bottom, looking for crayfish. The lollies were for dessert."

"Whoa," Lance said. He couldn't stop the warmth he felt from spreading across his face. "You lost me completely. What's a copper? What's a lollie? And what's a . . . Tuck shop?" He was enjoying this—just being himself. "And I never heard of a Promax, or a Hoadley's . . . aah, whatever you said." He was laughing so much now it was hard to keep talking. "And why would anybody wrap chips in newspaper? They usually come in foil bags."

"Not crisps," Angie laughed back, getting into the silly mood herself. "Chips. They're sort'a like what you call french fries, only fatter and a lot greasier."

"They sound disgusting."

"Don't knock it 'til ya tried it, ocka," Angie said, slipping back into her heavy Australian slang.

"I'm sure I'll regret this. But how does one go about trying it?"

"Well, mate. There ain't nowhere left to get the dinky-di. But I suppose we could try one of the fish-and-chips places along the way. May even find a chew-and-spew that remembers the good old days."

The two lovers were still laughing as they went up William Street, through Kings Cross, and headed toward Bondi Junction. It was a healing thing, even though they both knew it was a little forced. That didn't matter; it didn't make the release any less therapeutic. Laughter, Lance realized, was just *laughter*. It was always good for what ailed you.

By the time they reached Oxford Street, the laughter had eased. But the light mood remained.

Angie turned off the main road and scoured the shops on the side streets. She finally spotted a likely-looking old fish-and-chips shop and parked the car.

Lance had never been in a fish-and-chips shop before. He looked for all the world like a nine-year-old on his first trip to Disneyland.

The shop's entire front window was a glass-covered freezer. In it, at least a dozen different types of fish were stretched out, some still in their skins and others already skinned, cleaned and filleted. There was also a huge array of cooked prawns—most Americans called them shrimp— and lobster and crab.

Inside the spotlessly clean store, the front section of the counter held another glass freezer filled with more fish. Some of it had been covered in batter and deep fried.

The back section of the shop was taken up by two oil-filled cookers. Mounds of uncooked french fries—chips, Angie called them—were piled alongside them.

Angie approached the gray-haired old man behind the counter. "Two fish-and-chips, please," she said.

Both this sun-wrinkled old man and the elderly woman who worked with him were of obvious Italian descent. But when the old man spoke, his accent was a strange mixture of their native tongue and the Australian that Lance was beginning to take for the norm.

"You won'ta vinegar on that, love?"

"Too right," Angie snapped back. "And lots of salt. Oh, and do you think you could wrap it in newspaper?"

"We don't do that anymore," the old man said, but he smiled at the request.

Angie nodded her head toward Lance. "My friend's from America. I was telling him about the good old days. I think he thought I was crazy."

"Ah, America," the old man said and motioned in the air with his hands. "My cousin, Guiseppe, went to America. New York City."

"There're a lot of Italians in New York," Lance said, and the old man smiled.

Then he turned to his wife. "Momma, get some newspaper from the back."

The woman left, and the old man turned and scooped a heap of chips into a deep vat of hot oil. As the oil erupted, he grabbed two pieces of battered fish—Lance found out later they were shark—and dropped them into the oil as well.

When the chips and fish were cooked, the old Italian lifted them from the oil with a strainer and dumped them onto a metal tray. Then he shook copious amounts of salt over them from a giant shaker, squirted vinegar onto them from a plastic bottle, and wrapped them in white paper.

"I 'ave to put them in white paper first," he said and smiled as he turned to Angie and Lance. "It's a health regulation now." Then he took the newspaper his wife had brought him from the rear of the shop and wrapped the two packages in some of its pages.

"Two fish-and-chips, just'a like the old days," he smiled and handed the food to Angie.

Angie took it and offered a warm good-bye. Then, laughing, she took Lance's arm and guided him to the door.

"What?" he said. "No Hoadley's? Lollies?"

"Oh, be quiet," she said. "Let's just go sit in the park and eat."

"This is something else." Lance was staring at the scene in front of them as Angie drove the car down the hill on Campbell Parade.

Bondi Beach Park stretched out green and inviting to their right. Beyond it lay the beach, its golden sand glistening in the sun.

It wasn't the biggest beach in the Sydney area, Lance knew. There were some on the northern shore and others farther south that made this one seem small. But this was one of the best known, and maybe one of the prettiest.

Earlier he and Angie had driven into Centennial Park—an immense park near Bondi Junction—and had lounged along the shore of one of its lakes. By the time Angie had found the "right spot," the smell of the fish-and-chips had totally filled the car. And there was another smell that he couldn't quite put his finger on.

"It's the newspaper," Angie had said. "I told you, it gives the chips a special flavor."

Much as he'd hated to admit it, Angie had been right. The chips did taste different. Lance wasn't really sure if it was the newspaper or the vinegar, but he had been so hungry he'd wolfed down both the chips and the piece of fish.

Now they were back on the road again, and the grim reality of their trip was beginning to set in.

Angie nodded her head at a spit of land that jutted off to the right at the end of the beach. "Monica and Jessica live on that far point," she said. "In North Bondi."

"It looks like a nice place to live." Lance ran his tongue over the edge of his lips for at least the tenth time. They seemed to be lightly swollen, and he felt very thirsty. "I hope Monica has something cold and wet. My mouth feels parched, and my lips feel strange."

"It's the salt and vinegar." Angie deftly guided the Holden past a parked vehicle whose owner swung the door open without looking behind him. "*Idiot*," Angie shouted out the window. "A swig of soft drink will fix it," she told Lance.

Lance could feel the light mood was already beginning to fade. A few minutes later, when the car eased to a halt in front of a large old house on a street that ran off Military Road, they were both stone-faced.

Chapter 24

Monica Sheerlow smiled when she saw Angie and Lance waiting on the front step.

"I'm so glad you could come."

She stepped back and motioned them into the wood and brick house. Then she closed the front door, eased past them both and headed off down the hall. "Jessica is through here."

Lance and Angie followed Monica down the hall. As they went, Lance noticed the interior. The house had seemed old but well maintained from the outside, and the same was true within. But something about it bothered him. Even though everything was spic and span, there was a musty feeling. *It's understandable*, he thought as they moved silently down the hall. *Probably has a lot to do with all the wood panels and frames in here, and the salt water from the ocean.* Still, he couldn't shake off the oppressiveness he felt pushing down on him.

"Do you have a soft drink, Monica?" Angie asked. Lance squeezed her hand and sighed with relief. "We're both pretty dehydrated, but we didn't want to be any longer than we had to."

"Of course," Monica said. She veered to her right and led them through an archway into the kitchen.

Lance sat at the kitchen table and watched Monica open a large bottle of soda and pour two glasses. He couldn't help noticing how much she seemed to be *smiling* at them. At their first meeting she had been curt. The few words she had said to them were abrupt and far from friendly. But now she was treating them like old friends.

It didn't matter. He still got the same unpleasant sensation running up the back of his spine that he'd had whenever he'd looked at Robert Beresford. No. This was definitely *not* a comfortable place to be.

He was still feeling that way as he finished his drink, and Monica got to her feet.

"Jessica's in her nursery— aahh, room. Would you like to see her now?"

Lance nodded, and he and Angie followed Monica back out into the hall.

Jessica Beresford's room was spacious and clean and filled with beautiful pieces of very expensive furniture. The dressing table, the headboard of the huge bed, and even the silver-backed brush and comb set that rested on the bedside table were all fine antiques. The drapes were exquisite, and the wallpaper was in an old Tudor motif. There was even a huge floor-to-ceiling Renaissance statue of a man standing against the far wall.

But even with all its finery, this was still the room of a small girl.

Four dolls sat against one wall, each in its own tiny chair. Stuffed animals and cuddly toys were scattered everywhere with childish abandon.

Jessica was cradling an animal in her arms as they entered—a soft gray rabbit with huge floppy ears and a carrot in its paw. She sat on the edge of the bed, dressed in a pretty frock, hugging the rabbit and staring blankly off into space.

Lance was shocked by the striking beauty of this woman-child, just as he had been at their first meeting. *Under different circumstances*, he thought, *she would have pho-*

tographers clamoring to get her on film. But now . . . this way . . . He walked to the bed and stood looking down at his distant cousin, feeling sad and a little angry. *It's not fair*, he thought. *It's just not fair*.

"Jessica," he finally said as gently as he could. "It's Lance. Your cousin. I want to talk to you about—"

There was a loud thunk behind him, and Lance stopped in mid-sentence. There was something about the sound that sent a chill racing through him.

He turned to see Angie sprawled on the floor, blood seeping from a nasty gash on her forehead.

Monica was standing over her, her face twisted with hatred, her eyes blazing with an unnatural fire.

She held a long knife in her hand. Light glinted off its long, vicious blade. It was already red with Angie's blood.

Lance could only stare at her, stunned beyond action.

"W—what have you done?" he stuttered.

"She is not dead," Monica hissed in a strange, clipped English accent. "Not yet. She has something special waiting for her. She will know the joy of *real* pain before she breathes her last."

Lance knew the truth instantly. *It's not Monica speaking*, he thought. *The voice sounds like . . . like . . .* He tried to remember where he'd heard that accent, but Monica cut into his thoughts.

"But *you*. *You* must die, *now!*"

"What—"

Monica lunged at him, the knife aimed at his head. The whole affair had been too abrupt, too absurd—his reaction was painfully slow. Only base reflex made him flinch away from her blade; only her own clumsiness kept her from burying the hilt in his chest.

She fell to the carpet, rolled, and scrambled to her feet, panting fast and shallow like a small, panicked animal. In an instant she turned to him again, knife high, ready to lunge.

He was prepared this time. He moved into her path and

threw up his hands, seizing her wrists in his strong fingers. Pushing her back, he pinned her to the wall.

"Stop it," he grated. "Stop it before—"

Monica pulled her tiny hands from his tight grip with unbelievable ease, the knife still gripped in her fist. She slashed at him again, again straight at his face. Lance had to rear back and stumble to avoid the flashing blade.

Monica moved forward. Spittle dripped from her smile.

Damn it, Lance thought. *I don't want to hurt her—I'm sure it's not her fault. But she's too dangerous. I can't let her keep on like this.*

He hunched over and backed away from her, his eyes never leaving hers. As she tensed to leap at him once more, he stepped aside, moved in close, and bunched the fist of his right hand as tightly as he could. Then he let fly and his knuckles connected with her delicate jaw, making a dismayingly loud pop as they hit.

He didn't like it. Not one damn bit. The thought of hitting a woman bothered him more than he had thought it would—especially since the woman was trying to kill him—but the vivid image of being ripped open by the butcher's blade she wielded helped him overcome that feeling.

Monica shrugged off the hit and blinked hard. Then she straightened up . . . and hissed . . . and came at him again.

Lance had done some boxing in college; he knew his own strength. That blow would have dropped a man twice Monica's size. If anything, it had been a bit *too* hard; panic and desperation had kept him from pulling his punch.

But it had had no effect, she was coming at him again.

After being momentarily immobilized by outright astonishment, Lance shook himself from inactivity and threw himself from her path, sprawling out on the floor. Monica followed and the knife arced down and slammed into the wood only inches from where he had landed. The force of her thrust drove it a good three or four inches into the varnished pine.

Monica squealed and dragged on the hilt of the knife, frantically trying to get it loose.

Lance knew he had to do something . . . quickly. He rolled across the floor and drove a kick at her hand as she tugged at the knife.

Monica whimpered in pain, but refused to loosen her grip on the knife. Instead she braced her feet against the floorboards, let out a grunt, and pulled on the weapon with superhuman strength.

The knife popped from the wood with a sudden smacking sound, and without a moment's hesitation, Monica turned and hurled herself at Lance one final time.

He curled his knees to his chest the instant before Monica's weight dropped on top of him, and he tried immediately to kick her off, force her away. But she was possessed by a madness that gave her an impossible strength. She held his right hand with her left, to keep him from tearing at her, and tried to slash viciously at him with the glittering blade in her right.

It took all the strength Lance could muster just to keep her from driving the blade directly into his brain.

For a moment, the couple were frozen in battle, balanced as Lance had been in his struggle with the dream-leopard. And in that instant, Lance . . . *smelled* something. It was the same sickly sweet odor he had smelled before.

He shifted his attention from the grip on his assailant to her eyes—her deep, black, sparkling eyes . . .

Oblivion threatened to wash him away. He gasped, head suddenly spinning, and forced himself to pull his eyes from hers.

It's here, Lance knew in the flash of an instant. *The purple force that drove Robert. It's here again. It's taken over Monica and it's driving her to kill me.*

And worse, as with the leopard, he knew he couldn't contain Monica's inhuman strength indefinitely. Sooner or later he would slip or not be able to hold off her attack, and she would succeed in her efforts to plunge the knife into him.

Driven by desperation, he took a deep, ragged breath and coiled himself into a tight ball. Then, with every ounce of strength he had left, he kicked at Monica's chest with both feet.

The move caught her off guard. She vaulted back, suddenly standing again, and staggered into the doorway to stand near Angie's prone body.

One scrambling hand shot out to steady herself as she was forced to sidestep the motionless woman. "You'll never have it," she hissed. "*You'll never have it!*"

Monica threw herself forward . . .

But suddenly Angie moved. She had been stunned—maybe she'd even blacked out—but that had only been for a few seconds. For the last few minutes, she had watched the fight through slitted eyes, waiting for the right moment.

This was it.

Monica rushed forward, the knife poised to strike out at Lance.

Angie's hand flashed out and grabbed the crazed woman's ankle.

Monica screamed and stumbled forward, drawing her hands inward to cushion her fall.

The knife blade turned in her hand. She tried in vain to turn it away, to hold it back as she rushed toward collision with the floor, but . . .

Lance saw it happening. He shouted *"No!"* and lunged forward . . .

Too late.

Monica hit the ground with tremendous force, and the blade bit deeply into her stomach. Her body convulsed once as blood spurted from the gash. The movement only made the blade thrust deeper.

She let out a soft, surprised moan and grabbed the knife

with both hands. But her grip lost strength almost immediately. Her hands fluttered, then flopped to her side.

For an instant she looked up at Lance, her eyes filled with confusion and hate and a great deal of fear. Then she let out a huge sigh and lay very still.

"Lance!" Angie cried out and staggered to her feet. "Lance, are you all right?"

"Yes, I'm fine," he grated and got to his feet.

Angie looked down at Monica's motionless body. Blood oozed from around the hilt of the knife and formed a puddle on the polished wooden floor. "What's going on?" she said, her breathing labored. "Why would Monica attack us?"

Lance slipped his arm around Angie, and she buried her head into his shoulder. He was panting so heavily he couldn't talk.

"Poor Monica," Angie sobbed, burying her head even harder into his shoulder.

Her body suddenly stiffened in his arms. Then she pushed away from him and turned toward the bed. "Oh, my God, Lance. Jessica's been watching all this."

They both turned to look at the woman-child seated on the edge of the bed, still clutching the cuddly rabbit tightly in her arms.

Jessica stared dumbly back at them, her eyes still vacant.

"Maybe her condition is a blessing just this once," Lance said and rubbed at his eyes with his hand. "She probably doesn't even know what's happened."

Then Jessica moaned and the stuffed toy dropped to the floor.

Perhaps it was the only way she could express the grief and terror locked inside her; whatever the reason, suddenly her mouth opened wide, her hands came up in trembling fists, and she let out a long, hopeless, half-animal moan.

Lance hurried to her and knelt at her side. He told her it was all right, that everything would be fine . . . but she moaned even louder. The sound rose in both pitch and intensity. It transformed itself, twisting into a ululating scream that steadily grew to fill the room.

"Jessica, stop it," Lance said. The scream was beginning to hurt.

Angie covered her ears with both hands, but that didn't really help. Somehow Jessica's scream seemed to permeate every inch of her body. Her eardrums felt like they would split under the assault.

"Jessica," Lance shouted through the din. "*Stop it. You're hurting us.*"

He grabbed the idiot savant and shook her.

An invisible force seized him, lifted him into the air, and hurled him roughly against the nearby wall. For a moment he simply couldn't believe it—couldn't *comprehend* it—and his shout to Jessica caught in his throat.

The scream rose to a deafening *shriek*.

Angie reeled about, hands clamped tightly over her ears.

Lance pushed himself from the wall. He stretched, checking to see nothing was broken, then stumbled back toward Jessica.

The 500-pound Renaissance statue creaked loudly and shuddered . . . then, without visible means, wrenched away from its spot by the wall and hovered in the air a few inches above the floor.

Lance didn't hear it or see it. All he could hear was the shriek that now seemed to come from every direction. And the pain in his head from Jessica's screaming made his eyes water so badly that he was effectively blind.

Angie had gotten her back to the wall near the door. After two tries, she succeeded in opening her eyes . . . and wished she hadn't.

"*Lance, look out!*"

He turned to see the huge statue rushing toward him and had only an instant to drop to the floor and cover his head.

The statue slid over him with barely inches to spare and crashed straight through the wall behind him. The room behind the wall was instantly a shambles as the huge slab of marble kept right on going. It was still moving when he stopped looking and turned his attention back to Jessica.

And then Lance saw it.

Jessica was bathed in a purple glow. The presence that had already killed three other Beresfords was hovering around *her* now. It was somehow fueling her, *feeding* her as her scream rose even higher and higher.

It's using her savant power of concentration, Lance thought as his mind reeled. *I've got to reach her, I've got to get her away from this . . . thing.*

Lance staggered forward, his eyes watering. His hand stretched out to feel for Jessica.

The idiot savant raised a hand, palm up, and directed it toward Lance.

A bolt of pure energy leapt from her open palm and struck him square in the chest.

The world exploded around him in a blazing flash of purple, and he fell to the floor, writhing with convulsions.

Jessica's eyes had the same blank expression they'd had when Lance and Angie had arrived, but her hand kept pointing at Lance. Purple fire gushed from it, showering pain over him.

Lance began to scream, a scream so high and loud that Angie could hear it over the bedlam.

In an instant, she knew what to do. Never uncovering her ears—though never sure if it was helping in the first place—she staggered over to the bed and fell at Jessica's feet.

The sound was even worse here—more penetrating than ever. She forced herself forward, dragging herself up, using Jessica's legs.

Jessica didn't seem to notice Angie at all. Her eyes were locked in a blank stare. Her hand, still streaming purple energy, continued to point at Lance.

Angie screamed at Jessica and dragged her to her feet, but the screaming thundered on, the energy raged from her fingertips.

Lance writhed on the floor. His mouth hung open. His tongue darted out in thick convulsive thrusts, and froth formed at the edge of his teeth.

Angie slapped Jessica across the face.

Every window in the room imploded, spraying shards of glass throughout the room like miniature bullets.

The shrieking kept on, without pause.

Angie slapped Jessica again, as hard as she could.

The walls of the room begun to quiver, then shake. Dust rose from the cracks between the floorboards, and slivers of wood peeled away, hurling upward. Plaster dropped from the ceiling and dusted everything in the room like a snowfall.

A deep, guttural roar joined the shriek, and the walls started to bow wildly—first inward, then outward. Angie knew that only seconds remained before the entire room collapsed and buried them under tons of rubble.

She shouted at Jessica again. But when this had no appreciable effect, Angie gathered all her strength and smashed her cousin squarely on the jaw with her closed fist.

For an instant Jessica looked at Angie . . . *looked* at her with eyes that seemed to understand, that seemed to show true intelligence. Then she slumped backward on the bed, knocked unconscious by Angie's blow.

All sound in the room suddenly stopped with a snap like breaking bone.

The walls stopped shaking.

The snowfall of plaster subsided. Dust trickled and blossomed for a few more seconds, then stopped.

Lance's shoulders and knees flexed one final time . . . then his entire body relaxed. For a moment he lay perfectly still, perfectly poised.

Angie hurried to his side, terrified that he might be seriously injured, or *worse*. "*Lance*, are you all right?"

Then he moaned and shifted his aching shoulders. A moment later he was struggling to sit up.

But he didn't answer immediately. He swallowed hard, and the first sound that came from him was a painful little croak that was supposed to be a laugh.

"You seem to be asking me that a lot these days."

Angie wanted him to stay where he was, but Lance needed to get to his feet—if only to prove he could.

The scene swayed a little, but he stayed up. He leaned heavily against one wall and let his eyes slowly take in the room—or what was left of it.

"Jesus. Look at this place."

Then he saw Jessica stretched out on the bed. "What did you do to her?"

"I—hit her," Angie said, suddenly shy. "Really hard. I didn't mean to hurt her, but I didn't know what else to do."

"You did fine." Lance staggered forward a step, and Angie helped him over to the bed.

He dropped onto the bedspread and looked at Jessica, then searched for a pulse with a hand that was still shaking from the pain.

"She's still alive. But her pulse is very weak."

Angie's hand was steadier, and she checked Jessica's pale white wrist for a pulse, too. "I can hardly feel it. We better get her to a hospital."

"Are you up to it?" Lance asked, and Angie couldn't keep from smiling. He didn't look much better than Jessica did. His face was a mess of deep-red blotches, his eyes were ringed in heavy red lines, and his hands shook uncontrollably . . . and *he* was asking *her* if she could handle a trip to the hospital.

"If we do it together, and quickly, I think I am," she said, and helped Lance to his feet. "But we'd better not take too long, or I can't make any guarantees for either of us."

It took five minutes to get Lance to the car and get him settled in the front passenger seat. The attack had put an incredible strain on his system, but he seemed to have survived it and for that Angie was grateful. Still, he wasn't able to move, and it was Angie who had to go back for Jessica.

She lifted the unconscious woman with surprisingly little effort, and marveled at the effects of adrenalin on the system. "It's a darned good thing you're so fragile, my girl," she muttered to her unconscious cousin as she carried her down the driveway. "If you were any heavier, I think we'd both be in trouble."

She stretched Jessica out in the back seat, then climbed in behind the wheel and started the engine.

Lance was half-collapsed in the passenger seat, his breathing shallow.

"Lance," she said slowly, and put a hand on his shoulder. "Are you all right?"

He didn't stir.

She told herself not to panic. He was all right—he just *had* to be. "*Lance*," she said more firmly. "Can you hear me?"

He still didn't move. If anything, his breathing became even more shallow.

"Oh, my God," she said, only to herself. "Oh, my *God . . .*"

She screeched out of the driveway and sped toward the hospital at top speed, praying all the while that her cousins, *both* her cousins, would still be alive when she got there.

Lance opened his eyes very slowly. It was hard work—as hard as anything he'd ever tried to do before—and he had to blink to get them in focus.

He couldn't remember where he was, or what had happened to him. It seemed an interminable time before he could feel the rest of his body.

Finally it all came to him. He was stretched out on his back. His fingers could feel clean sheets. His head was on a soft pillow that smelled slightly medicinal.

So he was in a bed. Maybe even . . . a hospital?

Then he saw Angie. She was hovering over the bed, her face locked in a worried frown. There was a fresh bandage wound around her forehead, and one hand showed an angry red scrape across the knuckles.

It all came back to him in a single, cold rush, as if a dam had broken: Monica tried to kill them. Jessica had screamed . . . and *screamed* . . .

"*Jessica*," Lance shouted, and he sat bolt upright.

Angie put both hands on his shoulders and eased him back down onto the bed. "She's fine, Lance. She's being well looked after."

"Where are we?" Lance tried to move his head to see the room, but he had tried too much already. Everything was starting to spin, and there was nothing he seemed to be able to do to make it slow down.

"Take it easy, Lance. The doctor says you have to stay still for another few hours, at least." Angie tucked in the edge of the sheet and sat on a chair by the bed. "We're at the Prince of Wales Hospital."

"Are you okay?"

"My noggin feels like a rugga team has been using it for practice," Angie said, trying to make light of the situation. "But they only had to put a couple a' stitches in it, and the doc assures me nothing important spilled out."

Lance couldn't help smiling. It was the same every time she did that broad Australia accent. "I hesitate to ask, but what's a . . . rugga . . . team?"

"Rugby," Angie said as if that should be all the answer he would need. When Lance still stared blankly at her, she added. "Rugby football. You know."

"You mean that game we saw on television the other night?" Lance was happy to play along with Angie's bedside therapy; it saved his thinking of other things.

"Right, cobber. That's the one."

Even Angie couldn't keep a straight face this time. She broke into a wide smile and giggled like a girl.

But only for a moment. Then her laughter faded and a more serious look returned, almost of its own accord.

"Are you really all right?" Lance asked quietly.

"Yes, I'm fine."

"Jessica?"

"They have her heavily sedated. I couldn't tell them what really happened, they'd have put me in a padded cell. But I told them she had a violent seizure . . ." Angie looked down at the floor and almost whispered. "And that in the confusion . . . she . . ."

Her words trailed off, and she sat staring down at the floor.

"Monica?" Lance knew the answer before Angie answered, but he had to ask.

"Dead," Angie said, and she fought to hold back the tears. "The doctor said she must have died almost instantly."

"*Shit!*" Lance spat it out, then leaned heavily against his pillows and tried to run his fingers through his hair.

A bandage got in the way.

How many more people have to die because of this idiotic inheritance? he thought, raging. He wasn't sure how these senseless killings were tied in with Essie's estate, but he knew they were—somehow.

He thought briefly of all the casualties so far. *I can't feel any sorrow for Robert,* he decided. *He joined in willingly. He enjoyed it. But Douglas seemed like a nice guy. Monica? She put up a tough front, but it was only because she cared so much for Jessica. And Jessica . . . Jessica is a child.*

It wasn't any of them that did it. They were just puppets, just means to an end. It was the purple energy.

Lance had felt it behind Robert, and again when his mind had screamed out at Douglas. In this last mess, the purple . . . *thing* . . . whatever it was, had been so strong it had driven Monica to homicide, and when that didn't work, it had played with poor, defenseless Jessie, somehow concentrating her incredible savant power into a force that could lift a huge marble statue and drive it through a solid wall.

Suddenly Lance's thoughts flew back to Santa Barbara. *Was this what you were trying to warn me about, Mum?* A tear formed under his closed eyelid. *I'm sorry, love. I didn't understand. How could I? How could anyone? No wonder you were so frightened for me.*

It was as if his mind had cut loose from him; it drifted from recollection to recollection without choice. Now he was spiraling down to the present—to Australia, and all that had happened since his arrival.

It was simply too ridiculous to believe. Bizarre. Absurd. It was like watching an old, very bad horror movie.

But it had happened. It had all *happened*.

He kept his eyes closed and let his thoughts drift. Two questions kept presenting themselves for answers, and he had none. One had been niggling at the edge of his mind for days. The other was a new one.

"Where the hell did Robert get all his money?" he said abruptly, and opened his eyes.

"You know, that's a darn good question," Angie said. She sounded as if she had been wondering the same thing herself. "In all the confusion I'd forgotten, but Grandmother Beresford cut him off without a penny about four years ago. He was livid. For months he kept crying about how poor he was."

"Then where did he get the money to build that castle?"

"I don't know, Lance."

"Ummm." Lance had an idea where the wealth may have come from, but he kept it to himself. Instead, he asked his second question—but this time his voice was more gentle. "What about Jessica's parents?"

"Her mother died during labor," Angie said, then she hesitated. "Her father died . . . a couple of years ago." She sighed. "It was all pretty messy. Douglas's father died two months before that. My father was killed when I was a little girl."

She looked down at Lance, trying to hold back the fear she was suddenly feeling.

"You're the only male Beresford left."

"Don't forget Warwick." Lance rubbed at his chin with his hand, then shrugged. "Unless he was a hallucination."

Angie started to speak, then seemed to change her mind. The two of them were quiet for a long time.

It was Lance who finally broke the silence.

"You take it," he said. "Take the whole damn thing. I don't want it anymore."

"What?" Angie had been drifting; she didn't understand what he was talking about.

"The house. Beresford Hall. The entire estate. You have it."

"*Me?*" Angie was appalled. "I *never* wanted it!"

"Fine," Lance said. "Then let the lawyers decide who it belongs to."

Angie leaned over and hugged him. "Lance, I'm so glad. I've been so frightened for you. So afraid I'd lose you."

Lance held her close. Her perfume filled his senses, and he felt a huge weight lifting from him.

"I'm sorry, my love," he whispered into her golden hair. "You *are* going to lose me for a little bit."

"Why?" Angie pulled herself from his arms and sat up on the side of the bed.

"Benny and I have to go back to the States and get some . . . *things* straightened out."

It's funny, he thought. *Only a couple of weeks ago, the idea of facing up to Sammy Raines terrified me. Now, after all that's happened, it almost seems safe.*

"Take me with you, Lance."

"I can't do that. It could be dangerous. But don't worry, it won't take long. You can meet us in Europe a week after we leave. Two weeks, tops."

He wasn't being entirely truthful, but he knew it was best. Why frighten her? The fact was he didn't know what he and Benny were going to do in the States. He just knew he had to try to clear things with Raines.

At worst, he thought, *we can wrap up everything and go to Europe the way we'd planned in the first place.*

"Whatever it is, I'm sure I can help you, Lance," Angie said, beginning to sound stubborn. "Besides, I don't want to let you out of my sight—not now, not so soon after we've found each other."

"You won't lose me, Angie."

She tried to argue with him, but he could be stubborn himself. They finally agreed that she would fly to Europe and meet him as soon as he was free—but he had to go back home on his own, just he and Benny Haldane.

When she finally, grudgingly, accepted the terms, Lance breathed a long sigh and laid his head back on the pillow. Angie pouted for all of five seconds, then snuggled into his chest.

It's like I've known her forever, he thought, and that special warmth spread through him again. He felt it whenever she was close, and he loved it. He loved *her*.

After a few minutes, Angie's voice penetrated his reverie.

"It's a pretty rotten way to start a birthday, mate," she mumbled. "But we'll make it a good one yet."

Jesus, Lance thought. *In all the confusion I'd forgotten. Tomorrow's my birthday.*

"How about taking me to Taronga Park Zoo?" he said.

"Why not?" Angie murmured, smiling. "We'll take a hamper of food and spend the day."

"Lance?"

Angie's voice seemed to come from miles away. *She sounds like I feel*, he thought. *Exhausted, but happy.*

"What is it?" he finally asked.

"Do you like fried chicken?"

"Yes. Why?"

"Oh, nothing. I was just thinking about what to take with us in the morning." Her words were slowly fading as she drifted into sleep.

They were in bed, in Angie's apartment, and had just finished making love.

The doctor had finally let him get out of bed—but only after Lance had promised to take it easy. It took even more convincing to get a release from the hospital, but he had managed it with a little charm and a couple of lies.

Angie and Lance had gone back to the apartment and immediately climbed into bed. They were both so tired that sleep had seemed the only logical possibility . . . but after all that had happened, there was a deep need in both of them—a need to be close, to drive all the terror and evil away, if only for a while.

At first, their lovemaking had been intense. Passion had driven them both to the edge of rationality. But slowly the pent-up emotions—the fear and hatred from the horrors of the last weeks—had begun to fade. The second time, their lovemaking had been gentle, more tender.

Now both of them were drifting into peaceful sleep.

Tomorrow's my twenty-fifth birthday, Lance thought as he floated downward into darkness. *And I'm going to spend it with Angie. I've finally found someone I really love . . . somebody who loves me. This birthday will be special . . .*

Different than any I've ever had.

Chapter 25

Later that night, at exactly 12:00 A.M., Lancelot Sullivan-Beresford turned twenty-five years old . . .

And a silent, golden light exploded in his head.

He awoke with a start and found himself inexplicably sitting up in bed.

Angie was sleeping soundly next to him, but he barely noticed. He was busy trying to understand what was happening to him. There was . . . something . . . something very *strange* going on inside him.

If he had been able to put it into a thought, it would have been that he felt a golden warm glow surging through his veins—a glow that filled him with security . . . and dread.

But at that moment, in that state, he couldn't begin to put it into words. It was pure, powerful *emotion*, at a level he'd never experienced before.

It was as if the intellectual component of his mind had been overloaded—shorted out. He couldn't remember where he was, or even *who* he was. Everything he knew, everything he felt was wrapped up in one singular, irresistible compulsion.

There was somewhere he had to go . . . *now*. *Going* was the only thing that mattered in the slightest.

Without a word, he climbed out of bed and walked to Angie's vanity table. He reached into her open purse and found the car keys with the tips of his fingers, not looking down—not focusing at all. Then he turned and left the bedroom.

Angie rolled over in bed and mumbled his name. Her hand slipped across the pillowcase, past the place where his head should have been, and paused. She called again, disturbed even in sleep . . . but she didn't wake. After a momentary frown, and an uncomfortable shift, she turned and drifted back into a fitful sleep.

Lance was already gone. He didn't know where he was hurrying to—no conscious plan had formed in his mind. He only knew he had to *get* there as soon as possible.

He climbed into Angie's car and started the engine. Then he floored the accelerator and raced off into the night.

Wilmont made his way down the long staircase and shuffled toward the main doors of Beresford Hall.

He had been dragged from a deep, restful sleep by the persistent ringing of the front door bell. At first he'd tried to ignore it, hoping whoever it was would go away and return at a respectable hour. But he'd had no such luck.

"All right, I'm coming," he growled as he reached the bottom of the stairs.

The bell jangled on. It had been doing that for the last ten minutes, without pause.

Wilmont opened the door to find Lance Sullivan standing there, his eyes locked in a vacant stare.

"Young Master Lance, I—"

Lance bustled past him and vaulted up the stairs, two at a time, to the second floor.

"Mr. Beresford? What is it?"

Lance never turned. He never even called back. Instead, he charged down the second-floor hallway as if he were being chased by the devil himself.

"It's like some sort of . . . *trance*," Wilmont told Angie a few minutes later when he called her apartment.

''What did he want?'' Angie asked, still trying to rub the sleep from her eyes. What the devil was Wilmont talking about?

She had been dragged from a weird dream by the ringing telephone; she'd been halfway to her desk to answer it before she'd noticed, much to her surprise, that Lance was nowhere to be seen.

And now—what was he saying? Lance was at Beresford Hall? He'd barged in and done *what?*

''He did *what?*'' she said stupidly, struggling to catch up.

''Of course I quickly followed the young gentleman, to try to ascertain his plans,'' Wilmont said. ''He went straight to Miss Essie's old rooms. Naturally, I called to him. I informed him—quite politely, Miss—that the doors were locked and I couldn't let him in. But . . .''

The butler hesitated. Angie waited a moment, still a bit fuzzy. Then she said, ''Well? What did he do when he couldn't get in?''

''That's just it,'' Wilmont said and hesitated again. ''He . . . he *did* get in, Miss.''

''But you said it was locked.'' None of this was making any sense to Angie. She wedged the phone between her chin and collarbone and again rubbed the sleep from her eyes. ''Wilmont, excuse me, but what the *hell* are you trying to say?''

''It *was* locked, Miss Angelique. I check it every day. But when Mr. Beresford turned the handle . . . it opened.''

''What was so important inside?'' Angie said, suddenly concerned. She didn't like this. She didn't like how little sense it made, how quickly things were happening. Damn it, they were planning to have such a nice, quiet, *normal* day. And now, with the day barely *begun* . . . ''Why do you think he broke in there?''

''Miss, please, *please*. I don't mean to imply Master Lance *broke* anything, my, no.'' Wilmont's voice was such a soft whisper now that the light hiss of the phone line almost drowned him out. "It was the—the door. The door closed after him, and when I tried to open it, it wouldn't budge."

"What?"

"Miss Angelique, I swear to you, *I couldn't get it to open*. The key has always worked, but this time it wouldn't." There was a hint of hysteria in Wilmont's voice. From anyone else, Angie knew, it would have sounded normal—in fact, cool and calm. But for the highly reserved, virtually imperturbable Wilmont, this was a major emotional imbalance.

It frightened Angie more than screaming would have.

"I'll be there as soon as I can, Wilmont. And if Mr. Beresford comes out of the room before I arrive, hold him there, whatever it takes. Do you understand?"

"Yes, Miss," Wilmont said. He understood well enough; he just didn't like what he heard. Mr. Beresford was the heir to the estate. How in goodness' name was *he*, the *butler*, going to keep the heir of the estate from doing anything he bloody well *wanted* to do?

Wilmont found himself hoping that Mr. Beresford would stay in Essie Beresford's rooms, at least until Miss Angelique arrived. Otherwise, it could get very messy, he decided. Very messy indeed.

"*Lance?*"

Angie shouted her cousin's name and pounded on the door to Essie Beresford's rooms.

"Miss Angelique," Wilmont said. He had recovered now; he was his old, staid self. "You've been doing that, on and off, for over an hour now. Do you anticipate any real success, or is it simply a way to pass the time?"

She turned and glared at him, a wild look in her eyes. Wilmont was thoroughly cowed.

"Of course, if you'd prefer to pound on the door—by all means. Pound to your heart's content," he said, suddenly nervous.

Angie raised her fists to start again . . . and paused. She

thought for a moment; then she relaxed, falling forward heavily to lean against the wooden door.

Her entire body shook. Her breath came in sobs. Then she stepped away from the door and cleared her throat. "I suppose you're right, Wilmont. I'm just . . . worried about him. That's all."

"Yes, Miss. And I must say, I certainly understand your concern."

Wilmont wasn't just being polite—he meant every word. When Lance Beresford had first pushed past him and raced upstairs to his ex-mistress's rooms, Wilmont had thought the man was drunk—just a case of the young heir imbibing a little too much of the grape, celebrating his good fortune and all.

Now he wasn't so sure. Now he didn't know *what* to think.

The whole affair is dashed weird, he thought, as he saw tears fill Angelique's eyes. That was the third time she had been near weeping since her arrival, and it worried him. That wasn't like Miss Angelique—not at all.

There were so many things he wanted to tell her. *That door opened under Lance's hand the instant he touched it*, he thought. *I saw it. I SAW it! So why won't it open now?* Then he thought of something even more bizarre—something he hadn't told Miss Angelique. *She might insist on breaking the door down, and Miss Essie—God rest her soul— would never forgive me.*

He couldn't really explain it, but for some reason the idea of Miss Essie being upset with him, even though she was dead, was—well, it *frightened* him.

No, Wilmont decided. *If I tell Miss Angelique that the keyhole has disappeared, she will definitely call someone to break down the door. I won't do that. But—but it has disappeared. It's not just that the key won't function. There simply is no hole anymore.*

The two times Angie had asked him to use the key, Wilmont had pretended to insert it in the smooth metal plate. He had even made a show of "turning" it, or trying to. It was no good—and frankly, he wasn't even sure why he was trying to keep it a secret. But—but that was *Miss Essie's* room! No one should be in there in the first place, so why did he need a key?

A key . . . or a key*hole*?

A normal manservant, he realized with some pride, would probably have been downstairs packing already. But he was no ordinary butler. Wilmont had worked for Essie Beresford for fifteen years, and during that time there had been numerous occurrences that might have been considered . . . *unusual* by normal standards. He had weathered them all with grace and good manners.

It never occurred to Wilmont that he *under*reacted to the strange goings-on at Beresford Hall. He didn't realize then—or ever—that he had been kept under control by forces far larger than himself—that even now, he was being controlled.

Instead he thought that all was—well, if not quite normal, at least *acceptable*. He was doing it for Mistress Essie, after all, and though she had been a strange bird, he had loved her very much.

Angie shook his arm and snapped him from his reverie. "Wilmont? What is it?"

The butler smiled at her concern. *Poor dear*, he thought. *She looks so worried*. "I'm sorry, Miss Angelique. I'm afraid I was woolgathering."

Angie stared at the butler. "Are you sure you're all right?"

"Yes, Miss. I'm fine." Wilmont looked at her squarely for the first time . . . and realized something. *I've never noticed it before*, he thought, *but she has Miss Essie's eyes. It's as if she's looking right through me. I used to feel that from her grandmother so often . . .*

"Miss Angelique, would you like Mrs. Sallinger to make you some tea?"

Angie suddenly remembered what time it was. She let

her hand drop from Wilmont's arm and smiled, embarrassed. No wonder the poor man was drifting off like that! "I'm sorry, Wilmont. I forgot you were dragged from your bed in the middle of the night." She plopped down in the large leather lounge chair that sat against the far wall of the corridor outside Essie Beresford's rooms. "Look, why don't you go back to bed? I'll just wait here."

"If you don't mind, Miss Angelique, I would like very much to sit and wait with you," Wilmont said, smiling down at Essie's granddaughter. The Mistress had always liked this one, and Wilmont had to admit that he had developed—well, a bit of a soft spot for her himself.

Angie took his hand and squeezed it. Wilmont looked surprised by the gesture. "Thank you, Wilmont," she said, and rubbed at her bloodshot eyes. "I would appreciate your company."

"It would be my pleasure, Miss. But I must admit I'd forgotten the time myself. With your permission, I shan't wake Mrs. Sallinger. I'll just make something for us myself."

The butler turned and made his way down the hall, then glided gracefully—as always—down the stairs that led to the kitchen.

Angie watched him go, smiling. But after a moment, her eyes were drawn back to the door to Essie Beresford's rooms. She couldn't stop looking at them—she couldn't stop *thinking* about them. *I probably should have someone break the darned thing down. But it doesn't feel . . . right . . . somehow.*

I just hope you're okay in there, Lance.

There was no way she could explain to Wilmont about the bizarre series of events she and Lance had gone through in the last couple of days. Or why, after all that had happened, she didn't feel any real fear for Lance's safety at this minute. But it was true—she *wasn't* concerned. Oh, she desperately wanted to know where he was, what was happening—she was *burning* with curiosity—but that special link between them was still working, and somehow it was telling her not to worry.

As tired as she was, and as confusing as the situation appeared, she was sure he was all right. She knew he would come back to her as soon as he could. *And in the meantime*, she thought, as she shifted in the huge, comfortable chair, *I'll just sit here and watch the door. I won't take my eyes off it . . .*

When Wilmont returned ten minutes later, a tray of food in his hands, he found Angie fast asleep in the big chair. Without a word, he placed the tray on the small hall table and proceeded down the hallway to one of the nearby guest bedrooms.

A few seconds later, he returned with a blanket and gently draped it over Angie.

As quietly as he could, he returned to the bedroom. This time he brought back a wooden chair and silently placed it next to the lounge chair.

He checked on the young mistress one final time. Yes, she was sleeping comfortably. Wilmont allowed himself one good, long stretch. Then he sat down and poured himself a cup of tea from the silver service.

He sipped it slowly and munched on the sweet biscuits he had found in the kitchen, stifling a yawn with the back of his hand. Whatever was going on here, he decided, seemed to have paused for the moment. And young Miss Angelique needed her rest, that was obvious. He would stand guard, and alert her if there was any change in the situation. After all, that was his job, and he was proud to do it.

There amidst the witches and warlocks, the haunted houses and cosmic forces, there was always Wilmont. And Wilmont, above all else, was the best butler in Australia.

Chapter 26

Lance Sullivan blinked, shook his head, and tried to understand what was going on.

The last thing he remembered was lying beside Angie and thinking how lucky he was to have found her. Now, inexplicably, he stood in the middle of a large room he'd never seen before . . . and he didn't have the vaguest idea how he'd gotten there.

He ran his hands slowly through his mussed blond curls and let his eyes wander.

He appeared to be in a sitting room. To his immediate right, next to the main door, a huge bookcase covered virtually the entire wall. It was crammed with very old editions, most of them trimmed in what appeared to be pure gold leaf. From just a brief look, Lance was sure there were a number of rare collectibles among them.

Next to the wall, stretching away from the bookcase, sat a couch with polished mahogany armrests, covered with hand-embroidered silk also trimmed in gold. Next to the couch was an ornate walnut desk from the seventeenth century. A matching single chair with a crocheted shawl sat by a small window in the far wall. A polished oak table with a solid-brass lamp sat near the wall to his left, beside a second closed door. Everything in the room was covered with a fine layer of dust.

"I don't get it," Lance said to himself. "I don't get it at all." He almost crept to a bouquet of roses that hung limply in a Ming Dynasty vase perched on the windowsill. The blossoms had long since dried and shriveled.

He frowned at the flowers. Everything looked so old here—so *dead*. He eased aside the window's diaphanous silk curtain and looked out.

At first the view seemed just as new to him as the room itself. Then he recognized the aviary and the old-fashioned wrought-iron seat on the lawn.

Wilmont had shown him the aviary on the day they'd come to visit. He knew this place.

"I'm in Beresford Hall," Lance said into the dusty air. His voice had the deep throatiness of early morning, as if he had just awakened from a full night's sleep. "But how the hell did I get here?"

The hell with it, he thought. *That's enough questioning. Time for some answers*. Without hesitation, he wheeled about and strode purposefully back to the main door.

I'm getting out of here, he thought. *I'll worry about how I got here in the first place once I'm back with Angie, in more familiar surroundings*.

But the knob wouldn't turn, and when he wrenched on it the door didn't budge an inch. He cursed under his breath and bent down for a closer look.

There was no key in the door. There wasn't even a *hole* for a key.

It should have worried Lance. All it did was make him mad. "What the hell's happening here?" he said to the empty room. "And where in God's name am I?"

The answer came in a flash. He didn't actually think about it; it simply appeared in his mind, as if broadcast from a remote station.

I'm in Essie Beresford's rooms, he thought abruptly. And he knew it was true.

Lance didn't bother trying to understand *how* he knew. He simply *knew*—and the frustration of it brought his temper to the boiling point. He walked to the other door and put his shoulder to it as he twisted the knob.

This time the knob turned easily. The door swung open wildly and slammed into the wall behind it with a loud thud, and Lance strode purposefully through the doorway into Essie Beresford's bedroom . . .

And stopped, his mouth agape, his anger frozen in place.

An old four-poster bed with billowing drapes covered much of the far wall and filled the entire center of the room. A dressing table with three matching silver-inlaid mirrors stood against one of the other three walls, and a porcelain bowl was perched on a small chest of drawers near the far end of another. A satin-covered hope chest sat by the only window in the room and next to it stood what appeared to be an original Louis XIV chair.

But these furnishings barely registered with Lance. He was staring at a painting that was mounted in a hand-carved rosewood frame, hanging on the wall above the small chest of drawers and almost glowing in the light from the large chandelier hanging from the ceiling.

He walked slowly into the bedroom, his mouth still open, and stared at the picture.

Lance was no art expert. Benny had given him a basic overview of the field, helped him judge the value of rare and collectible artworks, but that was it: he knew he could be fooled by a forgery as easily as the next man.

But this . . . this was no forgery. There was something about the cracking paint, the flowing signature, the ancient canvas itself. The painter had breathed *life* into every single brush stroke. *God*, he thought. *It can't be a fake. Nobody could fake something like this.*

Benny had shown him a reproduction once, in a book on the lost works of the masters. It was just a rendering, made from surviving pencil sketches. The original piece was supposed to have been destroyed in a fire.

But here it was. Here it was in Essie Beresford's *bedroom*.

I'd bet a thousand dollars on it, he thought. *No—a hundred thousand.*

This is an original Rembrandt. A lost original Rembrandt.

Lance reluctantly turned his eyes away and looked again at the rest of the room. He was almost intoxicated by a realization. *None* of these were reproductions. Everything in this exquisitely decorated, opulent suite was original and in perfect condition. "The Getty Museum would pay millions for this room *alone*," he muttered.

Then the shock began to fade. *Okay*, he thought. *So I'm stuck in a multimillion-dollar museum. But I'm still stuck.* He was more curious than angry now, though. It was time, he decided, to search the rooms, starting with this boudoir. Maybe he could turn up something that would explain why he was here—or how he'd gotten here in the first place.

He walked to the chest and slid open the top drawer . . . and a new compulsion, more irresistible than the first, swept over him.

Go back to the sitting room, something told him. Instantly he turned on his heel and walked to the door, without even wondering why he was doing it.

A gorgeous young woman was waiting for him. She stood by the bookcase, draped in a golden aura, her long blonde hair glowing, her organdy gown warm and soft against her milky skin.

Lance stopped and stared. He hadn't heard her come in—he hadn't heard a thing, he realized, since he awakened in these rooms. But more important . . . he *recognized* this woman.

The last time he'd seen her she was a ghostly figure floating through the door of Essie's rooms—hovering in the hallway just outside the locked door. She had been trying, with no success and a good deal of consternation, to communicate something to him.

This time she appeared as solid as he was, and even more beautiful than he remembered now that he could see her clearly. She seemed to be waiting for him to speak.

"Can . . . can you talk this time?" he asked, half-expecting the vision to disappear again.

"Yes," the woman said, and smiled.

A feeling of warmth washed over him. Lance realized it wasn't just the vision herself, or her indisputable beauty, that made him so calm, so accepting—so *glad* to see her. It was something more than that.

She could be Angie's sister, he realized. *The eyes, the nose, the mouth that laughs loudly even when she smiles just a little. And something else. A feeling of . . . something. Something good.* He couldn't put his finger on it, but it was like the feeling he had known as a boy, when his mother had taken him inside the huge cathedral in Los Angeles. The acknowledgement of something good and true—something far larger than oneself.

"W—who are you?" he stuttered.

"I'm your great-grandmother, Lance. I'm Essie Beresford."

This was nonsense—it *had* to be. Essie Beresford had died an old woman only weeks before. This woman was young and beautiful, and very obviously alive.

It didn't matter. As much as he hated to admit it, something about what she said—about the *way* she said it—told him the words were true.

"B . . . but how . . . Uh, how could you . . . Essie Beresford is dead. And anyway, she was an old woman."

To his surprise, Lance found himself regretting his questions even as he spoke them. Whatever she might be now, he was sure she had once been his great-grandmother. He was foolish to question that. But—

"If you're Essie Beresford, or used to be," he blurted out, "then why did you leave such confusion? How did I get here? What the hell am I *doing* here, anyway? And why are you here, and what the hell *are* you, a ghost?"

He suddenly pulled up short. "Oh, God," he said suddenly. "I—I'm sorry. I just don't— I can't understand . . ."

He trailed off, feeling like an idiot. For the second time in as many minutes, he remembered what it felt like to be a little boy, and how stupid and small he felt when he was embarrassed in front of an adult he respected and liked. He felt like that now—and he didn't have the slightest idea *why*. "I'm . . . I'm just confused, that's all," he mumbled apologetically. "I'm incredibly *confused*."

"Not to worry, Lance. I've heard much worse in my life," Essie Beresford said. Lance noticed how strange and wonderful she sounded—how her words rang like tiny finger chimes. "And I will gladly answer your questions—all of them.

"You are here because I brought you here. I'm sorry that it had to be this way, but it took every bit of spare energy I had left and I couldn't take any chances. I just hope you'll forgive me when you know *all* the facts."

A frown crossed the beautiful face, and for an instant the golden hue seemed to dim.

The moment passed. In an instant, the vision that called herself Essie was once again bathed in a soft, orange-fire glow that turned her hair to a crown of gold.

"I never expected to have to do this," the vision said. "When I saw you in the hall the other day, I thought you'd understood the instructions in my letter and come to let me explain further. But you weren't prepared, and I couldn't communicate with you."

"What letter?"

"The letter I left with the will."

"All I got was a pile of ash," Lance said. He found himself pulling at the collar of the open-necked shirt he was wearing, suddenly chilled. He still didn't remember putting it on. "How could I make any sense from that?"

Essie Beresford said nothing. Instead she stared intently at him, and for a moment, Lance was struck by the absurdity of the situation. *What am I doing*? he wondered.

I'm standing here talking to—what? The ghost of my dead great-grandmother? Who just happens to look like a gorgeous twenty-two-year-old? This is nuts. This is completely nuts.

Essie's eyes suddenly grew wide and deep, becoming bottomless pools of black water. Lance couldn't look away . . . even when the room began to spin around him. It turned slowly at first—then faster and faster. Everything else was forgotten in his vertigo. All he could think of, all he knew, was the swirling water.

A strange prickling sensation rippled through his brain. It happened so fast he wasn't sure if he'd imagined it, like the sudden sweeping of fingernails over his skin.

"Oh, my!" Essie Beresford gasped. "I never realized! Lance, things have gone wrong—horribly wrong. I never intended for any of this to happen. I never meant for any of the horror . . ." She paused, sighing. "Poor Douglas. Poor Monica. They died horribly. Without even knowing why."

Lance snapped from the deep trance, and a new chill raced through him.

I didn't imagine it, then, he thought. *She somehow got inside my head.*

But Essie Beresford didn't notice his fear and anger. She was still puzzled by what she had . . . *taken* from him. "I don't understand," she said. "I left a letter explaining everything. What happened to it?"

"Why bother to ask?" he said harshly. "Why don't you just read my thoughts?"

Essie seemed taken aback by his sudden anger. Again, the golden glow that came from her seemed to falter—to flicker.

"That's what you did, isn't it?"

"I'm sorry, Lance," she whispered. "Truly I am. I thought it would be simpler—less painful for you. But I won't do it again without your permission. I promise you that. Now please, tell me. Was it Robert? Did he interfere somehow?"

Lance hesitated for a moment, curiosity and anger battling inside him. Finally he shrugged and said, "He took the letter as Josh Wilcox passed it to me. But he only had it for a few seconds."

Then he remembered how Robert had slid the envelope between the palms of both hands. He told Essie that, and she nodded sadly.

"Just so," she said, and sighed. "He must have used what little power he had to burn the letter in its envelope. I suppose I should have foreseen the likelihood of interception and made a contingency plan. But there was just no way to predict *every* possibility." For a moment she looked infinitely weary, infinitely sad. Then she straightened her shoulders bravely and smiled at him. "Still, I am responsible. I hope you can forgive me for the pain you've had to suffer because of me."

Lance had taken in everything so far—his sudden arrival, the remarkable room, even Essie's manifestation—with a stunned acceptance. But now he couldn't stand by any longer, struggling to understand bits and pieces of information that this apparition saw fit to give him. The anger and frustration was building again, a heat deep in his chest.

"Look, Essie—or whoever you are, *what*ever you are. I'm having one hell of a time accepting *any* of this. I need some . . . I don't know, some proof. Or even just a . . . a rational explanation would be great. But I need it *now*."

"Of course you do, dear boy," Essie Beresford said in a voice that seemed to quiver a fraction. Then, as she continued to speak, her body went through a complete transformation.

The soft, pearl-white skin on her face, arms and hands withered before Lance's eyes. The brilliant, flowing hair turned ashen gray. The tall, almost stately posture slowly

bent forward as if weighted down by the sudden passage of
time.

Within moments, the ravishing young woman was turning into a very old lady.

"Unfortunately, what I'm about to tell you doesn't come
under anyone's heading of 'rational.' I can only hope this
demonstration will convince you that my story is true, and
of vital importance to you—even though it *is* somewhat
melodramatic." The old woman smiled and almost cack-
led. "After all, the old saying is still true, isn't it? 'A
picture is worth a thousand words.' "

Lance couldn't hide his revulsion. If he had met Essie
looking this way the first time, maybe it would have been
different—he would have been expecting it. For an old
lady, she was not particularly hideous—she actually had a
stately kind of beauty. But Lance had been staring at a
stunningly beautiful woman just moments before, and to
see that woman age so quickly—so graphically—was more
than he could handle. *That's what it does to you*, he
thought. *That's what age does to us all.*

Essie saw his distress, and smiled sadly. "Would you
prefer me the way you first saw me?" she asked, trembling.

"Yes," Lance said softly. "I'm sorry, but . . ."

She shook her head. "Don't apologize. I prefer it that
way myself. There is so much pain in this manifestation
. . . so much memory of weakness . . ."

The metamorphosis occurred in reverse this time, and
Lance was even more stunned. It had been a shock to see
it happen so fast, but the process of aging, after all, was a
brutally recognizable thing. It happened to everyone.

This other thing, though—this *reverse* aging. It was
mind-boggling. In moments, the shoulders straightened
and lifted. The skin grew smooth and rosy again. The
fingers became steady and strong. Only the eyes didn't
change—the bright, sad, intelligent eyes.

He knew it wasn't true—it was an illusion, he realized
now—but, somehow, when the younger Essie was com-

pletely restored, she seemed even more beautiful than she had been before she'd made herself old.

"How did you do that?" he said when she had returned to her original form. He didn't realize it, but his words held a hint of the awe he felt.

"It's a quite long story, young Lance," Essie said. Once again, her voice sounded like the chime of perfectly tuned bells. "Nevertheless, it is one you must hear if you are to survive . . . even for the next few hours."

It didn't matter whether or not Lance wanted to hear the story Essie had to tell. He *had* to hear it. His life had been turned upside down in the last week . . . and finally someone had the answers.

First there were the dreams that had somehow become entangled with his waking life. Someone had called him in his Miami hotel room and warned him, and minutes later a man had died in his place. Then there was the letter from the lawyers that had found him in Texas, and the shower episode, and the Johnny Hancock delusion. Two days later his mother had died under strange circumstances, and he was beginning to wonder if her death might be connected to all that had happened since. In Fiji he had been accosted by the woman trying to warn him of what was about to happen in Australia—though he still didn't have a clue about what her last, shouted words had meant. The meetings with Warwick still made his head spin, and though Lance hadn't lost any sleep over Robert's death, Douglas and Monica had been innocent casualties.

All that and much more—and Essie had just said she knew why it was happening.

"I'm listening," he said.

Essie smiled that smile of infinite sadness, just as she had before. "Perhaps you should sit," she said gently. "This will take some time to tell."

Lance sat on the end of the couch. He felt numb, as if he had taken in all the hurt and pain he could stand. But he had to have answers or everything that had happened to him—to everyone around him—would be for nothing. And he was sure, in some special way, that this glowing visitor had those answers.

Essie did not move to sit. Lance wondered briefly if "sitting" meant anything to her now.

She reached up and flicked a strand of blonde hair from her eyes. Once again he noted the golden glow that formed around her, a warm and penetrating aura.

Then Essie Beresford began to speak, and in seconds everything else was forgotten.

Angie decided she must be dreaming. Somewhere in her consciousness she accepted that fact, so she wasn't too disturbed by what was happening.

It was the angle that bothered her. It was strangely high—foreshortened.

She saw herself sleeping in the lounge chair in the hall outside Essie Beresford's rooms. Next to her sleeping body she could clearly make out Wilmont sitting on a chair, his arms crossed. His eyes flickered to the door that led to Essie Beresford's rooms, then back to Angie, then finally checked the hall in both directions. He was on guard, and he was obviously taking his job seriously.

She looked down on him with amusement and affection . . . until she realized that she was looking *down*—from a vantage point somewhere near the hand-carved ceiling of the old hallway.

The realization was clear and sweet and somehow far from frightening; she was out of her body, just . . . hovering there, ghostlike.

She was still quite sure it was a dream . . . but Angie remembered reading about such things happening to other people. They had something to do with dying—the "near-death experience," they called it. She remembered being surprised at how many cases had been documented, by people who had died on operating tables, or in car accidents, or from heart attacks, and had been brought back to life through some extraordinary efforts by doctors or paramedics. For many, even their coming back was as big a mystery to the doctors as what had happened to them during the "near-death experience."

They all said the same thing—they all felt what she was feeling now.

It began when the spirit slipped out of the body. You would find yourself floating near the ceiling, looking down on your own physical form.

Like now, Angie thought dreamily. *Like me*.

Often they would watch doctors and nurses, or friends, trying to keep them alive. They would see what was happening in the "real" world, but in a new way—from a new angle. Most said they felt just as she felt now—as if they didn't want to go back into their bodies. As if this was the *right* thing to do—the *natural* thing.

Then, still floating in the corner of the hall, she remembered the next step: the tunnel.

Most of the others had talked about it—a huge, spiraling, blue-black tunnel that led toward an immense shimmering light. Many of them . . . *met* people then. The spirits of friends and relatives, long dead, who welcomed them into the Presence.

The Presence, she thought. The Face of God.

Angie felt herself begin to move . . . and for the first time she wondered if it was a dream at all. *Am I dying?* she thought suddenly. *Has something happened?*

There was a pressure—no, a *pull*, really. It was drawing her away from the hallway—away from the house.

Everything went black—and for a moment, her wonder turned to fear. *No*, she thought. *Not yet. This isn't the way it's supposed to work.*

But just as suddenly as the dark had closed around her, it was gone. She didn't travel down any tunnel, or come face to face with anything.

Instead, she soared through the air, like a bird on the wing, high above Beresford Hall.

I just dissolved through the walls, Angie thought. *That's why it got so dark.* And she began to realize that what was happening was far too logical, far too coherent to be a simple dream.

Then she saw it: a pulsing, glowing *something* that surrounded the entire Beresford estate. It was like a sentient fog, with long misty fingers moving endlessly in wide swirling arcs, covering everything with a thick purple mist.

She looked again and realized that that wasn't quite right. The fog extended across the area, penetrating the trees and houses and the town beyond . . . but it stopped at the edge of the estate. She looked up and saw it circle high above the mansion as well, hovering ominously . . . but the Beresford property was clear—almost golden, in fact.

"ANGELIQUE," an insubstantial voice called to her. It echoed inside her head, deep and booming, so profound it instantly pushed all other thoughts aside.

It was the single most powerful sound she had ever heard. Awe and wonder crowded out her fear. It set her heart racing, and her eyes filled with tears. Angie felt like falling to her knees—falling to the ground—and praying.

The voice spoke again. "COME TO ME," it echoed, "AND WE WILL BE ONE."

She was pulled like a moth to a flame. Angie soared toward the voice, towards the roiling purple energy that surrounded the estate.

I have finally heard it, she thought, filled with wonder. *The voice of God.* She strained to hurry, to get there sooner.

I'm dead, she thought as she swept happily forward. *My experience was a little different than the others', but the result is the same. He's calling to me. He's calling to me!*

But there was another voice—a tiny one, buried deep inside her.

"The purple mist," it whispered. *"Remember the purple . . ."*

"FOLLOW ME!" the Presence called, drowning out the other sound. If there was anything left but wonder, any doubt or fear, she couldn't remember it. And if she couldn't remember it, it couldn't have been important . . .

She was almost to the edge of the Beresford estate.

"COME . . ." the Presence said.

"*NO* . . ." the little voice called. "*The purple—*"

"COME!"

She pushed herself to cover the last few yards, to reach out a hand and touch—

"*COME!*"

A scream filled the air around her.

"*Noooooo!*"

Angie stopped, only inches from the bubbling purple field. *That scream*, she thought. *So horrible, so afraid—*

Then she realized the scream had come from her own mouth. It had risen up from deep inside her—from that tiny part of her that had resisted the call of the Presence.

And that sudden realization snapped the purple energy's control.

In a flash she remembered the glow that had hovered around Jessica when she had tried to kill Lance. She remembered *Lance's* memory—of the purple force he had experienced when he was locked in battle with Robert.

This purple *thing* was part of that. It came from the same source.

It was the cause of all their problems.

Angie shied back from where the energy boiled, only inches from her floating body. She willed herself to stop, to hover without motion and stare into the hissing, impenetrable mass.

My God, she thought, *it almost had me*. She had nearly rushed into the arms of whatever waited in the fog.

It sent cold shivers over her. Angie realized that it was all a lie—the voice, the Presence, the illusion of the near-death experience.

There's no death here, she thought, looking down at the

estate fifty feet below her. *It's out there, in the purple mist. The real Death waits there.*

Suddenly, wonderfully, she was warmed by a new sensation: a tranquility, a well-being with no hint of the fear she had felt before.

Her ethereal body hovered in the air, high over the far corner of the Beresford estate, and she smiled to herself, wondering how she could have missed this before.

The entire Beresford estate was wrapped in gold. The profound energy of this place—a deep, abiding strength, pure and whole—permeated every inch of the property: the house, the grounds, the stones themselves.

And that purple *thing* didn't—*couldn't*—breach it.

It wants to, she realized. *It's been pounding at the gate for eternity.* Now, abruptly, Angie could sense the driving compulsion of the writhing fog. *It's aching to rush in and devour the golden force—the power that holds everything inside it safe from harm. But it can't. It can't.*

She noted, almost as an afterthought, that the eerie purple force was pushing continuously against the edge of the golden energy. For as much as a minute, it would appear to move forward. But each time the golden fluorescence would eventually drive it back.

All is well, she realized, and smiled. *All is well.*

Later—much later—Angie would remember that final thought and curse her own ignorance. There was no safety in what she saw—no "wellness." There were two immense forces, locked in a deadly combat begun ages before. And at that moment, as she watched, the golden force that filled her with hope was in grave danger of losing, forever.

But she felt nothing like that now. She felt only peace and warmth around her, inside her. She laughed and stretched as she glided playfully, like Mary Poppins, above the strangely shaped chimneys of Beresford Hall. She would have continued to glide and soar there forever, but a sudden compulsion urged her to return to her sleeping body.

Reluctantly, Angie dived downward through air alive with the golden glow. She blinked and giggled as she passed through the darkness of the walls. In moments she was back in the hall outside Essie Beresford's rooms.

Back, she thought dimly, as a sudden, irresistible gravity pulled her back into her body. *Back where you belong*.

As she slipped into place—as her perception of the golden glow and the evil purple force slowly dissolved—a single, simple thought blossomed and faded.

I wonder if I'll remember this wonderful dream when I wake up, she thought.

Chapter 27

"The Beresford family was originally based in England, in an area known today as Northumberland," Essie Beresford said, beginning her long and bizarre tale.

Lance cut her off with a question. "Then what Warwick told me was true?"

He was perched on the couch in the late Essie Beresford's sitting room, in Beresford Hall, listening to a beautiful young woman bathed in a soft golden luminescence who claimed to be his dead great-grandmother. He tried not to think about that too much. He just tried to listen and learn.

"That statement was the only truth in Warwick's story, believe me," Essie said. "In fact, it may have been the only truth he's uttered in centuries."

Her soft blonde hair shone with a translucent sheen, and as she stared at him a small frown briefly clouded her features. "I must say, I still do not understand that meeting with him. Not at all."

She shrugged . . . and her entire body rippled. It was as if, for a scant second, she had shrugged off gravity itself—as if her body was about to separate into a thousand pieces and drift away in all directions.

The absurdity, and the wonderment, of it caught Lance

off guard. He had to fight to keep his mind on Essie's words.

"Still, let us not be distracted from our story, or you may never learn what you need to learn."

Lance's mind stopped its meandering. He focused instead on the mysterious man who seemed to stand at the center of the mystery. "Who *is* Warwick?" he said. "And how does he do that stuff?"

"*Lance!*" Essie's voice sharply cut off his question. For a moment it took on the serious, crackling tone of the old woman she had been just moments before. "There is too much at stake and too little time for us to play questions and answers. Now please, let me tell you what you need to know without further interruption—while there is *still* time."

Lance swallowed his other questions and sat quietly, and when Essie spoke again, her voice was once more like the tinkling of bells.

"As I said, the Beresford family was originally based in England. The distant past is shrouded in mystery, so unfortunately we can only take up the story in 1620.

"In that year a pair of twins—a boy and a girl—were born in Beresford Manse. They never knew their parents, and they spent the first twenty-five years of their lives under the tutelage of their Uncle Ramos. They were educated as few, if any, other English people of the times. They knew nothing of life outside the huge sprawling estate where they were raised, but aside from that omission—and a serious one at that—their lives were rich and full . . . and, at least to them, quite normal.

"The estate was huge and was separated from the surrounding territories by an impenetrable ring of hedges and trees. What little food and materials could not be produced on the property were brought in by Harold, the butler and all-around handyman. And there were books and games and—most important—each other to occupy their lives. For most of that first quarter-century, they did not miss contact with the outside world. In fact, they were rarely aware there was anything *to* miss.

"I say they were normal enough children, but that, of course, is relative. To themselves, and to their doting Uncle Ramos, they were normal as pie. By the standards of the Englishmen of the 1600s, they were something quite different—quite special—and rather frightening.

"Elsa, the cook, and Harold were the only other people the children ever knew. Faithful retainers since before the birth of the twins, these two were in virtual exile themselves, particularly Elsa, who rarely left the estate. It was a tidy world, and beautiful . . . and tragically artificial.

"The children grew to adulthood taking many things for granted that were not the everyday norm for the surrounding villages and townsfolk. They ate the best food and never went hungry; they were always dressed impeccably, and their clothes were replaced at the slightest sign of wear. Ramos was a good uncle—perhaps, in the final analysis, a bit *too* good, for he couldn't resist indulging their whims.

"The estate was a beautiful place—a sea of green. Three main lawns surrounded the house, and flower beds were scattered like jewels on velvet all about the grounds. And over the far hill they had their own lake where they could spend lazy summer afternoons boating, having picnics, playing and dreaming from dawn until sunset.

"Most of the trees and shrubs were fully grown and needed little attention, which was a lucky thing for Harold, since he seemed to have an endless stream of other duties. The twins, of course, never gave that a thought. Gardening, like everything else, was a *recreation*. No one *had* to do such things.

"However, the little girl *did* notice one idiosyncrasy about Harold and Elsa both. Neither of the adults could play the games that the twins played with each other. It was as if they didn't understand the rules—as if they didn't even understand what she was talking about when she tried to include them.

"She asked her Uncle Ramos why this was so, and he only shook his head and told her that both Harold and Elsa were entitled to their privacy. She never really understood what he meant—she was only eight years old at the time. As it turned out, she would be twenty-five before her simple question was answered—before *many* of her questions were answered, in fact. And then, she would be far from happy with what she learned."

Essie Beresford paused for a moment, drowning in recollection. She shook this feeling off—and for a moment, her body seemed to shimmer, to actually *glitter*. Then she looked directly at Lance again and smiled her warmest smile.

"The two young twins—Beresfords, like you—were raised as if they were royalty. Yet even with all the pampering and all the advanced education, they remained children in many ways—even until their shared twenty-fifth birthday.

"Then, at the dawn of their twenty-fifth year, it all ended. The twins became adults in an instant—between one heartbeat and the next—and their innocent childhood disappeared forever.

"The first step seemed innocuous enough. Uncle Ramos had them jointly sign the deed for the Beresford estate. 'It was your parents' wish,' he told them, 'and it is my wish as well.' And after they signed . . ."

Essie paused again, and her chest rose and fell—as if she were taking a deep breath, as if the next words came hard.

"After they signed, they learned that they were different—completely different from any other person on the planet, with the possible exception of their good uncle."

She looked at Lance and frowned slightly, her eyebrows drawing together in concentration. It was important he understood the next part, she knew. She was choosing her words very carefully. "Uncle Ramos told them they were the bearers of a special 'gift'—a gift that had lain dormant within them since birth.

"They possessed the innate ability to *control energy*—immense amounts of energy—with nothing more than their bodies and the force of their wills. And this energy was somehow centered in—somehow emanated from—the very house in which they lived.

"The twins were full of questions. Where did the energy come from? How did their 'power' work? Why did it appear only on their twenty-fifth birthday? Uncle Ramos couldn't—or *wouldn't*—answer their queries. He had a bad habit that way. Some answers, he said, would come with time and experience. Others . . ."

She paused again and ran her fingers through her shimmering hair. "I doubt the scientists of this century—or of the next—could answer some of those questions. Perhaps some are beyond answering at all. But the important ones—the ones that truly mattered—*did* come with time, just as Ramos had promised.

"The twins found that many of the games they had played as children had been meant to prepare them for their acquisition of power, particularly the ones they had played in their minds—when they had searched for secrets in each other's thoughts, or when they had joined their minds together to tell stories, lift objects, play tricks—"

"Wait a minute," Lance said. "I've kept quiet until now, but—read each other's *thoughts?* Moved *objects?* Are you telling me these kids were—what, *telepathic?*"

Essie smiled, almost embarrassed, and looked away when she nodded. "I believe that is the current term, yes. Telepathic and clairvoyant and psychokinetic and a number of other things not so readily labeled." She looked back at him, eyes sparkling. "That was the reason they were separated from the normal populace, even before their births. In those years, humans were only beginning to acquire a very basic, very faulty understanding of the power of the mind, and it frightened them." Her face hardened for a moment as she thought it through. "It frightens them still."

After a moment, she shook off the thought and continued, almost breezily. "Of course, the twins thought their Uncle Ramos was crazy—mad as the proverbial Hatter, though that term was still two hundred years from invention. Ramos, however, had foreseen this reaction and prepared for it. He had two men from the nearby town actually come onto the estate—under the pretext of delivering coal—just so that the twins could see them. They were waiting on the estate lawn, even as his revelations came to an end and the questions were cut off.

"The twins were amazed. Except for Elsa and Harold, they had never before met a person who wasn't a blood relative. It was a strange moment, that meeting—rather like the meeting you might imagine between two alien cultures.

"The children, after all, were legends in the surrounding towns. Rumors about their existence, and the reason for their isolation, were rampant. And the twins themselves had only seen drawings of peasants. Now, to see not one, but *two*, in the flesh . . .

" 'How do you do, gentlemen,' Uncle Ramos said to the workmen. 'I thought you might say hello to my niece and nephew before you leave.'

"The little girl thought the two workmen looked rather gentle, if a bit rough. They were covered in black soot—even their clothes and hair.

"The two colliers themselves were talking nervously, wondering aloud why Harold had always picked up the coal in town. 'It's no problem for us to bring it to ya,' the shorter one said—he had thinning hair and a strangely clipped accent. His partner was a rangy young boy with thick, long, jet-black hair. He was too frightened to speak and only nodded his agreement.

"Now, while he was speaking to the workmen, Uncle Ramos projected a thought into the twins' minds."

Lance started to interrupt again, but Essie anticipated his question. "Yes, Ramos possessed similar abilities, though not as extensive or as strong. Now just *listen*, won't you?"

Lance looked apologetic and sat back. *Talk on*, he thought. *It's a pleasant enough fantasy, I suppose.*

"Again, Ramos projected a thought at the twins, telling them to enter the minds of the two outsiders—to see what they were, and how they were different. 'But be careful,' he cautioned them. 'Be gentle. Remember, they are not as we are.'

"The twins were recovering from the surprise of meeting outsiders. Now they were both eager to explore—as all children are, I suppose.

"The stocky man continued his conversation with Uncle Ramos, totally unaware—as was his partner—that they were the subjects of a rather bizarre experiment.

"It was nothing new for the twins. They had done it often with each other and with their uncle. They reached out tiny mental tendrils—a bit like gently probing fingers—and touched the colliers' minds with their own."

Essie looked frankly at Lance, directly into his eyes—and again he was astonished by her similarities to Angie. That was *her* look—bold, open, blunt. "Lance, it was like entering an alien landscape. Like walking on the moon. The minds of these simple peasants, and the minds of these two gifted children . . . they were completely different. *Completely*.

"The men had no real psychic ability at all. They couldn't sense each other, or the world around them. They lived shrouded in a kind of befuddlement, a perpetual fear of the world. To the twins, it seemed as if the men were in prison—sentenced to a life in which everything they knew had to be forced through the tiny, inadequate pinholes of the physical senses—smell, hearing, feeling, sight. Both the children shuddered at the thought—what must it be like, they thought, to be so deaf and blind? The girl had to fight back tears at the thought of the unbelievable *loneliness* these two beings unknowingly suffered, cut off from the openness of mind-to-mind communication.

"Within moments, the children found they could 'skim' through the minds of these simple men—learning anything, *everything* they wished to know without effort or detection.

"The two young Beresfords communicated with each other as they continued their exploration. They wondered if this were some kind of trick, some test their uncle had arranged for them to unravel.

"Ramos assured them this was not the case. 'This is what the rest of humanity is like,' he told them, mind-to-mind. 'This is how different you are.'

"The twins had very different reactions to the revelation. The girl felt an empathy for these men and wished there were some way to help them learn the wonders of mind-to-mind communication. Very gently, she withdrew the tendrils of her mental probe and began to think, long and hard, about everything Uncle Ramos had told them.

"But the boy had other ideas."

Essie Beresford stopped. Her chest rose and fell again, in an agitated motion, and her eyes—deep blue, sparkling like sapphires—burned with rage.

"The boy felt . . . nothing. Only contempt for the ignorant men. From the moment of first contact, from the instant he accepted his own 'superiority,' as I suppose he would have called it, he saw them as little more than clever animals. Animals for him to *play* with.

"Very quickly, *too* quickly, he located the portion of the mind that controlled emotion. And he began to . . . *tinker*."

Essie stood and paced the room nervously. It was such a simple movement—so *human*—that Lance had a hard time remembering she was only a construct made strictly for his benefit, though it was more believable when he realized that she made no sound as she moved. No ticking of heel to floorboard, no whisper of cloth. Essie moved with perfect silence as she told her story.

"First, the boy invoked joy—a mad, mindless sort of joy. The two delivery men broke into laughter, one right in the middle of a sentence.

"But that was too easy. The boy wanted something *more* than that—something *deeper*. He tried . . . compliance.

"Quite suddenly, both men looked about as if they had lost something—as if they were awaiting orders. The stocky one blinked at Ramos and said, 'Beggin' your pardon, lordship. It's certainly my fault, and I do apologize, truly, but . . . what was it ya' wont us to do, again? Say it, gov, and it's done.'

"Ramos looked about, then shook his head. 'I never asked you to do anything,' he told them, looking confused by the question.

"The twin boy felt . . . *ecstasy*. It was as if he had suddenly discovered a special taste he'd never dreamed of—and with it, birthed a hunger that was deeper than any he'd ever known. He had to have more. More emotions of that certain kind . . . and *better* ones.

"So he induced *fear* in the men.

"Both men shrieked and fell to their knees, squeezing their heads in their hands.

"By now, of course, Ramos realized something was very wrong. He sent his mind rushing into the colliers' minds, but before he could intercede, the boy had pushed the level of fear to an impossible level—so great it overwhelmed the simple villagers. That panic—that *overload*—was what he had craved. When he felt it, when he'd drunk his fill, the boy withdrew.

"But it was too late. The men writhed on the soft, green lawn. They frothed at the mouth like beasts and twitched and screeched, and babbled until their bodies simple couldn't stand the strain."

Essie was standing at the window, staring out at the lawn. Staring . . . and remembering.

"It was almost an act of kindness when their hearts gave out and death finally eased their agony."

She looked out over the flower gardens of the estate a moment longer—then snapped away from them. When she turned back to Lance, the tears had disappeared from her eyes. She was brisk again, almost businesslike, and the sentences came more rapidly, as if time were running out.

"The entire fiasco began and ended in a matter of seconds. It could all have been a dream—a nightmare, really—if not for the sooty, twisted bodies curled up on the grass, lying in their own dung.

"No. It was no dream. Just the end of one, and the beginning of another that would last for centuries."

She stopped and stood, looking at her hands. Lance didn't speak; he figured the story wasn't over yet. But she needed a moment to gather herself, to think.

That's strange, he thought. *She seems . . . thinner, somehow*. It was an inadequate word, but it was true—somehow the apparition had lost substance. He could almost see *through* her now.

Essie's body, clothes and all, seemed to be . . . *fading*. She was becoming ghostly—but very, very slowly.

Lance opened his mouth to speak, but Essie's eyes focused on him again, and her body abruptly regained its solidity.

"The three Beresfords stood there for a long time, looking down at the bodies and not speaking," Essie said. "It was as if they were trying to hold onto the past, and they all knew the moment they spoke their happy twenty-five-year idyll would shatter. Things would never go back to the way they had been.

"Uncle Ramos was livid. He had warned them about being gentle, and the twins—the boy, at least—had chosen to ignore his instructions.

"The boy pretended to be sorry for what he had done.

He promised it would never, *never* happen again. But his sister knew the truth. She could 'feel' this new part of him—the part that had enjoyed the killing, that had *fed* on the vibrant intensity of fear in another being. And she could sense his hunger as well. She knew he could barely wait for the chance to continue his experiments on humans from the outside.

"Still, the girl said nothing to Ramos. She was, after all, a twin—half of a whole. She prayed that her brother's new obsession had been brought on by the sudden barrage of sensation—that it would pass with time. She *had* to hope that her other half would quickly learn to control his . . . *hunger*, and she was resolved to help him come to know it for what it was—a path straight to hell.

"Something else about the episode bothered the girl deeply. *Ramos had not been able to read the change in her brother*. Until that moment, she had thought her uncle to be all-powerful, consummately wise—infallible. Now . . . she didn't know. He seemed more like a man. More . . . *normal*."

Essie sighed bitterly and closed her eyes for a moment. "From that day on, the twin brother and sister truly *were* separated from the rest of humankind—far more isolated than they had been when locked inside the estate itself. *He* learned to draw sustenance from any petty cruelty. *She* prayed for the happy days of the past . . . but things were never, never the same."

She opened her eyes and looked deeply into Lance's. He felt a hint of the vertigo again, but it was different now—*self*-induced.

"No more guessing games, Lance. The male twin was Warwick Beresford. The female twin . . . was me."

"*What!*" Lance jumped to his feet and stared at her. "What the *hell?*" he said, and turned away.

What was she trying to tell him? That the old man he'd talked with a few days ago in the churchyard in Parramatta was born in the *seventeenth century*? That he . . . that *she* . . . that *they* were both over *350 years old!*

Disbelief raged in him. He knew that the manifestation of Essie Beresford was still there, staring at his back long and hard. And he had accepted so much already: prophecies, telepathy, clairvoyance, *ghosts*. Why not 350-year-old twins?

Still, it wasn't easy. And somehow he didn't think it was going to get any easier in the hours to come.

He turned back to her and smiled. It wasn't a warm smile, but it was there. "Okay," he said and shrugged heavily. "Okay. There's more, isn't there? So, go on."

A quizzical frown flickered across Essie's face. She knew the turmoil he was going through. To hear so much, so quickly—and all from someone whose presence itself seemed impossible.

But he was accepting it. Slowly, tentatively, perhaps only partially—but he was accepting it nonetheless. *There may be more to you, young Lance, than meets the eye*, she thought. When she began to speak again, the words were softer and gentler than ever . . . and the frown was gone.

"Uncle Ramos took care of the details," she told him. "We never saw the bodies again.

"The next day he tried to begin our education—our *real* education, in the ways of the Beresford legacy. It was supposed to have been a happy time, filled with discovery and joy. But the deaths of the colliers and Warwick's hunger changed all that. There was something . . . different in the way Uncle spoke. A deep sadness he could not hide.

"He told us he had been entrusted with raising us by our long-dead mother and father. It was the first time he had mentioned them without prompting in—well, in years.

"We did our best to interrogate him. We cajoled, we whimpered, we badgered, but he was adamant. Not a word about our parents. It had been their wish, he said, that we know nothing of either their lives or their apparently unexpected demise.

"Instead, he continued his explanation. His job, he said, was to take care of our education, to keep us away from the prying eyes of a world that would misunderstand us and probably burn us at the stake, and most important, on our twenty-fifth birthday, he was to tell us of our legacy and begin training us in its use.

"I remember it vividly, even now. We were sitting in the stuffy, opulent main hall of Beresford Manse, even though it was a warm day. We couldn't bring ourselves to go outside—even the thought of going into the yard brought back memories of the deaths—so we stayed seated in the high-backed chairs in front of the fireplace and whispered about . . . *power*.

" 'The talent,' Uncle Ramos told us, 'must remain secret and be used sparingly.' It would take many years to explore even the surface of it, he said. We should be prudent, and cautious. We could be surprised like any other human. We could *die* like any other human as well.

"Warwick didn't care. The deaths of the colliers had opened up something deep and awful inside him. At first I didn't want to believe it, but somehow his mind had been . . . *twisted*. He was already desperate to feed again.

"Two weeks later, he went to the kitchen and tried to take over Elsa's mind. But he found what we had known since we were eight years old. Both Harold and Elsa were able to block their minds from us, in some way we couldn't comprehend.

"Seconds after his attempt, Uncle Ramos burst in. He told Warwick that the two retainers had been protected all these years by *him*, at our parents' request, so we wouldn't learn too early of our gift.

"Warwick was livid. He drew himself up to his full height and demanded that Uncle Ramos free Elsa's mind, and then immediately tell him everything he needed to know about the power that was his legacy.

"Uncle Ramos refused to remove his protection from the servants. He even tried to laugh off Warwick's demands, reminding him of the time and careful planning and practice it would take to control the 'energy' that was his birthright.

"But Ramos had underestimated the strength of Warwick's demented mind. Without really understanding how he was doing it, Warwick formed his thoughts into a weapon and lashed out wildly. It was a clumsy attempt at best—more like, more like a huge broadsword than a rapier—but the effect was devastating.

"Had Uncle Ramos been prepared for it, the attack would probably have done little, if any, damage. But it was so soon—we were so, so *young*. He wasn't ready. *None* of us were. And the psychic blow came as a complete surprise. It sent him reeling back against the wall of the kitchen, his mind badly injured, his defenses critically weakened.

"Warwick drove on relentlessly, tearing at our uncle's mind. He drove his mental weapon deeper, without concern or conscience—without *reason*—trying to force Ramos to tell us everything. I knew then that the child who had looked up to this man, who had loved him and cared for him, was completely gone. A monster had taken his place.

"It was a battle of wills—the first, but far from the last, that I was to see. Compared to other, later, conflagrations, it was all rather minor, really. I'm still convinced now, as I was then, that Uncle Ramos could have struck Warwick down. But he had been charged with the job of protecting us—he had done so all our lives—and I don't believe he could bring himself to harm the boy.

"On the other hand, he couldn't allow Warwick to triumph, either—he didn't dare reveal everything he knew to a madman. So he just . . . turned himself off, rather than let someone as sick as Warwick have the knowledge that lay stored deep in his mind.

"I ran in just as Ramos was . . . *receding*," Essie said,

her voice quavering. "I still remember seeing him sprawled out on the stone floor, gasping his last breaths. I remember it, God help me, as if it were yesterday."

There was a tear in her eye. "He looked at me," she whispered, "with such love. Then he said, 'Essie, what have I done to you?' And he died.

"I tried to join minds with him, to tell him I loved him and that he mustn't go like this, but he was already sliding away into darkness. I couldn't . . . reach him."

Essie had to fight to hold back a sob. Lance didn't know what to say, so he said nothing. He knew this feeling. He had felt it himself only weeks before, when his mother was suddenly gone from him forever.

Finally, Essie looked up. Her eyes were clear again; her body solid and full. "I was shattered by Uncle Ramos's death," she said. "Warwick pretended not to be affected, but I think he was shaken by what he'd done. Not shaken enough to *change*, of course, but . . ."

She shrugged and looked down at her hand. "He began a tirade that lasted for days. He stormed around the huge manse screaming obscenities into the air—at Uncle Ramos, at our unknown and unremembered mother and father, at everything in general—just for the rotten turn of events that had overtaken him. Naturally, he never admitted his own role in it all—never thought for a moment that *he* had brought all this on us.

"He was my twin, the other half of me, and yet I was suddenly frightened by him. I locked myself in my rooms for days at a time, but I couldn't block him out. Even when I covered my ears I couldn't stop his anger from raging in my mind. We had been too open to each other for too many years.

"I didn't eat. I couldn't sleep. I couldn't think. And most of all, I just couldn't comprehend what had happened. In reality, I suppose I was a pampered child who refused to accept that things had changed—that they would never be the same again. It took me a long time to admit that whether I liked it or not, my childhood was over.

"Of course, I had no real option. It was either change, accept responsibility and face up to things, or die.

"So, after five days of listening to Warwick's raging, I marshaled my senses and consciously thought about what to do. One possible answer came to me. I began to methodically catalog every minute detail of the—the *block*, the mental barrier, that I'd felt in Harold and Elsa.

"I turned it over and over in my mind, looking at it from every conceivable angle. Though I didn't know it at the time, I had begun using a part of myself that was unique—an ability I did *not* share with my twin. I could *analyze* the mechanisms of the power. I could take it apart, understand its nature, and use it constructively—creatively. Warwick could only wield it as a blunt instrument or as a siphon. It was a purely emotional experience for him— deep, supremely powerful, but *crude*.

"What I was doing, Lance, was *learning*. At the advanced age of twenty-five, I had begun to take on the responsibilities of an adult—and to take the first small steps toward understanding the immense power that was my inheritance.

"Two days later, weak from hunger but enthused by my efforts, I sat on my bed and gently raised a barrier around my *own* mind—around the essence that was uniquely me.

"The insane raging of Warwick's mind slowly faded . . . and finally it was gone. For an instant I knew a relief like none I'd ever experienced. Then another feeling swam over me.

"*Loneliness*. Lance, for the first time in my life, I couldn't hear other people's thoughts, or feel the closeness of another being. I felt blind and deaf and dumb—*crippled*. I realized that, for the first time, I was just like the two coal men.

"The emptiness ripped at me with such savagery that I instinctively began to pull down the block—it was that painful, that frightening. I probably would have succeeded if Warwick hadn't inadvertently intervened.

"He began pounding on my door and shouting obscenities at me. The pain in his words reflected the separation I was feeling as well, but there was such intensity in his voice—that *hunger* again—that I knew for certain that he was mad. If, at that moment, I had let him in—into my room, into my mind—he would have killed me. I was sure of it.

"My resolve strengthened. The block became a part of me . . . and it has saved my life a hundred times since.

"Warwick pounded on my door for hours, but the external noise didn't compare to his mental tirades. The noise was easy to ignore—so easy, in fact, that I wasn't conscious of exactly when he gave up and went away.

"Over the next three days, I experimented with the blocking technique and found I could control it in subtle ways. I could ease it open, in a sense—crack it just enough to reach out again, while still protecting myself.

"Days passed—days of study, and thought, and fear.

"When I finally felt strong enough to reach out for Warwick, I found his mind strangely subdued. I left the room and went looking for him . . . and found him slumped in a chair in front of the fireplace in the main hall, awake but . . . *still*.

"I tiptoed past the open archway that led to the living room. I could see Warwick, but he didn't seem to notice me as I quickly made my way to the kitchen. Once there, I wolfed down a piece of bread and sucked on a withered orange for the juice. As my hunger began to ease, I realized that the stealth was unnecessary. Warwick hadn't even flinched. He wasn't the least bit interested in me.

"Only then I noted the drastic change in the kitchen. It was a mess. Cooking utensils were littered about. Containers had been emptied and dropped on the floor. Even the fire in the stove was out. I knew Harold and Elsa would never have let things get that bad, if they had any choice."

Essie closed her eyes and breathed deeply. *An odd thing for a ghost to do*, Lance thought. He still couldn't decide how much of this he could believe—if he could believe any of it at all.

"I found the bodies of the two retainers outside the kitchen door. Without Uncle Ramos's protection, they had been easy prey for Warwick. From the looks of . . . things, they had been dead for at least a day or two. And there was little doubt as to how they had died.

"I sat in the kitchen and cried. They had been family to me, Lance—almost *all* my family. I told myself there must have been something I could have done to help—*what* I didn't know, but *something*. I thought of the years of joy that were gone forever. I realized that my only living relative—my only connection with the world—was the madman slumped in the next room.

"Finally, I pondered what I was to do. It was obvious now why Warwick was no longer screaming at me. Without interference from our uncle, he had been able to satisfy his hunger—the only force that drove him now. For the moment he was like a lion after a kill. He was . . . *content*.

"But what would happen when the hunger returned? Would he go into the village? Would he dare leave the manse?

"Or would he come for *me?*

"And what about the simple necessities of day-to-day living? After the grief and shock had passed, I investigated what was left of the kitchen and pantry. Elsa and Harold had always kept food made in advance, but Warwick had eaten or destroyed much of that. Harold was no longer there to get more, and nobody would bring food to us. No one ever came there.

"I realized that our isolation was a blessing in some very important ways. It had probably already saved our lives. Still, we had to eat—and neither Warwick nor I had ever set foot outside of the estate. Where did one get food?

How did Harold pay for it? For that matter, which of the three nearby towns did he visit on his shopping days?

"There were an endless number of questions, and not an answer to be seen. And, of course, there was the most important question of all. What would Warwick do when the hunger returned?

"The unbelievable irony of our situation suddenly struck me. I couldn't help it—I just had to laugh. There we were, potentially the most powerful humans on the face of the earth, and we didn't even know how to feed ourselves.

"The laughter spread through me—but there was no humor left to fuel it. It was a dry, ugly laughter, one that hovered on the precarious edge of sanity. For a moment I teetered there on the edge. I believe even now that if I had fallen over the precipice, at that moment, I would never have made it back to normal.

"But I held on—barely. After what seemed like an eternity, my laughter subsided. Then I sat on the giant wooden table in the kitchen and let my legs swing gently in the air.

"I remembered how I had sat and done this many times, since I was a small girl, watching while Elsa cooked a meal or baked something for the family. The simplicity, the familiarity of it, gave me an unexpected anchor—something to hold on to.

"I recovered. Slowly, *very* slowly, I recovered. And as I did, I began to understand what I had to do—to protect myself, to escape, to *survive*.

"I realized that, before anything else, I had to face Warwick.

"As it turned out, my fear was premature. My brother was having a harder time with the isolation of his own thoughts than I had ever had. After all, I had *chosen* to cut myself off. It had happened to him without thought or consultation, and it *hurt*, Lance, it hurt us both. Even drifting in that animal euphoria that stole over him after his

. . . fits . . . his numbed mind realized how much he needed me. For a while, at least.

"It was obvious to me that, twin or no twin, Warwick couldn't be trusted. But I had never been truly alone before, and after the brief mental encounter with the two coal men, I knew that I might have a hard time finding anyone I could even talk with. Still, I had to do *something*."

Essie Beresford looked about the room, her eyes not really seeing anything there. She absentmindedly twisted her golden hair with the fingers of her right hand.

Lance saw her nervousness and understood. For the first time, he felt a real empathy for this lady who might well be one of his ancient ancestors. *It must be hard*, he thought to himself, *going over memories hundreds of years old. Especially memories like these.*

Then he stopped himself and realized what he had just been doing. *My God*, he thought, *I'm actually beginning to believe all this stuff.*

Essie looked at him—a deep, penetrating, almost amused look. "How are you?" she asked.

He took a deep breath. "I'm hanging in there," he said slowly. "Keep going."

He knew at that moment that if she could have, she would have reached out and taken his hand. The look on her face told him that much—and the look itself was enough. She smiled and began to speak again . . . and now Lance listened with a truly open mind.

"Even with all his faults, Warwick was the only surviving family I had. In a strange way, we needed each other.

"I did not fool myself into believing it was anything more than a temporary truce, but at the time it was a necessary one. And, in some ways, events had given me a lucky edge. Warwick was virtually incapacitated. I had to be the one to take the bit in my teeth, as it were.

"I started by going through Harold's notes and receipts. I discovered a good deal about what he shopped for and where he shopped for it. Even with that, it was hard—*very* hard—to hitch a horse to the sulky and drive down the road that led away from the estate.

"I'm not sure what I expected to find beyond the walls. Maybe a different world—something huge and exciting and very tidy—like the estate itself, only *bigger*. Whatever it was, it was a foolish expectation. Despite the weeks of insanity and my own newfound maturity, in many ways I was still a babe in the woods."

Essie smiled as she thought back on that time. Even in the midst of this dark story, Lance realized, she was somewhat enjoying herself. He wondered if she had had anyone to talk to in her last years of life—whether she had reminisced like this *before* her death. He felt a sudden rush of affection for this woman he would never really know.

"We had studied history," Essie said. "And we had been told of the present situation in the world outside. I'd always thought the history of mankind was not much more than an endless string of wars, with virtually no time to rest between them. So perhaps I was expecting to find armies poised outside the gates, ready to attack.

"What I found instead were open fields and a great many trees—very much like the view *inside* the estate. After a short while, however, the dusty road led me past a variety of wretched farmhouses—little more than hovels, really—and cattle so thin and diseased they could barely stand.

"It wasn't until I reached the nearby village that I saw any people at all.

"My first visit to the village of Norald was an experience that rivaled anything I'd ever known. The village itself was pathetic—nothing more than a long series of meager shacks with thatched roofs and stone walls. But to me, at that time, it seemed huge. I'd never *seen* so many people in my life. And though we'd read about village life and all it entailed, the books hadn't prepared me for the noise, or the colors, or the smells—or any of it.

"Do you know what the most astonishing thing was,

Lance? *Dogs*. There were *dogs* there—skinny little things that sniffed at everything and barked incessantly. I'd never seen one before. I hadn't even *imagined* them correctly. I had this silly image in my head that was half lion, half hound-of-hell.

"Looking back on it now, I know it was a pitiful little town filled with poor wretches eking out a bare-bones living, but it was like a county fair to the eyes of a young woman who'd never seen a town before.

"And it was during that first contact with humanity that I learned how lucky I had been to install my mental defenses against Warwick. The block had become as much a part of me as brushing my hair. I knew, after all, that I could never let it down as long as Warwick lived—that he could attack me at any time, perhaps from any*where*.

"In Norald, I imagined I was safe—at least I *hoped* I was. As I slowly drove the rig down the crowded central street, I felt something nudge the shield, and I began to investigate it.

"I was curious to know what it was. Carefully, slowly, tentatively, I lowered my defenses . . .

"Thunder exploded between my temples. A blaring babble of shrieking voices slammed into me. My last conscious act, before I blacked out, was to raise the shield to full strength again. It was all that saved my sanity, and possibly my life.

"I awoke to find myself stretched out across the leather seat of the sulky. A girl with flaming red hair, dressed in a cotton blouse and a billowing frock, was dabbing at my forehead with a wet rag.

"It smelled terrible, and it was probably far from hygienic, but it felt wonderful. When I was finally able to sit up and look about, I found a group of townspeople crowded about the sulky, staring at me.

" 'Who are ye, woman?' said a burly man wearing a leather apron. He had a booming voice and an accent much like the two colliers'. 'And where 'ave ye come from?'

" 'Don't bother 'er with stuff like that,' the girl with the rag snapped. Her voice was loud and harsh, and I remember how shocked I was to learn a woman could sound like that. 'Can't ye see she's a lady?'

"I finally explained who I was," Essie said. "I already knew, from the thoughts I'd read in the two colliers' minds, that the people hereabouts knew about the estate and had heard rumors of Warwick and I. But I was still surprised when the crowd moved back from the sulky, hardly able to hide their terror at the thought of my being there. I had never encountered group fear before, or the results of village gossip.

"The girl with the rag turned on the group, hands wedged at her hip, and sneered. 'Look at ye. Grow'd men and women afraid of a tiny slip of a girl. Do she look like a monster to ye? Look at her.'

"The man with the apron was the first to step back toward the sulky. The others soon followed, though some made sure there was always someone else between them and me.

"I told them that Harold and Elsa had left our employ, and that Uncle Ramos had been called away unexpectedly on business.

"They were basically kind and simple folk, and after hearing my story, they welcomed me to town—I can't say it was a rousing welcome—and offered to help in any way they could.

"When the hubbub around my arrival had died down a bit, and most of the townsfolk had returned to whatever they were doing before my collapse, I had an opportunity to consider what had happened to me when I'd lowered my shield.

"It was blatantly obvious once I gave it just an ounce of thought. I hadn't been prepared for the chaos of a group of untrained minds suddenly charging at me. The pressure had been more than I could bear, and I'd simply . . . shut down.

"Now, at last, I understood why our uncle had kept us isolated. There was no way we would have survived such an onslaught as children. It would have crippled our abilities at best, or driven us mad at worst. Even now, Warwick was wholly unprepared for intercourse with the outside world—just as Ramos had tried to explain. He would need careful preparation before he could safely leave the estate.

"I also realized, as I climbed down from the sulky and stood in the dirt street, that in a strange way I owed Warwick a debt of thanks. If he had not raged at me, day after day, I would not have been forced to learn how to block my thoughts. I had no doubt that the babble of noise that exploded in my brain would have killed me outright, or left me with no brain at all, long before I could have understood what was going on.

"The girl with the rag told me her name was Meg. She made a rough attempt at a curtsy and smiled, showing off a row of nearly perfect teeth. Both Warwick and I had healthy teeth as well—we had always been in excellent health—but visiting Norald had shown me how unusual that was in that time. When the townspeople had bunched around me, I had noticed most of them had mouths full of rotting stumps and blanched gums. And worse, many of the people I'd seen were more blatantly physically deformed, with everything from small growths on their faces and arms to twisted and humpbacked bodies. Some had been injured, but many appeared to have carried their deformities from birth. I made a mental note to go through Uncle Ramos's books to try to discover a way to help such people."

Essie paused and shook her head, half-amused and half-embarrassed. "Oh, Lance," she whispered. "I was so young then. I never dreamed . . ."

"I know," Lance said—and he did, he understood all

too well. That burning desire to change the world, and that horrible realization that the world changed *you*.

"At any rate," she said, shrugging, "I was really concentrating on Meg.

" 'Have ye ever done this shoppin' afore, Miss Essie?' she asked, patting her flaming red hair.

"When I told her I hadn't, and that I didn't even know how it was done, she was astounded. How could a woman grow to adulthood and never learn to shop for the things she needed? How could she put meals on the table?

" 'It's a good thing the fates had ye fall upon me,' she added and laughed lightly. 'Ye would be easy pickin's for the likes a what ye have to deal with in Norald.' Then she curtsied awkwardly again. 'I don't mean no offense, but ye best leave the bartering to me, Miss Essie.'

"I quickly assured her that I wasn't offended in the least, and that I thought it was a sound idea indeed. She smiled widely, tucked the rag into the top of her skirt, and happily led me down the muddy street.

"As we made our way, Meg told me she lived in a house not too far from our estate and worked in the nearby tavern. She happily chattered about her horrid boss, her sluttish fellow barmaid, and the obnoxious and lovely and evil men who populated her world. I found as we walked and talked that I actually *liked* this woman—the first woman my own age that I had ever known. Despite her rough exterior, she had a good heart beating in her chest and a zest for life that was contagious. I was soon laughing out loud at her village witticisms—the few of them I understood at the time.

"It was soon obvious that Meg had been right about the merchants of Norald, and that it was indeed my good fortune to have found her. The game of barter was an art learned over many years, and if not for Meg, the merchants would have robbed me blind that day.

"This was not just conjecture on my part. As Meg and I walked from place to place in the town, I began experi-

menting with my mental shield—easing it back the tiniest
amount and peering out through the crack. It was easier
than I thought; by the time we reached the local butcher, I
had perfected it enough to be able to read the surface of his
thoughts and still block out the din of the other minds in
town.

"The butcher was upset that Meg had taken me in hand.
She was known as a shrewd bargainer, but still he tried to
browbeat her into paying more than he thought the meat
was worth—simply because I looked as if I could afford a
bit more.

"Meg would stand for none of it. She dug in her heels
and dealt with him as stubbornly as if she had been buying
the food for her own family. The deal she finally struck
was one that Meg and the butcher both believed was the
best they were going to do . . . though, strangely, neither
of them seemed quite as happy about it as they might have
been.

"It was there, at the butcher's, that I first felt—how
shall I put this delicately, Lance? Where I first felt *lust*.

"Once the bargain had been struck, the butcher relaxed.
The 'business' portion of his smallish brain relaxed, and
he began to look at Meg and me as . . . something else.
Suddenly we were *women*, not *customers*.

"Meg made it easy to get the two confused. Her open-
front blouse showed a good deal of cleavage—a fact that
shocked me when I first noticed—and though the butcher
appeared to barely notice, the mind behind his piggish
eyes was racing.

"I saw—no, I *felt* what he was thinking as he pictured
her in his mind. First she was bare-bosomed, then completely naked. Suddenly he was thinking long and hard
about just how thick and just how red her pubic hair must
be.

"Then he looked at *me*. Though he had heard the
rumors and a part of his mind held a ring of fear, he was
now thinking of me only as a woman. I was dressed in a

high-collared dress that reached well below my knees, and though it did show off my figure—I was a rather shapely lass, Lance—it was far from alluring.

"This minor detail didn't deter the butcher. In fact, it seemed to stimulate his imagination even more. In his mind he saw the two of us in the rear of his shop. I, of course, refused his advances, but he tore my dress and underclothes from me. Then he dragged off his own rough clothes and lept at me, naked and roaring like—

"—I slammed my shield between our minds.

"My shock and humiliation must have shown through. Meg suddenly turned to me and said, 'Are ye all right, Miss Essie? Ye look pale, all of a sudden.'

"I told her I was fine, though that wasn't exactly true. My pulse was racing, my palms were sweaty, and I felt a strange throbbing in my body that I'd never felt before.

"At the time, of course, I would have denied it was anything other than pure revulsion. But later, looking back on it, I realized that my own nascent sexuality had been aroused for the first time—I was *twenty-five*, after all. One day I would have to come to grips with that, I knew, but at the time I was trying to understand so much that I pushed the feeling away.

"By the end of the afternoon, I had acquired the goods we needed and paid for them with a bag of coins I'd found in Elsa's cubbyhole in the kitchen. The sun was slipping behind the trees by the time I returned to the sulky and prepared for my trip back to the estate.

"Meg and I had become friends, of a sort, and she made me promise that when I next came to town, I would come to her tavern, if only to say hello. I gave her a coin for her trouble, and though her mind told me she wanted it, and needed it, she refused to take it. I insisted until she finally agreed, and then I left.

"As the sulky made its way down the long dirt track toward Beresford Manse, I found myself brooding. The excursion had been fun, but it had made me ask as many questions as it had answered.

"I needed to know what the financial situation of the estate was. We obviously would need to pay for things, and I'd already used most of the coins I'd found in Elsa's hiding place. In fact, I realized, I needed to go through any papers Uncle Ramos had left. Besides money and information about running the estate, he may have left some inkling of the legacy itself.

"I was so deeply involved in my own thoughts that I never noticed the approaching men until they were next to the sulky. They must have cut across the fields as I'd made my way around the winding road.

"One of them grabbed the head of the horse. The other rode behind and grabbed for me. His thoughts told me of his intent even before he reached the edge of the rig, and the violence and cruelty I felt terrified me.

"The two had been in the crowd in Norald, and they had decided I would be easy prey for robbery. At the time, I realized, that was all they had hoped for. But now, as he looked at me, his thoughts began to remind me of the butcher's.

"I was terrified, Lance. I wanted to strike out and hurt these two men, I admit. And not just because they wanted to take the food I had worked all day to buy. But because they saw me as little more than a female animal, something put on the earth to satiate their male desires.

"I remembered Uncle Ramos, and what he had said. 'They are not like us,' he had told us. 'They are fragile.'

"But it didn't matter to me—not then. I wanted to make an example of these two, so when I returned to town others like them would know enough to leave me be.

"The first man reached up to grab my arm, and in that instant I reached out and took his mind in my hands.

"I thought of . . . *fire.*

"In his mind's eye, he saw me bathed in flame, with eyes that glowed like hot coals. The image opened its mouth and breathed fire at him, and he felt the skin on his face singe and wither in the heat.

"In an instant, he was on his knees, feeling all the pain he would have endured if his body had truly been burned. And as he wept and writhed, I sent the image to the second man.

"I let it continue for both of them for more than a minute. I can't imagine how long it must have been for them. Finally, my own anger abated. I eased my control and stopped the flames. Then I spoke directly into their minds, in a voice so loud they clapped their trembling hands over their ears.

" 'YOU HAVE BEEN WARNED,' I boomed. 'GO NOW. TELL THE OTHERS TO LET THIS GIRL BE!' The men struggled to their knees, whimpering, and scrambled into the bush like wounded rabbits. I remember feeling good about that—*good* about their fear and pain."

Now Essie didn't look pleased about it at all. "It was crude manipulation," she said, sounding almost apologetic. "But at that time I was amazed I was able to do it.

"The next time I was in town, a brief touch of two or three minds was enough to tell me my plan had worked. Most of the townsfolk had heard the tale of the two would-be thieves. The general consensus seemed to be that the two fools had drunk too much ale and imagined the entire episode. Still, these were simple people who were deeply afraid of the unknown. This new rumor, added to the vague one that had circulated for years, was enough to make many of them give me a wide berth.

"Even the butcher watched his thoughts when I was around. I think a small part of me was strangely unhappy about that, but I would never have admitted it to myself.

"Back at Beresford Manse I set about putting things in order. First I cleaned up the kitchen; then I made food for Warwick and I. A part of me realized I was using the situation. Since Warwick was dependant on me to prepare his food and look after him, he would have to leave me alone. And as long as he continued to vegetate, having fed on the violent emotions until he could stand no more, I was free to rummage through Uncle Ramos's things without interruption.

"After a full day of hunting, I found our uncle's personal papers hidden in a small space behind a loose brick in his bedroom. The deed for the estate that Warwick and I had signed on our twenty-fifth birthday was there. It was tied to a thick stack of other papers related to the family finances.

"The estate, it turned out, was very rich. The notes led me to a huge fortune in gold coins hidden deep in the dungeonlike wine cellars of the manse itself, and in London there were three different brokers who did little else but manage our holdings. The income from any one of them would make Warwick and I wealthy beyond most people's wildest dreams.

"There was one other set of documents bundled with the financial papers—a stack of old texts and handwritten notes, some of them dating back hundreds of years.

"In every waking hour during the next month—except for the times I went to Norald and spent the day with Meg—I studied those texts. From time to time, I would reach out and gently touch Warwick's mind, constantly aware of his location, his temperament, his thoughts—or lack of them.

"With each passing day I felt him changing. He was slowly returning to life, and the more animated he became, the stronger his unholy hunger became.

"It had already driven him to kill on three different occasions. I knew it would lead to more—not tomorrow or the day after, but *soon*. And I noted with a weird fascination that Warwick's bizarre appetite and the sensation I had felt lurking in the village butcher—the glee and satisfaction he felt when he dreamed of attacking me—were horribly similar. Warwick's twisted hunger was not so unusual after all, I decided. The only difference was that he possessed the power to make his worst dreams come true.

"About five weeks after our twenty-fifth birthday, the respite ended and the nightmare began anew.

"I remember pulling myself from hours of study. When my mind stretched out to check on Warwick, he wasn't in his usual chair in front of the huge brick fireplace. A quick mental check showed he wasn't anywhere in the house.

"I had never tried to connect with my brother over any great distance, so I decided to find out if it were possible. I sent my mind outwards, striving to locate the complex pattern of thinking I had come to know as Warwick's.

"I found a faint mental trail that felt like his, but I could only follow it for a short distance outside the estate. Beyond that, the confusion of other minds grew too intense.

"I wasn't even sure if I had been following Warwick at all—but if that had been his spoor, he had gone off in the direction of a town to the south of Norald.

"I continued my quest, stretching toward that small village. And as I extended myself, I examined the ability I was using. The power itself has always fascinated me, Lance—how it works, what it *does*. But with every yard I extended beyond the estate itself, my power waned. I realized that I had certain physical limitations, apparently bound by the property itself, or my misuse of the legacy, and the farther I strayed from our familial home, the weaker I became. I was forced to end my search and draw my mind back into my body. Even that comparatively simple act was so exhausting that, upon my return, I collapsed onto my bed and fell into a deep, trancelike sleep.

"Later that night I awoke and sent out a light tendril of thought in search of Warwick. What I found horrified me.

"He was in an open section of the wine cellars, and his mind was literally bursting with hunger. Hunger . . . and *lust*.

"Through his mind's eye, I saw the young girl he had

strapped to one of the brick walls of the cellar. I heard her howl in pain as his mind drove spikes of force deep into her brain, and I felt Warwick's own twisted ecstasy as she grew more and more terrified.

"But there was something worse there, Lance. There was Warwick himself, and the satisfaction of his hunger. With each wave of agony that radiated from the girl, he—he *fed*. He took it in, sucked at it, *loved* it in a way I can't describe—in a way I don't *want* to describe.

"And I felt it, Lance. I felt him *feed*. It was an abominable thing. The worst thing I had ever felt in my innocent twenty-five years on earth; it is still among the worst memories I carry after almost fifteen times that long."

Essie paused and hugged her arms, swallowing against the revulsion she had conjured up.

The power of it made Lance pause himself. *It must have been very bad*, he thought. *To remember it like this after more than three centuries . . .*

She swallowed once more and took up the tale again. "I dragged my mind from his and lay on the bed, shaking uncontrollably. My first thought was to help the girl, but there was nothing I could do. The sheer animal force that drove Warwick had already killed Uncle Ramos; I wasn't stupid enough to think I could face up to insanity like that and survive.

"What I could do was study even harder—to continue to sift through the notes and texts that Uncle Ramos, our parents, and the other unknown Beresford kin had left behind. I knew then that I *had* to find some answers about the legacy and how I might use it to help Warwick. Without the knowledge—and the power it created—I was a prisoner in the manse. A prisoner whose continued existence relied entirely on the good graces of a madman.

"It had already become painfully obvious to me that none of my ancestors had truly understood the power. They had tried to explain its effects, to codify its eccentricities and put into words all they knew about it, and though that was much more than I knew, it didn't really tell me what I wanted to know.

"One small paragraph buried in the notes left by my great-uncle Darius before he was murdered—the notes never said by whom, or how—hinted at a possible origin of the power: a connection to some other world, some other . . . *dimension*, I suppose. He believed the Beresford Manse to be a kind of gateway, which would explain the geographical limitations of the power. But his notes gave no clue at all as to how the power had come to be, and how he, Darius, had decided this point of fact, or even conjecture.

"The writing of these ancient scrolls and texts was often hard to understand, and the language was always obscure. Still, I was learning. I found that the power of the Beresfords will allow us to live a very long time—centuries, if we're careful. Being careful, however, was not a Beresford trait, it seemed. It appeared that most of the Beresford heirs had been murdered or had suffered bizarre 'accidents' long before they were due to inherit the gift. After what had already happened between Warwick and me, I was beginning to understand why that might be . . ."

And from what Angie said the other night, it appears that trend continues, Lance thought wryly.

"I also discovered that the Beresford Manse hadn't always been the building it was in the 1600s. It apparently was once a large thatched-roof hut, and before that something else—though what I couldn't ascertain from the notes.

"A short section in one of the scrolls sent me on another, related search. Since I'd read all there was to read in the notes left behind by Uncle Ramos, I went to the library and began to read through hundreds of different volumes on the history of the Beresford clan. I was totally free to work, since Warwick was in his satiated state once more, lolling about as if drugged. All I had to do was cook, read . . . and try to forget that girl, and the cellar, and the . . . the *feeding*."

Essie paused again, then turned suddenly and pointed at the bookcase beside her. "Many of the books you see here are the originals. Much later, I had some of these printed from the scrolls and texts I found there."

Essie reached out to take a book, but her hand passed through the leather binding and the bookcase itself. She quickly extricated her ghostly hand from the case, as startled as Lance himself. "I keep forgetting," she mumbled. "Such a bother." Then she looked at Lance, as if expecting him to say something.

He smiled rather blandly. He was past being surprised . . . by anything. And he didn't want to start asking questions now, or he'd never hear the end of the story.

"All right," she said graciously, realizing how quickly her time was passing. "I will go on. I continued to study and survive, but Warwick's . . . *trysts* were becoming more frequent and more intense—if that were possible. Toward the end, he went out more and more often, until he was out 'hunting' every four weeks or so.

"I knew what was happening," Essie said, "but I tried desperately to block it out. The books were what was important—the knowledge they held. If I let my emotions take control of me, if I tried to fight him before I was ready, I would only fail, and even more would die later. So I let the women perish. I hated myself for it—I still curse those days locked up in the manse—but I had to, Lance. I *had* to let it happen."

She looked at him as if begging for forgiveness. *It's not me who has to forgive you*, he thought, looking deeply into her cobalt eyes. *It's you. You have to forgive yourself.*

He couldn't tell if she sensed his thoughts. She simply looked away and went on with her story . . . though her voice trembled more than before. "On one of my trips to town," Essie said, "Meg talked about a new panic that was gripping the entire countryside. Young girls from the surrounding areas were being killed, she said, and the local authorities couldn't figure out who, or what, was responsible. They weren't even sure how the murders were being committed. The nude bodies of the girls were always found out in the fields, but no one ever saw anything. Meg herself thought it was witches, since the bodies were being mutilated.

"The news shocked me, though it shouldn't have. I had thought Warwick's attacks were always mental—fear, psychically induced, until the mind itself burned to cinders to feed his hunger. I didn't realize he had sunk even lower— that *physical* pain satisfied him as well.

"Again, I chose to ignore it—I was *forced* to ignore it, if only for a short while longer. Then, even as I was stumbling toward the first threads of an idea that might help me escape and help neutralize Warwick, I inadvertently discovered exactly what he was up to.

"One night, after a long session of reading and note taking, I reached out and found my brother in the cellar.

"Again he had a girl tied and hanging from the wall— but this time, I knew, she was naked. I tried to pull away, but somehow I couldn't. There was something . . . *profound* in the pain—something awful and fascinating at the same time. And what's more, I simply couldn't believe what I was seeing—that anyone, even Warwick, could carry out such an evil enterprise.

"He was beating the girl with a whip. As each slash of its leather tails tore at her soft flesh and blood splashed from the wounds, her fear grew larger and hotter. Waves of it pounded from her in a hideous tide . . . and with each wave, Warwick shuddered with pleasure.

"When the girl's fear of the lashes began to reach a peak and level off, Warwick threw off his own clothes and attacked her, as the butcher had dreamed of attacking me. Again and again he drove himself at her, like the wildest of beasts.

"And with her body invaded as well as her mind, the girl's terror reached unimaginable heights. Her mind tried to collapse, her body tried to die, but Warwick would not let it happen—not yet. He kept her mind from collapsing. He held her body together. He drew energy from . . . *somewhere else* to keep her heart from bursting in her chest and her brain from breaking through her skull. He wanted to feel every nuance of the pain he was inflicting.''

Essie's voice was harsh with pain. *This is the hardest part*, Lance realized. *Every word is agony for her*.

"And even that was not enough," she rasped. "When even with this . . . *strategy* . . . her fear began to peak, he renewed his physical attacks with obscene metal objects. Her horror, her panic, her revulsion, soared higher. And higher. And *higher*. And through all this he drained the emanations of her fear, like a demonic parasite.

"And Lance . . . I was locked inside it *with* him. I felt his pleasure—his *ecstasy*. And though it revolted me, I couldn't help but share it—even *understand* it. I saw how close we were—how close *all* humans are—to the edge of the darkness. And that terrified me more than Warwick ever could.''

Essie ran her fingers through her sparkling hair and sighed. "It seemed to go on for . . . forever. I couldn't escape from the waves of sexual and mental stimulation that gushed through his being. My own body . . . *reacted* to this pleasure in ways I would never have dreamed possible, driven by its own insatiable need. They triggered my first . . . orgasms. It was horrible. It was . . . horrible. And wonderful. And I will never, *never* recover.''

Lance could only stare at her, and thank God he had never felt it himself. He prayed it would never happen again . . .

And then he remembered that the brother she spoke of still lived—that Warwick Beresford was *here*, in Australia, in *Sydney*—and that everything she described could happen again. Today. *Now*.

"I was part of it, Lance," she said hoarsely. "I hated it, and I loved it, and it wasn't my fault, but I was *part* of it. Still . . . I wasn't Warwick. Even when it took me over—as it did for a time—I was still myself, still whole. And eventually, through an act of will I have never been able to duplicate, I was able to break free.

"During the last seconds of turmoil, I saw the face of his victim. It was that face—that *face*—that drove me mad.

"A scream rose in my throat. I threw caution to the wind. I cursed my cowardice and inaction. I formed my will into a single, solid battering ram of force and threw it at him with all my might.

"I tried to stop him . . . but I had completely misunderstood the *nature* of the strength that flowed through my brother. My intellectualized, carefully crafted energy was nothing compared to his bludgeoning force. It was so minute, so *fragile*, that he barely acknowledged the main assault.

"At first he paid me little heed. Then, when he noticed my intrusion, he languidly turned his attention to me and hurled me from his thoughts as easily as if he had been swatting a fly.

"I tried again. And again. But my repeated attempts were even less successful than the first. I found I couldn't even reach into his thoughts. I had misjudged his power *that* much.

"I withdrew, trembling and filled with disgust at my weakness and naïveté. I rushed from the library to my bedroom, threw myself on the bed, and cried for hours, shedding tears for so many things. For the stupidity that let me believe Warwick could be saved. For the audacity I had displayed in thinking I was the only one who might learn to use the power—undoubtedly Warwick was somehow channeling it to his will. For the twin I had grown up with, had run and played with, who was now little more than a beast.

"But most of all, I cried for the girl I had come to call a friend.

"I cried for Meg, the latest victim of Warwick's disease."

Essie looked up at Lance. His eyes were wide, his mouth agape. "I wanted to tell her it wasn't witches at all," Essie whispered thickly. "Not witches at all, Meg. Just my brother."

Essie stood up and turned away. For a time, neither of them spoke. It was too hard.

Finally Essie shook her head and turned back, and the intensity he had sensed in her earlier returned with greater force. Time was running out; they both knew that now.

"The next few days I stayed locked in my room, formulating a plan. Then, while Warwick lay in the stupor that always followed his . . . *meals* . . . I made my move.

"I went to him and told him I knew what he had been doing. I told him that unless he did exactly as I said, I would bring the townspeople to Beresford Manse, now, while he was in his weakened state.

"At first he barely heard me. Finally the reality of it—and the threat I posed—began to sink in.

"Next I carefully explained to him what would happen if they decided he was a warlock. I described what it would be like to be burned at the stake.

"He tried to argue, but in his condition, he could barely hold up his head.

"I told him he disgusted me, and I explained a plan whereby we could each be rid of the other. I would be gone, and he would be free to do whatever he pleased with his life—and the lives of others.

"My plan was to split the house into two. Since it had two wings that were virtually identical—mirror images of each other—we would both still have a Beresford Manse, of sorts. The power, I theorized, would be retained in both segments, and exactly halved . . . but half of infinity is still infinity. I even agreed to transport my portion of the manse as far away as I could—around the world, if need be. Even that would be too close by my own estimation.

"Of course, he scoffed at my idea. But I persisted,

nagging him, continually reminding him that his alternative was a fiery death.''

She smiled grimly. ''I was very lucky,'' she said. ''And he was very confused, and being satiated, was not thinking clearly. Finally, he acquiesced. I could take my half and go—but I knew I would have to do it quickly, before the hunger returned. Before his thinking cleared and he realized what I was up to.

''I joined minds with Warwick, and using the techniques I had unraveled in the notes and books, I tapped into the power of our legacy.

''It was a huge gamble on my part, Lance. Even now I marvel at my *audacity*. I suppose it's the kind of bravery reserved for the young, equal parts foolhardiness and desperation. Still, I had little choice. I couldn't leave without some fragment of the power—I wasn't equipped to live like a regular human being. I knew I would die in a matter of weeks. And I couldn't leave the entire legacy to a madman like Warwick—this hideous compromise was some small improvement over surrender. And I knew that I couldn't stay in the manse and do nothing. It was too unbearable to endure . . . and, God help me, too *attractive* to the worst part of me.

''I gambled that Warwick's weakened state would cloud his thinking . . . and I was right. I don't believe he realized that linking our minds as we did when we were children would unleash a vast source of power—one that either of us could control in total, if our wills were strong enough. Instead he dreamed about his *feeding* and his sickening perversities. Until it was too late—far too late.

''It took every ounce of my energy and skill to succeed. But fear and desperation can be horribly efficient motivators, and I persevered.

''We split Beresford Manse into two parts—mirror images—and the part with my rooms, the library, all the notes and the gold from the cellar was teleported here, to Australia.

"After the mammoth effort, I hovered close to death for weeks. I had known of the danger; I knew that neither Warwick nor I was trained to handle the power properly, and that it could destroy us in an instant. Naturally, I hadn't explained that to Warwick. Part of me, I think, *wanted* him to be taken. After what I'd seen him do to Meg, I didn't really care.

"And I had lied to him as well. I had told him that the power itself was infinite, limited only by one's imagination and force of will. I had told him that separating the two wings would not affect his energy levels at all.

"It did. It crippled him—at least compared to the nearly limitless power he had wielded before. Splitting the house had diminished the power of the legacy, and by a great deal *more* than half. It meant that even if he survived the separation, he could not continue on with his depraved rituals, since he had been inadvertently using the power based in the house to draw the life-force from his victims.

"He would still have the hunger, but no way to feed it. God forgive me, but I thought that would be enough. A kind of . . . poetic justice, perhaps?

"At the time, I believed that was the end of it. I had removed myself from his proximity—from England altogether—and at the same time, I had stopped his evil crusade."

Now she hid her face in her hands, and the light from within her dimmed more seriously than ever.

"I was wrong, Lance. I was horribly wrong. It was more than a century before I learned the truth. Warwick *did* survive. And, since I had removed his ability to continue his twisted pastime, I had also ended his euphoric states of inactivity.

"I made myself a formidable enemy, Lance. Once he was fully awakened, Warwick came to understand what I had done . . . and he set about finding a way to rejoin the two halves of the house—to bring together the full power of the Beresford legacy, under *his* control.

"For more than three hundred years, he has been obsessed with two things. First, the reunification of the manse. Second, my death." She suddenly looked up and frowned. "No. Not my death, exactly. My total and absolute domination. He wants to take over my being and torture me . . . *endlessly*. To repay me for what I've done to him."

She smiled wearily—almost jauntily, Lance thought. "Of course, I found out about all this much later. In the beginning, after I was well enough to realize I wasn't going to die, I was too busy with setting myself up to think about my brother.

"At the time of my arrival, this area was covered in bush. There were trees as far as the eye could see, alive with snakes and exotic animals. The aboriginals were no problem for me. To them I was a sky-spirit who had flown down from the stars and settled nearby. They felt it was a special blessing and always treated me with respect—from a distance. Still, it took a long time to get everything in running order.

"But I had a long time. I *thought* I had all the time in the world . . .

"I used a good deal of it to study the nature of this energy even further. Though the house was split in two, there was still tremendous power available to me. Over the years, I slowly gained access to it, coming to appreciate many of its idiosyncrasies, though never really *understanding*.

"Some of the mysteries remain exactly that—mysteries. I was never able to find out any more about its origin than I had known in Northumberland. The backgrounds of my parents and more distant ancestors are equally unknown to me . . . but over the years, both of these questions seem to have lost their importance for me.

"I used the power of this 'birthright' to stay hidden until the first modern settlement came to Parramatta and to secure long-range investments. Then I carefully orches-

trated my induction into the 'elite' of the city. Before lon
it was a well-known fact that the hermit woman who live
in Beresford Hall had been one of the first settlers, that sh
disliked visitors, that she was blue-blooded aristocracy an
best left to herself. Some years later, it was a relativel
easy job to stage my death, then appear as my own grand
daughter from England, come to take over my holdings.

"Through the years, my abilities to control at least som
of the power grew. I found I could free my mind from m
body and send it outside the estate without suffering an
significant draining of strength. At first I watched silentl
as progress took its toll nearby—in Parramatta and th
surrounding areas. Then, as the years went by, I was abl
to stretch farther afield, to send my mind soaring vas
distances, looking down like some great bird.

"It was truly wonderful, Lance," Essie said, lookin
him squarely in the eyes. "There's nothing quite like it.'

Then she took a long, sad breath and added, "One day
as I was gliding over the tips of the French Pyrenees, I fe
another presence. At first I was surprised and a little take
aback. Of course, this hadn't been the first time I'd eve
felt a presence other than my own. While it wasn't
common thing, I had noted other mind-travelers before
But this presence was different. This one was not ju
flowing freely, enjoying the wonderment. It was intent
Seeking. Driven by madness.

"Then I realized—it was searching for *me*.

"At the first touch, I instantly recognized him. Warwick—
damned, mad Warwick. He hadn't died. And worse, h
had learned to use the power.

"I sent my essence racing back to my body, and sa
here, in this room, trembling and terrified that Warwic
was right behind me.

"After an hour, I admitted to myself that I had bee
very lucky. But only a fool would have rested on that luck
So, that same day, I began working on ways to strengthe

my mental shield. Over the next few years, I achieved considerable success.

"But, once again, I had underestimated the strength of a mind driven by insane purpose.

"One day, almost three years to the day after my encounter over the Pyrenees, I suddenly felt a massive thrust against my personal shield. Warwick had found me.

"We spent hours in that first, critical battle. He battered at my protective wall for hours, just to demonstrate how much his power had grown. And when he felt the illustration was complete—for the moment—he suddenly withdrew.

"Some days later, he returned . . . and this time he spoke to me, even though I tried to block him out. He said that his strength and ability had grown, and he insisted we rejoin the house. If I refused him, he said he would kill me.

"I had no doubt he might very well be able to carry out his threat—if not immediately, then at some time in the future. In any case, it was obvious that my demise was a certainty. Either he would continue to struggle against me and win—and I would die—or I would grow so weak that I would succumb to his wishes—and he would kill me.

"That was the summer of 1957. I was desperate, with only the barest fragments of a plan—a small possibility.

"It centered on James Beresford. Your father, Lance.

"Through the centuries, I had followed the progress of some of the more obscure lines of the Beresford clan. And, of course, after two different liaisons of my own, I watched closely over my immediate family. Evidence of our special gift exists everywhere, if one knows what to look for: in the triumphs of the French Revolution and the American War of Independence; in the tragedies of Napoleon's rise to power; in Hitler's bloody holocaust; in the dark mysticism that has warped Russian history since the time of the czars. And there is that mysterious crater in

Tunguska that speaks of a battle almost beyond comprehension . . .''

Lance was burning with questions, but he held them inside. It was *hard*, but he held them.

"It was obvious to me that the Beresford gift was very strong in your father, Lance—dormant, but strong. I spoke to him, told him of the legacy, and offered to tutor him in the use of the power in exchange for his help in putting an end to Warwick's plan.

"Your father agreed, but I underestimated the mental bond between twins. Warwick picked up a hint of our plans and killed James in what appeared to be a simple car accident.

"Your father had told your mother everything that I told him. After his death, she blamed me for it. I knew she was carrying a child—carrying you, Lance—and even from the womb, you showed signs of power at least as strong as your father's. So I blocked my thoughts from Warwick, and while under attack from him, I helped the two of you escape to America.

"I kept even the hint of your whereabouts hidden from him for almost a quarter of a century. For years, your mother continued to move around the country, always changing names. Finally she went to stay in Santa Barbara . . . and that was where I found her, only a few months ago.

"I waited, hoping there would be more time. But Warwick's attacks on me became more frequent, more intense. Finally I learned he was on his way to Australia to face me . . . and that his insane strength had grown to a point where it appeared I could never hope to win the coming battle—at least not alone.

"So I brought you into play—far earlier than I had hoped—and set into motion this whole series of events that has led us . . . here. Now. To the inevitable confrontation with Warwick."

Lance stared at Essie, waiting for her to go on. She

seemed again to be lost deep in thought, and he gently nudged her with, "Do you mean to tell me this was all *on purpose?*"

She smiled briefly. "Of course not, young Lance. I made a grave error, and the cost was great—very great."

Her words were barely a whisper, but Lance heard them clearly.

"My first step was the will, and the specific instructions for contacting you. Then I . . . *died.* Actually I entered the state in which you find me now. Call it a kind of . . . 'limbo,' for lack of a better term. It is a state that allows me to conserve what little energy I still retain, while keeping watch on the events in my native plane. I had hoped this unexpected twist might confuse Warwick and give me a chance to move you into place before he even knew of your existence . . . and it worked, if only in part. I believe my plan *did* confuse him as I had hoped . . . but not for long enough. And my miscalculation did damage far exceeding any minor tactical benefits."

"I'm sorry," Lance said, shaking his head. "I don't understand what you mean."

"I know, Lance. I know. It is pitifully simple, really. Soon after I entered this state, I found that my awareness of the world outside these few rooms was drastically diminished—far more so than I had anticipated—and that my ability to use the power I had left was so limited that it took virtually every ounce of it just to stop Warwick from blasting through my shield and swamping me.

"My plan had been to come to you. To warn you. To explain everything you needed to know, right there in America. Then I would protect you until you could get the will and sign the deed. Instead, I could make only the most feeble connections with your undermind, and what little strength I could exercise was expended just keeping you alive.

"You were in danger from killers sent by Sammy Raines. At the time, I thought it was an unbelievable bit of bad timing, but now I'm not so sure. At any rate, I had to save you and create a diversion, since the . . . 'hit team'—I believe that is the term?—was told to make doubly sure you were dead. I called you and gave you the password, 'Crossfire.' After that I misdirected the killers to a man who was in fact the backup hit man. To add to the confusion, I temporarily manifested a set of papers, saying he was Arnold Perpoint, and placed them in his wallet.''

"I'll be damned," Lance said in a soft whisper, hardly realizing he had spoken.

"You and your friend Benny had already decided on the identity you would use at the rendezvous point," Essie said. "It was no problem for me to assure that both of you carried out those plans, though it was a little hard convincing Benny to go to the hotel, since he thought you were dead.

"I had already sent you a dream that should have prepared you for everything that was to come. I used the dream form because my fading energy could only be employed in short bursts, and sending the information into your subconscious meant you would be able to assimilate it at a much greater speed.

"To my consternation, contact with you was shaky at best, and for a long time after using what energy I could muster, I wasn't able to reach you at all, or know anything of what was happening to you. Still, as I lost contact, I knew you had been saved from death and believed you had received my message.

"When I next touched you, you were at the hotel. I was horrified to learn that the dream had been turned into a garbled nightmare and that Warwick was using it and other methods to try to turn you away from your inheritance. At that time I was powerless to do much more than watch. Eventually I lost contact again.

"During this blacked-out time, I came to the conclusion that Warwick couldn't find you either—but he *was* able to follow my lead to you. This, I thought, would explain the distortion of the dream, and possibly his bizarre attacks on you in the shower.

"But it seems that, even in this, I underestimated Warwick's strength and tenacity—though I didn't know that until you got here and I was able to 'read' some of the situations that arose after my first contact with you.

"It now appears Warwick had already found you, and may have been responsible for the attempted murder. What's more, having distorted my message and used the dream to terrify you once, he employed it again and again in hopes of stopping you from coming here to talk with me. It would seem he also had you take on another identity—and urged your subconscious to keep it permanently. I can only guess at his motives, but I assume he hoped to lock you into the new personality, or to drive you insane, or even just to delay things until he could find a way to finally overcome me.

Essie stopped and sighed deeply, and Lance was surprised to see tears in her eyes again—tears of weariness and apology and defeat. "I'm afraid I was of little help to you, Lance. I couldn't stop your mother's death. I wasn't able to intercede when one of the ancients tried to warn you, in the islands of Fiji. In fact, my only real assistance was in eradicating a worm that had followed you to the airport when you left America.

"It would seem now that Warwick had long ago enlisted Robert, probably with the promise of power and wealth. I imagine, at first, it was to help in his battle with me. Then, when you came along, Robert became the perfect frontline soldier. And he died for it, just as Monica did. Just as . . . so many. So many . . ."

She was starting to fade completely—to disappear from view. Lance wasn't sure if it was some limitation imposed by her state of "limbo" or simply the weight of all the grief and self-loathing. *It would be enough to kill a normal woman*, he thought bitterly. *But what do you do if you're already dead?*

He had a million questions, and he was beginning to think that few of them would be answered here and now. But one kept nagging him. "Why all the deaths?" he asked quietly. "Doug, Monica, Robert? All dead . . . and who knows the damage that's been done to Jessica."

Essie Beresford shrugged, and for an instant she almost disappeared from sight. "As Beresford offspring, they each carried the essence of the legacy—though it may have been minute in some cases," she said. "I admit, I don't know why Warwick continued to use them—and other surrogates—against you. It is baffling to me. It's as if he is hesitating to face you directly—almost as if he's *afraid* to."

"But with all the power at his disposal, why would he fear me? I don't even know what it *is*."

"There are many things I don't understand, young Lance," Essie said, her eyes showing the pain she was feeling for him. "Perhaps he fears you and Angelique together. Her power is formidable. Three times she has helped you overcome Warwick's assaults, though she barely realizes it herself. Perhaps together you are even more powerful than we twins. I simply don't know. I'm sorry, but I don't."

"But I never met Angie until I arrived in Australia—" Lance suddenly stopped, mid-sentence, as the full weight of what Essie had just said finally clicked in his mind. "What do you mean . . . *together*?" he blurted out. "You can't really still believe that *I* have any power? Look how easily Warwick has trampled me and those around me. I've messed up everything you tried to do."

Essie sighed and leaned back, smiling wryly. "Have you heard nothing I've said, young Lance?"

"I don't understand what you mean."

Essie took on the tone of a great-grandmother, trying to explain something vitally important to a young, naive relative. "A maniac, wielding a portion of what might well be one of the greatest forces in the universe, has been raging against you for weeks, frequently working in ways even I don't understand. And you have been able to survive. You look on that as *failure?*"

"But a lot of innocent people have died." Even as he was speaking, Lance knew in that place deep inside himself that there was something not quite right about his reasoning. But he just couldn't believe that he was anything more than the person he had always thought himself to be. Oh, naturally he'd had dreams of being more than he was—one of them even entailed being master of the universe. But everyone daydreamed like that . . . that's all they were, *daydreams*.

Essie could see the confusion in Lance. After a long pause, she spoke again, choosing her words very carefully. "In a war there are always casualties. Don't fool yourself, Lance, you *are* in a war, and you have been since Warwick discovered you existed."

Essie's next words carried all the love and gentleness she felt for her great-grandchild . . . and a hint of the fear she had for his ultimate survival. "If there were some way I could do what must be done, I swear to you, I would. But I cannot. And though there is much I don't understand, I am certain of two things. The first is that if you run, if you die, Warwick will gain control of the house, reunite the two structures, and attain all the power he craves. Hitler was an abomination, Lance, but believe me when I tell you that Warwick, possessed of the full Beresford power, would make him look like a saint."

Lance swallowed hard. "And the second?" he said, trying to sound unmoved. It was becoming normal for Lance to be right in his gut assumptions these days, and right now his gut told him that he didn't really want to hear what Essie had to say. But he asked anyway. He had to.

"I know this is all an enormous shock," Essie said. "You probably wish you could wake up and find it is just another bad dream—a particularly sick nightmare." She leaned forward and tried to put her hand on his . . . but it passed through without slowing.

Lance *did* feel something though—a tingling, a sweetness, an echo of vitality unlike anything he'd ever felt before. "You think you can't take any more," she said, her voice deep and rich. "And I wish with all my heart there had been time for you to have slowly assimilated the knowledge you need. But we have no such liberty. Now that he knows of you, Warwick can never allow you to survive.

"You see, Lance, you are the only one who can possibly stop him. And if you don't . . . the world and everyone you love within it will die . . . or *worse*."

Chapter 28

Benny Haldane awoke. Still, it was a few long dazed minutes before he shook the sleep from his eyes and climbed out of bed.

"God, I feel like shit," he mumbled to himself as he grabbed his pants from the back of the nearby chair, pulled them on, and made his way down the hall to the bathroom.

After a quick shower, he began to feel almost human again, and a shave helped, too.

A few minutes later he wandered out into the kitchen. The clock on the wall said it was after eight, and the light in the sky said morning, but he had no idea what day it was.

He padded, barefoot, through the apartment, knocking on doors and calling as he went, but Angie and Lance were nowhere to be found.

"Where the hell would they go, so early in the morning?" he said to the empty hallway as he made his way back to the kitchen.

He busied himself by making coffee and scrambling some eggs, then sat down to relax and eat.

Lance and Angie still hadn't returned by the time he had finished breakfast and done the dishes, so he decided to go back to his hotel and get a change of clothes.

Before he left, he scribbled a note telling them where he'd gone, and that he'd be back in an hour or so. Then he grabbed the spare key from the hiding place in the freezer—it was exactly where Angie had said it would be—and left the apartment.

The jewelry store was in the walkway off the foyer of the Australiana Hotel. It was just opening when Benny passed, and he couldn't resist taking a quick peek at what they had on sale.

He had been to his room and changed clothes, and now he was feeling a good deal better—at least three-quarters human. *The brown jacket and camel slacks always make me feel like a million bucks*, he told himself as he brushed back the sides of his hair and made his way across the thick carpet of the walkway.

While he had been in his room, he had called Angie's apartment. She and Lance still hadn't returned, so he was feeling no urgency to rush back to Kirribilli. Instead, he made his way inside the small, but elegant, jewelry store and walked slowly down the length of the long glass showcases.

A girl with big eyes and a warm smile stood behind the counter. It was the beginning of the day, so she still had the spark of freshness that would usually be gone by lunch, as customer after customer wore her down. Benny liked shopping at this time of day. People actually seemed glad to be out and around, glad to be working.

Benny's expert eye catalogued the pieces as he went— the ones that looked nice but weren't really top quality, the ones with nice stones and awful settings, the ones with awful stones but nice settings—from the A+ quality to the C- junk.

It was just a personal quirk, a force of habit. Since Lance had come into his fortune, they had both decided to quit—how had Lance put it?—"exercising their special skills." Still, Benny couldn't keep his eyes from noticing good jewels when he saw them sparkling at him from their fancy cases. Or mediocre jewels. Or *bad* jewels, for that matter.

Then he noticed something else, and all casual thought was instantly gone.

The man in the three-piece suit, hovering outside the window, had looked at him just a touch too long. He straightened his dark-blue tie, using the store's front window as a mirror, and tried to appear casual, but it didn't fool Benny for a minute.

He knew this guy. He had been one of the passengers in first class on the flight to Australia.

Of course, there was always the chance of coincidence, but Benny's senses told him that that wasn't the case—not this time. This man had followed him from America. He was hoping Benny would lead him to Lance.

The son of a bitch had been sent by Sammy Raines.

Benny felt like he'd been duped. It didn't matter if the guy were a pro; it didn't matter if he hadn't offered a single clue to tip Benny off. The fact was, Benny was a professional, and he'd made a mistake. Pros in his line of work weren't allowed to do that. Often one mistake was all you got.

Well, he thought, *it ain't goin' no farther*. Obviously he had to lose this guy, and fast. And it had to be thorough. For all Benny knew, there might be a confederate nearby.

No, he decided, *what I need is a diversion*. He looked down at the jewelry in the case under his hands, and an idea popped into his head. *Ah-hah*, he thought. *Perfect. Now if only this guy will be cooperative.*

As if on cue, the man in the three-piece suit ambled casually into the store and began looking at a pendant in the case near the door. Then he moved slowly down the row, pretending to be seriously interested in what the cases held, but all the while watching Benny from the corner of his eye.

Benny knew as well as anyone that speed was often

your best friend in situations like this. Without seeming to break his stride, he wheeled about and hurried over to the newcomer.

Then he grabbed the man in the three-piece suit by his arm and started shouting. "Miss," he said sharply to the wide-eyed girl behind the counter. "Call the police. This man is a thief."

The girl was stunned, though not nearly so much as the man who was following Benny.

Benny pulled his wallet from his coat and flashed it at the girl. "Come on, girl. Call the police."

The flustered salesgirl did even better than that. She stepped on an alarm button on the floor, and in a few seconds a security guard came running down the walkway and into the store.

"Officer," Benny snapped, trying to sound as officious as he possibly could, "this man just stole a diamond bracelet from that case." Benny pointed to a nearby cabinet—one of the ones with the A+ items in it.

"Are you crazy?" Joel Thanner said. "I haven't stolen anything."

"It's in the inside pocket of his coat," Benny said, intent on keeping everything moving rapidly.

Thanner objected, but the security guard patted down his coat anyway . . . and felt something nestled under the left breast.

"What do you think you're doing?" Joel Thanner said indignantly. "I'll have your job for this."

"You're welcome to it, mate," the guard said wearily as he reached his hand into the inside coat pocket of the man's suit and pulled out a diamond bracelet.

Next, the guard held the bracelet up in the light. It sent sparkling starbursts of light off in all directions. "You want to tell me how this got in your pocket, mister?" he said gruffly.

Then he turned to the salesgirl. "Is this one of yours, Miss?"

The salesgirl quickly checked the velvet tray in the case Benny had pointed out. It was, of course, empty. "Oh, my goodness. Yes, it is, officer. I only got it from the safe a few minutes—"

Benny cut her off. "Officer, hold this one. He had a confederate. I'll get him."

The security guard was somewhat flustered by what was happening, but still had his wits about him. "Wait a minute. Who *are* you?"

"The name's Willis. Agent Chuck Willis," Benny snapped back. "I'm an FBI man, here in your country on a holiday. I saw this man take the bracelet and just did what I've been trained to do." Now Benny looked urgently at the outside walkway. "But his partner's getting away."

"You got any ID?" the young security guard asked, feeling a little dwarfed by the idea of being in on a bust with an FBI man.

Benny showed him his ID: a perfect forgery of FBI identification in the name of Charles Willis, with his photograph in the appropriate spot.

This was enough for the young guard. He wasn't about to stand in the way of the Bureau, even if Willis *was* on holiday.

He motioned Benny to go. "I'll hold this one."

"Good work, officer," Benny said and hurried away down the hall and around the far corner.

He could still hear Thanner's voice echoing through the lobby as he hurried to the elevator and went straight to his room.

It took a little more than three minutes to pack his bag, and one more minute to call the desk and have them prepare his bill. It took another three minutes to pay the bill in cash, leave the hotel, and jump into the first vacant cab he saw.

Two blocks from the hotel he left the taxi, walked two

blocks north, and caught another one. This one went six city blocks, then he walked some more.

He changed cabs five times, until he was absolutely sure he wasn't being followed. Finally, he gave the driver of the last cab the name of the main street two blocks over from Angie's place.

As the Ford Falcon cab wound its way through the bustling city streets and onto the onramp for the Harbor Bridge, Benny eased back in the comfortable rear seat and thought back on what had just happened.

He imagined he heard the voice of his long-dead mother, and thanked her yet again for the priceless advice she had given him when he was a boy. "No matter what you do, Benjamin," she would say, "prepare for it properly and try to take along everything you might need. You'll never go wrong that way."

"Bless you, Ma," he said, grinning. Before leaving the States he had done just that, and the fake ID had been part of the emergency preparations. He had thought it might come in handy, and sure enough . . .

He pulled off his Carrera sunglasses and wiped them clean, then he slipped them back onto the bridge of his nose. He couldn't help smiling, thinking of the shocked look on the face of Sammy's man when the security guard pulled the bracelet from his pocket.

In all the confusion, it had been relatively easy to plant it there.

Benny chuckled at the thought of the man being hauled off to jail. Of course, he'd probably get out when they couldn't find any Agent Willis working for the FBI, Benny thought, but at least he should be out of circulation for awhile. Besides, you could always look on the bright side: maybe the guy had an outstanding warrant or something. *That* would keep him nice and cozy for, say, three to five years.

*   *   *

"Angie, is that you?" Benny said into the receiver of the phone in Angie's kitchen.

He'd heard the phone ringing as soon as he opened the door with the borrowed key. He even left his bags on the step just to get a head start on the phone, and it had been a good move.

"Yes, Benny, it's me. I'm at Beresford Hall." The connection was terrible; her voice was almost lost in a series of clicks and hissing.

"Where's Lance, Angie? I have to talk to him."

"He's here, Benny. But he needs your help. He's locked himself in one of the rooms and he won't come out."

"What! Whatta ya mean?" That didn't sound like Lance at all. *Still*, he thought, *the kid has been acting kinda funny since he got to Australia, what with this mumbo-jumbo stuff and all. But locking himself in a room?* "Why would he do that?"

"I don't know, Benny." Angie's voice sounded close to tears.

"Hey, Angie. Don't let it get to you. I'm sure there's a perfectly good explanation, you'll see."

"Benny, will you come out here? Maybe if he hears your voice he'll come out."

"I'm as good as on my way, Angie. Just tell me how to get there. And don't you worry, you hear me?"

Benny hung up the phone, and much of the optimism he'd been using to cheer up Angie left him. He remembered what they had told him the night they had dinner at the hotel. Then he remembered the car trying to run them all down. And that . . . *thing* in his hotel room.

"Jesus, Lance," he said, speaking into the air. "Ever since you got this inheritance, things have been well and truly messed up."

A few minutes later, Benny was flagging down a cab on the main street two blocks from Angie's. He gave the driver the address Angie had given him, and worried that,

on top of everything else, he was going to have to give
Lance the bad news about Sammy Raines's man.

It never occurred to him that Lance didn't care abou
Sammy Raines any more . . . or that Sammy, tenaciou
though he was, was a very small player in a very larg
game.

Chapter 29

"You have to let me possess you—let me *become* you for a short time," Essie Beresford told Lance. "We will . . . merge, join together, in a way so complete that it cannot be expressed in words. During this . . . joining, I will be able to impart all the knowledge I have to you. You will know all I know. Then, perhaps—*perhaps*—you will be able to defeat Warwick."

Lance looked slowly around the sitting room and blinked, as if he was waking from a long, deep sleep. He was surprised to see morning light streaming through the window in thick golden bars. The apparition in front of him sparkled and flickered—far less substantial than it had been when he'd first seen it hours before.

And now she wants to possess me, he thought distantly. *But only temporarily, of course.*

He ran his fingers through his hair and tried to piece it all together. He had listened to Essie's bizarre story . . . and as ludicrous as it seemed, he *believed* it.

A part of him wanted to push it all away—to stand up, pound on the table, then state clearly and succinctly that he thought it was a crock of shit and that he simply refused to swallow it.

The problem was, he couldn't do that. Every detail of her story rang true. Every instinct he had told him to trust this woman . . . and enough incredible things had happened to him in the last few weeks that he knew he *couldn't* ignore what she said, even if he wanted to.

Still, he wasn't overjoyed at the idea of suddenly absorbing 300 years of Essie Beresford's knowledge. It sounded a little like being force-fed. *On the other hand*, he thought grimly, *I don't want to face this maniac relative of mine without knowing as much as I can . . . and it looks like I'm going to have to face him, like it or not.*

"What will you do if I say no?" he asked, his voice surprisingly steady.

Essie thought about it for a moment, then decided. "I will have to tell Angelique what I have just told you and pray that *she* will be able to withstand Warwick . . . somehow," Essie said. "But I have grave doubts about her ability to succeed."

Lance had a sudden sinking feeling in the pit of his stomach. The little he knew Angie was enough to convince him that she wouldn't care about her chances of success or failure. She was just enough of a fool to try and stop Warwick, no matter what the odds.

But how could he be sure about Essie herself? How could he *trust* her without—

"You are wondering if I am telling you the entire truth," Essie said, smiling wisely. He started to protest, and she held up her sparkling hand. "No, I haven't read your mind—I promised you I wouldn't. It is easy to see on your face, Lance. You still are not sure if the story is true. *I* could be the enemy here, not Warwick. Isn't that right?"

It was exactly right, and they both knew it. Lance could only shrug and say, "So, how *would* I know?"

"By using that part of you that has always instinctively led you down the safe road. It is a common quality in Beresfords, and it is particularly strong in you."

Damn it, he thought. *She knows me too well already. I do want to trust her. I feel as if I have to.* "All right," he said grudgingly. "If I do as you ask—if we 'join'—what will happen to *you?*"

"What should have happened long ago," she told him. "This world in which I now dwell is already very much like death. After the joining—and one final appearance—I will pass through the gateway to the final rest."

"And after that?" he persisted. "On the other side of the—the gate?"

She smiled sadly and shook her head. "I don't know, Lance. I have no more idea about that than you do."

"Are you ready for that?" he asked, watching her closely. "Are you ready to . . . finish dying, just to get at Warwick?"

She grimaced. "It's more than that. This is more than simple revenge—though I won't deny there's some element of that in it. I am trying to protect you—and my other offspring, and quite likely the whole world. I am trying to make amends for my mistakes and hesitations in the past. And if it means giving up my final, faint connections to this plane . . ." She shrugged and sighed. "I suppose that is as it should be. I have enjoyed my life a great deal, Lance. It has been singularly long, and rich, and challenging. But I know that even now—even knowing what he has become—I cannot draw any pleasure from destroying my brother. I will not enjoy seeing his death . . . but it *must happen.*"

"*He* may destroy *me,*" Lance said.

"That must not happen, young Lance," Essie said, suddenly very serious. "It just *can't.*"

Lance got up from the couch and walked over to the window. Outside he could see the early-morning sun illuminating the flowers that filled the gardens of Beresford Hall. It was a beautiful sight. Simple, but beautiful.

All over the world there are places like this, he thought. *Places where children can still safely play. Secluded spots where lovers can tell each other their feelings and plan their future. One day soon I may sit on a bench just like that one by the aviary and ask Angie to marry me. But if Warwick gains access to this "power" Essie talks about, there won't be any safe havens any longer. There won't be any aviaries, any parks—any Angie.*

Hell, it's not a great world now. There are already too many places where life isn't worth living—where death comes without warning to everyone, adults and children alike. But at least there's still a chance we can make it work, somehow. What are our chances if Warwick takes the legacy in hand? What are my chances if I don't try to stop him?

He sighed and turned away from the window. There had never been a choice, Lance knew—not really. From the beginning of this entire mess, he realized, he had been moving steadily toward this moment—toward this decision.

"All right," he said, knowing that Essie already sensed his decision. "What do I do?"

Essie beamed at him. The energy blazed bright and full in her for the first time in hours. "Thank you, Lance," she said.

He shrugged. "Nothin' to it," he told her, trying to make his words sound brave, but failing dismally.

She told him to sit back on the couch and relax. "There will be no pain," she promised.

For a moment, fear clutched at him. He knew that what he was doing, at that moment, might be the biggest mistake he could ever make. In that moment of doubt, he thought about trying to resist, about jumping up from the chair and running, just *running*, before she took him over . . .

Then a feeling of intense well-being washed over him, and all his doubts disappeared.

The essence of Lance Sullivan-Beresford—the shining fragment that was unique to him—suddenly burst open like a blooming rose.

One second the shard of consciousness was a single piece, separate and distinct. In the next, it was . . . *more*. Something had come to join it—to *increase* it. He was still a single entity . . . but how great, how *vast* an entity he had suddenly become.

Everything was bathed in a golden warmth as Lance and Essie became one mind. The two possessors of the Beresford gift reveled in open communion.

In one clear flash, the mind that was Lance *knew* Essie had told him the truth . . .

While the mind that was Essie Beresford gasped in shock. "*I see it now*," the thought said . . . and Lance saw it, too. "*No wonder Warwick hesitated to attack you directly. Your potential dwarfs us both. Even undiscovered, even untrained, it is . . . awesome. He would never have risked a direct attack that might somehow trigger your dormant potential—not unless there was absolutely no other alternative.*"

Now Lance saw in himself what Warwick had seen— what Essie was seeing. A few seconds before it would have shocked him beyond understanding. Now he noted the golden force throbbing deep within him as if he were examining a stranger . . . and he acknowledged the vast potential there. The potential in *himself*.

The two minds, still entwined, drifted and shared. Lance drank in Essie's knowledge. In a timeless, flowing stream of consciousness, he relived her birth, her childhood, her growth to adulthood. He saw firsthand the fiasco with the two colliers, and he witnessed Warwick's slow mutation, culminating in the murder of his own uncle. He watched the life-force being ripped from Meg. Then he soared to the edge of the Beresford estate and, briefly shrouded from Warwick's view, looked into the purple mist that bubbled at the edge of Essie's golden shield. He saw—he *touched*— the horror that Warwick Beresford had become.

Now he slowed his journey. Now he stopped. It was time to be more methodical—to go step by step through

Essie's understanding of the Beresford legacy, from the very beginning.

He read with her as she assembled the notes left by Uncle Ramos and the other ancestors. He read all the books and catalogued the knowledge with astonishing ease. He went through the splitting of the house and recovered his strength slowly, just as Essie had.

And, finally, he dared to explore the essence of the power itself.

At every step, immense new comprehension expanded within him. Essie had understood a great deal—but she had missed much as well. They reexperienced three hundred and fifty years of life *together*, and together they learned new ways to wield the energy, gained new insights into the mechanisms that controlled it—all nonverbally, all innately.

When the stream of knowledge that Essie had acquired came to an end, the being that had once been Lance Sullivan slipped away from her with consummate ease, astonishing grace. He took the accumulated knowledge of their joining and drew it together into a vibrant whole . . . then he reached back into Essie and helped her send out fingers of energy that strengthened her private shield. *I can help this much*, he told her as they worked. *Any more and he may become suspicious and be alerted to what we are trying to do.*

It was done subtly, pervasively. Warwick would not notice any drastic shift—but it made it impossible for him to make any inroads in his attack on the shield, or eavesdrop within the estate. Now all that happened within these walls would be hidden from him. They no longer needed to fear his invasion, and Warwick would remain unaware of Lance's contact with Essie Beresford . . .

Until the time is right, Lance thought.

The communion continued for slightly more than two and a half hours. To Essie and Lance, it was both an eternity—and a blink of an eye. Finally, filled with regret and relief and anticipation, they separated, returning to their singular selves . . . in some ways the same, but in most different, *far* different than before.

Lance understood how different he was—how much had changed within him. But he hid the metamorphosis for the moment. One of his greatest strengths, he realized, would be surprise, and he couldn't jeopardize that.

Even so—even "disguised"—he saw the world as he had never seen it before. He sensed he had been permanently heightened; his ability to hold and comprehend had expanded to an impossible scale.

He stood in Essie Beresford's rooms and saw the world for the first time. "Incredible," he whispered, looking everywhere at once. "Incredible . . ."

Essie, on the other hand, had faded to a barely discernible outline—a ghost of a ghost. "One last task," she said faintly, and smiled.

Lance turned to her and saw her power and goodness clearly now. He smiled back and nodded, then walked to the door that led to the hallway.

As he turned the knob and opened the door without trouble, he turned and looked over his shoulder at the fading nimbus near the bookcase.

"Hold on," he whispered. Then he left Essie's sitting room.

"What's going on?" Benny Haldane asked Angie.

"I wish I knew, Benny."

They were in the foyer of Beresford Hall. Wilmont, the butler, stood nearby, looking weary but solid.

Benny had rushed to the hall from Kirribilli, and Angie had met him at the front door, looking as if she had slept in her clothes. Wilmont was by her side, displaying his best stiff-upper-lip demeanor while she quickly told their story.

"Wilmont called and told me Lance was out here, but by the time I arrived, he'd already locked himself in

Grandmother Essie's rooms. I knocked for hours. Then I fell asleep on a couch in the hall . . . but Wilmont assures me Lance never left.''

"That's correct, sir," Wilmont said shortly.

"You don't have *any* idea what he's doing in there?" Benny said, his head swimming. This entire thing was getting more mysterious by the minute . . . and Benny *hated* mysteries.

Angie shrugged. "Not a clue. I tried to wake you before I left the apartment, but you were dead to the world. So I came out alone." She looked exhausted and crestfallen; Benny couldn't resist putting a hand on her shoulder. "It's no use, Benny," she said softly and sighed. "I haven't done *anything* to help."

"All right," Benny said, taking control of things. "Why don't you show me where he is? I'll try to talk him into coming out. And if that don't work, we'll go to Plan Two."

She looked blankly. "Plan Two?"

He grinned. "We'll break down the damned door."

"That won't be necessary," Lance said as he walked slowly down the staircase from the second floor.

Angie spun to see him, and her face lit up like Christmas. "*Lance!*" she cried. Then she covered the distance between them before the echo of her shout could die away and threw herself into his arms. "Thank God you're all right!"

The embrace was long and fierce, and it ended as abruptly as it had begun when she pulled herself back and looked severely into his face. "You *are* all right, aren't you?"

"I'm fine, honey. Never felt better," Lance said, and gently eased her back to him.

He meant it more than she could know . . . but he couldn't tell her. Not yet . . .

"What the hell's been going on here, Lance?" Benny was more than a little miffed that he hadn't gotten the chance to play leader for more than a few seconds. *That damn Sullivan kid is so friggin' capable, it's disgusting*, he thought half-seriously.

"It's too hard to explain right now, Benny. But I'm fine, I promise."

"Great," Benny said. "Then let's get the hell outta here."

"Yes," Angie quickly added. For some unexplained reason, she suddenly felt afraid—not for herself, but for Lance. She had an overwhelming compulsion of her own: they had to leave the house, *now*, and never come back. *Ever.* "Let's go back to the apartment, Lance. Right now."

"No," Lance said quietly. He slipped his arm around Angie's shoulders and hugged her close. "This is my place now."

He turned to Wilmont. "Thank you for looking after Angie for me, Wilmont. I realize you're tired, but there is something of great importance that I need you to do before you rest. Do you feel up to it?"

Wilmont's entire body snapped to attention. Even the creases in his uniform seemed gone.

There was something in the boy's voice, he realized. Something he had missed. After all, he had been without mistress or master for many weeks, and it was his job—his *life*—to serve a master.

Now he had one. There was no question: Mr. Lance was ready for him, and he was ready for whatever would come. It was his station. His joy. His duty.

Lance saw the effect he was having on Wilmont and realized he had committed a faux pas. Wilmont was ready to do his bidding, whatever it might be. This surprised and cowed him more than a little. "Fine," he said, not wanting to embarrass the butler—or himself—any more than he already had. "Then ask Mrs. Sallinger to make breakfast for Miss Angie, Mr. Haldane, and myself."

"Yes, sir," Wilmont said briskly, turning to go.

"Wait!" Lance said. "There's more." *This instant obedience is going to take some getting used to*, he thought.

"After you've talked with Mrs. Sallinger, I'd like you to go and clean up. I will need you to hand deliver a letter. When that's done, take the rest of the day off. I would like to have the house to myself today and tonight. But I'll see you here bright and early tomorrow morning so that we can get formally acquainted."

Wilmont didn't hesitate for an instant. "Yes, sir," he said. "Thank you, sir." He turned to leave.

"Oh, and Wilmont," Lance called after him. "Please inform Mrs Sallinger that once she has served us breakfast, I would appreciate it if she would also spend the entire day away from the house."

"Very good, sir," Wilmont answered, not breaking stride as he hurried away.

Angie knew she should be worried. Lance seemed . . . *different*. But since his arm was around her, holding her close, she couldn't seem to find the fear that had swept through her just seconds before.

Still, she thought, *I would like to know what happened in those rooms* . . .

She didn't get the chance to ask. In the next instant, Lance moved off toward the breakfast room, towing her along. "Come on," he said. "I'm starving. Let's eat."

Benny trailed behind Angie and Lance as they made their way down the hall. His expert eye absentmindedly catalogued the furnishings and artworks; he figured the estate had to be worth a pretty penny, but his mind wasn't really on it.

This whole thing, he thought, *is just too goddamn confusing for a guy like me*. A moment ago, Angie had been crazy with worry about Lance . . . but now she was smiling. And *Lance* had just locked himself in some deserted bedrooms for hours on end . . . but everybody was acting like that was okay, too.

I better wait until after breakfast to tell him about the

guy at the jewelry store, Benny thought. *Why spoil a good meal?*

"Fine, Mr. Holdsworthy," Lance said, speaking into the old-fashioned phone. "I'll expect him at five o'clock." Then he placed the elongated receiver in its large black cradle and walked back into the breakfast room of Beresford Hall.

Angie and Benny were still seated at the table, sipping coffee. As he entered, Angie's eyes met his over the rim of her cup.

Mrs. Sallinger, it turned out, was a wonderful cook. The breakfast had been huge and fragrant and delicious. But shortly after the scrambled eggs had arrived, Lance had gotten a phone call.

Angie had tried to question him about it, but he had evaded all her questions, telling her he would explain it all to her later, when there was time.

Now he had received a second call, from Warwick Beresford's solicitor, and Angie couldn't contain her curiosity a second longer. "Lance, why have you invited Warwick here this evening? I thought you said you got a weird feeling from him?"

"It's a business transaction related to my inheritance," Lance said easily, and munched on a piece of toast and jam.

He's telling me the truth, Angie thought, sure that her instincts were accurate. *But I'd swear it's not the whole truth. And anyway, why has he suddenly decided to accept the inheritance? The last thing he said was that he didn't want it.*

She sipped at her coffee and glared at Lance across the table. "I guess I'll just have to make up my own mind when I meet him, won't I? You're obviously not in the *mood* to talk about it."

Lance reached over and put his hand on hers. "I don't mean to be evasive, Angie. It's just that things have changed. And now there's something I have to take care of, that's all . . .''

Angie tried to understand. She nodded and smiled softly and tried to let it go.

"And I have to do it alone. I want you and Benny to go back to the apartment and wait for me."

Angie's smile faded abruptly. She stiffened and pulled her hand away from Lance's.

She was hurt, of course. They had promised to stay together—they *needed* to stay together. But it was something more than that. It was another deep, instinctive feeling. An unassailable conviction that Lance might need her—*soon, today*. But how could she help him if she wasn't there?

"I don't want to go, Lance." The words weren't enough, but her love for him was clear.

He understood. "I know," he said softly. "I really do. But I have to do this alone."

Her mouth was already open to protest, but he cut her off.

"Please, Angie," he said. "Do as I ask."

She wanted to argue. She wanted to scream at him, to tell him all her instincts were on fire. But something about the way he asked her—about the look in his eye . . .

"All right," she said, her words sounding stronger than she felt. "But promise you'll call as soon as this . . . *business* is finished."

"I promise."

Lance had to struggle to keep his real feelings hidden from Angie. He didn't want her to go. Three times now she'd pulled him out of scrapes, and this one would probably be bigger and messier than any of the others. But he had to do it right—he had to do it *alone*—and he wasn't sure he could handle it knowing she was nearby, in possible danger.

Benny Haldane watched the entire exchange without comment. He just sipped his coffee, ate two helpings of scrambled eggs, devoured a stack of pancakes, and finished off with toast. He hadn't had a good meal in days, and he wasn't about to turn one down now. Still, normally he would have gobbled everything down in minutes. As it was, he dallied at every step.

He didn't want to bring up their . . . *other* little problem. Lance seemed to have enough troubles already, though Benny could barely understand—or *believe*—half of what they'd told him so far. Besides, he'd worked with the kid for a long time; he'd gotten to know when he was bothered, when things were getting to be too much for him. Lance was getting to that place now—Benny could tell— and he didn't want to be the one to push Lance over the edge.

Still, he thought sourly, *some bad news you just gotta give, and let the chips fall where they're gonna.*

He took one last swallow of coffee and cleared his throat. "Lance," he said, "I've got some pretty rotten news." He said it quickly, before he thought up some good excuse to wait. "Sammy Raines knows where we are."

Lance looked at him and blinked. There was none of the shock in his expression that Benny had expected—none of the borderline panic he'd seen in the kid back in the States.

They looked at each other for a moment, each expecting the other to speak. Finally, Lance spoke.

"Is he?" he said mildly. "How do you know that, Benny?"

Benny Haldane gave him a very strange look. "One of his men flew out here on the flight with me," Benny said slowly. "I missed him at the time, but this morning, when I went back to the hotel, I spotted him."

Benny went on to explain what had happened, though Lance seemed distracted the entire time. When he finished, he sat and stared at his partner, waiting for a reaction—*any* reaction.

It was a remarkable anticlimax. Benny had expected

Lance to freak, to bolt, to head for the nearest exit. He was prepared to calm him down, get him thinking again, and then huddle with him for as long as it took, so they could decide what to do about this terrible development.

Instead, Lance thought about it for a short time . . . then he brushed it aside. "Benny," he finally said, "would you go back to the apartment with Angie, and wait there until I call?"

If I call, Lance thought to himself. *If I'm even able to call.*

Benny couldn't believe his ears. "But, Lance. *Lance.* What about Raines?"

"Later, Benny," Lance said.

Benny started to protest . . . then he got a clear look at the boy and changed his mind. He'd heard the tone of voice before. He'd seen that face.

Something big was going on here, Benny realized. They weren't talking about some petty little business deal, or some visit from a long-lost relative. This was *important* shit.

He finally got the message: whatever it was, Lance didn't want Angie around for it, and he was asking Benny to take care of her.

A part of Benny still wanted to holler, "*What about Sammy?*" But he didn't do it. Instead, he relaxed and did what Lance asked him to do.

They were partners . . . and friends. And he knew his partner would explain things to him as soon as he could.

He just wasn't sure if he really *wanted* an explanation. Not about all this crazy voodoo crap . . .

Chapter 30

"Come in, Warwick," Lance said, and moved aside to let his distant relative enter.

"Thank you, Lance."

Warwick was dressed in a tweed suit with a matching hat, and as he stepped inside, he chomped down on the briar that jutted from the side of his mouth. The entry alcove was suddenly filled with a sweet, acrid odor.

That smell, Lance thought. *I know that smell.* He wondered how in hell he hadn't made the connection between Warwick and all that had happened to him before, when they'd met at the church in Parramatta. There was no doubt about that odor. It was the illusive, almost sickly sweet smell that had been haunting him at different times over the last few weeks.

Never mind, he told himself. He had been stretched to the limit at the time. Things were different now.

At any rate, he *hoped* things were different now . . .

"That's an interesting blend of tobacco you've got there," he said, fighting to keep his voice steady.

"I'm glad you like it," Warwick said, and smiled. "It's my own blend. Very old, you know, but made specially for me."

Warwick Beresford could barely hide his greed as he glanced about at the foyer of Beresford Hall. For over 300 years he had waited to stand where he now stood. And in a few moments, he knew, he would have title to the other half of what was rightfully his—the inheritance his unholy bitch of a sister had stolen from him all those years ago.

Then everything will be different, he promised himself. *Everything*.

Warwick had to resist the urge to lick his lips. Just *thinking* about what he would do with the combined strength of the two mansions made him burn with hunger. He had studied for so long—studied and waited an interminable amount of time—just to revenge himself on that bitch of a sister.

It would happen soon, he told himself. Wherever she was hiding, he would find her, no matter what it took. He would find her and make her *pay*. And when that was finished—though it would take a very long, very enjoyable time—he would be free to set himself up as . . . as . . .

A god, he decided. *A god capable of anything*.

Anything.

His head was spinning. He felt dizzy just thinking about it.

Lance broke into the old man's reverie. "I have all the papers upstairs," he said, and motioned toward the second floor.

For the last few hours, Lance had sat by himself in the huge living room of Beresford Hall. It had taken him over an hour to finally get Angie and Benny out of the place. After that, he had sat in the quiet and prepared himself for the ordeal that lay ahead. He could have spent the time with Essie—what little remained of her—in her rooms, but he had decided reluctantly to stay downstairs. He had needed to be alone, if only for a little while.

During this quiet time, Lance had remembered his boyhood. He had returned to his special place on the ridge in the Los Padres National Forest . . . and to his mother.

If things had been different, he had thought, *she wouldn't have had to die*. But he hadn't dwelt on that—he couldn't. It had happened; he had gone on. And the one responsible for her death was going to pay for it. So, instead, he had remembered the good times they had spent together, and her wonderful sense of humor.

Finally, reluctantly, he had brought his thoughts back to the job at hand.

He'd only seen Warwick twice, physically. It had been during the other time, the time when he merged with Essie, that he had learned the most about his notorious relative. Thinking about Essie's experiences had filled him with a sense of doom. He had felt weak, inadequate— nothing at all like when the power had surged through him during the joining. He had had to use all his strength just to keep from jumping to his feet and rushing out of Beresford Hall, never to return.

But as the day wore on into late afternoon, he had slowly resigned himself to the fact that he *would* face Warwick. And that it was likely only one of them would survive.

Then it had been 5:00 P.M.

Now. Lance and Warwick made their way up the stairs and down the long hallway to Essie's sitting room. When they reached the doorway, Lance entered without a pause . . . but Warwick hesitated. He stood outside and moved his head back and forth in sharp flinching movements.

He's feeling Essie's presence, Lance thought. But aloud, to Warwick, he said, "Is something wrong?"

Warwick stared intently at him, and Lance felt a sharp metal probe snake into his mind.

He was prepared. They had expected Warwick to wonder at Essie's absence, to suspect her close proximity, but they were sure that, though he might be able to sense her presence, he wouldn't be able to know what form she took, or to pinpoint her exact location.

Lance hoped they were right. For the moment, all he could do was stare back at Warwick with a blank look.

An uneasy tickling sensation rippled through his skull. He had an almost unbearable urge to scratch his head—the same infuriatingly intense itch he'd felt when he'd broken his arm as a boy and had had to wear a plaster cast on his arm for six weeks.

He fought the urge, and his hands stayed loose at his sides. He didn't dare flinch—he didn't dare show any sign that he was aware of what was happening.

Warwick straightened and shrugged off his worry. This boy was no problem, he decided. The trace of the Beresford legacy was definitely there, but it was so deeply buried it would never come out of its own accord. He had misjudged the situation before; he had let his concern over the boy's potential get the better of him.

But that was behind him now. Now he was in the house and free to do as he pleased.

As soon as the papers were signed, he would find that meddling sister of his. She was hovering about here, somewhere, still trying to stop him—that much he knew. But he also knew it wouldn't work. She was powerless, *powerless*. And thinking about the pain he would inflict on her brought a smile to his lips.

"No, everything's perfect," Warwick said, and walked into the sitting room. "Just perfect."

"What time is it, Benny?" Angie said. She jumped nervously to her feet and walked to the large window in the living room of her apartment. Though she stared out across the harbor, she didn't really see anything. She was too preoccupied.

Benny sighed loudly. He didn't even bother to look at his watch. "Like they say in the movies, it's thirty seconds later than the last time you asked."

She turned back to him, a blank stare on her face. "Four o'clock," he said gently. "And if you keep jumping up and down and pacing back and forth like that, you're gonna need a new carpet."

He got to his feet and went to stand beside her. "Angie, he'll call when he's finished with whatever he's doing. You'll see."

Angie wasn't really listening to Benny. Her mind was racing, fighting a battle with itself.

She and Benny had come back here to Kirribilli, just as Lance had asked. Since then she had counted practically every second that had gone by . . . and with every second it was harder for her to do as Lance had asked her to do, to stay out of it.

She had told him she would, and at the time she had meant it. But now . . . she . . .

"Come on, Benny," she said, and she stalked across the room. She grabbed her handbag without breaking stride as she passed the small coffee table.

"Where to?"

"Beresford Hall, of course."

"But Lance said—"

"I know what he said." She swung open the door to the apartment. "But he's in trouble, and he might need our help. What good are we here?"

Benny shrugged, but Angie never saw his movement. She was already hurrying down the stairs.

"What the hell," Benny said to the air. He made sure the door was locked as he closed it behind them. "It beats sitting around watching you wear out the rug."

Angie was already in the car and putting it into gear when Benny hurried down the stairs. He had barely slid into the front seat of the Holden beside Angie before she had sent it racing out onto the street and speeding toward the far corner.

He didn't get the door shut properly until she screeched to a stop at the first traffic light. Angie was clutching the steering wheel so hard that the whites of her knuckles stood out, and the glare in her eyes made Benny grab for the seat belt.

This is gonna be a rough ride, he thought as the car shot past the corner and made an erratic turn into traffic. *A real rough ride.*

Lance was sitting on the couch where, earlier that day, he had listened to Essie tell the tale of the Family Beresford.

He didn't allow himself to remember that as he smiled briefly at Warwick, who was seated in the small chair by the window.

"I'm so glad you decided to allow me to purchase the property," Warwick said, his words as sickly sweet as the smell of his tobacco.

It was strange, Lance thought. Warwick bore no resemblance to Essie at all—at least none he could discern. Had time changed them both that much? Had their different uses of the power made them that different?

Lance nodded and picked up a leather pouch sitting on the desk before him. He opened the flap and slid out the deed to Beresford Hall.

Warwick's eyes glistened. *In one minute*, he thought gleefully. *In one minute it will be mine.*

Lance took a fountain pen from his pocket and flipped through the pages until he found the lines for the signatures. It was a simple procedure: the new owner signed on the first line; the current owner acknowledged the transferal on the second.

Warwick leaned forward on the couch, his hand outstretched, the smile still on his face.

Now, Lance chortled. *Now!*

Before Warwick realized what was happening, Lance signed the first line himself and held the pen up near his right shoulder.

Essie Beresford materialized beside him, took the pen

from her protégé's hand, and signed over the estate to Lance Beresford himself.

Lance turned to watch as his ancient relative straightened and sighed. For an instant, her hand came out and penetrated his shoulder, and the honeyed, golden warmth of her light filled him.

Goodbye, he thought to her.

I love you, she said. *Thank you*.

And Essie Beresford disappeared forever.

Warwick Beresford was frozen with astonishment.

It had happened too fast—*too fast*. One moment he had triumphed. The pup was about to sign the property over; the weakened bitch of a sister was waiting to be trapped.

And now . . .

Now . . .

He jumped to his feet, his fists trembling. "What have you *done*?" he growled, his voice low and dangerous. "*What have you DONE?*"

Lance started to answer him. His hand came up; his mouth opened—

And he began to fall.

Without preface or explanation, he was filled with the sensation of falling through space. Darkness spun around him; he seemed to be turning in the darkness, end over end.

Then, as suddenly as it had begun, the disorientation ended. Now he was stable—still floating, somehow, but *steady*.

Golden waves of color washed over him. The bristling charge he had felt when he was merged with Essie returned, but this time it was much stronger. This time, he realized, *he* was the one receiving the generated warmth.

His senses were spiraling about, flowing in a current of throbbing golden power. Alone this time, Lance struggled to understand and control the enormity of what was happening. For a moment he was lost in it—blinded by the beauty, overwhelmed by the sheer joy of it. Only the memory of what Essie had done when they were joined—how she had molded the power to her will, how she had *shaped* it—helped him overcome.

Slowly a sense of control returned, and he reached out to make tentative contact with the power itself. As hundreds had done before, he opened himself to the full force of the Beresford legacy.

For the first time, he was truly the *scion* that Essie Beresford had foreseen.

Every solitary atom of his being glowed warm and golden. He saw the world in all its true and wonderful potential, and joy welled up in him—true, unalloyed *joy*. The world was a wonderful place to be—wonderful to be a part of. Life itself was a flowing river of pure power—twining auras that flowed through him in a constant blinding current. He could see those lines of ineffable force. As each passed, he tried to grasp it, to draw it inside himself, but they were swift, and beautiful, and elusive.

Finally, he caught the edge of one swirling Neapolitan rainbow, and—

He was standing back in the drawing room, looking at Warwick.

It took a tremendous effort to drag himself into the moment. He felt . . . *light*. Like a . . . a bird. A bird that longed to soar upwards, away, and feel the thrill of diving and climbing, of riding the winds, of seeing the world in a way he'd never dreamed of.

"I changed my mind," he said to Warwick. "Essie told me you were planning to tear down the house, and I couldn't let that happen." He continued to play at the game of being an innocent, secure in the belief that Warwick did not suspect just how powerful he had become. "Angie and I have decided to get married and live here instead."

Warwick was livid. As Lance watched in astonishment,

the old man's features distorted and twisted, flowing like hot wax.

In an instant, the friendly old Briton was gone. In his place stood a different creature entirely—an evil caricature of a handsome young man.

Warwick's face was lined with layer upon layer of wrinkles, pockmarked with thick bristles of twisted hair. His eyes were set deep under hooded brows. His teeth were a twin row of razorlike incisors. The fingers that had reached for the pen were now taloned claws.

Lance finally understood just how different this twin was from the sister he had joined with. And the cost—it seemed there was a cost for everything in creation—of using the negative side of the Beresford inheritance. There was little left to recognize of the small boy playing happily by the lake that he had seen in Essie's mind's pictures of her childhood.

When the new Warwick spoke, his voice was a hiss. "You miserable fool," he spat. "You *child*. You dare deny *me?* You *dare?*" An ominous blue fire swirled about him and his eyes glowed a deep red. "I'll squash you like an insect!"

Lance barely had time to prepare himself before Warwick screamed out—

"DIE!"

And conjured up a throbbing ball of pure energy.

One second there was nothing. The next, there was a shimmering sphere of purple fire enveloping Warwick's crooked fingers, pulsing and expanding with every heartbeat.

Warwick gasped in ecstasy and hurled the ball at Lance's face.

Without Essie's knowledge, Lance would have died there and then. Instead, as Warwick bellowed his rage and triumph, Lance stumbled back, feigning confusion, and threw out an invisible shield just as his great-grandmother had shown him.

His barrier forced the sphere a fraction from its intended

course, and it caromed violently off the far wall, spraying sparks in all directions. The sparks themselves faded a moment later without ash or ember, as if they had never been there.

Warwick stared at his young relative, momentarily confused. The sphere should have put an end to this pup, he knew. But somehow, yet again, the boy had cheated death.

Incandescent anger burned in the breast of the earl of Beresford. *Enough*, he decided. He would put paid to this would-be usurper once and for all.

Warwick drew on the power bubbling within him and sent another ball of energy scorching across the room. It flew straight and true this time; there would be no hairsbreadth escape.

Lance Sullivan-Beresford knew it was time to stop hiding. As the second sphere of energy formed in his uncle's hand, he stood to his full height and allowed the power of the legacy to come forth, unbridled.

In the instant the purple sphere flew towards him, Lance raised his arms and sent a bolt of blazing golden fire roaring from his fingertips. The knowledge he had gained from Essie Beresford helped him form it; his own talent energized it; his remarkable will sent it straight for Warwick's heart.

The blow caught the older Beresford full in the chest, unaware and unprotected, and threw him back against the marble fireplace. He staggered and fell to his knees, gurgling like a man in the throes of death.

In the same instant, Lance dodged the oncoming sphere of purple energy. It shattered harmlessly against the wall behind him.

Deep within the golden inferno, Warwick Beresford realized he had been tricked. He recognized the stink of his bitch-sister in this. The boy had been prepared—he had been trained in secret, damn her!—and a direct attack could cost Warwick dearly.

Lying bastard, Warwick thought. *Two can play your game.*

Warwick stayed on his knees. His hands flew to his pitted cheeks as blood spurted from his nose, then from his ears and even from his eyes. He clutched blindly at the back of the chair he had taken a moment earlier, fighting for each breath. His wrinkled skin blanched, a sickly gray now, as he slowly slid down the chair and crumpled onto the carpet.

Lance was stunned. He knew the power he had inherited was great, but he hadn't expected such a blazing fire to erupt from him. It had been . . . *too easy.* He had killed the man with a single bolt . . . and though he thought he had prepared himself for this, it was *horrible* to watch someone die by your own hand.

And from the look of it, Warwick *was* dying. The battle appeared to be over almost before it had begun.

I used too much, he thought. *And I don't even know how I did it.* He stood over the body, stunned and confused . . .

And Warwick used the hesitation to his advantage.

So, he thought as he crouched on the carpet. *The pup was not that well prepared.* He knew it took centuries to truly understand the power, and this boy was new to it—painfully new.

As Warwick lay deathly still on the carpet, a pool of blood slowly forming around his head, he sent tendrils of thought out, each with a specific order.

He sent the nightmare for Lance one final time.

Darkness swept over him. It kissed him. Engorged him. Embraced him. Sucked at him like a hungry beast. His heart pounded in his chest. A cold and bottomless sensation swelled inside him and threatened to engulf him forever . . .

Lance stiffened and swayed under the sudden onslaught. The cold. The dark. The horribly familiar fear . . .

I know this, he thought. *It's the dream, and I mustn't give in to it. I have to . . . fight it.*

The darkness eased, but now the entire room was draped in a slate-gray gloom. A wet, bone-chilling coldness numbed his senses. And in this fog, he felt something evil waiting—something poised, ready to strike at him, to tear the very life from him.

I can beat this, Lance told himself.

Droplets of mist formed on his face, gathering in his eyebrows, running in rivulets down his cheeks.

I can beat this.

The unearthly mist seeped into his clothes, making them stick to his skin. The numbing cold spread like arthritic fingers through his body. Where it penetrated, all sensation fled.

I can . . . BEAT THIS.

Lance concentrated. He used a technique Essie had taught him—one she had used herself, centuries before—and gathered his thoughts in a spot near the center of his forehead, between the eyes. Every fiber of his being fought to drag him into the fear, to throw him into the darkness that would tear the very life from him . . . but he held on, keeping himself seated at the spot.

He remembered the warmth he had felt when he touched the power, and he called upon it for help. *Now*, he thought desperately. *If I ever needed you, I need you now . . .*

Shards of warmth rose inside him—slowly at first, then more rapidly, expanding to touch every part of his body. As the golden energy spread, the cold, ominous fear abated. The gray fog began to dissipate.

Seconds later, sunlight shone in the room again.

Warwick was at the door now, all signs of his injury gone. But for the first time, the earl of Beresford felt a tinge of fear himself.

The pup had broken free of the dream with seeming ease. There was obviously more to him than met the eye. *Maybe I was right the first time*, Warwick thought. *Maybe the power is in the boy.*

Suddenly . . .

Wonderfully . . .

Warwick sensed something new in the house. Downstairs. At the front door. *There.*

He realized what it was . . . and laughed. Then, without a word, he turned and rushed from the room.

Angie and Benny were downstairs.

"Lance?" Angie called out. "Lance, where are you? Benny and I are back, and we're not going to leave until you explain what's going on. Lance? Lance!"

In the same instant, Lance drove off the last of the gray fog, saw Warwick exit the door, and heard Angie's voice echoing through the house.

His heart sank in his chest.

The old man, the *bastard*, had tricked him. He hadn't been badly injured—simply stunned, if that. He had recovered enough to mount a new attack, and escape. And now he was heading downstairs . . .

Toward Angie and Benny.

Benny was still shaking over the crazed ride from Kirribilli. Angie had driven like a madwoman: running red lights, passing traffic on the inside, darting between trucks and buses that were three times the size of her car . . .

It had been awful. He had found himself actually praying that a cop would stop them. Even that would have been better than dying in a ball of flame when she finally came across something she couldn't push aside or swerve around.

He'd barely believed their good fortune when they'd pulled into the mansion's driveway. Angie hadn't even let the car stop; she'd just jumped out of the driver's seat and let the Holden coast into a hedge while she vaulted up the porch steps three at a time and burst through the front door.

Benny had hurried after her, and they had immediately begun to search for any signs of Lance . . . but there were none to be found on the ground floor.

Angie called out for Lance, then turned to Benny. ''He must be upstairs. Come on.''

They turned to climb the staircase—

And Benny saw something race onto the landing. He saw it, but he didn't believe it.

It was a twisted . . . *thing*, human in stance, but animal in nature—or at least that's what it appeared to be—dressed in a tweed suit and bleeding purple energy like something out of *Star Wars*. As they stood at the bottom of the stairs, dumbfounded, the creature swooped downward, like a luminous bird of prey, its clawed hands outstretched.

Lance was right behind Warwick, charging down the hall at full speed. He knew he was going to be too late to help; his mind screamed out, seizing Angie's awareness and projecting with all his might.

''*Angie! LOOK OUT!*''

Angelique Beresford saw Warwick and instantly recognized the purple energy flowing from him. It was the *thing* that had attacked Lance—the source of all their troubles.

Warwick sent a massive bolt of energy coursing toward Angie and Benny. It burned the air as it traveled . . .

And Angie heard Lance's voice, not as a normal voice, but *inside her head*, shouting the warning.

She had no time to do anything more than cross her hands over her head and think of the golden shield she had seen so vividly in her dream.

In the instant before the purple fire reached them, a stream of golden color raced from Angie's crossed arms and struck the evil bolt head-on.

There was a hideous, blinding flash of golden-purple light, and the sound of an explosion too large to survive . . .

Then the air cleared suddenly, and the energies were gone. Dissipated. Balanced.

Canceled out, Angie realized, understanding what had happened.

Warwick cursed aloud and came down heavily on the landing, halfway to the bottom floor. Again he sent tendrils of thought stretching ahead of him, seeking . . . seeking . . . and *finding*.

The banisters that stretched up either side of the large staircase were hand-carved from ancient hardwood. So were the two matched eagles that perched on the base posts in silent immobility.

Immobile no longer, Warwick thought, and gestured.

Hardwood eyes, carved by a master craftsman in the sixteenth century, suddenly blinked and blazed with a purplish-red glow.

First one eagle, then the other, began to move. The wood creaked and groaned as the birds stretched their wings. Their carved skins crackled like paper as heads turned and beaks clicked.

They were still wood, as before . . . but now the wood had life. And the wooden birds had a purpose.

Angie heard the cracking sound as the wood shifted, but she was watching Warwick bustling down the stairs two at a time. The sudden movement of air at her back made her turn—

Just as the wooden eagles leapt up with a strange, creaking shriek.

The creatures took to the air, circled tightly and dived at Angie and Benny.

Angie tried to duck, but Benny stood where he was. He couldn't believe what he was seeing—he *refused* to believe. His feet were solid as stone.

The first eagle plummeted downward, talons outstretched, and slashed at Benny as it rocketed past. Blood gushed from two vicious wounds on the counterfeiter's face, and still he stood, transfixed, unable to respond.

'Sa dream, was all he could think. *'Sa friggin' dream* . . .

Angie threw herself forward and tackled him to the ground as both birds streaked by a second time. She gritted her teeth at the burst of putrid wind that slammed at them as the eagles swooped by with only inches to spare.

Frantic, she scanned the area looking for a weapon,

anything that might help, as the wooden birds circled for another attack. But there was nothing within reach that could help.

The wooden attackers moved closer together now, their stiff wings almost knocking. For an instant, they seemed to hang in the air, as if on strings . . . then they dropped, hard and fast, their claws like wooden knives hurtling straight for the unprotected pair.

Lance arrived at the top of the stairs just as the final dive began. He could see that the wooden creatures weighed at least ten pounds each, and now it didn't matter if they were alive or dead: sharp, heavy instruments like that, falling from such a height, would be enough to skewer both Angie and Benny like marshmallows on a stick.

The panic rose in him again, but Lance remembered the fog—and something Essie had told him during the joining.

He held himself at the top of the stairs, stiff as a statue . . .

And he thought of *fire*. He pictured yellow and orange flames licking hungrily as they danced—rising and falling, only to flare upward again, destroying everything they touched. He imagined pure fire, seething and bubbling inside his hands . . . growing more and more intense . . . *white hot* . . .

Then he pictured the wooden eagles in his mind's eye, conjuring up every tiny detail of their intricate carving. They were falling even faster. Falling straight for his friends . . .

He slammed the two images together.

The wooden eagles burst into raging fireballs. For a moment they screeched, wood shrieking against wood, and fell even faster, trailing smoke.

The explosion that followed was brilliant white and bloody red. It lasted only an instant in a startling rush of sound and light—and then it was gone. Nothing was left, not even a sparkle. One second they were matching incandescent balls of flame, streaming downward, the next they were vaporized.

A gust of hot air slammed into Angie and Benny, but that was all. They rose slowly, dazed by the battle, but unhurt.

Warwick knew he had lost—for the moment. *But not forever*, he told himself as he ran across the foyer. *I'll be back. I'll get them yet—*

He flung open the front door, his mind racing with plans for escape . . .

And a wall of golden energy stopped him in his tracks. It was a solid barrier that stretched from top to bottom. And now, as he turned to look through the casement windows, the french doors, the skylight, he saw that it was everywhere—*everywhere*.

He couldn't pass through it. He didn't even dare touch it. He remembered what the twin bolts of power had done on the landing—they had *canceled each other out*. He wasn't going to let that happen to *him*.

He had walked into a trap.

Lance stood at the top of the stairs and thought, *Thank you, Essie*. In the final moments before she had faded away, she had carried out the last part of their joint plan—something Lance had thought might come in handy. She had reached into him and shown him how to erect a shield just as strong as her own—stronger, actually, since Lance was using her knowledge to create the barrier, but his own immense power to energize it.

Now the old man could only stand before the coruscating barrier and gape . . . and his consternation gave Lance exactly the respite he needed.

He rushed down the stairs and held Angie tightly in his arms. "*Damn it*," he told her, "*I told you to stay away*." As glad as he was to see her, to hold her, he was terrified for her safety.

"*I'm sorry*," Angie said. "*I thought you might need my help again*." Then she motioned to Benny, who was sitting on the bottom step of the staircase, his eyes glazed in shock. *"Benny's been hurt."*

In their confusion and urgency, neither of them noticed that they weren't speaking at all—that they were communicating as Warwick and Essie had communicated centuries ago: mind-to-mind.

"I'm sorry, my love," Lance said . . . and then he sent a special, irresistible command to them both.

"Sleep," he told them.

Angie immediately collapsed in his arms, and Benny slumped against the stairs and began to snore. Lance was astounded at how easy it had been—*too* easy, in fact.

When Angie wakes up, she'll skin me alive, he thought. *But it's better this way.*

He set Angie down on the stair next to Benny and raised his hands above them. Fire flew from his fingertips and formed a glistening shell of golden light around the sleeping figures. Slowly, almost reluctantly, it solidified. When he finally lowered his hands, the translucent shell remained, pulsing quietly in time with its occupants' breathing.

"Stay safe," he told Angie, mind-to-mind. *"I'll be back."*

Then Lance Beresford turned to his ancient enemy and called out his name.

"Warwick!" he boomed. "Face me!"

The ancient Beresford stopped glaring at the golden barrier. He looked down at the floor, his head bowed, his shoulders slumped. For a moment, Lance could almost believe the old man had given up—that he was ready to surrender—

Then, without any warning, Warwick spun on his heel and lashed out at Lance and the two sleepers simultaneously.

Purple fire played across the golden shell, making it ring like a bell . . . but no cracks developed. It stayed whole. Lance himself raised one arm and deflected the purple bolt toward the far wall. It sizzled against the wallpaper without damaging it, just as before.

After a moment, Warwick saw the futility of his gesture, and he let his arms fall. For the first time, he looked truly defeated.

"You're trapped," Lance said, his words projecting a boldness he didn't feel.

But Warwick knew more than Lance. He now understood what had happened—how he had been lured into this carefully planned trap. He had to admit it: the boy was crude in the ways of the power, but he got the job done.

For centuries, Warwick had believed himself to be the most powerful man alive, even without possession of the other half of the house. But he was no fool. He had seen the power in this boy, and he would never had taken the risk of direct confrontation if he'd thought there was the chance of defeat, no matter how remote.

How powerful am I now? he thought bitterly. He had driven his full strength against the shield that blocked his escape, and though he knew that Essie had helped put it up, it was the *pup* that held it in place.

Face the facts, he told himself. *Essie is gone. Dead.* Warwick had felt the life ebb from her as she'd faded from the room upstairs. Now it was the boy. He was untrained in many ways, but his connection to the power was vast.

There was only one chance. Warwick had to get away. To retreat and regroup. And he had to do it quickly, before the young pup realized just how vulnerable he was inside this golden shield.

With a fierce howl, Warwick waved his hand in a wide circle. Purple energy gushed from his fingers, and the circle hung in the air, its interior swirling with a thick mist. Suddenly the circle expanded until it was larger than a man—until it almost filled the entry alcove.

Before Lance realized what was happening, Warwick stepped into the mist and was gone.

And just as quickly, Lance followed.

He didn't think it through—there wasn't time. It was an

instinctive reaction, pure reflex, that made Lance reach out with his mind as the circle began to close.

The instant before the roiling sphere disappeared, Lance reached it and . . . held it open. He didn't try to understand how he did it, or even exactly what *it* was. Instead, he sent his consciousness probing into the swirling mist with only one thought driving him. *Find Warwick.*

Inside the mist, his probe felt the presence that could only have been Essie's twin. He didn't think about it; he didn't ponder his action. He simply stepped into the mist.

It was as if Warwick had ripped the very fabric of space itself and thrust himself into a different world. The mist wasn't mist at all, Lance realized, as he stepped through the far side. It was a *gate*—a gate to a different plane.

A moment earlier he had been in Essie Beresford's house—*his* house. Now, an instant later, he found himself in a landscape of wildly brilliant colors and exotic shapes.

He looked up at the blood-red sky and saw that he was standing beneath what appeared to be a perfectly square mountain of red rock that stretched straight upward. Its top was miles away—so far it was literally out of sight. Next to the square mountain were smaller versions of it, and their tops, too, were lost high in the red haze.

Warwick was standing fifty yards away. He turned at the sound of space tearing and gasped when he saw Lance standing in the middle of the plane, dazed and awestruck.

Terror gripped him. The boy should never have been able to follow, but there he was.

There was nothing else Warwick could do. He struck again without warning, convinced he was fighting for his very existence.

His body suddenly expanded. In an instant, he appeared like one of the giant mountains—unbelievably huge, massive.

Lance turned just in time to see a foot as big as a house stamping down out of the sky at him. He shouted in surprise and jumped high and far . . .

And landed thirty feet away as the heel of the huge boot slammed into the ground with tremendous force.

Lance didn't have time to wonder about the giant—or about his own incredible leap. He just scrambled to his feet and *ran*.

Warwick laughed like thunder and reached out for more energy. He would crush this boy like a . . .

Like . . .

A wave of weakness swept over him. He paused, squinting down at the tiny figure of Lance Beresford scrambling away . . . and found he had made a grave error in his calculations.

His plan had been to escape the constricting golden shield by forming a gate and sideslipping into an adjacent world—which had *worked*. But here, far from their native reality, he was equally far from the house in Britain—his ultimate source of power. Here, he was even more cut off from the energy than he had been in Australia, and if this parlor trick didn't work . . .

It took all the strength he could muster to topple one of the mountainlike structures on top of Lance. He had to do it quickly. He lunged forward, shoved at the blood-red column of stone with all his might, and forced it over, straight down, to slam into the speck of a pup as it ran.

He didn't stop to survey the damage. There wasn't time. Instead, he ripped open reality once again and tried to return to earth.

It didn't work—not the way he planned. The gate yawned. He stepped through.

But he found himself floating out in galactic space, his normal size again.

His weakening power had let him down. He had made the journey back to his own dimension—that much had been accomplished—but he was in the wrong portion of space. He was thousands, perhaps *millions*, of lightyears from home.

He floated like a ghost, unaware of the cold, unaware of

the vacuum around him. *My only consolation*, he thought bitterly, *is that the boy is dead. When I find my way out of here and get back to the house in England, I can devise a plan to steal the energy, one way or another. I will still win.*

But Lance wasn't dead. When Warwick had grown to enormous size and slammed the column down, he had just *thought* himself somewhere else. The crashing tower of alien stone had fallen only on red dust.

And now he was . . . where? In darkness, that much he knew. But even in the darkness he felt himself growing inexplicably stronger. It was as if he were being fueled by the very alienness all about him.

He hadn't really had time to arrange his own rescue. It had been only a blink, a single thought—and he was gone. Now, though he was submerged in a darkness like nothing he had ever known, he felt no fear.

He was finally beginning to understand the limitations of his power. In fact—impossibly—it seemed to have *no* limitations.

He pushed that aside. He would think about it later, when there was time—*if* there was time. At the moment, he had to find Warwick . . . and he now knew that if he just concentrated, if he focused his thoughts on his ancient relative . . .

Warwick was feeling weaker, but he knew he could make it. *Just take a moment to get your bearings*, he told himself. *You've traversed space before. There is always the beacon, the light from the manse itself, to lead you home.* He made himself turn in space, spin slowly, seeking a lighthouse, searching . . .

Lance appeared a few feet away, bristling with power.

"*No! No, damn you!*" Warwick cursed, and immediately projected himself into another nearby dimension. It took even more of his waning power, but there was no choice—no choice at all. He couldn't face the boy, he knew. Not now.

This time he was deep in the pit of a furnace—a world of fire and melting stone that would rival hell itself.

Seconds later, Lance was there.

Warwick fled. It was all he could do. Another gate, another projection, and . . .

Warwick took them to a plain that stretched endlessly in all directions. Ruins of vast cities covered every inch of the landscape, which was still steaming from a devastation centuries old.

Lance arrived at the same time as Warwick did, but behind him—out of sight for the moment. The elder Beresford looked older, he noticed, and very tired. But when he turned and saw Lance, he drew himself up to his full height and slammed a massive bolt of radiant death straight for Lance's eyes.

Then Warwick shifted again.

And again.

And still again.

Each new dimension was even more exotic than the last. Some had huge fiery suns; others were swirling nebulae of colors so vast and varied that they sent waves of vertigo through Lance's mind.

But with each shift, Warwick grew weaker . . . and Lance grew stronger.

Warwick paused in a glittering pocket dimension, where motes of living light swarmed around them like sparking moths. "How are you doing it?" he shrieked, waving his fist in frustration.

And, standing on an ocean filled with liquid the color of stainless steel, he paused again—shoulders drooping, chest heaving. "How," he panted, "are you doing it?"

"Doing what?" Lance asked, golden energy flickering between his fingers.

"Don't toy with me, boy," Warwick hissed. "You grow stronger by the minute. What have you learned that I don't know? How are you drawing on the energy when we're both cut off from the source?"

It was true, Lance knew. He *was* growing stronger. And it was equally true that he was cut off from Beresford Hall. But he hadn't given a moment's thought to *how* it was happening. It just . . . *was*.

Warwick couldn't stand the silence. It was too much like the grave. "I am dying, boy," he gritted out, staring down at the silvery liquid that easily held their weight. "I can only last a little while longer. Please, take me home. I don't want to die out here, cut off from all I know."

It almost made Lance laugh. "Do you think I would trust you? Do I seem *that* naive?" He hovered above the shining ocean, black against the salmon sky. "If I took you back, you would just draw new energy from the house in England and start this crazy war all over again."

"No, I won't," Warwick whimpered. "I swear."

Lance knew the beast couldn't be trusted. Deceit was written all over his writhing face—hell, it was etched in the man's cells. He had been permanently twisted by the Beresford legacy. There was no rehabilitation possible.

But a part of Lance—perhaps the part he had taken from Essie, the part that loved a long-dead little boy—still felt something for Warwick Beresford . . . or for what Warwick Beresford had once been.

It was pity, pure and simple—and an appreciation of how anyone, no matter how strong, could be seduced by the immensity of this power.

Lance made his decision—but still, he was no fool. He took a minute and prepared himself . . . then he floated to Warwick's side.

"All right, Warwick," he said. "I will take you back. But the instant you do anything foolish, I will show no further mercy."

Lance sent his thoughts to the house in Australia, and then he pictured Warwick and himself there.

"Now," he said. "Let's try to come to some—"

Even as they broke from the other dimension, into their own reality, Warwick struck.

He gathered every iota of energy left in him and transported himself to England.

Lance had been ready. He instantly found the trail and followed the traitor to England.

In the next instant, he was standing on the ground floor of Beresford Manse. It looked very much like the hall he had known in Australia, but over the years Warwick had made changes. Now it was draped with banners depicting vile acts of torture. Vicious weapons of war hung all about. And everything was permeated with that sickly sweet stench that had plagued him for weeks.

Warwick was surprised to see Lance there with him. The pup was even better at the subtleties of tracking than he had imagined.

Still, it didn't matter. Warwick was *home* now. This was the source of his power, and nothing could stop him here. *Nothing*.

In the blink of an eye, he drank it in, filling every inch of his being with energy. It washed over him in a rich, penetrating purple current.

Then, finally, he turned and faced Lance, more powerful than ever before. And more hideous.

Now this ancient ancestor finally showed Lance the real depths to which his depravity had dragged him, the entirety of the *beast* he had literally become. Large pustules, exuding a disgusting yellow fluid, covered most of his sagging flesh. The claws that once were hands were twisted and gnarled, and the talons huge like matched sets of razor-sharp knives. The dark, brooding eyes were huge, their whites streaked with scarlet, and were set deep under shrublike eyebrows. The *thing* that had once been Warwick Beresford was perpetually stooped in a hunched crouch. Though Warwick had appeared beastlike after the confrontation in Essie's rooms, at least he had still seemed human—if only somewhat. Now, all trace of humanity was gone.

"You are a fool, boy," the beast hissed. "You should

have struck me down while you could. Now I will destroy you, and then I will decimate this planet.''

Lance looked at him, a sad look on his face . . . and *shifted*.

In the next instant, they were facing each other on a featureless plain, in a featureless world, in a featureless universe. It was Lance's own little world, tailored to this special purpose.

He had given his ancient relative one final chance to redeem himself, and Warwick had failed the test.

Now they would fight on *Lance's* terms.

The beast that was Warwick looked about frantically, astonished at the transport. It had never happened so fast—so *completely*. There were intermediate stages, there was the creation of the initial gate. How could Lance—what did he—

The beast tried to leave, but there was no point of reference—no interdimensional landmark to start with. They seemed to be . . . nowhere. It was as if the boy had found a brand-new place—as if he were trapped in the pup's *mind*.

He turned and looked at Lance, burning with hatred. *All right*, he thought. *It's over. I've lost. As long as I'm trapped here—wherever "here" is—the pup has me.*

But does he think I'll give up so easily? Does he think I've survived this long by letting go?

The beast had one trick left, and he intended to use it *now*. He lifted his arms, closed his eyes . . .

And Betty Sullivan appeared a few feet from where Lance stood on the plain. She smiled and put up her hands, beckoning to her son. "Lance," she said, "it's me. Your mother. I'm here."

Lance gaped at her. For an instant, he hesitated. *So much power*, he thought. *So much energy*. Could it be? Had the bastard actually found a way to bring her back from death?

For a fraction of a second, Lance let his shields down to

probe the apparition's mind. If it was his mother, if it *could* be—

No. In the next moment Warwick's cruel construct shimmered and disappeared—and at that same instant, Warwick hurled every last erg of stored energy directly into Lance's unprotected brain.

Pain exploded like a bomb in Lance's mind. It tore at every fiber, every atom, as if his entire being was trying to explode and implode at the same time.

His vision blurred. Blood pounded in his ears. He stumbled about on the gray-green plain of his personal universe, clutching his head and whimpering, unable to think, or to feel, or to *act*.

Lance struggled against the pain as long as he could, but it was no use. Finally, he fell to his knees, exhausted. He cried out softly to Warwick for mercy.

So close, he thought, choking on bile. *I almost had him . . .*

But Warwick was not Lance. There wasn't an ounce of compassion left in his twisted mind. He continued to pour purple fire at the wounded man, determined to destroy him, to reduce him to ash . . . even if it meant being stranded in this nothingness forever.

Lance forced himself to think, if only for an instant. He managed somehow to step back from the pain and observe it, just as Essie had taught him.

His body was being tortured by every last ounce of Warwick's purple energy. In moments, he knew, his physical integument would collapse under the attack and be destroyed.

But . . . *the body wasn't him any longer*. He stood in some remote, shielded part of his mind and realized that the power had made him *more* than that—that the blood and bone and flesh he had always thought of as Lance Beresford was just a, a cloak. A housing.

He hadn't been able to see it before—there had been too much pain, too much confusion—but in many ways the body was a *damper* on his potential. It limited the way he thought, his means of expressing the power. It didn't matter if Warwick destroyed the shell. The essence, he knew, would survive. The essence would soar out to . . . out to . . .

For an instant he knew where his essence would fly. It was . . . *there*, in a particular place, far out in the distant reaches of space.

It was a different world, he knew. A different way of thinking, of *being* . . .

Then he thought . . .

He thought of . . .

Angie.

He saw her in his mind—or, he wondered, had *she* seen *him*? Was she dreaming of him, wrapped in her golden shell? Was she worried, was she . . . ?

It didn't matter, he realized. It amounted to the same thing. He wasn't ready for the—the *new* place. He would go there one day, and willingly, but right now the body was still important. *Survival* was important.

And knowing that, he knew he could defeat Warwick Beresford in an instant.

He reached out and renewed his contact with his physical form. For a nanosecond the pain ripped at him, but he turned it off—just *turned it off* with a trick he never knew before—and got to his feet.

Warwick was astonished. He stepped back, the purple energy faltering and fading. "How—" he said.

Before Warwick knew what was happening, he was suddenly grasped in a huge invisible fist that lifted him fifty feet off the gray-green plain, dangling him in the dusty air.

Even then he strove to destroy Lance. His hands flashed final beams of energy as he howled defiance at the scion of the Beresford clan.

"Never!" he bellowed. "Never! NEVER!"

There was no way to avoid this, Lance knew. It had to be done.

He centered his thoughts. He gave the command.

Die, Warwick, he commanded . . .

And a brilliant sword of light illuminated the plain. It leapt from Lance's hand and hovered above Warwick's head—pulsing, incandescent, neon-white, so bright no human eye could see it.

Warwick was still screeching defiance when the sword streaked down and pierced him. It exploded, flaring like a nova as it consumed the plain, the sky, the entire dimension of nothingness . . .

And Warwick Beresford died.

Multicolored nebulae wheeled through space as they had for eons—slowly, inexorably sliding down the walls of the universe as they had forever, as they would forever.

Galaxies burned against the black tapestry of space. Stars and planets—some billions of years old, some relatively new—rolled like thunder in silent ellipses, waiting and growing and dying.

The mute, immense residents of the firmament were unmoved by everything that had happened. It had happened before; it would happen again. Time was a human construct; it fell below their notice.

But it mattered to Lance Beresford. As he streaked through space, swimming mutely among the spinning stars, Lance was moved.

He had been surprised by his own final attack. He hadn't known how it would happen—what it would mean. But he knew now.

The blazing sword had literally blasted an entire dimension out of existence. Only Lance himself, its creator, had survived. He had been hurled away from the destruction, back into the universe of mankind.

Now he was doing the impossible: soaring through unknown space without a ship or a suit or a clue as to his location, traveling at equally impossible speeds . . .

He knew where he was going. He wasn't even *concerned* about his goal. He was obviously all right. He was just going . . . *somewhere*.

Then a thought crossed his mind. This "somewhere" he was going. He hadn't chosen it—didn't *know* it. Was he going *home*?

The answer came into his mind, clear and bright and— *outside* himself, somehow. "*Yes*," it told him. "*Home*."

For a moment Lance was content to watch the universe turn around him. Then, for some reason, a second question formed in his mind. *This home*, he thought, *is it . . . earth?*

All forward motion stopped. He drifted in the vacuum of space—suspended, uncertain.

The answer was a long time in coming. He seemed to know it even before it formed in his mind.

"*No*," the answer came. "*Not earth*."

He continued to float in space—motionless, contemplative. He knew he could stay there forever, or move "forward," toward the new place. Or . . .

Or . . .

After a timeless moment, Lance thought of Angie. He brought her image into his mind and held it there.

Instantly, he returned to earth. One second he was somewhere in the distant reaches of space, the next he was floating above Beresford Hall.

A distant, exquisite sensation brushed across him. He felt . . . *loneliness*, a sorrow without depth, from . . . somewhere else. *From the new place*, he realized.

Someday, he promised himself. Then he looked down on the Beresford estate and smiled.

He felt a wave of energy streaming up from the house. His senses expanded like a flower's petals opening to the sun. It was as if he'd never really seen or felt anything before in his short, squalid life. He could start anew, now—*really* start, he realized.

And yet, even with this influx of energy, he felt an . . . emptiness. The house seemed truncated, incomplete without its twin in Northumberland.

Lance took a deep breath and *thought*. Then he was hovering above the English countryside.

With a surge of joy, he finally grasped all the power— Essie's and Warwick's, Beresford Manse and Beresford Hall.

All of it.

For a moment, he saw through three sets of eyes. There was the fading viewpoint that had once been Warwick's, as it dwindled to oblivion in the netherworlds. There was the luminous essence of Essie Beresford, still vibrant and whole inside him, helping him—guiding him. And there was his boundless, indescribable sight of Beresford House— the massive, hidden consciousness of the power itself, rejoicing in union for the first time in centuries.

Lance knew instantly that what he had accomplished so far—until this moment—represented only a tiny fraction of his capability. He could reunite the houses in a second. He could clutch a continent, the planet—the *continuum*—in the palm of his hand. Change the past, the present . . . perhaps even the future.

He, Lance Sullivan-Beresford, *was* the Beresford legacy. He was the inheritor of a power that had grown steadily stronger since the dawn of human thought—an energy inherently human, but not governed by the laws that governed humanity.

He could exist with or without his body, in any number of different and exotic forms. He would live forever, if he chose. Or he could die a thousand times.

He was finally what Torikka had called him that day at the Nadi airport.

He was the scion. *The One*.

Chapter 31

In the foyer of Beresford Hall, Lance stood and looked down on the sleeping forms of Angie and Benny, still wrapped in the protective golden womb he had placed around them.

He smiled, thinking of Angie, and was suddenly very human. Then his mind wandered to the lady who had so much reminded him of her.

Had Essie made the right choice? he wondered. She had used him to stop a monster from possessing the world. But had she turned him into something that might become equally twisted? It was an immense power—a *seductive* power. And she had trusted his ability to resist the darkness and cling to the light.

But was she right?

Lance pushed the questions aside and knelt down beside Angie. Then he lifted the sleep from her and from Benny.

Angie yawned and opened her eyes. "Are you okay, Lance?" she asked sleepily.

"*I'm fine*," he smiled.

"Warwick?"

"*He's gone for good.*"

Angie smiled and tried to sit up. "What was that you said about marriage?"

"*It seemed like a good idea at the time.*"

"So, have you changed your mind already, or—?"

Angie stopped and blinked. Then she blinked again. There was something . . . something *not normal* happening. Then she realized what it was.

"*Your mouth wasn't moving when you talked,*" she said directly into his mind.

"*I know,*" Lance said, and as he smiled this time his dimples showed. "*Don't be frightened. It's just a special gift we both have.*"

Angie thought about it for a minute and realized she wasn't frightened by it. It was more like . . . a surprise. A pleasant surprise.

At the same time, Lance was remembering when he'd mentioned marrying Angie. It hadn't been to her, or even when she had been nearby. It had been upstairs, during the confrontation with Warwick.

So, he thought wryly. *It appears we both have a lot to learn about each other.*

The pair stared silently at each other, communicating without words.

"*My God, Lance. What happened to you?*"

"*A hell of a lot, my love. I'll explain later.*"

"*But—*"

"*And by the way,*" he thought to her. "*I haven't changed my mind. I just wondered what kind of marriage it would be. Will we somehow split the Beresford power and end up like Essie and Warwick, fighting for domination?*"

Angelique Beresford laughed into his mind. "*I don't know what you're talking about, but I ain't about to be dominated by anyone, mate. Not even by you.*"

He beamed at her. "*Glad to hear it, my love. But forget about all that. How would you like to be Lady Beresford?*"

"*Oh . . . I don't know,*" Angie thought to him, the

touch of a joke in every word. "*We'll have to talk mor about this dominance bit.*"

Now the pair laughed out loud.

Benny was having trouble shaking the sleep from hi body and trying to decide what to do about the two cuts o his face. A part of his mind remembered how they ha gotten there, but he refused to think about that. He wouldn' believe it—he *couldn't*. It was easier, healthier, to simpl blot it out.

He wiped the caked blood from the wounds with hi handkerchief and noticed Angie and Lance for he firs time. They were standing in each other's arms, just starin at each other. At first it seemed a little unusual to Benny He'd heard of young lovers gazing into limpid pools an all that crap—hell, he'd done it himself a couple doze times—but for so long? Like *this?*

"Well, don't just stand there thinking about it," h grumbled, "*kiss* each other and get it over with!"

The couple turned and looked at Benny in surprise Then Lance grinned. "Whatever the man says," he laughed and they locked in a long and passionate kiss.

It embarrassed Benny more than ever. When they finall broke from the kiss, he looked up and cleared his throat.

"I hesitate to ask what's been going on here, because don't think I'm going to like the answer. But . . . what th *hell* is going on here?"

Lance looked at his friend with new insight. He realize now that Benny's flippant attitude only half-hid his ver real fear. Benny didn't really want to know. He wa terrified by the unknown element of all this.

"It has to do with what we talked about at your hote the other night," Lance said, choosing his words ver carefully.

"You mean that voodoo mumbo jumbo, right?" Ben ny's smile froze on his face, keeping up the front.

"Yes." Lance smiled back.

"Then I don't *want* to know, okay?" Benny said truth

fully . . . and Lance *knew* it was the truth. "Just tell me this. Do you own this house and all that money fair and square, or what?"

"Fair and square," Lance grinned.

"Then—pardon me for askin'—but *what are we gonna do about Sammy Raines*, goddamn it? He knows we're in Sydney somewhere, and he won't rest until he finds us. I don't know about you, but I'm not too knocked out by the idea of looking over my shoulder for the rest of my life—short as that may be."

Lance was still feeling the euphoria of unbridled power. He couldn't resist teasing his uncertain friend.

"Well," he said, giving it some thought. "We *could* just give Sammy the money he thinks I lost for him, if he promises to leave us alone."

"Hey, that's a great idea," Benny said.

But Lance wasn't finished. "Or I could turn him into a frog."

"*What?*" Benny was totally taken aback by Lance's words.

"Or I could send him to a bargain-basement version of Dante's inferno for a few million years. Can you imagine it? Burning every piece of flesh from his body, *very slowly*, while heightening his senses so that he feels every tiny nuance of pain? Every intense, agonizing, gut-wrenching, soul-searing—"

As he spoke, Lance drifted into his mind and began to picture his thoughts. It was intoxicating, to know how easily he could dispose of the man who had caused him and Benny so much trouble.

Angie punched Lance on the arm . . . *hard*. Then, when he didn't stop, she hit him again, even harder.

"Cut that out," she said. "It's getting a little *too* real."

She had seen and felt everything he had conjured up in his imagination, and she didn't like it one bit.

Lance blinked and brought his mind back to the present. Benny, of course, decided it was a joke. What else could it be? "Couldn't happen to a nicer fella," he said in his W. C. Fields impression.

Lance turned a surprised look to Angie and momentarily blocked his thoughts from her.

Well, well, he mused. *Essie wasn't so dumb after all.*

There hadn't been a perfect answer available to her. Her whole bloody scheme was risky, at best. She had to hope that he wouldn't break apart at his acquisition of the Beresford legacy—or worse, turn into something as twisted as Warwick. So she gave him all the help she could . . . and a safety valve, an extra conscience, in the shape of a beautiful, blonde angel.

If the temptation to rip reality to shreds becomes too great, Lance thought, *then Angie will be there to stop me. But can she really control me? Or will she even want to?*

Then he wondered for an instant about the strange twinges he had felt. A tugging . . . *something* . . . from out there, in the endless void of multidimensional space. It felt . . . maternal, almost, as if he were being called home by a parent.

Angie was suddenly frightened. One moment she and Lance were joined, and the next he was . . . *gone.*

The thoughts that had raged in his mind were terrible . . . but this emptiness was much worse.

They had joined minds. They had touched each other in ways that were special and unique—they had communicated in a way unknown to normal humanity. But now—now he was gone, and she felt empty, drained, without him.

She tugged frantically at his arm, unable to put her fear into words.

Then, as suddenly as the darkness had enveloped her, it was gone. Lance lowered the barrier and the two lovers' minds joined again. They sang together, swept up in the joy of reunion.

When they finally returned their thoughts to the house and to Benny, it was Angie who spoke first.

"Let's just pay the man, okay?"

"Okay." Lance reached out and hugged Angie close. Then he smiled and winked at Benny. "It's probably easier that way."